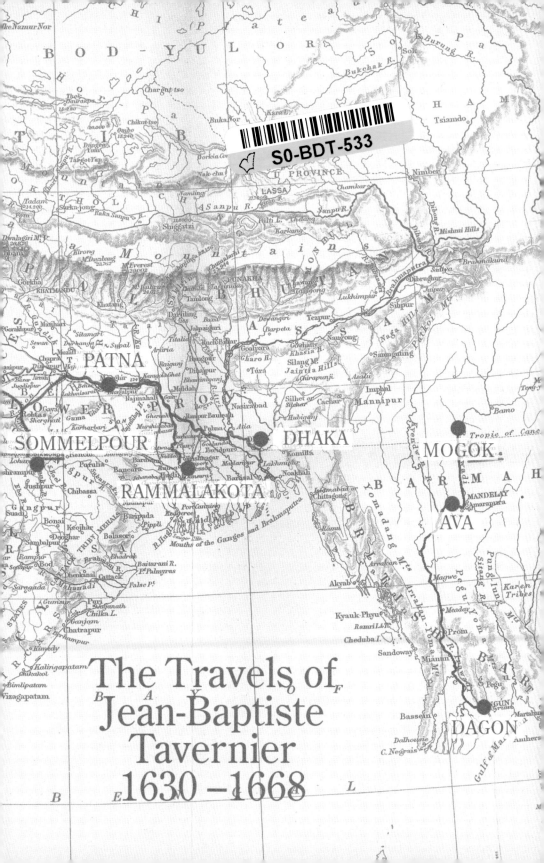

The Travels of Jean-Baptiste Tavernier 1630–1668

The French Blue

A Novel of the 17th Century

For Bo

Richard W. Wise

Also by Richard W. Wise

Secrets Of The Gem Trade

The French Blue

A Novel of the 17th Century

By Richard W. Wise

BRUNSWICK
HOUSE PRESS

Published by Brunswick House Press
Lenox, Massachusetts

Figure 1: Jean-Baptiste Tavernier in Asia from the Dutch edition of Tavernier's
Les Six Voyages, Amsterdam, 1678.

Figure 2: Drawing: Procession of the Queen of Tonquin from the 1st English edition of Tavernier's The Six Voyages.

Library of Congress Cataloging-in-Publication Data

Wise, Richard W.
    The French Blue/Wise, Richard W.
    p. cm.
    Title: The French Blue
    LCCN: 2009927861
    ISBN: 0-9728223-6-4   813.5422
    978-0-9728223-6-7

Jean-Baptiste Tavernier, Baron. (1605-1689)—Fiction. Louis XIV (1638-1715)—Fiction. Thirty-Years War—Fiction. Dutch East India Company—Fiction. Shah Jahan (1592-1666)—Fiction.

Book & cover design by Harry Bernard
Edited by Jacquelyn Malone & Rebekah V. Wise
Front cover image: Portrait of Jean-Baptiste Tavernier by Nicolas de Largillière, 1700.
Hope Diamond image (front cover) ©Tino Hammid.
Back cover image: A reconstruction of the medal of the Order of The Golden Fleece with the French Blue Diamond. Reconstruction painted by Pascal Monney ©Muséum National d'Histoire Naturelle. Used with permission.

Published by: Brunswick House Press
81 Church Street, Lenox, Massachusetts 01240:
SAN: 255-1365

Email: sage@secretsofthegemtrade.com
Website: www.thefrenchblue.com
Printed in Singapore

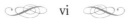

To: Rebekah Bean Tressel (Ma. T.)
with love, deepest respect and admiration.

List of Characters

Actual historical figures marked with *

Abbas II: Shah of Persia, drinking buddy of JBT.

Achmed: Servant of Madeleine de Goisse.

*Akil Khan: Eunuch, keeper of the Emperor Aurangzeb's jewels.

Arash Abdul-razzaq, (Sheik): Pearl dealer in Bahrain.

*Aurangzeb, Emperor of India: Son of Shah Jahan who ascended the throne after defeating and killing his three brothers and deposing and imprisoning his father.

Bharton: Armenian trader and head of Šahrimanian family who befriends JBT.

*Bourbon, Philippe de: "Monsieur", Duke of Anjou later Duke of Orleans. Younger brother of Louis XIV.

*Butler, Walter (Colonel): Irish mercenary in service of Ferdinand II.

Butler, Suzanne: Wife of Colonel.

*Colbert, Jean-Baptiste: Mazarin's secretary, Finance Minister under Louis XIV.

Chenault, Jean Jacques (Captain): Assistant to Père Joseph, younger brother of Marquis de Feuquières.

Dhawan, Hiresh: Banian dealer from Rammalakota, source of the French Blue.

de Goisse, Geneviève: Madame Twelve Tomans, French courtesan, mother of Madeleine.

de Goisse, Madeleine: French/Persian courtesan, wife of JBT.

Danush: JBT's loyal Persian servant .

*De Bie, (Vice Admiral): Dutch, In charge of sea fight of Dui.

Dellon, Alain: Physician who accompanied JBT on 2nd voyage.

Devereaux, (Captain): Officer in Butler's regiment at Eger.

Dulac, François: Master diamond cutter at Torreles.

Farid, (Nakhoda): Captain of sambuk owned by Mohamed Abdul-razzaq.

*Feuquiéres, (Marquis) de: Ambassador to Heilbronn League.

*Gordon, (Lt. Colonel): Deputy Commandant under Butler at Eger.

Ja'far: turquoise dealer and son and factotum of Sheik Yamani.

*Jahanara (Princess): Daughter and favorite of Shah Jahan.

*Joseph, (Père): Capuchin monk, Eminence Grise of Cardinal Richelieu.

*Jumla, E(mir): Persian adventurer in service first to King of Golconda then later with Aurangzeb.

*Kinsky, Wilhelm (Count): One of Wallenstein's senior commanders, assassinated at Egra.

Louis XIV: King of France.

*Maatsuiker, June: Governor of Dutch port of Pointe de Galle, Ceylon.

*Mazarin (Cardinal) aka Guido Mazarini: Italian protégé of Cardinal Richelieu. Raised to Cardinal and succeeded his mentor as 1st Minister under the regency of Ann of Austria, the mother of Louis XIV.

*Mohammad Ali Beg: Turncoat Armenian Nazir of Persia.

*Montespan, Athénaïs de: (Marquise), mistress of King Louis XIV.

Ortiz, Pedro: Ruby dealer gone native in Masulipatam.

*Orléans, Gaston de: Brother of Louis XIII. Duke of Orleans.

*Pindale: King of Ava.

*Raphael (Father): Head of French Capuchin order in Isfahan.

Richelieu (Duke Cardinal): First Minister of France under Louis XIII.

Shadeh, Circassian courtesan: Madeleine's maid.

*Shaista Khan: Governor of Gujarat, maternal uncle of Emperor Aurangzeb.

*Shah Jahan: Emperor of India deposed by his son Aurangzeb.

*Sao Yun Pha: (Sabwa) of Momeik and Mogok, Prince of the ruby mines.

*Tavernier, Daniel: JBT's younger brother, dies in Batavia.

*Terzky, (Count): Wallenstein's brother-in-law and senior commander, assassinated at Egra.

Torreles, Pierre: Jeweler, distant cousin of JBT.

Rochambeau, Noelle (Countess): early mistress of JBT.

*Van Goens, Rijckloff Volckertz: Admiral Dutch fleet (Dui).

*Van Roosendael: Captain of JBT's ship (Avenhorn) at Battle off of Dui.

*Wachtendonck (Herr): President of Dutch factory at Patna.

Wallenstein, Albert von: Duke of Friedland, Generalissimo of Holy Roman Emperor, Ferdinand II, assassinated at Egra.

Yamani, Sheikh: Turquoise dealer in Madan.

Yusuf: Pearl diver. Killed in shark attack.

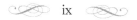

The Early Years

Chapter 1

Reminiscence

 tall walnut case with long slender drawers was set against a whitewashed wall in the first floor shop of the building my father shared with a sail maker. In it was stored my father's stock of maps including his meticulously hand-drawn copies of the work of famous Dutch cartographers: Fredrick De Wit, Van Ceulen, Ortelius and the great Gerardus Mercator himself.

My father was a cartographer. He made and sold maps and nautical charts. Paris was not as it is now. It was the second largest city in Christendom, but it was still a medieval town contained within its ancient walls. The streets were unpaved open sewers and there were no street lamps.

He drew maps of exotic places. Yet all my father knew of the world he had learned secondhand from studying the masters and from information picked up from mariners, merchants, scholars, travelers, and other wanderers who visited the shop. Vienna, Persia,

India—the mere mention of these names instilled a deep longing in my breast.

"Father," I asked, "do you not pine to see the wonderful places you draw on your maps"?

He only shrugged and smiled affectionately. "Jean-Baptiste, I am too old to have such dreams. Dreams are for young men. I have you, your brothers, and your mother to look after."

"But, Father, don't you, didn't you ever dream of traveling to these far off places, even when you were young"?

My father turned pensive then, his eyes took on a far off look, and his lips curled into a little smile. He ruffled my hair. "Tell me, Jean-Baptiste, where will you get the money for all this travel? How will you make your living"?

"I don't know, Papa," I said haltingly, "perhaps … perhaps I will become a merchant and buy and sell jewels and other precious and wonderful things."

Marcel, the sail maker's son, was my best friend. We would dream together by the hour, tracing the routes of our make believe voyages to exotic places that were, for us, only names that appeared on my father's maps.

One subject in particular interested my father: the Terra Australis Incognita, the great unknown southern land. It is a land supposed to exist at the very bottom of the world. Ptolemy first postulated its existence, and every map of the world made since shows it. The great Ortelius made a chart in 1570 that shows a well-defined group of islands southeast of the Spice Islands and further south, an unknown land that girdles the world. How did he know of this land? Ortelius, like my father, never traveled. My uncle Melchior, who was the great man's apprentice, tried to wheedle from him the source of his information, but he never explained how he obtained this knowledge.

Some have claimed to have visited the Terra Australis, usually in a ship blown off course by the savage gales that stalk the southern oceans, but none truly knows its size or extent. A Dutchman named Tasman has since published a map of the southern ocean showing half a continent or a large island labeled "Australis," but Tasman's rendering differs markedly from that of Ortelius, and who knows how accurate it is? My father spoke of this mysterious land often. He was obsessed with it. It was his great ambition to be the first to describe it with accuracy.

One who claimed to have visited this southern land was a Portuguese sea captain, Santos by name, who found his way to my father's shop. My father quickly took the unusual step of inviting him to dinner.

The captain raised his fingers to his lips and kissed them. "Senhora, this stew, it is ambrosia."

My mother's face flushed. She was a gruff woman who regarded all foreigners with deep suspicion, but she was inordinately proud of her cooking. Before the end of the meal, Captain Santos had her laughing and simpering like a girl. The captain had found her weak spot, and he shamelessly exploited it.

As soon as supper was finished, my father ushered our guest to a pair of chairs fronting the hearth. After I finished my chores, I crept softly over to a wood bench set in the corner of the hearth, near enough to hear the conversation. The night was chill, and the air was unusually damp. The fire in the hearth danced and the bricks threw off comforting warmth. I arranged myself—all legs, knees, and elbows—with my back against the bricks. As heat seeped into my body, I settled myself quietly to listen.

Affecting to ignore me, my father offered our guest a brandy and took down two of his long clay pipes from the mantle. Soon a pungent haze of blue smoke formed a magical aura that surrounded us in the dancing firelight. Glasses were refilled; the captain sat back in his chair, hoisted his high sea boots onto the hearth, crossed his legs, and commenced telling his tale.

"You have asked me, senhor, about the Terra Australis. I believe that I have visited this unknown land. In fact, I am sure of it. I will tell you my tale, all of it true, I swear on the soul of my mother, and you shall be my judge."

Chapter 2

The Tale of Terra Australis Incognita

I am the second son of a grain merchant. My older brother João stood to succeed to the family business. My father hoped I would become a priest, so I was enrolled in a Jesuit school, but as I could not manage to parse a single Latin verb by my fourth year, the priests told my father that I had no vocation for the Church. My father then decided that I should seek my fortune at sea and purchased me a berth as a cabin boy when I was thirteen.

"Nothing could have pleased me more. In those days everyone in our village had heard stories of men who had shipped out to the Indies and returned covered in gold and precious gems. I have, senhor, a true love of the sea. I worked hard, learned, and I did well.

"It was mid September, and we sweltered in the hot breath at the tail end of the southwest monsoon. My ship, the Santo Inez, a small but sturdy two-masted caravel, was outbound from our enclave at Goa with a cargo of powder and shot for the Portuguese forts at Madras. By this time, though I was only twenty-five, I was second in command, the piloto.

The captain smiled at me with a buccaneer's gleam in his eye. Here was a man who was actually doing what I longed to do–traveling, seeing the world! I leaned back against the warm stones and listened with rapt attention.

"We ran the ship along the Malabar Coast with plans to put in at the Indian ports of Mangalore, Karnaqapalli, and, perhaps, Trivandrum to look for trading opportunities and with luck to catch the beginnings of the northeast monsoon. We planned to round Cape Comorin and make our way north along the coast to Madras. The breeze held a steady southwest at fifteen knots for many days, but on the afternoon of our sixteenth day, it suddenly began to veer southeast and freshen. This was not unexpected. Toward the end of the monsoon season, the wind becomes like a woman, fickle and difficult to predict.

"Our ship, she was running downwind, and as the wind grew stronger, the captain reduced sail. The Santo Inez was square rigged. I am not sure, Senhor Tavernier, how familiar you are with our Portuguese ships. They can be square rigged like your cogs, or lateen rigged like an Arab dhow. The square rig is perfect for running downwind; the lateen allows us to sail upwind, which your square-rigged vessels are not able to do. This is why we Portuguese were the first to round the cape and to sail to the Indies.

I looked at my father, who smiled, winked, and turned back to Captain Santos.

"The sky turned to lead, and the wind blew stronger. Toward evening, huge seas began to batter our stern, slipping beneath the hull and causing the ship to buck like an unbroken horse. The wind continued to freshen, growl, and then to howl. The ship's waist was awash, and the seas broke over our poop. The wind drove us further and further south, and, as I said, with the square rig we had little choice but to hold steady and run directly before the blast.

"The storm lasted for ten days, and as it began to blow itself out, we found ourselves at night in unfamiliar waters. After spending many days and nights on deck, I rolled exhausted into my hammock for an hour's sleep between watches. To the east, the next morning, we could just make out the outline of land shrouded in blue mist. I thought it must be an island.

"Two days sailing with the shoreline in view made it clear that this was a large landmass. I altered course toward the land, hoping to find a settlement or a landmark that would help me to fix our position. After almost a month at sea, we were short of fresh water. Alfonso, the ship's boy, was about ten years old and had the sharpest eye on board—much like your son, full of life. I ordered him into the main crosstrees to keep a lookout for signs of water, a stream or river where we could fill our casks.

My father turned to me with a smile. "You hear, Jean-Baptiste? Would you like to be a cabin boy, go to sea? Perhaps the captain could be persuaded to take you with him."

I sat up straight: "Oh yes, father, I am ready."

"Ha, ha, did you hear that, Captain? Could you use a boy who gets seasick on the ferry crossing the Seine"?

"Father," I protested, my face turning scarlet. "That is not true, and besides it was only once, and the day was very windy."

Captain Santos lifted his hand and gestured for quiet. He looked at me appraisingly. "Hmm, he is still young, yet, senhor, and skinny. Perhaps in a year or two. How old are you, boy?"

"I am nine."

"Nine next month"! my father interjected. "Enough, Jean-Baptiste. Please continue, Captain."

The captain rubbed his chin. "Hmm, yes, well, no more than an hour passed when Alfonso called down. He had spotted a stream flowing into a narrow sandy cove a point or two off the starboard bow. Through the glass I could make out a cluster of unfamiliar looking trees growing along a riverbank. Beyond the watercourse for miles in either direction all that could be seen was a deserted stretch of rock-strewn beach with no sign of any sort of village or settlement.

"We had no idea what country this was or what manner of people we might encounter. Still we needed water. The Captain decided upon caution. We would stand offshore and send the ship's boat with myself as coxswain to reconnoiter the shore. I chose six oarsmen. My first choice was Da Silva, the bosun, a lanky black-haired brute of a man with a livid scar running halfway around his throat, the souvenir of an unsuccessful attempt on the part of the Indian officials to hang him. Alfonso begged to go along, so I put him in the bow as lookout.

As I listened to Captain Santos' story, I closed my eyes and the sky turned blue. I could hear the harsh cry of gulls and smell the sharp tang of the sea. I was the lookout.

"I armed the crew with musket and cutlass. As an officer, I carried my personal weapon, a rapier of good Toledo steel that had fallen from the hand of a dying hidalgo, or so he called himself."

Captain Santos smiled wolfishly; a single gold tooth gleamed in the firelight. "The man insulted me, then foolishly tried to draw the long blade in the close quarters of a ship's passageway."

He shook his head. "You must understand, senhor, every Portuguese butcher's son, once he rounds the Cape of Good Hope, is magically transformed into an aristocrat and demands to be addressed as Dom. Such foolishness, no? A nobleman indeed! Was I to bow my head to the son of a butcher? No, but I was still a young man and hot headed. My dagger was buried in his guts before he could clear his scabbard."

He shrugged. "It seemed a shame to waste such an excellent blade, but I did not wish to make the same mistake as the late hidalgo. I had the blade shortened for shipboard use by an armorer in Goa, who also made me a fine dagger with the remains."

Captain Santos returned to his story.

"The cove was narrow, but there was enough water for the Santo Inez to anchor just within the shelter of the headlands, which would protect her from the north, south, and east.

"To the left and right of the river, there was a rocky beach two-cable lengths in width. Fringing the beach, an unbroken line of dunes stretched as far as one could see in both directions. The dunes were so high they blocked our view into the interior. The only touch of color in this dun-hued vista was the small copse of spindly trees grouped on either bank of the river.

"The trouble began as our prow scraped up on the shore. The ship's arrival had been observed. A large party of natives appeared on the peak of a dune. I raised my glass to get a better look. There were about twenty of the devils, some armed with spears, others with clubs. They trotted toward us.

"These were people such as I had never seen before. First of all, senhor, they were black and wooly headed like Africans, but unlike African men, who are often huge and muscular, these men were short, bandy-legged with broad squashed noses, thick lips, and deep set eyes. There were a few women, with flat teats that dangled almost…" He abruptly stopped speaking and looked in my direction! "Ah, senhor, I ask your pardon," he said. "Perhaps these are matters that should not be discussed in front of the boy"?

My father laughed, then stared for a moment into the fire and slowly shook his head. "No Captain, continue. My son will someday be a man of the world. Such things are, I fear, an important part of his education. It is necessary that he see things as they are."

My heart swelled with pride at hearing my father's words: "Father, I…!"

My father raised a restraining hand. "Jean-Baptiste, two more logs, if you please. The fire grows dim and not one word to your mother, not one about what you hear tonight." He picked up the bottle: "Senhor, your glass stands empty, and talking is thirsty work." Our guest gratefully accepted another portion of brandy and raised his glass in a toast to his host. The logs blazed and the two men drank while I squirmed in my seat, impatient for the captain to resume telling his story.

"Ah, that is better! An excellent brandy," he said with a smile and a wink in my direction. "And now where was I? Oh yes, Madre de Deos, senhor, how does one describe such people?

"The natives stopped about fifty paces from us and started doing some sort of dance—shouting and cavorting and making threatening gestures with their spears. We could understand nothing of their barbarous gibberish, but it was very clear that they desired us to leave, and, if we did not, they proposed to attack us. I stepped forward and attempted with sign language to signal our peaceful intent. My efforts were ignored.

"One man, perhaps the leader, rushed forward several steps, stopped and began shaking his spear, and pointed toward the ship. He was the ugliest of the lot, covered in dung with idolatrous symbols painted all over his face and body. These hostiles seemed not at all interested in any sort of parlay. The group paused a moment, then started forward in a body to join their leader. Something had to be done before they came within spear range.

"My best tactic—allowing them within range of our muskets but keeping beyond the range of their spears—was not working. The savages edged ever closer. They appeared to be working up the nerve to charge us. I remember thinking that they probably had never seen a musket. I turned to Da Silva and ordered him to fire over the head of the chief, who continued to cut his capers, muttering and dancing about like a rabid monkey.

"The bosun smiled, lifted his musket, aimed, and fired. The gun's report paralyzed the devils. The chief opened his mouth as if to speak, staggered, and cupped his hand around the wound that sprouted like a red blossom over his heart. He reeled once and toppled over on his back. Seeing their headman sprawled out on the beach, the savages broke ranks and took to their heels, running until they were lost from view over the top of a dune. The boat crew cheered!

"'Silencio !' I bellowed, staring into the bosun's eyes. 'Da Silva, I ordered you to fire over the man's head, did I not'?

"The bosun stared back at me as if I were an idiot. I repeated the question.

"He shrugged. 'I do not understand, Senhor Piloto. The savage was about to attack you. I acted only to save your life.'

"I heard a snicker or two from behind me. 'Silencio'! I ordered again glaring at Da Silva.

"The bosun had killed the native as one would swat a fly with no thought of remorse. What could I say? I was within a hair's breadth of ordering the same thing myself. Perhaps he was right. As the padres say, such creatures are damned, and it is no sin to kill them, but something in me balked at killing a man in cold blood, no matter that he was a savage. This was something I could not say to my men, you understand, they would think me weak or, worse, a fool. Still, it hurt my pride. I ordered them back to the boat.

"Capitan Rodrigo walked over to where I stood at the rail, brooding, watching the men ferry our casks back and forth to the river. He clapped me on the back. 'I believe we put the wrath of God into those savages, eh, Fernando'?

"'I wonder, capitan, It seems too easy.'

"'Have you seen anything more of the creatures'?

"'No, Dom Rodrigo, I have seen nothing. Perhaps they are waiting for the night.'

"'Yes, perhaps. The captain set his jaw. He might have been a handsome man, but his face had been cruelly marked by the pox. I have ordered the two starboard cannon to be loaded and I will set a watch.' He stroked his chin. 'If they come back, we will be ready. A round of grape will put the fear of God in them.'

"'You are wise to take precautions, Dom Rodrigo."

"The capitan nodded and slapped his palm on the rail, his gaze traveling up and down the rocky beach. 'They will not be back, believe me. They have lost their leader. It will take time to pick another. I will send a hunting party ashore. Jorge is a steady man. He will lead them. We need fresh meat, Fernando. I am sick to death of salt pork.'

"The captain's plan gave me a bad feeling. I started to argue, to make a protest. 'But, Dom Rodrigo, we know nothing of the interior of this country. There may be thousands of savages just beyond those dunes.'

"'Thousands? I do not think so. I sent Alfonso to the maintop. His young eyes see nothing. Look at this God forsaken land, Fernando. Madre de Deos, what would they live on, hey?'

"Our hunting party returned at sundown with Alfonso running far in the lead, as usual.

"'Alfonso, have you seen any sign of the savages'?

"'No, Senhor Piloto.'

"Captain Rodrigo smiled. 'There you see, Fernando. They are still running, ha, ha.'

"The party had bagged two odd furred creatures that looked like a cross between a giant rat and a rabbit. Jorge, the second mate, swore that it stood upright like a man and hopped along, making great strides on its muscular rear legs. The animal had shown no fear, and it had been easy work to put a musket ball through its head.

"The prospect of fresh meat put all hands in a festive mood. The captain detailed two men to remain on board, one on deck and the other in the crosstrees as a lookout. The rest of the crew went ashore. The men gathered drift wood and built a large fire on the beach. In the general merriment, the confrontation with the savages was all but forgotten. This was to prove a terrible error.

"The meat was tough and stringy, but it was meat, and after four weeks of salt-pork and ship's biscuit, it tasted like the finest beef. A keg of rum made its way ashore. This was a bad mistake, senhor. Stupido! We were intruders in an unknown land among hostile savages, but Dom Rodrigo ignored it.

"When I was a young man, senhor, I slept like the dead. I would fall asleep and know nothing until the morning, but, this night I could not sleep. And since that night, I have slept like a cat. Every breeze, every change in the motion of my ship, I feel it.

"There was little wind that night. The sea lapped gently upon the sand, and the moon was about to set. The men were lying down to sleep; I left the fire and wandered up the beach to bathe in the warm sea.

"This night was sultry. The sky overflowed with stars, and the heavens looked like an upturned bowl or a knitted cap pulled down over the brow of the world. I walked along the sand just at the water's edge, feeling the warm seawater lapping and sucking about my ankles. I stripped off my clothes and swam out beyond the breaker line, turned over on my back, floated, and studied the sky.

"A pilot uses the sky; I love it like a man loves a woman. To look at it brings me closer to God. In this place, the constellations were all wrong. Many I had never seen before. One I remember was very beautiful, four bright stars almost directly overhead formed a perfect cross. We had come, senhor, very far south. Perhaps to the Terra Incognita that is marked on the charts. I do not know, but, then, what else could it have been? If it was an island, it was a very large one. And the people! I have visited many places, remote islands, places few white men have seen, but Madre de Deos, I have yet to see any people who look like these, with nothing on, naked, covered in filth, just as God or, maybe the Devil, had made them.

"Just then I had a feeling—I cannot explain it—like a cold finger running down my back. Something was wrong at the camp. I stopped and listened, but I could hear nothing. I swam to shore, threw on my clothes, picked up my pistols, and began to run up the beach. The moon had set, and all was dark. This was bad. It meant our sentries had gone to sleep and let the fire die down. But, I knew, senhor, something was not right. I was young, strong and much lighter than I am today. I ran as swiftly as I could.

"At first I could see nothing amiss. The fire still emitted a faint glow, which, added to the bright starlight, made it possible to pick out large details. Then I noticed many large dark clumps surrounding the perimeter of the camp. They looked like bushes, but there were no bushes on this beach. Half a cable length away, I could see they were men, many men.

"Running at full speed, I cocked my pistol and fired into the first clump. The shot ripped through the still night like a clap of thunder. The bush became the shape of a man, screamed, and fell to the ground. Another shape loomed up in front of me. My second shot caught the savage square in the face and threw those nearby into confusion. It also woke up the camp. The attackers scattered left and right, panicked by the pistol shots. I ran into the camp and grabbed some dead branches and threw them on the fire. Flames blazed up, illuminating a lurid scene of confusion and death.

"My shots only stunned the savages for a few moments. They quickly resumed their attack with spears, rocks, and clubs. They had planned well and held the advantage of surprise and numbers. There must have been a hundred at the least. Some of my men had gained their feet, but they were groggy from drink, and I saw several shipmates broken on the sand, the black blood gleaming in the star light. I found my bedroll and snatched up my rapier just in time to parry a spear thrust. I impaled the bastard on the point of my sword, then wheeled right and slashed the throat of another.

"The battle became a series of images momentarily caught in the firelight. Shapes rose and fell, danced together briefly then separated. Screams of pain and rage pierced the night. Some of the men grappled blindly with attackers, who swarmed over them like flies on a dead fish. One or two of our men managed to grab muskets, and several of the savages lay writhing on the sand. Da Silva, who earlier seemed dead drunk, clubbed one of the savages to the ground with the his musket, then roaring like a rabid beast, picked up another and broke him over his knee like a rotten stick. A few of our men were up and fighting with cutlass and dirk. The fight seemed to go on forever, but in fact lasted barely half a glass.

"I inflicted the greatest damage with the point of my rapier, using its length in a classic stoccata lunga to slip through my opponent's guard and stick him like a ripe melon. A thrust to a depth of only three fingers into a vulnerable part—the throat, the heart—is all it takes to kill a man. During the time it takes to extract a stubborn blade from a deep thrust, a man is virtually defenseless. In a fight against several attackers, this can lead to his ruin.

"From the ship they could see that a fight was going on. Our gunner, thanks be to God, was officer of the deck, and, though half-drunk himself, he had the presence of mind to take the action that preserved us.

"The moon had set and with only the light from the fire, the gunner could not really tell what was happening. He dared not fire with grape lest he destroy our own people, so he levered up the gun that had been loaded with ball, aimed the shot well over our heads and touched off the fuse. The cannon belched a tongue of flame. The explosion, coming from so close inshore, was deafening. For the savages it was as if a thunderbolt had been hurled from the heavens. They froze, dropped their weapons, and ran like the Devil himself was at their heels."

As the captain finished his story I found that I was almost out of breath, and the sweat rolled down my face. How could such a story fail to stir a young man's blood? This was so much more than words drawn upon a map. From that day, I knew my destiny.

1st Voyage

(1631-1633)

Chapter 3

The Siege of Mantua

 ow could a steady diet of such tales fail to inflame a young man's soul? My father hoped that I would enter the cartographer's trade. He enrolled me in a Huguenot school in Paris. But, like Captain Santos, I was an indifferent student. Schoolwork bored me. By the time I turned fifteen, my father surrendered and gave me his permission to travel. By my early twenties I had visited most of Europe and learnt its languages.

Travel was my true education. For several years I served as a page in the court of Phillip Raab, the viceroy of Hungary, who treated me with great affection. While in the viceroy's service I had an opportunity to meet the Count d'Arc, who was the ambassador of Mantua to the court of the Holy Roman Emperor at Vienna, and came to know a solemn dark-haired young man about my age who was to become the Prince of Mantua. When he and the count departed the court, he invited me to come to Mantua and take service with his father, the Duke of Nevers.

I had been with the viceroy for about four years, and I was restless. Court life in Hungary and at Vienna had lost its appeal, and the prince's kind offer seemed to me a good opportunity to see something of Italy. I applied to the viceroy for his approval of my plan. With some reluctance, he released me from his service with a handsome gift of a horse, a brace of pistols, and a purse of gold ducats.

When I arrived in Mantua, I found the city under siege by the French. The prince, who had gone on ahead, expressed great joy on seeing me again and kindly offered me a choice of an ensigncy or a commission in a regiment of the duke's artillery. I accepted the commission in the artillery. The prince, whom I had told of my desire to see the world, agreed that I might be released from this service whenever I wished.

The siege was a dull affair, except for one event. One day the prince ordered me to pick eight men to form a squad to reconnoiter the width and depth of a ditch the enemy had dug to defend a fort they built outside the city walls. The men were reluctant, and only after I agreed to lead them would any step forward to volunteer.

"My lord, I have chosen the men. Here are the seven, plus myself."

The prince frowned. His dark eyes clouded. We had become good friends, and he feared for my safety. "Tenante Tavernier, I admire your zeal, but you are too valuable to me here. Pick another man to go in your place."

"If it please, Your Highness, I beg to be allowed to accompany my men."

The prince motioned me forward, put his hand on my shoulder, and whispered quietly. "Jean-Baptiste, this is a very dangerous mission. The fort is well manned, and I fear for your safety. Pick one of the sergeants from your company to lead the men, I beg you."

"Thank you, Your Highness, for your concern, but in order to get volunteers, I promised these men that I would personally lead the mission. I beg you to consider that my honor is at stake."

The prince gazed at me with his sad eyes. "Very well, my friend, I see that you are set upon taking a foolish risk. But at least do this, go to the armory. I will order the armorer to provide you with the finest quality steel breastplate and whatever other armor you can carry." As he had ordered, I called upon the armorer, who gave me my choice. I selected the lightest cuirass I could find.

I gathered the squad at sunup the next morning. "Our mission is to probe the enemy defenses and measure the distance from the moat to the wall. There is to be no talking. None! We will be walking into enemy territory. Look to me, I will guide you with hand signals, and I want no mistakes. All firearms will be left behind. We will carry only our swords and dirks."

"No guns!, What if there are patrols, tenente"?

"We must avoid them or meet them hand to hand. A single shot will bring the whole French army down on us. We will have good cover until we clear the marshes on the other side of the moat."

"And, after that"?

"We must trust our luck."

It was November, and a cold thick fog hovered over the marshes. We worked our way as quietly as we could through the reeds and soon found ourselves up to our knees in muck. I began to regret the weight of my cuirass.

The chest deep water chilled my bones. On the other side of the moat, the ground was firmer, and we cleared the reeds without incident. We were now on open ground, less than fifty yards from the wall. I counted off the paces. Was the fog thinning? I could just make out the bulk of the wooden embrasure through a curling veil of mist. I looked around and gestured for silence. We were now so close that I could hear the sentries pacing the rampart. One cleared his throat and spoke; another answered. Their voices hovered above our heads like disembodied spirits. A drop of sweat stung my eye, but I dared not even raise my hand to wipe it away. A few short steps and the mission would be completed. We could turn around and withdraw to the safety of our own walls!

Just as I reached out to touch the base of the wall, a young corporal who was a pace or two behind me stepped into a marshy spot and cried out in surprise as he pitched forward. We froze and held our breath. All was quiet for a moment. I began to hope; then a sharp whistle pierced the damp air.

Suddenly the quiet morning was filled with the sound of pounding boots. Then the sharp pop, pop of muskets. Lead balls whizzed through the air like angry bees. I grabbed the corporal to pull him free of the mud. His eyes rolled back and stared at me. Blood dripped from his mouth.

I looked up at the rampart. The fog was lifting. Just above us soldiers were crowding the walls, jostling each other, eager to get a shot at us. To my right, a scream!"

"Retreat, retreat," I shouted! Another man fell at my side! As I turned to aid him, a sharp blow to my heart drove me to the ground. I tried to rise, but another sharp pain just below my ribcage knocked me down again. I staggered to my feet and looked about; men were falling all around me. I panicked. I had only one thought—run! Somehow I managed to reach the moat and wade across—I don't recall how.

Three of us emerged dripping onto our side of the ditch and ran toward the city walls with our sodden boots squishing across the marshy ground. Sweat rolled down my face beneath my helmet, and my breath came in ragged gasps. We were now out of range of the enemy's musketry. I stopped, caught my breath, and staggered toward the postern gate. When we gained the city, I noticed that both of my two remaining men were wounded.

After we were safely inside the walls of the city, I examined my cuirass and found two deep dents in the steel, one just to the right of my left breast and another just below. To be sure, the prince's order had saved my life.

If I had any lingering doubts, it was that experience which decided me against any sort of military career. I had lost my nerve and let down my men. Others, including the prince, tried their best to convince me otherwise, but a young man's conscience is a hard master. Some say that a truly brave man does not know fear. I believed that then, but now I know that it is untrue. Only fools are immune to fear. It is how a man handles the fear that is important.

I decided I would no longer put off my travels, and when the enemy temporarily gave up the siege on Christmas day, I went to see the prince and applied for my discharge. The prince provided me with a passport and an armed escort as far as Venice. From Venice I made a tour of Rome, Florence, Pisa, Leghorn, and Genoa, where I embarked for Marseilles. From Marseilles I returned to Paris, then entered Germany. I went to Breslau and took the route to Glogau, where on the road to Stettin I fell into the company of an Irish Colonel named Walter Butler who employed me as a translator.

Chapter 4

The Road
to Persia

he colonel, a mercenary in command of a regiment of Irish Horse, was with the army of the Holy Roman Empire. The Imperial army was on the move, the objective to prevent the King of Sweden from occupying the city and conquering Pomerania and the lands of the southern Baltic. The Swedish king was Protestant, and he had formed an alliance with the Protestant electors of Germany against their emperor, who was an ardent Catholic.

The colonel was a man of pleasing countenance, full bodied, red haired with bristling mutton chops. "Lord, but this army moves like the turf drying. You say you were at Mantua, Jean-Baptiste? Tell me of the siege."

"It was a complex affair, Colonel. I was merely a junior officer in the duke's artillery."

"It still goes on, I hear."

"I believe so."

"You are well out of it then." At that moment a courier rode up, saluted, handed the colonel a note, and spurred his horse onward. "Sweet Jesus, can you believe it? We are ordered to stop, camp here, and await further orders. By the time we reach Stettin, all the women will be pregnant with Swedish bastards."

"We have covered barely a league since we broke camp this morning. At this rate Colonel, I fear that the first crop will be grown and enlisted in the Swedish army."

The Colonel threw back his head and laughed heartily, then waggled his finger at me. "You have a wicked tongue for a Frenchman, my friend. I'd not be surprised if you don't have some Irish blood in you. But we must look on the bright side. Now I shall have me revenge for the way you buggered me at the chess board last night."

We traveled companionably together for some weeks. Though robust in appearance, the Colonel confided he had lately sustained an unfortunate wound.

"What I am about to say is a bit difficult, Jean-Baptiste. About a year ago I took a musket ball here," he said pointing to his groin.

"Does the wound still bother you, Walter"?

"No, no," he waved his hand dismissively. "Fit as a fiddle, can still sit a horse, ah, except for one thing. Look here, Jean-Baptiste, I have told no one about this, but I consider you a good friend. The fact is I can no longer, ah, fulfill my responsibilities as a man, if you take my meaning."

"My God, Walter, I had no idea. A temporary condition, surely"?

"Not if you believe the doctors, but here is my problem. You know my wife, and you have no doubt noticed the difference in our ages."

I nodded. Suzanne, the Colonel's lady, was traveling with us. She was a beautiful young Irish girl, perhaps twenty years younger than her husband, with snapping brown eyes and a flowing mane of red hair.

"Well, she is a young, full-blooded lass, and I believe she is beginning to look elsewhere, if you follow me. I can't really blame her. There are a lot of young bucks among my officers, and a woman has her needs just like a man. The thing is, I can't have it. Cuckolding the commanding officer, aside from the embarrassment, is bad for discipline. I don't think anything has happened yet, but it's just a matter of time, and if I find out about it, I am honor bound to call the man out and challenge him to a duel."

I nodded. I really couldn't think of anything to say.

"Well, the thing is, Jean-Baptiste, Suzanne likes you, and I like you. And you are not one of my officers."

With that Colonel Butler gave me a meaningful look and spurred his horse off toward the head of the column.

I did not see the colonel for the rest of the day. That evening the colonel ordered our tents pitched in a copse of shade trees somewhat away from the main force. After it grew dark and the fires were banked, I, like, most of the men, had turned into my bedroll. Listening to the song of the cicadas, I began to write in my journal by the light of a candle when I heard a light scratching sound at the tent flap, then a whisper of silk, and a fragrant shadow slid through the open flap. I stood as she put a finger to my lips.

"Madame"?

"Shh, quiet, Jean-Baptiste, and please no more *madame*. If we are to be friends you must call me Suzanne." Her deep brown eyes smiled into mine. She was dressed only in a shift. She reached up and kissed me. The colonel's wife was not some slip of a girl; she was ample and curved with an imposing bosom like a Greek nymph as they are rendered by the court artists.

Suzanne was also not shy. She performed some sleight of hand and her dressing gown slid from her shoulders, revealing a pair of milk-white breasts with nipples of a deep cherry red. She smiled, lifted one, and offered it to me. I buried my mouth in its softness.

The next morning the colonel met me with a tight smile. He was affable enough, but our relationship had changed. Where there had been camaraderie, there was now a certain awkwardness. The army broke camp, and we continued toward Stettin. The evenings followed the pattern of the one just described and passed very pleasantly indeed. Madame Butler turned out to be a lady with much skill in love making. She taught me a great deal.

After several more weeks we were not more than four leagues from Stettin when we received word that the Swedes had entered and were engaged in fortifying the city. This news created much disarray in the emperor's army.

As the weeks passed, the awkwardness grew, and I became more and more uncomfortable. Hardly surprising, I suppose. Walter Butler loved his young bride, and I believe she loved him. The Swedish victory provided me with the opportunity to take my leave from the Colonel and continue my travels with a view toward eventually seeing Constantinople and the court of the Turkish grand seignior.

Fortune smiled upon me once again. Passing through Regensburg I renewed an acquaintance with Père Joseph, whom I had met in Paris, a Capuchin monk now in the service of Cardinal Richelieu. He was kind enough to introduce me to two prominent French travelers, Monsieur l'Abbé de Chapes and Monsieur de Saint Liebau, who were on their way to Constantinople and thence to Palestine. These two gentlemen were willing to include me in their party—a favor I was able to repay as both needed passports to travel through the lands of the Holy Roman Empire. I went to see my old patron, the emperor's viceroy, who was pleased to see me again and provided passports for me and both these gentlemen.

Not counting the route around the horn of Africa that bypasses Persia, there are four overland routes that a traveler may take from Paris to The Orient. We took the route through the emperor's capital at Vienna. This city is situated half way between Paris and Constantinople. To reach Constantinople from Vienna, you must travel roughly southeast, passing through the cities of Altenburg, Raab, Comorre, Buda, Belgrade, Sophia, and Adrianople. This journey occupied us fifty-five days in all.

Chapter 5

The Turquoise Mines of Madan

I spent eleven months in Constantinople and the best part of two years in Persia, and had an opportunity to see a good deal of the country. I visited all the principal cities. On one occasion I visited Mashhad in the extreme northeastern part of the kingdom and from there went on to the town of Nishapur.

I still had a small purse of gold ducats I had saved from my service with the viceroy and the Prince of Mantua, and I had my eye out for items of trade that I could profitably take back to Europe. Many important Persian men wore turkey-stones, gems that the Persians call turquoise, in their sword hilts and in jewels affixed to their turbans. I decided to seek out the turquoise mines I was told were situated three days journey west, just outside the small village of Madan. To this end I secured a guide, a young man named Danush, a native of the region who had been apprenticed as a weaver to a rug merchant with whom I had made acquaintance.

Danush was all thumbs, a restless youth who was unable to sit still for more than a few minutes. He was long and thin, reed-like, with a gaunt triangular face, prominent cheekbones, widely spaced, deeply set dark, almost black, eyes, an olive complexion and a hooked nose. Danush made a poor apprentice and the merchant, in a rush to rid himself of the youth, made much of the fact that he was the youngest son of a family of poor turquoise miners. A Persian would call this fate, *kismet:* the merchant rid himself of an inept apprentice, and I acquired this gem miner's son who set me on the course I would follow for the rest of my life.

Like all Persian men, Danush wore no undergarments. His outfit consisted of a pair of dirty cotton *salvi,* drawstring pants that fell to his ankles. This loose fitting garment has no opening in front so it is necessary to undo them before making water. He also wore a soiled *pirhan*, a sort of undershirt, and over that a thread bare *kirdi,* a short sleeved tunic that fell to his knees.

The lad was eager. "Danush," I said, "what do you know of the quality of beasts? Do you know an honest hostler from whom you can hire another pack camel and a riding horse for yourself"?

"Oh, yes, aga," he said, fawning like a eunuch. "I know all about camels and horses, too, and I know every hostler in Nishapur. You may put your trust in me, aga. By this afternoon I shall acquire two beasts of the very highest quality."

Despite his boast, the boy proved to be a poor judge of both horses and camels. "Danush, what have you brought me." I looked at the two ill-fed beasts the boy led back to the caravanserai and shook my head. The camel was an ancient graybeard with at least one hoof in the grave, and the horse's back was so covered with sores that my unfortunate guide could not get a saddle on him. He did, however, have a powerful kick. "These two will be dead before the day is out," I said. "Or you will."

The boy was crestfallen. "Please forgive me, aga, there was very little to choose from. I brought you the best the hostler had on offer." He dropped the saddle blanket, his shoulders drooped, and he hung his head.

It was impossible to be angry with the boy. I put my arm around his shoulders. He had done his best. I returned with him to the hostler's and did little better as the selection was so mean. Finally I chose an aged swayback nag that could, at least, be ridden. We kept the camel.

Our beasts picked their way delicately over the rocky trail. I shaded my eyes and gazed over the parched landscape. There was no sign of water, much less fodder for our animals. This did not bother the camels, but we had to carry grain for the horses, and the poor beasts suffered from thirst. The nights were often very cold, but once the sun rose, the days turned hot. By the end of the third day, my own elderly mount had grown so weak that it refused its duty, and I was obliged to ride the camel back.

Danush was quick with languages. The boy had a gift. Loafing around the town square he had picked up bits and pieces of many tongues. Throughout the trip he jabbered away in a mixture of French and trade Farsi.

"Aga, the finest turquoise, *à la vielle roche* (of the old rock), are found in the valley where I was born. The valley is very famous. It is called Abu Iskagi, which means "father of Isaac."

"Is that the Isaac of the Christian Bible"?

"I am sorry, aga. I know nothing of Christians except that they are infidels and must all burn in Hell because they do not accept the prophet Mohammad, may all peace and blessings be upon Him."

"Most Franks are Christians, Danush"!

"You are a Christian? Oh, I beg your pardon, aga. Please forgive me. I did not mean to say that all Christians will burn in Hell—at least not forever. No, I can see you are a good man, so perhaps Allah will let you out of Hell after only 10,000 years."

"That would be very generous of him."

"Indeed, aga, Allah is all merciful."

"Tell me more about turquoise. I wish to purchase some to take back to my country."

"Of course, aga. I am an expert in turquoise. The best is called *angustari*. These have the blue of the afternoon sky and are without flaw. The second quality is of the same color but with spidery lines running through it. The first quality is very difficult to find, and the shah demands that we sell all that we find to him. He keeps a detachment of soldiers in the village to enforce his farmān, but the shah's officials pay very little, and it may take months to receive payment, and to get even then, we must pay *baksheesh*. My brother says that the shah means to keep us poor while he grows rich on our backs."

"Dangerous words"!

"Yes, aga, my mother has warned him many times. He is the eldest, but sometimes he says very foolish things."

"Do you think you could find me some of this angustari turquoise?"

Danush gazed at me narrowly for a moment, then smiled. "Yes, aga, I think so. I will try. If you wish to buy turquoise, your humble servant will help you. When we get to my valley, I will tell my brothers, and they will put the word out among the other miners." Danush's face became very serious. He looked to the left and right, then lowered his voice, speaking barely above a whisper. "We must be very careful, aga. The shah's men have ears everywhere and if you are caught…" He drew a finger across his throat.

"Tell me more."

"Aga, you must trust your humble servant. I shall be your guide, and if you take my advice, you will become a very rich man. Leave me at my home, and go on to the village. Many people will show you turquoise stones. Because you are a *Ferenghi,* they will cheat you. Look, see as much as you can, ask prices, but do not buy. After a week, come back to my valley. That will give my brothers time to find the best stones. Trust me. I will get you better prices from the miners."

I decided to trust Danush and left him at his family's hut in a rocky valley several miles outside Madan and entered the town with my servants and pack animals and established myself at the caravanserai on the edge of the village.

Once I was situated, I took a stroll outside the gates where a small gaggle of poorly fed hawkers squatted in the dust, hoping to entice travelers with some poor trinket. The town shimmered in the afternoon heat, a few sun-baked dwellings arranged in a square pasted on a rocky hillside. Some of the vendors offered poor quality turquoise. As Danush advised, I scornfully dismissed the goods on offer, hoping to establish my interest in finer quality turquoise.

Very early on my third morning in the village, as I strolled casually outside the gates, a stocky young man approached me. His name was Hafez, he said. He stroked the scraggly beginnings of chin whiskers with dirty nail-bitten fingers. His deep-set dark eyes darted about nervously. He seemed uncomfortable about being seen talking with a Frank. He spoke trade-Farsi and had enough Portuguese and French words to convey his meaning. He politely asked if I was interested in fine turquoise, and when I nodded, he invited me to accompany him to a house situated only a short walk toward the farther side of the village.

We passed through an arched gateway into a pleasant courtyard that belied the ill-kept outer façade of the house and appeared, in the ghostly half-light of early dawn, to be planted with flowers and fragrant vines. There was the delicate sound of running water. We passed through a second arched doorway and entered the house.

The interior chamber was small but beautifully appointed. An elderly gentleman rose from a slightly raised platform set against one wall on a fine thickly woven carpet, one of several that covered the floor. Beautifully brocaded leaning cushions formed a circle at his feet. Tallow lamps lighted the room. The walls and vaulted ceiling were covered with a plaster so finely ground that it shimmered like silver in the lamplight.

Sheik Yamani was the village headman. He was clad in the usual baggy *salvi*, an over-shirt and waistcoat like that worn by most of his countrymen, but made of richer stuff. His turban was richly colored silk brocade that was decorated with a golden turban jewel, a *jigha* in the shape of a feather, enameled and set with a single but exquisite turkey stone. He sported a silvery tuft of beard below his chin.

An old woman brought two steaming glasses of hot tea. The sheik and I sat facing each other, carefully sipping the boiling liquid, smiling and nodding. He spoke only Farsi, but with smiles and gestures welcomed me to the village. I understood very few of the words, but I did recognize *piruzeh,* the Farsi word for turquoise, and smiled each time I heard it. Hafez sat next to the old man and did his best to interpret.

Sheik Yamani opened a small-decorated box sitting on the carpet at his right hand, and, with a gesture and smile of encouragement, placed a small cloth satchel in my hand. I gently shook the satchel and three turquoise pebbles rolled into my palm. They were rough with a whitish crust and each had a section that had been polished. I held the pebbles, one after another, up to the light. I expected a bright rich azure blue, but what I saw was chalky and lifeless. I was disappointed but not surprised.

Danush, my font of eastern wisdom, had explained to me in painstaking detail that by custom, buyers are shown the poorest quality first and in great quantity. This is known as "washing the eyes." When the buyer is finally shown a bit better quality, he will often pay a high price for gems that are little better but seem to be much better by comparison. I replaced the pebbles, slowly retied the satchel, and passed it back. I carefully met the sheik's eye but kept my face expressionless and made no comment.

More tea was poured and several more parcels presented, but the quality did not improve. After about an hour I rose, bowed, and made it clear that I had other business to attend to.

The sheik smiled serenely. Hafez, however, was clearly agitated. "There is nothing you wish to buy? Did you not like the gems"? he asked.

I replied with a bow and looked directly to the sheik. "Please thank His Excellency for his hospitality. "The gems you have shown me are interesting." I opened my hands. "But, unfortunately, they are not for me."

"But, aga, these are the very finest gems. Perhaps you might wish to select a few"?

Affecting an air of sincere regret, I again looked directly at the sheik. "Alas, Your Excellency, I am only interested in gems of the old rock. I believe the term in your language is angustari."

Hafez's eyes widened for the briefest moment. He had taken me for a neophyte, but he was now confused. He opened his mouth to speak, but the sheik, whose face remained placid throughout Hafez's harangue, gently placed his hand on the younger man's arm and spoke a few words to him in Farsi.

The younger man swallowed hard and bowed his head.

"Please, accept Sheik Yamani's apology for the poor quality of the goods you have seen today. The aga is obviously a lord with deep understanding of the turquoise. If Your Lordship would condescend to return early tomorrow, His Excellency will attempt to find merchandise more suited to the discerning eye of a great lord and peerless merchant."

The subtle interplay of resentment and respect led me to believe that Hafez was probably the sheik's son. My lordship would certainly condescend to return.

I spent the rest of the day sorting my personal effects and attending to the many little chores that travelers often neglect, but the day was hot and toward afternoon I grew restless and wandered outside the walls of the caravanserai. It was a poor place: brown stucco walls, just barely a roof and a series of small arched windowless chambers surrounding a dusty courtyard. A caravan of merchants was camped just outside.

To my young mind these men were the heroes of romance. Where had they been, and where were they going? I longed to meet them and to be in their company, but I did not yet speak much of the language, and I was too shy to approach them.

Servants tended the livestock, watering, mending tack, and generally preparing for departure. Brown smoke and the pungent fragrance of roasting meat rose from a cooking fire where servants basted a small spitted lamb and prepared other dishes in large blackened pots. Heaps of goods were stacked around the camp. A group of men sat conversing beneath a large awning, sucking smoke from a water pipe.

One of the men rose, detached himself from the group, and strolled in my direction. He was not a tall man, but he was broad and strongly built, dressed in a long hooded Arab caftan. He smiled and touched his right hand to his lips in the Arab manner.

"Greetings, Ferenghi. I was told there was a Frenchman in the camp. I am called Bharton. I am an Armenian and, as you can see, a poor merchant."

To my surprise, he spoke to me in perfect French.

"I see you are surprised to find an educated man at this dusty backwater. And you are…"?

"Your pardon, monsieur." I introduced myself.

"Ah, an interesting name. I have noted among the Franks it is custom to have two, even three names. This can be confusing, no? My family name you would find difficult to pronounce. I am simply Bharton. In my tongue that means 'the seller,' and it will do for all purposes. Your name means "tavern keeper," does it not"? He raised his hands skyward. "What I would not barter for a tavern in this remote wilderness. If I may make so bold as to ask, what brings you to this dusty village"?

I blurted out that I was simply obeying an urge to travel and that I much admired intrepid merchants like himself.

"Admire me," he laughed. "Surely, my young friend, you have spent too much time in the sun. What is there to admire in the life of a merchant? Dust, deserts, mountains and freezing snow, lazy servants who steal from you when your back is turned, fat, greedy officials with their soft hands always extended. And that is before you meet the real bandits and thieves." He had a hearty laugh.

"I hope to be a merchant one day."

"In this case, monsieur, you must honor me by dining with me this evening in my tent. You will hear the true life story of Bharton, merchant extraordinaire, and perhaps I can do you the service of dissuading you from your mad intention."

I bowed and immediately accepted his offer. We shook hands, and he strode off laughing and gesturing in the direction of his tent.

The tent was tall and commodious, its floor covered in fine Persian carpets. Several richly embroidered cushions sat about its center, and burnished copper lamps lit the interior with a warm flickering glow. I judged that three camels, at the least, would be required to carry just this tent and its contents. My host rose and greeted me heartily.

"Welcome to my humble abode."

I looked around in awe. "Humble? Your tent is magnificent."

He laughed again. "This, Monsieur Tavern Keeper, is where I spend more than half my life. Should it not be comfortable? Come, sit! We have much to talk about."

It is my custom to keep a supply of wine whenever I travel. It is an excellent way to make friends. As a present to my host, I brought along a borracho filled with shiraz wine and another of French brandy. Bharton's eyes lit up with joy.

"What is this, my friend, manna from heaven? Sit, sit!" He handed the wine to a servant to open and rubbed his hands together in anticipation. "We must have a glass and drink to your health."

We seated ourselves on the cushions with knees apart and the soles of the feet together in the Persian manner. A servant brought glasses and decanted the wine.

My host lifted his glass: "I drink to my new friend and guest, Monsieur Jean-Baptiste Tavernier, Frank," he shouted, laughing. He sipped the wine and smiled more broadly. "Ah, nectar of the Gods! I must amend my toast: To Jean-Baptiste Tavernier, wine connoisseur, man of the world, and prince of Franks."

We drank another toast, in fact several more, before dinner was served. The food proved delicious; roasted spring lamb basted with honey, lemon, and herbs accompanied by several other dishes, pistachios, fruit and, of course, pilaf.

With the food and the wine we talked much and settled into a casual trust. He began to tell me the story of his people.

"We flourish because the young shah does not trust his own subjects. His grandfather, Abbās, was of the same opinion. He established the policy his grandson, the current shah, follows. The old man was a great warrior. First, he took Tabriz and all the silk-growing regions from the Turks. Then he took control of the silk trade. He issued a royal farmān that all the silk grown in Persia must be sold to the crown. He became the biggest merchant of them all. Imagine, monsieur, never has a ruler done this before. Then he gave the silk to my people to sell. Of course, he knew that we Armenians are the finest merchants in the world. Who does not? But Abbās gave us a monopoly on his silk for another reason. He was a canny dog. We had the silk but he had us. Shah Safi does the same. With our family connections we bypass the Turks and sell the silk in Venice to merchants from all over Europe. Even" he said with a wink, "to the Franks."

"So this is how you learned to speak French?"

"Yes, but of course. My father left me for a year in the care of our French factor in Smyrna. I speak many languages, but French is by far the most beautiful."

My host arranged himself more comfortably on the cushions and poured another brandy. "Now we have our own settlement in the capital at Isfahan. Under the shah's personal protection we have our own mayor and practice our Christian religion without interference from the Persians. We call it New Julfa and at present we prosper, but it has not always been so."

"What do you mean?"

"Have another glass of wine, my friend, and I will tell you the story." He took a swallow from his own glass and began. "For many years we lived in Julfa in our own country. It is on the river Aras near the mountain where Noah landed the Ark. After he defeated the Turks, the devil Abbās himself visited our town. At first he was greeted with great joy. For three days our most prominent citizens entertained him. He then announced to our people that as a special sign of his favor, they were to be moved from Julfa and resettled at his capital, Isfahan. They would be given three days to pack all their goods and cross the river Aras, after which he would order his army to burn the town. Oh, Jean-Baptiste, as you can imagine there was much sorrow, much ringing of hands, many tears, but the shah was implacable. Nothing would move him."

"Sixty-thousand of us started out, but many died. I was very young, but I remember riding in a wagon with my mother. And I remember the wailing of the women and the choking smoke when we looked back and saw our beautiful town buried in flames. The soldiers assisted us. We were told to cross the river, but it was too deep to ford, and we had no wood with which to build rafts. The shah's men were impatient, and those who could not swim were thrown into the river. Many of us drowned, and much of our goods were swept away and lost."

"Some, at least, of the promises made by Shah Abbās were kept. We were given the silk trade, and we have prospered. But now we have the man's grandson, this new Shah Safi. So far it has been as it was under Abbās, but we Armenians have few illusions, my friend.

We are a cup full of Christians in a Moorish sea. And they hate us, oh, yes, many of them, the mullahs, the merchants. They are jealous of our special relationship with the old shah. And who can blame them? But what can one do"? Bharton raised his hand, sighing with resignation. "Isfahan! You have been there, my friend. Is not Isfahan the most beautiful city on earth?"

"Yes," I answered, "of all that I have seen thus far."

"Jean-Baptiste, I did not mean to run on. Please forgive me. I like you, and I hope that you will consider me your friend. I will give you the address of my home in Isfahan. When you are next in my beautiful city, please call on me, and I will leave word with my family to aid you if ever you are in need. I will be home in two months, perhaps three; I hope we will meet again then."

It was with a promise from me that I would, without fail, call upon him when he returned to Isfahan that I bade goodbye to my friend, Bharton.

The next morning I woke at my accustomed hour just before dawn. My mouth was filled with cotton. Nevertheless I dressed rapidly and found the patient Hafez awaiting me at the entrance to the caravanserai.

The men gathered on the bench in the courtyard were brokers. Most of them were fairly young and poorly dressed—obviously not the owners of the stones. I was surprised at how public this whole process seemed given that selling to anyone other than the government was strictly illegal. The military garrison was close by, and soldiers regularly patrolled the town. I began to suspect that the officials in charge had been bribed, and statements made by Hafez when I asked about all the coming and going of brokers confirmed this.

Parcel after parcel was placed before me, and I politely rejected them all. The stones seemed to lose their gray overtones and to grow bluer and more intense as the morning wore on. I began to see a true azure color, like the sky at sunrise. The sheik sat quietly, serene as a porcelain doll. Hafez did his best to follow his father's example but could not help fidgeting. This was a test of patience and will, and the question was, which of us would blink first.

The endless glasses of tea began to do their work. "That sheik,"

I thought "must have a bladder made of bronze." I felt ready to explode. Test or no test, I rose and signaled to Hafez of my urgent need. Sheik Yamani said something to his son. Hafez announced that we would stop and politely informed me that a noon meal of special delicacies had been prepared in my honor.

He then showed me through a door to a small tiled chamber and began, with obvious pride, to demonstrate its use. It was an indoor privy. I had never seen the like. Not only was it situated right inside the house, but it had running water. Rather than squatting in the usual way, I sat on a large porcelain bowl with a hole in it. When I finished, I pulled the lever set in the wall and a great gush of water ran through the bowl carrying away the filth. This was truly a marvel! To keep the air sweet, a large vessel filled with flowers sat in a niche in the wall.

In the main chamber, colorful hot and cold dishes lay on a leather apron spread on the floor between the cushions. There were several pilafs, a dish I am particularly devoted to—some flavored with dates and raisins, others of a rich saffron color. The men gathered around the apron and took up pieces of flat Persian pita bread, which is both soft and supple, and using the bread to dip and scoop, we broke our fast. There was sorbet to drink and once the meal was finished, a servant brought tiny bowls filled with hot water scented with rose petals to clean our hands.

The dishes and apron were cleared. Hafez placed a carved rosewood box before the sheik. He opened the box and with a smile of encouragement presented me with a small parcel. Inside were eight pieces of rough turquoise. The color was the azure blue like those I had seen inlaid in daggers worn by nobles of the court. Here finally was the quality I was seeking.

My heart began to beat faster. I held each piece up to the sunlight which, thankfully, was streaming through the latticed windows and etching intricate patterns of light and shade across the chamber walls. After I finished my examination, I took a moment to stretch my arms and back, and took several deep breaths to calm myself. In my early years in Asia, sitting cross-legged for long periods on the floor was difficult. I glanced at the sheik. His face betrayed nothing.

"These," I said, making an offhand gesture toward the little pile of heavenly pebbles, "are of some interest." The sheik nodded gravely. "What," I enquired, "is the price"?

Hafez was at pains to explain to me that his father was showing me the finest *angustari*, so fine that it was normally reserved for the exclusive use of His Majesty, Shah Safi.

I nodded, imitating, I hoped, the sober countenance of the sheik. Was there a slight twinkle in the old man's eye? My hands began to sweat. I felt as transparent as a mountain stream.

A price was stated. I thought about it, picked up each piece and examined it once again, took a deep breath and offered one third of the price asked. From the look on Hafez's face you would think that I had kicked his wife or worse still his favorite camel.

"Aga, you must understand this is the *finest* of the fine. It is very rare. His Excellency is risking his head even showing you such treasures."

My patience was at an end. I looked Hafez in the eye: "I have been sitting here for the better part of two days, my friend, waiting to be shown goods of interest. Now, finally, you show me something I can use, and you ask a ridiculous price. I am a serious man, and I know the price I can pay." I started to rise.

My outburst surprised the young man. "Please, aga, don't be offended. You must understand that turquoise of this quality is difficult to find, very, very difficult. Please, sit down. I only meant to say that the risk is very great."

"I understand, but I have been offered cut gems at a better price in Nishapur." I lied.

After much bargaining involving the usual talk of starving families, children in rags, profitless trades, and imminent insolvency, together with appeals to God, we struck a bargain. My final price was a bit less than half the original asking price.

I awoke with a start. It was still dark. The excitement of that first purchase had brought back a boyhood dream. I had just found a priceless gem. The dream had been so vivid that it took me a moment to recall myself. I patted the small lump at my waistband, rose, and woke my servants. In the cool predawn darkness we quietly packed up our beasts. The sun found us half way along the road to Danush's valley. We arrived at the tiny cluster of huts just before noon.

Danush greeted me outside his family's hut. "Aga, your poor servant has been anxious for your safety."

By this he meant he was concerned for the state of my purse.

"Have you news"?

"Yes, aga, Allah be praised. Your poor servant has walked all over this mountain and found some excellent merchandise, which I hope will please you. But first, aga, you must rest and take refreshment."

I dismounted. My camel exhaled a long sigh of relief as Danush led it away. I settled myself in the shade of a lone plane tree a short distance from the hut while my servants unburdened, fed, and watered the animals.

The sun was high, and there was no breeze. I eased my back against the tree trunk. The village, if it could be called one, was a cluster of five huts built of the same dun colored brick as those in Madan, though these were even smaller and meaner. It was the dusty height of the dry season. A few spindly goats wandered freely, dancing nimbly over the rocks and rooting among the few sparse outcrops of burnt grass.

Danush brought a skin of water and stood smiling benevolently down at me as I raised it to my lips. His smile resembled that of a man preparing to take a big bite out of a juicy melon. He was bursting with impatience to brag of his accomplishments.

"Aga, acting on your behalf, I have summoned my brothers and several of the other miners who have gems to sell. They will come here to my father's house this afternoon while the light is still good. I have told them that you are a very important lord among the Franks and that they should bring only their finest goods."

"I hope you are right, Danush. I wasted a great deal of time looking at very poor quality turquoise while I was in Madan."

"A thousand apologies, master. Ah! but did I not warn you of the tricks that these greedy villains will play upon a poor Ferenghi? You must listen to your humble servant. But do not worry master.

Allah is with you. The miners have struck a large vein. You will see. I myself have put aside some beautiful stones."

"Yes, yes, Danush. I am sure that you have done well, and you will be well rewarded if these stones are as fine as you say."

"Oh, thank you, aga, thank you, thank you," he said bowing and smiling. "May I ask, aga, if you found anything of interest in Madan"?

My response was noncommittal. "A few things, but hardly enough to warrant the time spent."

Danush thought about that for a moment, opened his mouth and then shut it again, bowed and prepared to make his exit. "I will leave you to rest now, aga. Sleep well; I will wake you when my brothers arrive."

In my travels I have learned that it is best to keep one's business private. Servants should be told what they need to know and no more. Not that Danush was dishonest. True, he was poor and ambitious, with a desire to better himself. That did not make him either a thief or a liar. Still, a man ought to be cautious.

I looked carefully around. My men were busy with their chores. I tugged the small pouch out of my waistband and shook the rough turquoise into my lap. Had I bought well, or had I been duped? Buyer's remorse—every trader is familiar with it, but this was my first acquaintance. Perhaps Danush has found better stones at a better price. Vigorously, I rubbed my hands together. "Stop it," I scolded myself. "You are acting like a greedy pig." Well, pig or not, I could feel the blood coursing through my body. I had never felt more alive.

I awoke with a start and found Danush urgently shaking my shoulder.

"Aga, aga wake up, wake up!"

In a panic I looked down at my lap. I had, at least, remembered to tuck the pouch securely into my waistband before I fell asleep.

"Master, my brothers are here."

"Where? Danush, I am awake. Stop shaking me!" I shaded my eyes and squinted up at my servant's anxious face. "Where are your brothers?"

Following his finger I saw a group of five thin raggedly dressed men standing quietly about half a cable length away.

"With your permission, aga, I will invite them to come and sit here. The light is much better in the shade."

"Very well," I said hiking myself upright, with my back straight but resting firmly against the tree trunk. This was likely to be a lengthy negotiation. "There are too many men. I will speak with your brothers, but your two brothers only."

The two brothers shambled over. They were dressed in filthy turbans, dusty salvārs, and singlets, and their hands were rough and scarred with knurled fingers and broken nails. They bowed respectfully, and I motioned for them to be seated. Danush laid a tanned goatskin across the ground between us and his eldest brother spread out a large parcel of rough turquoise. They were mostly knobby pebbles, the largest the size of a woman's fist. It was a mixed lot but included several pieces that showed excellent color, as good as or better than the lot I had purchased in Madan. The finest piece was no larger than an English walnut and, even in the shade, glowed a pure sky blue. Many were low grade, but there were several large nodules that showed the same fine color, some with a network of inky black lines like a spider's web. I found these patterns intriguing and, with my newly found confidence, I decided to make an offer for them.

Danush's brothers stated a price and clearly expected me to purchase the whole lot.

"Danush, please explain to your brothers that I have a long way to go. There is a lot of weight, and I have no market in my country for poor quality stones." Danush translated this, and the two miners nodded their heads gravely but began to fidget and exchange solemn looks.

Danush cleared his throat. "Aga, it is the custom to sell only by lot. If you will take my advice, do not confuse them, or they will ask too high a price. Buy all of it. The price will be good, and I will help you to sell off the pieces you do not want when we return to Nishapur."

I nodded reluctantly. "Very well, Danush, I will do as you suggest if you are sure we can sell the poorer stones. But after what

I saw in the village, your brothers' price is too high."

"Perhaps you could offer half"?

I offered one third, and, after some haggling, the sum I agreed to was just about two thirds of the total amount I had paid in Madan.

Danush stood up. "Aga," he said, his eyes shining with pride, "you have done well. You bargained well, and you have won my brothers' respect. Could you give them a few coppers in part payment?"

I reached for my purse.

"It need only be enough for a small celebration and to purchase a little food and supplies for their families. It is best, master, that they not be seen as having too much money. The village elders might become suspicious, and that would be very bad. My eldest brother will come with us. We will pay him, and he can buy what is needed at the shops in Nishapur."

Danush was proving himself to be a canny young fellow. I handed him my coin purse. He counted out mostly smaller copper coins with a few silver ones, which he divided among the miners, who bowed happily and hurried away.

One of his brothers put his hand on Danush's shoulder, spoke to him in rapid Farsi and pointed East. "Aga, my brother says that now that our business is finished, we should go. We should leave now while it is still light. It would not be good for us to be seen here."

"Are we in danger?"

"No, aga, not yet. But men talk, and word of a foreigner in the valley will travel quickly. The shah's men have long ears. The moon is just past full. We can travel through the night and be many miles away by sunup. My brother knows a place where there is water. We can rest comfortably during the day tomorrow."

An hour later we were on the road. Other than Danush's continuing struggle with his mount, the return trip was without incident. As we picked our way along the rocky road, without the least warning, the obnoxious animal would begin to buck and rear, throwing Danush—who was at best an indifferent horseman—to the ground. Danush rose angry and cursing. He confronted the animal, bringing his face within an inch of the horse's nose, sputtering and threatening and lecturing it angrily. Danush's brother found this all hilarious and would laugh until tears carved small rivulets through the dust as they ran down his cheeks. The horse, for its part, seemed to give heed to the young man's words. The beast would stand like a truant schoolboy with large brown sorrowful eyes, and listen attentively to my guide as he ranted and raged. Then properly chastened, he would stand docilely and allow Danush to remount, and a few hours later, buck him off again.

After two days and numerous repetitions of this treatment, Danush picked himself up from a particularly bad fall, calmly dusted himself off, walked up to the now placid beast, hauled off, and punched it full in the snout. The animal stepped back, shook its head, staggered once, then dropped in its tracks, and lay still.

I was riding just behind. I stared in wonder. "Danush, you have killed your horse."

I could hear Danush's brother, who was just behind me, choking with laughter.

I dismounted and rushed over to Danush, who stood stunned with his mouth hanging open, looking down at his horse lying flat on its side in the dust, seemingly dead.

Danush's face had a look of such total bewilderment that I too burst into laughter. Tears welled up in my eyes. Danush just stood, staring down at the horse. A few moments later the dumb beast began to show signs of life and eventually staggered to its feet. The horse was apparently much chastened by the experience. Not once during the rest of the trip did he give my guide even the slightest trouble. I did note a subtle change in Danush. His walk took on a swagger, and the horses began to treat my scrawny young servant with a new respect.

As we got closer to Nishapur, Danush grew increasingly excited and, in his usual fashion, began lecturing me about the proper way to get our turquoise cut into gemstones.

"You must be careful, aga. It is very easy for the gem cutters to steal from you. You must find an honest lapidary and pay him a fair price for his services. Otherwise he will simply steal enough to make his work worthwhile."

After I secured lodgings and began to unpack, I let him take a bag of samples, and he and his brother disappeared into the bowels of the dusty mountain town. He soon returned, chattering like a crow.

"I have found the place, aga. The master's name is Kambiz. He has been cutting turquoise for many years. My brother knows him and says that he has a very good reputation among the miners."

It was not so different from the scene in a Paris lapidary except that the workmen did not sit in chairs but squatted Persian style over wheels set just off the ground. Several young boys were employed turning the large gears that powered the wheels.

Six cutters, shirtless, their chests thick with dust, were at work toward the rear of the shop, and the harsh buzz of the wheels made conversation difficult. We crouched at a small wooden table that had been knocked together and placed in the shade of a tall palm tree.

I spent most of my time over the next couple of weeks sitting in the shade of that old palm watching while my turquoise was slabbed, marked, fashioned, then polished. Each finished stone was placed in the appropriate box: angustari, barkhaneh, and arabi, according to their quality. I carefully studied the division.

There was much talk of *zat*. Zat is a quality that is impossible to define. I could not see it at first. Then one day I watched a cutter rubbing a likely stone with leather to bring out the final polish, and suddenly there it was. It was like the dewy glow on a young girl's cheek, and it is impossible to see until the final polish. It is a quality in turquoise that is akin to the water of a pearl.

Finally the cutting was finished, and Kambiz laid out all the cut stones on polished brass trays for my inspection. He placed one tray on the old table and spoke briefly to Danush. My servant smiled and nodded his head vigorously and translated.

"Aga, Master Kambiz asks if you would care to sort these stones."

"The best ones"?

"Yes, aga. Kambiz has seen that you have studied the sorting. He wishes to see if you have polished your eye."

"Polished my eye"?

"That is how it is said among dealers."

"Very well." I squatted over the tray and, trying not to think too much, divided the stones into three groups and stood up.

Kambiz stood for a moment stroking his beard. He pointed to the group I picked as the best.

"Aga, Master Kambiz asks if you would be so kind as to divide the first group."

Without speaking further I divided the pile that included the best into three smaller piles. I pushed one stone to the side. It seemed finer than all the others.

Kambiz scratched his beard, snorted, turned to me, and bowed deeply. He addressed Danush in rapid Farsi.

"Aga," Danush said reverently, smiling, his face glowing with pride, "the master says that you are a devi. He swears by the beard of the Prophet, may peace be upon Him, that your eye is perfect."

"A devi," I laughed. "What is a devi? Is it like a jinn? Please tell Master Kambiz that he need not flatter me."

"No, aga, truly it is not flattery. The master is no honey-tongued Armenian who will shamelessly praise a buyer to make a sale. Your humble servant agrees. Have I not taught you myself. Yet though I have worked with the turquoise all my life, it would take me much longer to do what you just did. I marvel at your eye," he said reverently. "A devi is a blessed one, aga. It is a gift from God."

"Devi, indeed! Danush, you have done well," I said to change the subject. "Much of what I have learned I owe to your honesty and guidance. You recall that I promised you a reward if the buying went well." I pointed to the parcel of very small barkhaneh gems and one of pale, greenish arabi. "You may keep the coppers that I have given you, and you shall have these parcels to trade on your own account."

Danush clapped his hands with glee and bowed. "Oh, aga," he said looking up at me with tears in his eyes. "You are indeed a prince among Franks." He kneeled and grabbed at my leg. "May Allah bless you; I am your slave forever."

On his knees, groveling in the dust, with his large brown eyes looking up at me, he was a comical sight, and I could not help but laugh. "Get up, you worthless cur. Serve me faithfully, and you shall benefit even more. Now get up!"

The next morning I slept late and woke with a slight headache from too much wine. Several cups of dark Persian coffee set me right, though I still felt cranky. Danush was nowhere in evidence. I found my servant at the workshop. He had procured a stack of cheap cotton bags and squatted by the table deep in concentration, dividing the turquoise I had given him into small piles.

My arrival startled him. "Danush, what are you about"? I croaked.

"Aga," he said, jumping to his feet. "Forgive me for leaving before you. I only wished to get this unworthy business out of the way so it would not disturb you."

"Sorting the parcels again? I thought we had done with that."

He smiled slyly. "Sit please, aga, here in the shade," he said, beckoning me to settle myself beneath the tree. "Allow your poor servant to demonstrate. Here you see I have divided the arabi stones by size and quality, and here the barkhaneh into three grades."

"Now what"?

"Now I make my parcels, aga."

"Hmm."

Danush smiled that smile that told me I was in for another lecture. "Of course, here you see, aga, I divide each parcel into three parts."

"Now I make three new parcels. The largest part of each parcel is the poorest quality arabi stones. Then I add to each a few of the better quality arabi. Then just a few of the finer from the small parcel of barkhaneh your lordship so generously gave your poor servant. These better stones must be divided carefully among the three parcels because they are the eyes. You see, they make the whole parcel look better." He took a small bag from his girdle and shook three small indigo blue stones into his hand. "These are my best, and I shall sell them by the piece only."

Put together, the poorer quality stones seemed to draw color from the better gems. "You see, aga, now your slave can make a good profit, and these," he said pointing to a pile of poor quality leftovers "I have already spoken to my friends, Ali and Mohamed. They will sell them cheaply to the tradesmen in the square—Kambiz says that I may work from his shop, and he will give me some parcels to sell."

I nodded approvingly. "So you are about to become a gem merchant in Nishapur."

Danush grinned. "Y Allah, I thank God each day for bringing us together, aga."

"I suppose then that you would not be interested in remaining in my service and traveling to Isfahan"?

Danush jumped to his feet. "You will take me with you to Isfahan. Oh, aga, no, I did not dream that you would take me to Isfahan. I mean yes, of course, did your poor servant not say that he was your slave forever? Our turquoise will bring much better prices in Isfahan. You will take me with you. Oh thank you, aga, thank you." He dropped to his knees and began to knock his head against the ground.

"Enough, you are a worthless servant. I will take you, but only if you stop babbling. Get up this minute and pack up these goods, but before, get me a pot of coffee."

Chapter 6

The Pearl Trade

The tall dunes seemed to undulate and the heat rose from the sand in waves. The sky was a cloudless, seamless blue all the way to the horizon. I found myself wishing fervently for a cloud. Tiny black specks of seabirds that rose, wheeled, and floated across the sky were our only clue that we were drawing closer to the sea. We had been traveling across the desert for three weeks. Ahead and toward the east, visible from the barren hill on which I sat upon my camel, the barely visible whitewashed walls and minarets of a small coastal town shimmered in the morning sun.

We departed the Persian capital with ten camels, four to carry my goods and four to carry myself, Danush and my two servants, with two animals as spares. The caravan consisted of more than one hundred-fifty merchants, our small retinue almost lost among the thousand men and beasts bound for the port of Bander Abbās on the Persian Gulf. My own goal was the island of Bahrain, the center of pearl fishing in the Gulf.

On caravan, each morning is much the same. The most devout
of the Arab camel herders unrolled their rugs in the direction of
Mecca and prayed. Danush was not the most devout of men, but he
could not resist the pointed glances of his co-religionists. Sullenly he
would unroll his prayer rug and with a surly sideways glance, kneel,
and join their devotions while I stood silently beating my arms and
stamping my feet to drive the cold from my night-stiff limbs.

Once the prayers were over, Danush prepared breakfast. First
he added small chips of dried camel dung to build up the fire
that had been carefully banked the night before. He filled a fire
blackened pot and boiled tea. Then he then dug up the pita, the thin
flat bread that had been mixed, kneaded, flattened, and placed in
shallow holes scraped in the bare earth, covered over with dirt and
hot ashes from the fire. Raw onions, tangy hummus, the warm pita,
and bitter green tea were our usual fare.

Most of the merchants were clad in Bedouin attire: long robes
and headdresses that covered a man from head to foot. I purchased
a suit of these garments. They provided some relief from the heat.

The camel drivers, dressed like desert bandits, their *kiffiyeh*—
masks—drawn up over their mouths and noses to keep out the dust,
began prodding the stubborn beasts with birch switches, forcing
them into line. Each animal was attached by stout cord to the beast
in front of it. They stood braying and shitting, and the pungent odor
filled the camp. I gave Danush the job to make sure the servants
had our beasts up and our goods loaded when our turn came. If
a merchant is not ready, another will claim his place. With over a
thousand camels, I pitied those timid souls near the end of the line
who ate dust and endured the stink of dung for the entire trek.

The presence of a Frank among the travelers was the cause of
not a little curiosity. My explanation that I was traveling for pleasure
with a desire to see strange and faraway places was simply not
believed. Persians have little curiosity about other countries and no
desire to visit them. The merchants I met believed that, like them, I
sought trade and profits, and officials I met assumed that I was a spy
sent by the Frankish king.

The trip had begun with a decision: I would become a gem
merchant and travel to the Persian Gulf to learn about pearls. I had

promised to visit Bharton, the Armenian merchant I had met in Madan, and I determined to seek his advice. As luck would have it, he was at home.

Bharton lived with his family in an impressive mansion in New Julfa, the Armenian suburb of Isfahan, the richest and most beautiful neighborhood in the city. To reach the suburb you must pass along a broad scenic boulevard called Chahar Bagh. It is here that the rich promenade and take the air much as they do along the Seine in Paris. The avenue is more than thirty paces wide, shaded with Tamarisk trees, resplendent with gardens and water courses, and punctuated by fountains at regular intervals along the center length of the avenue.

Bharton's house was a grand, rectangular, flat roofed structure with three floors and a roofed central portico supported by tall columns. A vaulted, two-story glass entranceway was recessed within the portico, and the entranceway walls were lined with two tiers of recessed niches, each decorated with a beautifully painted fresco.

"Jean-Baptiste, my friend, how good it is to see you," Bharton said, enfolding me in a bear hug. "Sit, sit!" He put his arm around my shoulders and guided me to a couch made in the French style. Bharton took a chair facing me. There was a low table of carved sandalwood between us. "Tell me about your adventures since Madan. How did you fare after I left you."

"Ah," I said sitting back and stretching, "it has been so long! It feels good to sit in a proper chair again. As a matter of fact, I bought several parcels of turquoise."

"Turquoise, yes. I recall that you mentioned that you were interested in the stone, but buying, as I am sure you found out, can be difficult. You did business with the sheik"?

"Sheik Yamani, do you know him? Yes, and I bought a lot from another source as well."

"Yamani"! he said, his face clouding, "Yes, I know him well. He is a wily devil. I should have warned you, but I had no time. The caravan was leaving, and I had to be on my way. I hope you were not cheated too badly."

"As to that, Bharton, I was hoping that you might be willing to examine my purchases and give me your honest opinion. Please, do not spare my feelings."

"Of course."

I drew the parcels from a bag, opened them one at a time, and laid them out on the table. Bharton looked each over carefully, picking up one or two pieces and holding them up to the light.

"What did you pay?"

I told him. He sat back and gazed thoughtfully at me without saying a word.

"Well, what do you think?"

"You have done well, surprisingly well. You are my friend, so I must tell you honestly. When you first spoke, my heart stopped. Forgive me, my friend, but I was sure you had been skinned by that dog Yamani, but you have done very well. Several of these parcels are excellent, and this one"—he said as he held up one of the stones from my best parcel and examined it closely— "these gems are magnificent, as fine as any I have ever seen. You could throw all the rest away and still make a good profit from this parcel alone."

"What sort of profit, do you think, might be made in Paris?"

"Paris, Hmm." Bharton stroked his mustaches, gazed into my eyes and considered the question. Like all Armenians, he could do complex calculations in his head and give you the sums in eight different languages.

"I believe, on average, that you could realize four hundred percent selling these gems right here in Isfahan. I would pay you that much, but in Paris no less than eight hundred percent, perhaps a bit more for the two best parcels."

"Eight hundred percent! By the beard of the Prophet, that is an excellent return on my investment."

"Ha, ha, by the beard of the Prophet or the Pope's nose, but first you must get them and yourself safely back to France." Bharton was grinning, his dark eyes twinkled. "Jean-Baptiste, you must have Armenian blood. I am sure of it, but enough talk of business. You are my honored guest. You look and, forgive me for saying so my friend, you smell like a camel. What you need is a steam and a bath."

"It is true. I came here as soon as I got to Isfahan, and I can still taste the grit of the desert in my teeth. A coffee, perhaps several, would do wonders."

Bharton clapped me on the back. "Well come, you shall have both. First, a bath. Then we will talk. My servants will bring sherbet and coffee."

We sat facing each other on a submerged step with only our heads and shoulders above the steaming water. I leaned back and closed my eyes. The cool tiles felt good against the back of my neck, and I could feel the sand oozing from every pore in my body.

"So, my friend, what are your plans"? Bharton asked. "When do you return to Paris"?

I opened my eyes to find him smiling benevolently from the other side of the pool. "I am not yet ready to return to Europe. If you would do me the favor, I would like to leave my goods with you. I plan to travel to the islands of the Gulf of Persia, to the pearl fisheries. I am with child to see and learn something of pearls.

Again, Bharton's dark eyes gazed silently at me from across the pool for a few moments. "So now that you have become an expert in Turkey Stones, you wish to learn about pearls."

"I wish to learn all I can. I have decided to become a dealer of rare jewels, Bharton. I believe I have found my calling."

"A gem merchant"! Bharton's booming laugh echoed off the walls. "An excellent choice, my friend. I approve. It is a good plan. Gems are small, and they require fewer stinking camels to carry them, and an astute trader can earn a fine profit. As it happens, you have come to the right man. My family has a strong interest in the pearl trade. I know just the man to help you; he is an associate of mine. Tonight we will drink wine, and tomorrow I will write you a letter of introduction. And, if you will, you may do me a service on your return."

As I got to know Bharton better, I learned that the Armenians do nothing without a purpose, but then, who does? Bharton was grooming me to carry and sell pearls in Europe and India, and though I did not know this at the time, this trip to the Persian Gulf was to be a test.

Sheik Arash Abdul-razzaq gazed at me steadily across the table. He was a middle aged man of medium height, with a short black beard, a long hooked nose, and closely-set, dark, piercing eyes that gave him the look of a bird of prey. Nonetheless he had a pleasant demeanor, and I liked him immediately. He read Bharton's letter through twice, then rubbed his chin.

We sat directly facing one another. He had my letter spread out on the table before him. "Bharton says you are an honest man and will honor our confidences." Not for the last time the piercing eyes questioned mine. "Is this true; are you a man of honor as my friend says"?

"Yes, sheik," I said meeting his eyes. "I believe that I am, and I will work very hard and devote myself to learning all that you are willing to teach me"!

He held my eyes for a few moments. Then he slammed his open palm down on the table. "Good! Good! Bharton is a man of respect, and he calls you his brother—that is enough. I see you have a servant with you; we will make room for him as well. You have arrived at the perfect time. We sail with the evening tide. And so, Senhor Jean-Baptista, we make ready to sail. Allah Karim, your education begins!"

The pearling season is short. It begins in June, when the waters of the Gulf are warm enough for diving, and ends in mid October when the waters grow cold. The sheik owned a *sambuk*, a single decked, ocean going dhow that he used for pearling in deeper waters, but it drew too much water to work the shallower shoals. It was roomy and comfortable, and Sheik Arash, who often spent several weeks to a month at a time on the banks, used it as his headquarters, keeping a smaller dhow for traveling between the fleet and shore, and for visiting among the fleet. Both of these vessels were equipped with sweeps and, depending on the wind, could be either rowed or sailed.

Our beamy little boat had been loaded to the gunnels with provisions for two months that included a small herd of sheep, along with several hundredweight of fodder, half a ton of rice, barrels of freshwater, five dozen bottles of sherbet, two hookahs, a barrel of tobacco and one of sweetmeats, fourteen human beings, and a chest of silver abassi stored in a dark space beneath the poop. We each had our own sleeping mat, a cloak for foul weather, and a small rug. Leaning pillows were set out along the poop.

There was a stiff breeze; Sheik Arash smiled and hopped about the deck roaring orders, obviously delighted to be off. "First, my friend, we will off-load stores onto my sambuk. Then we go where the wind and the will of Allah take us. We roast sheep, sleep on the beach under the stars, and buy pearls."

The fleet was huge; twenty thousand men and a thousand vessels of all sizes bobbed like corks in the protected waters. The ships were clustered around the shoals like bees around a honeysuckle bush.

The sheik's sambuk had eight sweeps on each side and could manage sixteen divers in the water at one time. The divers worked in two shifts, each making ten dives and resting for ten, requiring a total of thirty-two divers onboard. I made friends with Yusuf, the lead diver. He told me each diver made one hundred twenty dives between sunup and sundown.

Yusuf, like most of the divers, was a debtor for life. Each season his *nakhoda*, as a captain is called, advanced him money to pay for his food and supplies. The diver owned the pearls he found, but good pearls are very rare, and Yusuf usually ended the season in debt, obliging him to dive the next season to pay it off. Then, of course, he would need more supplies. Debts flowed down the generations. When a diver died, his son inherited his debt and was required to dive in order to pay it and usually in the course of a season, he incurred a debt of his own.

The nakhoda might be the nominal owner of the dhow he captained, but he is not the real owner. The broker who finances the nakhoda is in debt to the merchant who finances him. All who search for pearls are entangled in this web of debt. At the top of the pyramid sit men like Sheik Arash, who, in partnership with powerful and well connected Armenian merchant families, like Bharton's, run the pearl trade as their personal fiefdoms.

On most mornings, we set sail in the small dhow after the dawn prayer. The greater part of the day was spent calling around the fleet, pursuing rumors of fine quality pearls that usually proved to be false. At night we beached the small boat, roasted a sheep, and slept on the beach. Often we spent a day or two among the tents of Arab Bedouin of the sheik's acquaintance, lolling about drinking camel's milk. Sheik Arash swore by the milk and considered it a sovereign remedy for dropsy and the binding up of the bowels. It is thicker and whiter than cow's milk and has a sharp, smoky, somewhat salty flavor that I do not enjoy. I wore traditional dress, and after a few weeks in the desert sun, I was as dark as an Arab.

Almost at once it became clear to me that Sheik Arash sought not good pearls at fair prices but fine pearls for next to nothing. There was no such thing as a fair price, only a low price. This strategy worked fairly well. The nakhoda was a seaman, not a merchant; he had only a dim idea of the value of the pearls he fished. Fine pearls were rare, there were many buyers, and competition was fierce. The rumor of a particularly fine pearl traveled on wings.

The trick was to get there first and make a bargain. A pearling captain preferred to sell at the end of the voyage, once he had time to sort and value the pearls correctly. But after a month or more at sea he was often short of cash and in need of supplies.

The sheik was well aware that time was his enemy. We came aboard with a present for the nakhoda, a sack of tobacco or a pound of sweetmeats. Coffee was served, and the talk began and touched every subject other than the business that brought us. Eventually a small box was fetched from its hiding place and the pearls brought forth, wrapped in scraps of dirty cloth, each with the mark of the diver that owned them. When the negotiations began, work stopped, and the divers gathered around and watched.

The sheik sat in the Persian manner, straight backed on the bare wooden deck with the soles of his feet touching. He wore his buyer's face, which seemed cut from a block of dark wood. I sat at his right hand, and he passed each parcel to me when he finished examining it. The nakhoda, an ancient Arab by the name of Khalid sat stony faced and affected little interest in the proceedings. He had a broad nose, flowing gray beard, and a ragged turban. The sheik asked, in an offhand way, the price of a few parcels. The nakhoda pretended not to hear. Finally the sheik turned, looked directly at the nakhoda, cleared his throat, and spoke:

"Khalid, are your pearls for sale?"

"Perhaps, if the price is right."

"Then name your price."

"Do you wish to buy all?"

The sheik laughed. "All! How long have we known each other, my old friend"? He gestured to the largest group of parcels that had somehow moved together in a larger pile. "Of what use are these?"

The sheik had one cardinal rule: "The buyer never makes the first offer."

"Perhaps I should wait. It is early in the season. I am told that the market is good in Goa."

"By Allah, it is not! Where have you heard such a thing. Have you been visited by a Jinn? Two years ago, yes. But you are sadly out of date, my friend. The market in Goa has been dead since the English broke the power of the Portuguese infidels. The best market is in Surat, and it is not good."

The sheik's repost brought a murmur of appreciative laughter. Sheik Arash was playing to the audience of divers who sat huddled in a cluster just behind our circle, like the chorus in a Greek tragedy.

"The price is 600"! Khalid said sullenly. He was not pleased to have his crew laughing at him.

The sheik laughed dismissively. "Six hundred abassi! What fool would pay such a price? By Allah, I will pay 200, and that is a gift. The market is bad, bad, bad! By Allah I am being generous." This time the chorus remained mute.

"We have been working for three months, and this is all we have to show. These three alone," he said, pointing to one of the sacks "are worth 600." The chorus murmured its agreement. They were now firmly on their nakhoda's side.

The sheik put his hand on my shoulder. "Please, my friend," his hands now raised in supplication, "do not make me look the fool in front of this Frank. He is a great merchant, and I will lose all respect if I pay such a price."

The nakhoda ignored me. "The price is 600."

Khalid was no fool. Frustrated, Sheik Arash gestured to his clerk who passed him a pair of copper sieves and a small scale. Working deliberately, the sheik measured, then weighed each pearl. The sun dropped lower on the horizon. A servant brought more coffee. Finally the sheik addressed the nakhoda. "Khalid, my friend, you know I cannot pay more than these pearls are worth. This is my last offer. I will pay 300 abassi, and, by Allah, you know that it is fair."

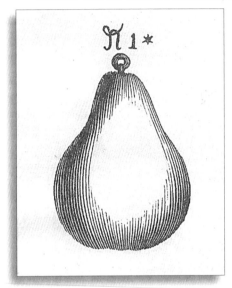

Figure 3: Tavernier's drawing of a pearl found in the fisheries at Al Katif in the Persian Gulf. The Shah of Persia paid 1.4 million French livres for the pearl. This is the highest known price paid for a gem at this time—far more than the price paid for the Sancy diamond (the largest diamond in Europe at that time).

The nakhoda shook his head and smiled slightly. "I know that I can get my price in Bahrain, but there are two more months and we need supplies. Five hundred abassi, my final price."

"Five hundred !" The sheik rolled his eyes and lifted his hands toward heaven. Then he turned to the clerk who passed him a bag jingling with silver. "Five hundred , never! This is my last offer." He carefully counted out 350 abassi and placed them in a pile on the deck in front of the nakhoda. The silver gleamed in the late afternoon light. "Allah Karim, this my final offer, my last price. Take it or leave it."

Khalid sat motionless for a long moment, mumbling to himself and gazing at the pile of silver coins. Finally he sighed, shrugged his shoulders, reached over, and gathered up the silver.

Once we returned to our vessel the real valuing began. Sheik Arash took our growing cache of pearls, lay them out on a white cloth, and compared them to the most recent purchases. It was amazing how much a pearl's value increased once the sheik had purchased it. A pearl worth one toman when owned by the pearler was suddenly worth two or three once the sheik had taken possession of it.

He spoke to them, rolled them around, held them to the light, and gloated over them. Some were white, but many had a yellow cast. In Europe, as with diamonds, the whitest pearls bring the highest price. We Europeans prefer all things white, the whitest bread, the whitest women, and the whitest pearls. White pearls were earmarked for Europe. After bleaching in the sun, those pearls that retained a yellow tint were traded in India where the color was more flattering to the darker skin of Indian women.

A dealer always remembers the finest gems he has seen, particularly if he was not able to have them. The finest pearl I have ever seen was owned by the reigning Prince of Muscat. This pearl was finest, not for its size—it only weighed twelve and one-sixteenth carats—not for its perfect roundness, nor for its fine milk-white color and lovely pinkish overtone, but for its translucence—you could see light through it.

One day after the noon meal Sheik Arash and I were reclining together on the poop of the sambuk. We had been buying for well over a month. The day was hot and sunny, with a pleasant wind blowing from the west. A canvas tarpaulin above our heads provided shade. The seas were calm, and the pearlers were working their way downwind along a narrow shoal. The hollow sound of the chanting crew and of oars creaking between the thole pins floated across the water.

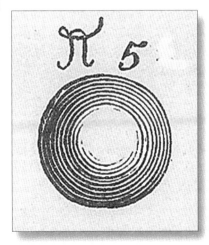

"Senhor Jean-Baptista, let us see what you have learned about the grading of pearls. Here," he said. He drew his leather bag of pearls from his girdle and handed

Figure 4: Tavernier's drawing of "a round pearl of perfect form the largest I know of and it belongs to the Great Mogul".

me the bag. "Please, be so kind as to sort these pearls."

The request took me completely by surprise. Sweat broke out on my forehead. "Sheik Arash, I have indeed learned a great deal from you about negotiating a sale, and I have watched you closely and listened to all you have taught me, but..." I believe he caught a faint irony in my response, and his hawk's eyes regarded me silently for a moment. Then he threw back his head and laughed heartily.

"Si, my friend," he said smiling and shaking his head. "You must remember there is no such thing as the correct price. There is only what I will pay, and what the seller will accept. You are a most amusing fellow and a most observant one as well. So now, here are the pearls. We must move on to the most important part of your education."

"But, sheik, I...." I was not a little nervous.

The sheik held up his hand for silence. "Do not worry, my friend. So far you have done well, very well. What I am asking you to do does not require the learning of books. Judging a pearl is like judging a woman. At first, you need only an eye for beauty."

"At first"?

"Yes," he said, his eyes twinkling. "A pearl is more beautiful than the most beautiful woman; do you know why, senhor?"

"No, I do not."

"Because, a pearl cannot speak"! At this he laughed even more heartily, then spread a large white cloth on the bench between us, took the bag from my hand, and emptied it onto the cloth. "Now, my friend, do not think, only sort. Then we will talk."

I began to sort the pearls one by one. I created several little piles. Those with the best luster and the roundest shape, I placed to my right in the first group, then separated those with blemishes into a second group, just to the left of the first. Baroque shapes I divided in a similar fashion.

The sheik looked at my selections approvingly. "Yes," he said nodding, "you have done well! You have a good eye, senhor. You see that the finest pearl is the one that is most beautiful. Now," he said, "choose the one that you believe to be the finest of them all."

Sweat was running down my face from the strain. Two of the

three whiter pearls in my best lot showed a faint blush of rose when viewed from certain angles in the early afternoon light. From the three I first picked up the one gem that I most admired. It was beautiful, perfectly round, small—no broader than my smallest fingernail—and as I moved it from the light into the shadow, I could see that the delicate color seemed to come and go, being most apparent on the cloth in the shaded sunlight. The other two were also beautiful. One was much larger and also showed the delicate rosy glow. The third seemed to have finer luster. It had an inner glow like the skin of a newborn babe, and it was larger than my first choice, though perhaps the slightest bit off round.

I gazed at the sheik. "So," he said, "make your choice"!

I took a deep breath and made my selection. Instantly I knew I had made a mistake. The sheik shook his head. My heart sank. Sheik Arash patted me kindly on the shoulder. "I saw you hesitate. Why did you not choose the one that first spoke to you?"

The sheik smiled at my look of surprise. "I, I don't know Sheik Arash, I was unsure."

He tapped my forehead gently with his finger. "You think too much! That is a problem and the most important lesson! When you think too much, you begin to doubt yourself." He spoke with gravity, but his eyes were kindly. "Do not look so disappointed. You have done well, very well. The three you chose are unquestionably the finest. My younger brother, Farid—I despair of him—has worked with me for ten years, and he could not do half so well as you have after only two months. But, Inshallah, very few have the eye, and, in fact, you were not exactly wrong. The pearl you chose would likely bring the higher price due to its size. In any transaction much depends on what is most important to the buyer.

"In the pearl trade," he said, "a perfectly round pearl we call an 'eight way roller.' Such pearls are very rare. Always test the roundness of the pearl, but you must do so subtly so that the seller will not observe your technique. Remember, the seller is your enemy. Roll the pearl back and forth each way, like so"! he said, pushing the pearl with his finger, first this way and then that, as a child might roll a marble.

"Play with it as if you are simply amusing yourself, roll it in all eight directions. If it rolls smoothly, it is truly round. You must learn to trust your heart. Here, you see. It is not quite perfect. Very fine, yes, larger, yes, but not quite perfect. Perfection is the goal, though nothing is perfect except the will of God. Here," he said picking up my first choice. "This one is, *Y Allah*, so it is the finest."

"But Sheik Arash, I thought you just said that perfection is not possible. Nothing on earth can be perfect?"

The sheik shrugged. "You ask the strangest questions, my friend. Do I look like a mullah, that I can spend my time thinking about such things?"

During the course of the voyage, I sorted the sheik's bag many times. Each time Sheik Arash would teach me a bit more about pearls and a great deal more about life.

Chapter 7

The Diver

The sun had just shown its face when I ambled out on deck.

I found Yusuf the diver standing alone, shivering on the foredeck. He wore a threadbare sarong that covered him from his waist to his knees but provided little warmth. His thin arms hugged his undernourished body. He stood looking down at his tender, Nejdi, who squatted by the rail, methodically opening Yusuf's catch with his knife. The diver's shells were always left overnight; they opened easier the next morning. It was a thankless task—perhaps one shell in a thousand held a pearl. Yusuf's teeth chattered in the hot morning sun.

Portuguese slavers kidnapped Yusuf when he was a child and forced him to dive for pearls. He escaped but was still diving. Nearing forty years, he was quite old for a diver, though he looked much older. He spoke good Portuguese, and we became friends.

"Good morning, Yusuf."

He raised his head and smiled. "Dôm Joâo, good morning. May Allah's face shine upon you"!

"And you, my friend. Any luck"? I asked, gesturing toward the shells piled up beside him. I stood next to him at the rail. "You look troubled."

He hugged himself closer. "A dream, a nightmare. I can't seem to be rid of it."

"I have had such dreams. Sometimes it helps to speak of them."

Yusuf nodded but said nothing. He stared at the deck. High in the sky the gulls wheeled and dived. After some moments he lifted his head. "My dream is always the same, and lately it comes to me every night. A shadow pursues me. A noise comes with it like the sound inside a shell when you hold it to your ear. It roars like the surf as the shadow comes closer. I try to flee, but my legs are like lead, and I cannot get away. Last night was the worst. When I wake up I am dripping with sweat. I think the dream is a sign foretelling my fate. If I dive today, the shadow will catch me, and I will die."

"Then, you must not dive."

He shrugged his thin shoulders. "I am the lead diver. I cannot refuse to dive, and it would do no good. What is written is written. The other divers would just laugh at me or worse. Please do not speak of this, Dôm Joâo. The divers might think I am possessed by a Jinni and shun me."

"Tell Sheik Arash you are sick."

Yusuf put a date in his mouth and chewed slowly. Divers fear cramps. They eat little while they are diving. A few dates, coffee. He shook his head. "No, I thank you, my friend, but if it is not today, it will be tomorrow. A man cannot escape Allah's will, *inshallah*."

Just then Nejdi let out whoop. Yusuf squatted down and looked at the shell his tender was holding. I too squatted down to look. Imbedded in the oyster's soft tissue was a pearl, a big pearl. The diver gingerly picked up the pearl, held it in the sun, and squinted at it. It glowed like the moon, round and white with a blush of pink. I had never seen one so perfect. It was more beautiful than any of the pearls in the sheik's horde. I clapped Yusuf on the back. "Give you joy of your pearl, Yusuf. How is your luck now, my friend?"

The diver grinned. The other divers clustered around, murmuring like a covey of doves. The men moved aside making way for the nakhoda, who was drawn by the excited talk. He squatted next to Yusuf, took the pearl, hefted it, rolled it around in his hand, then held it up in the sunlight.

"Allah Karim! God is indeed merciful," he said, laughing and patting Yusuf on the back. "You are a lucky man, Yusuf; this is a good one, a very good one."

Perhaps now Yusuf could buy his own house, something he had dreamed about. He told me of his landlord, who leered at his wife and was always threatening to increase the rent on the tiny hovel where they lived.

Yusuf did not dive that day. By custom when a diver finds an important pearl, he is given the day free. He spent most of the time lolling in the sun. He was much caressed by the sheik and the nakhoda. That night he was invited to eat with the nakhoda and his mate. After dinner they played dice, a game Yusuf dearly loved. I saw him on deck the next morning kneeling with the other divers around the small fire of camel thorn, kept going all day to warm the divers. He greeted me with joy.

"Last night the dream did not come, and I woke up today a rich man. I think my luck has changed. Y Allah, today I shall dive. Perhaps I will find another pearl."

The first three dives went well. Yusuf came up with his basket brimming with shell. He wrapped his leg around the weighted drop line, adjusted his nose clip, waved to me, and nodded. The tender released the line, and the diver splashed into the water. The rock attached to the end of the line towed him rapidly to the bottom.

A current was running, and Yusuf's lifeline streamed quite far astern. On deck the day was perfect. The sun shone and small puffy clouds scudded across the sky. The sea was soft azure blue. All I could see was his distorted shape in the water. Then a dark shadow moved swiftly over the shoal. Then another, and there was a frantic tugging on the line. This was the danger signal. The tender standing at the stern oar began to point and gesture. "Shark"! he yelled, and began hauling in Yusuf's lifeline, hand over hand. Crew members on both sides of the boat sprang into action, pulling in their divers.

By the time Yusuf was hauled to the surface, there was little left. The sharks had torn off both his legs and had bitten through half of his upper torso. His face was twisted in a grimace, his dark eyes open and sightless.

That evening we buried Yusuf the diver. He was wrapped in his sarong and gently laid in the center of the tender. He made a pitifully small bundle. We silently rowed the jalboot to the beach and carried him a few yards above the tide line into the sand. The wind had died. All that could be heard was the cry of the sea gulls. Yusuf was buried in a shallow grave just before the evening prayer. There was no mullah on board. Sheik Arash said a few words.

The sheik and I sat together in the stern of the skiff as it was rowed back to the sambuk.

"It is a sad thing," I said, to break the silence.

The sheik raised his head and regarded me with a smile. He placed his hand on my shoulder. "All things, my friend, happen as Allah wills."

"Surely Allah did not wish the death of this poor man."

Sheikh Arash shrugged. "You are a Nazarene, my friend, and though you are people of the book, you do not understand the true faith. We Moslems believe all we do is written in God's book and cannot be changed."

"You do not believe in free will"?

"Is that what you Christians believe? Free will? How can a man have free will if God knows everything"?

"We believe God loves us."

"Loves you? Allah does not love. Why should he care for such insignificant creatures, for it is written that Mohammed one day took up two handfuls of earth and scattered them. 'So,' he said, 'God empties His hand of His slaves, a portion for Paradise and a portion for the blaze.'"

"Forgive me, sheik, I mean no offense, but that seems a bleak doctrine."

Sheik Arash sat silently for a moment rubbing his chin. Finally he nodded his head. "Bleak? Yes, perhaps so. Very bleak! But is this not the world as it is? Everywhere you see suffering. Your doctrine doubtless brings you comfort, but look around you, my young friend. Love? Where in this world do you see love"?

"At least his wife and sons will have the money from the sale of his pearl."

Sheik Arash shook his head. "No, he lost money last night playing dice with the nakhoda and the serang."

The sheik would inform Yusuf's widow and his two young sons of his death when we returned to Bahrain, and the next year his oldest son would dive for Sheik Arash to pay his father's debt. Inshallah!

Chapter 8

A Good Bargain

hen I reached Isfahan, I went straight to Bharton's home, still dressed in my Arab robes. I found him preparing for another trading journey, his luggage and supplies stacked in heaps on the floor of his office.

He clapped his hands for a servant. "Coffee, Salim. Bring us a pot"!

"Come, sit down, my friend. What have you brought me from Bahrain"?

He read the letters the sheik had written, nodded several times, then asked to see the pearls. We sat in chairs, the first I had sat in since I had last been in his house. I spread the pearls on Bharton's writing desk on a piece of white silk cloth.

"Upon my head, Jean-Baptiste, you have done excellently. The sheik speaks well of your abilities, you understand. I believe he wishes to adopt you. He says that you have the eye, and it appears that you have brought luck to the buying as well. This is the finest crop of pearls I have seen in ten years."

"I thank you, Bharton, for the opportunity."

"First, the turquoise and now pearls, I believe your servant is correct—you are a devi"!

I fear my face turned red as a flame. "You should not listen to Danush, Bharton. He talks a lot of nonsense."

"Humph. Tell me, now that you have visited the Pearl Coast, what are your plans"?

"I have been thinking a lot about Paris lately. I have been away from home for a long time."

"Hmm. So now we shall take the next step. Some of these beauties would be best sent to Europe. So here is what I propose, a partnership."

"No Bharton," I protested," I have made no investment! These are your pearls, and you have already done much for me".

Bharton gazed across the table smiling broadly. He raised his hand to cut off my protests. "Hear me out, Jean-Baptiste, if you please. You are quite right in one respect: the investment is mine or rather my family's."

"We could sell these pearls in Venice. If we were to follow our usual pattern, we could make a fine profit, you understand. But if you take them back to France, we could make an even greater profit. The Venetians control much of the trade between Persia and northern Europe. They keep the finest pieces for themselves, and the rest they sell. The Franks must buy from them, you understand, and they make immense profits."

"Here is my proposal. You take the best of the white pearls directly to France. It is an excellent parcel. You will sell the pearls for a much higher price than we could ever get in Venice—so much higher that, even splitting the profits, we will make more than we ever could selling to those money grubbing Venetians."

"Then I will sell them for you, and you shall have the profit in return for the opportunity you have given me."

Bharton raised his hands in a gesture of helplessness. "Jean-Baptiste," he laughed, "you are an amazingly stubborn fellow. No, my friend, no. It is important that you also share in the profits. Before you protest, you must understand I have two reasons for this. First, you are my friend and I wish to see you again, and second, in business it is important that your partners make money. Someday you will find yourself badly in need, and if you have followed my advice, you will always be able to raise the capital you require."

Finally it was agreed. Bharton set the cost price on the parcel. The profit realized above the cost would be split evenly between us. The Armenians maintain a spider's web of commercial associations throughout the world and a very settled manner of doing business. A letter of credit with Bharton's signature was as good in Surat as it was in Amsterdam, and money paid in Paris could be easily transferred to Isfahan.

Chapter 9

Return of the Prodigal

aris seemed much the same. Summer had come early. The trees lining the streets were blooming; the tender moist green of their leaves spoke of youth and promise and stood in contrast to the gray stone facades of the houses that lined the muddy street. It was early morning, and the air retained a bit of a chill. My mother stood on the stoop with a kerchief wrapped around her hair, sweeping the stairs as I rode up. Sweeping was a chore she always insisted on doing each morning, a habit left over from her childhood in Antwerp. As I prepared to dismount she looked up, shading her eyes with her hand. Her eyes widened with surprise.

"Jean-Baptiste, is that you? Is it really you"?

"Yes, ma mère," I said, folding her in my arms. "It is good to be home."

She stood back, held me at arm's length, and squinted at me. "You have lost weight. Oh, my son, we have been so worried about you. You have been gone so long. Forgive me, but I thought you might have been killed."

"Well, here I am, and, as you can see, very much alive."

"Yes, yes, wait a moment." She turned and shouted up at the second floor window. "Papa, Papa, wake up, you sleepyhead! You will never guess who is here. Come down quickly! Our son has returned."

My father's sleepy face appeared at the window. "Jean-Baptiste, you are home! Welcome, welcome! Woman, do not keep our son standing in the street. Come in, come in! I will be down directly."

We sat down around the hearth. My dear mother looked much the same as always, with her white matron's cap and her hair pulled back and neatly made up in a bun. Was her hair a bit grayer? Her eyes lit up with delight when I presented her with a small but exquisite pear shaped pearl of fine water, which was hung on a light gold chain. It had been a parting gift from Sheik Arash.

My father kept shaking his head. He was finding it hard to believe that his little boy had grown up, traveled to Persia, and returned a wealthy man. Truth to tell, I was far from wealthy, but my denials, I fear, were somewhat halfhearted. Who does not wish his parents to judge him a success in life? The fact that I had returned with bags full of pearls and turquoise impressed them and, in more self-indulgent moments, impressed me not a little as well.

I was rich in goods but had little ready money. I could, of course, use Bharton's letter to borrow ready cash, but I preferred to sell some of my goods. I knew nothing of the gem business or, for that matter, the current prices for turquoise and pearls in the Paris market. I hit upon the beginnings of a plan.

During my stay in Isfahan Bharton had made me a present of a suit of clothes in the Persian style, fit for a prince. I recruited two young cousins, sons of my uncle Melchior, and dressed them as lackeys. They were to play the part of my servants. I set out with my retinue for Le Marais–dressed in a purple over-shirt, and a yellow, long-sleeved, silk overcoat embroidered with purple threads. Yellow leggings matched my overcoat. My turban was also yellow silk but richly embroidered with purple and blue.

Le Marais, "the place," as we Parisians call it, is the most elegant and fashionable quarter of Paris. Richelieu built a townhouse there as did many noble families. It is close to the King's residence at the Louvre.

Fashionable shoppers stopped in their tracks and stared open-mouthed like bumpkins while, together with my retinue, I, a vision in oriental dress, sauntered regally along the boardwalk that fronted the shops. One

Figure 5: Browsing the shops at The Place du Cardinal from a 17th Century engraving.

elderly lady of fashion, decked out with a fur pelisse, gaped and tripped, sprawling over a display of millinery goods as we passed.

Several jewelers were set up among the forty or so booths along the arcade, but the day was perfect—sunny with the scent of spring in the air–so that I saw no reason to hurry. I took my time making my way from one to another.

The second jeweler's shop advertised a specialty in pearls. When I entered I was approached by a thin pinch-faced little man dressed in a frayed waistcoat of indifferent quality. He bowed. "My lord, how may I be of service?"

My lord, indeed! One young cousin, who had followed me into the shop, could hardly contain himself and was about to burst into laughter. I shot him a poisoned glance and at the same time struggled to maintain a straight face.

"My good man, I have a problem. Perhaps you can help me."

"A problem? Think nothing of it. There are few problems that Jacques cannot solve. How may I be of service to you, my lord."

I had brought with me an exquisite choker-length pearl strand that was part of Bharton's consignment. The gems were round, well matched, and of fine, lively water. I fished the strand from my purse. "Here is my problem," I said, extending my hand, the strand dangling from my forefinger. "I purchased this strand in Italy as a natal gift for my wife. I hoped that would be the end of it. Unfortunately," I sighed with what I hoped sounded like exasperation, "she prefers an opera length strand, and I am seeking pearls of similar quality to lengthen it. You understand, monsieur," I said, rolling my eyes heavenward in my best imitation of a foppish aristocrat, "women are never satisfied. What can one do"?

Jacques, the jeweler, took the strand, withdrew a glass attached to a cord from beneath his waistcoat, and made a great show of examining the pearls. He twisted his lips into a conspiratorial smile. "Very fine pearls, sir. May I congratulate you on your superior eye? I believe we can help you." He bowed again, exposing a bald head with a few thin, greasy strands of hair plastered across his bare pate. "If you will kindly step this way."

He plucked a silk handkerchief from his breast pocket and dusted off the top of a stool in front of the counter. "Please, monsieur, take a seat." He stepped behind the counter and from a rear shelf produced a rectangular board engraved with a series of parallel grooves, such as pearl sorters use in Bahrain. He placed a white porcelain platter next to the board and signaled an assistant who brought a chamois pouch, from which he poured a large quantity of pearls into the platter. He took my strand and laid it along a groove in the sorting board, picked up a pair of wooden tweezers, rapidly selected a line of pearls from the pouch, and set them in a groove alongside.

The gems he selected were very close in size and symmetry but of vastly inferior water. When he had picked a number sufficient to create the length I requested, he looked up and spread his hands. "Voila, my lord," he said with a flourish.

"Hmm," I said. I took my chin in my hand and pretended to study the pearls. "And the price, monsieur"?

"My lord," he said, looking me in the eye for a moment before shifting to study his layout. "I can see that you are a connoisseur of pearls. For you I can make a special price, a very special price."

Considering the quality of his pearls, the price was astonishing. I could barely control myself. I wanted to scream, to spit in his face: charlatan! idiot! Did this fool believe I had just fallen off the hay wagon? With difficulty I pretended to consider his offer for several minutes, idly fingering the pearls, taking one, then another, and holding them up toward the light while I considered what to say next. Finally I hit upon it. "Monsieur," I said, "I am afraid these will not do. Perhaps you have something of better quality"?

The smug smile drained from his face. The little man was clearly unprepared for my response. "Better, monsieur? These are the finest. I do have a few single pieces put aside… but the matching"!

I produced an indulgent smile.

The jeweler snapped his fingers, the assistant returned, and the jeweler whispered something. Moments later, he returned with another, smaller pouch. This parcel was of better quality, though less than half the number needed and still inferior in all respects to the gems in my strand. Once again, I asked the price. His answer nearly caused me to pitch headlong off my stool.

I took several deep breaths, then swallowed. "Are these," I inquired in a soft voice, "the best you can show me"?

The oily little fellow barely concealed his exasperation. Again a snap of the fingers followed by a brief whispered exchange with his assistant and a single pair of round pearls of fine water were placed before me.

"With regret, my lord. These are my finest pearls. They are very rare, the finest oriental quality. Perhaps, a pair of earrings would please your lady wife? But you must understand, my good sir, the price!"

"Beautiful," I exclaimed, and they were, with a lovely skin and beautiful water—a good match for my strand. The price was, of course, astonishing.

I knew what I needed to know. Bharton had been right. These Parisian jewelers were asking prices five times what I expected. My only regret was that I had not bought up every mean little pearl I saw in the Persian Gulf. "Beautiful," I said again, "I will keep them in mind for another occasion, but" I tried to look hapless "you understand, monsieur, my wife is not to be diverted, and so I must continue my quest. I bid you good day."

The smarmy little man bowed again and presented his calling

card, somewhat mollified by the possibility of a future sale. I lifted my chin, sniffed as if I detected a bad odor, and made a slow, dignified exit.

My retinue had lost interest and wandered off. I had to search around a bit, but I gathered them up, gave each a shiny silver penny, and we continued our stroll. At each shop that displayed pearls, I would produce my strand and make a similar enquiry. I was shown trays of gems. I priced pearls and, where I could, turquoise as well. Turkey stones were scarce in Paris at this time, and the prices were also quite astonishing.

Much of what was available in pearls came from the West Indies fisheries. They had a different look from the Persian Gulf. When I requested Persian pearls, I was either given excuses or assured that the pearls on offer were certainly Persian. If the Parisian jewelers were getting such prices, our profits were assured.

Figure 6: Jean-Baptiste Tavernier dressed in a Persian khalat. Portrait by Nicolas de Largilliére Herzog Anton Ulrich-Museum Braunschweig

Finally I made my way to a shop owned by Monsieur Torreles, who was a well-respected diamond cutter and a distant cousin of my father. The shop had an impressive inventory of diamonds, pearls, and divers gemstones, including turquoise. The salon was larger than the first jeweler's and led to a second room with a dozen artisans, both goldsmiths and lapidaries, at work. I asked to speak to the proprietor and was introduced to Pierre Torreles, a slender man of middle years, several inches taller than myself with a full head of dark hair and graying muttonchops. He regarded me frankly, with blue eyes the same shade as my father's, and a hint of a smile playing around the corners of his mouth. He showed me to a small private office.

"So," he said, "you are my cousin, Jean-Baptiste, the traveler. I have heard of you. I must say," he said with a broad smile, "you look like the crown prince of Persia in that costume."

I managed a sheepish smile.

"Yes, and all day I have been hearing that a genuine oriental potentate was shopping in our humble arcade. That, I suppose, would be you"?

"Yes," I said. "I suppose so."

"Ha, ha! Well, Your Excellency, it is a pleasure to meet you at last. How may I be of service"?

I handed him my pearl strand.

"What's this? Lovely! Where might I ask did you obtain such a marvelous strand"?

I liked this man so I told him a bit of my Persian adventures and the story of my sojourn with Sheik Arash Abdul-razzaq.

"Incredible, cousin. Such a tale"! His eyes danced. "I am sorry I made sport of you, Jean-Baptiste. I hope you will forgive me, but you know you do look rather like something out of the Arabian Nights in that get-up. We must have dinner together. I must hear more of your adventures, but is there something I may do for you today?"

"Two things, cousin. I brought back from Persia a fine parcel of oriental pearls and several parcels of Persian turquoise that I wish to sell."

He sat up straight in his chair. "You have more, of similar quality, and, you wish to sell them to me"?

"If you are interested."

"Interested? I am with child to see the goods you have brought from Persia."

I returned that evening after the shop closed with my goods and laid them out on the office table. Pierre lit several tallow lamps and placed them around the table.

"Incredible, Jean-Baptiste, incredible! Have you truly visited these places? It seems the stuff of legend." Pierre regarded me silently for a moment, then smiled. "So, cousin, now for the bad news," he said, fingering a parcel of pearls. "Tell me your price."

Pierre haggled like an Arab. I could tell he really wanted the parcel. "Come, cousin," I said, "at this price you can easily double, even triple your money. I have a friend, a very wealthy Persian prince, who knows your market well, and he assures me that, not only is the quality exceptional, but there is nothing to match these pearls anywhere in le Marais."

Pierre regarded me with a sour look. "So that was the purpose of your masquerade. You are a subtle devil, Jean-Baptiste, and Mon Dieu, a relative. But," he laughed, "unfortunately you are also correct, and so I agree to your price. Now," he said, rubbing his hands together, "let us discuss the turquoise."

"On the turquoise, I will give you an excellent price, and in return I would ask you a favor."

"Of course, cousin." I could hear the tiniest bit of uncertainty in his voice. "What sort of favor"?

"Not to put too fine a point on it, cousin, I wish to become your apprentice."

Pierre tilted back in his chair and regarded me very seriously for a moment. "Apprentice, Jean-Baptiste, I am flattered. But why? Surely you do not…"

"Pierre, you are a fine jeweler, and you are family. My dream is to return to the Orient, perhaps to India, to buy diamonds. Someday I believe, I will find a fabulous stone, and I wish to pursue that dream. But my knowledge is sadly lacking. I need a good teacher.

Pierre sat back in his chair and regarded me silently for several minutes. Finally he spoke. "Yes, Jean-Baptiste, I can see that you are a dreamer. You have been lucky, but I suspect more than just lucky. Frankly, had you come to me with such an idea before your voyage to Persia, I would have called you a fool and dismissed you out of hand. But with what I see before me, you have proven yourself and I believe you will achieve your dream. So I accept your offer, and I will tell you that I believe I have gotten the best of the bargain." He put out his hand. "Welcome, Jean-Baptiste Tavernier, to the House of Torreles. Next week you become my junior assistant and in a few years, who knows, perhaps on your trip to India, you may have a partner."

Chapter 10

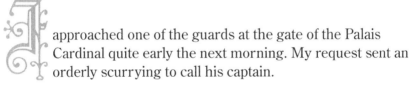

The Red Cardinal

I approached one of the guards at the gate of the Palais Cardinal quite early the next morning. My request sent an orderly scurrying to call his captain.

"What is your business, young man?"

"I wish to make an appointment with Père Joseph." This was the Capuchin friar who introduced me to Monsieur l'Abbé de Chapes and Monsieur de Saint Liebau, with whom I had traveled to Constantinople. The friar made me promise him that I would call on him when I returned to Paris.

The officer looked me up and down and sniffed as if he detected a bad odor. "And what, may I ask, is your business with His Excellency?"

I don't think the officer believed me.

"I have strict orders, monsieur; Père Joseph is accepting no appointments."

I bowed, and as I left, I proffered my calling card. Perhaps the Gray Eminence had forgotten me. Everyone in Paris knew of Père Joseph; he had a fearsome reputation as a canny political operator deep in the councils of Cardinal Richelieu, the first minister of France. My hope was quickly dashed. Early the next morning my father shook me awake.

"Jean-Baptiste, wake up, wake up. A soldier in livery just delivered this note." His face was ashen. "Mon Dieu, it bears the crest of Cardinal Richelieu himself."

Indeed it did, I was to present myself at the palais that very morning.

I handed my invitation to the guard. The man looked at the crest and snapped to attention. It was "very good, sir," and "this way my lord." The captain was called, a page was summoned.

The page led me up the grand staircase to a landing where the staircase split left and right. He was a serious young man dressed in the cardinal's distinctive red and yellow livery. On the wall was a huge carved rendering of the cardinal's coat of arms. We ascended to the right and walked along a long hallway with arched windows and a vaulted ceiling, with colorful scenes from Greek mythology painted on an ultramarine blue sky. The end of the hall widened into an antechamber with a tall double door decorated with the cardinal's arms in gold leaf. On either side of the door a richly caparisoned guard dressed in the duke's livery stood as straight as his polished halberd. The page offered me one of the chairs that lined both walls of the anteroom and hurried off.

I sat down and looked about. There were a number of other men about the room. Some sat idly while others clustered in small groups talking quietly. All were richly dressed. I made myself as comfortable as I could and waited. About a quarter of an hour later, one of the gilded doors swung open and a severe looking, plainly dressed man emerged and came toward me. The room went silent.

"Monsieur Tavernier?"

I bolted to my feet, hat in hand.

The secretary made a curt bow. "His Eminence will see you now."

"His Eminence, but…I…?"

The secretary ignored my confusion, turned on his heel, and strode toward the ornate doorway. I hurried to catch up. "Surely," I thought, "there is some mistake," but once through the first set of doors, I was ushered through another set of doors every bit as grand as the first and found myself in a richly decorated chamber standing before a huge wooden desk behind which sat Cardinal Richelieu himself.

"Your Eminence, Monsieur Tavernier!" the black clad lackey announced with a deep bow. He backed toward the doors, bowed again, and slipped out, softly closing the doors behind.

"Monsieur Tavernier," the cardinal addressed me without looking up or rising from his chair.

I bowed deeply. "Your Eminence," I said, addressing the diminutive red skull cap atop the cardinal's thinning gray head. "I do beg your pardon. I thought I was to meet with Père Joseph." The cardinal wore a plain unadorned red cassock.

"Unfortunately, monsieur," the cardinal said, looking up, his dark eyes holding mine, "Père Joseph is otherwise engaged." He smiled thinly, his lips remaining tightly closed and slightly pursed as if he had just tasted something sour. "I am afraid, monsieur, that you must make do with me."

I bowed.

"I am informed that you recently returned from a trip to Constantinople and Persia."

"That is true, Your Eminence."

The cardinal rose from his chair and walked around the massive desk. He was a slender, severe looking man with a bony face, wide cheekbones and a pointed chin that was accentuated by dark, carefully trimmed mustaches and goatee. "Come," he said. He lightly grasped my elbow and gestured toward two chairs with a low table set between. "Sit down. I wish to hear something of your travels."

The interview seemed quite long though I don't believe it lasted a half of an hour. Did I say interview? Interrogation was more like it! The cardinal was very well informed. He knew my history, knew of my service with the Viceroy of Hungary and with the Duke of Mantua. He was most interested in the Persian court and state of the shah's army, subjects about which I knew almost nothing. He also wished to know about the state of the roads, the difficulties of sea travel, and the time it took to go from place to place. He kept his eyes fixed on mine and listened attentively to my descriptions of the turquoise mines and pearling in the Persian Gulf. He nodded his approval several times when I spoke of my plans to return to Persia and visit the East Indies.

"Monsieur Tavernier?" the Cardinal hesitated and regarded me thoughtfully for several moments. "Monsieur Tavernier, you are a subject of the king of France, yet you have taken service with two foreign princes, one with whom France is currently at war. You are also a Huguenot, I believe. If you were called upon by your king to serve your country, where would your first loyalty lie, with France or with those whom you have served?"

My face began turning red. I could feel the sweat breaking out at my hairline. "Your Eminence, I don't understand, I…"

The cardinal raised his hand, "Do not be alarmed my young friend. I merely ask a question. There will be no repercussions." His eyes seemed as dark as the pit. "Take a moment, consider carefully, and answer truthfully."

If the cardinal had meant his last statement to reassure me, he had not succeeded. I knew that his was more than just an idle inquiry. All France knew this man's reputation for ruthlessness. He had proven so at La Rochelle. Four fifths of the town's population, some twenty thousand Protestants, died in that siege. Yet he was also known as generous to those who served him well.

I was angry. What had I done or said that my loyalty to my country should be questioned? I raised my head, took a deep breath, met the cardinal's eye and made my answer.

"Your Eminence, I have served those who have offered me employment and opportunity. In no case have I, to my knowledge, done anything against the interests of my country. Yes, I am a Huguenot, but I do not believe that my Protestant faith automatically makes me disloyal any more than the Roman Catholic religion automatically makes a man a patriot. I am a loyal subject of His

Majesty, Louis XIII."

Richelieu's cold eyes searched mine for what seemed like hours when, in fact, it could not have been more than seconds. He nodded thoughtfully, picked up a little bell set on the table between us, rang it, and stood up. I jumped to my feet.

"Well spoken, Monsieur Tavernier, well spoken. I can see that you are a brave and thoughtful young man. Père Joseph was correct in bringing you to my attention. Your plans are ambitious, but I believe you will carry them forward, and I wish you to keep me informed. Kindly come and see me again before you depart on your next journey. If there is anything I can do to help move forward your plans, I wish to know of it. Thank you, monsieur, and good day."

I stifled several questions, bowed deeply, and thanked his eminence. Moments later I found myself following the narrow back of the young page down the same long corridor. I felt completely drained and not a little bit puzzled. The cardinal had asked many questions but revealed almost nothing. What was it this man wanted of me? I felt like I had won a reprieve although from what I knew not. One thing seemed very clear; though Cardinal Richelieu did not say a great deal, he left the impression that everything he did say he meant.

The next week I began work for my cousin Pierre. Over my mother's tearful objections I took rooms in the Quarter Marais, not far from Pierre's atelier. I was too old and had done and seen too much to live beneath my parent's critical eye. I sold most of my turquoise to Pierre at a price that delighted him and gave me an excellent profit and that, together with my share from his purchase of a portion of Bharton's pearls, would keep me in reasonable luxury for several years.

Pierre also sent me to his friend, a tailor who had a passion for gems. A pair of fine Turkey stones made up as earrings for his wife was more than enough to provide me with several handsome outfits, including a plumed chapeau and other items in the latest fashion. Next came footwear. Shoes were out of style. A man of fashion wore knee-high boots of the finest leather. I visited the cobbler and had several pairs made. I fear I strutted a bit in those days. Fine clothes, as they say, make the man.

Pierre set me to work in this lapidary under the direction of his master diamond cutter, François Dulac.

"Monsieur Pierre says that you have a plan to make a voyage to India to go to the diamond mines yourself and buy rough diamond."

"Yes, monsieur, that is my plan."

"He also told me that you have lately come from the lands of Persia and that you bought Turkey stones at the mines and visited the islands of the Persian Gulf and watched men dive to the bottom of the sea and bring up pearls."

"Yes."

He shook his head. "Such wonders! I am a simple man, monsieur. I have never heard such tales, much less met a man who has seen such wonders, but Monsieur Pierre showed me your pearls and, mark you, they are as fine as any I have ever seen, and the proof of the pudding is in the eating. You want Dulac to teach you about diamond rough? That I will do willingly enough."

"I do, Master Dulac. I plan to visit the diamond mines of India and seek out gems. Do you think the plan is sound?"

He eyed me oddly, then shook his head. "How should I know? Sound enough if you come back at all, I guess! So far, monsieur, you have had the Devil's own luck, but luck has a way of changing, if you take my meaning. If it's diamonds you want to learn, I will teach you what I can. I don't want Monsieur Pierre thinking that I have been speaking out of turn."

"Thank you. I shall work hard and learn all that you are willing to teach me." I believe that Master Dulac regarded me as a dilettante and did not expect me to last very long in his workshop. I was determined to prove him wrong.

The next morning I reported to the master dressed in a linen shirt and an old woolen doublet, plain cotton stockings, and a pair of beaten leather boots that had seen half of Persia. He looked me over, nodded, and handed me a leather apron.

"Look here, my lad," he said pointing to a very heavy rectangular frame made of thick wooden beams about man high. The frame held two flat metal wheels, each the size of a pie plate, which were spinning like tops.

"This here is René, and these are what we call laps." A serious looking workman in a thickly spotted leather apron stood balanced with his legs spread apart, both hands putting pressure on a slender steel armature that held what appeared to be a small rough diamond against one of the spinning wheels.

I became absorbed in the work, and spring passed into summer then into fall. One day in late autumn, Pierre called me into his office.

"Ah, there you are, cousin. Tell me, Jean-Baptiste, how you are getting along? Are you enjoying your life here in Paris?"

I said that I was enjoying having my own bachelor quarters and working at the atelier, but that I had time for little else.

"Hmm, Jean-Baptiste, no one can complain about your dedication. You work hard and you are doing very well. I meant how are you getting along socially? You are a young man. Have you found friends," he winked, "perhaps a young lady?"

"No, cousin, I have not had the time."

"No time? Nonsense Jean-Baptiste! You are a Frenchman! A man cannot work all the time. He must have diversion. I do not wish to see you making yourself ill. What is it the English say, all work and no play! You need to have some fun, isn't that so?"

"Well yes, Pierre, I suppose so," I said a bit helplessly.

Pierre had a large smile pasted across his face. "Well, cousin, I have an important errand for you. I wish you to take this pair of earrings," he gestured at a lovely pair of drop pearls set before him on a velvet pad, "to a very old and important client, the Countess Rochambeau. Her husband is on a diplomatic trip to England and will not return for several months. I have told her about you, and she has expressed an interest in meeting you and hearing the story of your travels. The family keeps a chateau here in the Marais. I have made an appointment for you this afternoon."

"Today! Very well, Pierre, I shall put my best foot forward."

The smile remained fixed to his face: "Yes, yes, of course, my dear boy. I know you will. I depend upon it. So go along now and, Jean-Baptiste," he winked, "take your time. Take the afternoon if necessary. With her husband away, the countess is a lonely woman;

if she wishes to engage you in a few hours of conversation, do not feel as though you must hurry back. We shall get along well enough."

I gathered together the merchandise and set out on foot. I can still recall the warm sun of high summer on my back. The Rochambeau Palais was quite near; it sat on the corner of a tree-lined street just off the Rue Cardinal. It was but a quarter hour's walk from Torreles.

I was expected. A footman in livery admitted me and showed me into a richly decorated salon, bowed, and made his exit. I had just begun to examine a particularly fine Flemish tapestry when, with a rustle of expensive silk, madame swept into the room. I was dumb struck. I had been expecting an "old" client, but though the countess may have been an old client, she was certainly not old. Countess Rochambeau was a vision in scarlet. Honey gold hair the texture of spun silk framed a wide brow and heart shaped face, with beautifully sculpted full red lips that turned up at the corners, large deep blue eyes shaped like almonds, and a naughty smile. She offered her hand. I completely forgot my fine manners but managed a kiss and a bow.

"Enchanté, monsieur," she said showing a perfect row of pearly teeth. Her hand lingered in mine for just a moment longer than necessary. "Pierre is an old friend, and he has spoken to me often of his adventuresome cousin. He knows of my devotion to all things Eastern. But you see I am so excited," she said and smiled her beguiling smile, "that I have forgotten my manners. Come, won't you sit down, monsieur?"

She placed her hand behind my elbow and guided me across the room to a couch and chair, both upholstered in light blue silk and set by a window with rich, full length, red velvet draperies. She sat on the couch and invited me to take the chair opposite her.

"You will take tea, monsieur?" My arm tingled where the countess's hand had touched it.

"With pleasure, my lady, if it is no trouble." She picked up a silver bell and shook it gently. "No trouble at all, monsieur." She smiled and her eyes looked deep into mine. "I simply adore Persia. I hope that I don't bore you with questions, but you must tell me everything. Where you went, what you saw, everything."

"Really, madame, you have visited Persia?"

She laughed. "Oh no, monsieur. I am afraid that the nearest I have been to Persia is this carpet upon which your feet currently rest. I have only heard tales. The rugs and the embroidered fabrics, such a palette and the workmanship…!"

She paid close attention and laughed with delight at my description of the follies of my servant Danush which, I confess, I embellished somewhat. I found myself prattling on and on, entranced, wishing only to see the smile on those beautiful lips and hear the delicate music of her laughter. Do I sound smitten? I surely was.

After I had talked on for perhaps two hours, the countess interrupted me. "How delightful, such a raconteur. I shall have a soirée and you, dear Jean-Baptiste, shall be the guest of honor."

"Then I shall have the privilege of meeting your husband, the count?"

She shook her head sadly. "No, I doubt that the count will be in attendance. He has been gone for almost a year, and I am not certain when he will return. I am a lonely woman, monsieur, very lonely. Your visit has raised my spirits. You are so young and handsome; I wish us to be friends. And please, no more, madame. My name is Noelle." She patted the cushion next to her and smiled soulfully. "Here, Jean-Baptiste, won't you join me?"

I was so surprised by her offer that I stumbled and almost fell onto the couch. The hour was getting late and the afternoon light was beginning to fade into shadow. The divan was small; we sat with our shoulders almost touching. I hardly dared meet those lovely eyes; I looked down. Her gown was cut low, exposing a lovely décolleté and soft breasts that rose and fell enchantingly with the rhythm of her breath. She smiled shyly and took my hand. Her scent made my head swim. I swallowed several times. My hand shook as I raised her hand to my lips as somehow she slid into my arms, and I tasted the honey of her mouth.

As I am a gentleman, I will not say more except that this was the first of many assignations with the lovely Countess de Rochambeau.

The count, her husband, returned from his mission but was rarely at home. He preferred to be off gambling or pursuing one or another lady of the court. This is the way of the aristocracy. They play at love as they play at everything. Each man has a wife whom he ignores and a mistress upon whom he lavishes his attention. It is the same with the women. Each is expected to have a besotted suitor to pursue her.

I went to work as usual the next day. I half expected that Pierre would have something to say about my prolonged absence the previous afternoon. Instead he greeted me with a broad smile and a knowing wink and then without another word returned to his work.

I had tucked away the meeting with the first minister in a corner of my mind when I received another summons to the Palais Cardinal.

This time the summons bore the signature of Père Joseph. The friar's chamber was quite plain. He sat behind a simple wood table dressed in the dour gray habit of the Capuchin order. He got right down to business:

"Monsieur Tavernier, I summoned you here today on behalf of the first minister of the realm, His Eminence, Cardinal Richelieu. In your interview with His Eminence, he asked you if you considered yourself a loyal subject of His Majesty." His pale eyes bored into me. "Do you recall your answer?"

"I do."

He nodded curtly then continued. "The Cardinal has asked me on behalf of His Majesty to inquire if you would be willing to do your country a service. I must warn you before you answer that what I am about to ask will be difficult and perhaps dangerous. Please consider your answer carefully!"

The Cardinal! His Majesty! Such great personages required my help? If I had been older and wiser, I might have thought my answer over more carefully. This was to be one of the most important decisions of my life, and yet it was made almost instantly.

I said, "Yes."

Père Joseph nodded, favored me with a wintry smile, and then went on in a formal tone.

"Very good, my son. I believe you are well acquainted with the court of the Holy Roman Emperor, Ferdinand II."

"Yes, Your Excellency. During the four years I served the Viceroy, I spent more than a year at the Emperor Ferdinand's court in Vienna."

"You are also friendly with a number of officials of the court—the Governor of Vienna and an Irish mercenary, a Colonel Butler, who is currently in the Emperor's service."

I was astonished and not a little frightened by the depth of Père Joseph's knowledge. "Your Excellency is very well informed."

"I believe you mentioned the colonel during our conversation in Ratisbon."

"Well then, Your Excellency, I must compliment you on your excellent memory."

Père Joseph smiled thinly. His feverish eyes always looked directly at me. "It is you who deserve compliments; you, monsieur, are a very subtle courtier. You are a Huguenot, yet you somehow managed to survive and remain in the Emperor Ferdinand's favor for some four and a half years. During this same period he expelled all the Protestant priests from Bohemia. How did you manage that, monsieur?"

"Well, Excellency, not to put too fine a point on it, but I was never one to flaunt my religious convictions."

Suddenly Père Joseph threw back his head and laughed. "Not to put too fine a point on it, indeed. I suspect that you never mentioned them at all."

"I don't believe, Your Excellency, that I was ever asked."

"Silence was golden in this case, Jean-Baptiste. You were familiar with the political situation in Ferdinand's empire prior to your journey to Constantinople?"

"It has been several years, Your Excellency, since I have been in Vienna, and much has changed, I am sure."

Père Joseph eyed me sternly. "Indeed, monsieur, I am about to bring you up to date, but first, let me warn you: some of what I am about to tell you is common knowledge, but much of it is a state secret and is known only to His Majesty and a few of his most trusted ministers. It is to be shared with no one, no one at all. If you were to repeat this information, it would be considered treason against His Majesty, do you understand?"

I swallowed with difficulty and nodded my head.

"Now tell me, what do you know of the political situation in Germany?"

"I know little of the current state of affairs. As Your Excellency is aware, I have been traveling continuously since we last met. I was in Germany with the imperial army as an interpreter with Colonel Butler's regiment when the king of Sweden invaded Pomerania. The king seems to have been a great military leader. He defeated and killed General Tilly and might have made himself master of all Germany had he not been killed in the battle at Lutzen by the imperial army under General Wallenstein."

"Very good, my son, you have the sense of it. Now let me give you our...that is, His Majesty's view of the current situation: As of this moment, a Habsburg sits upon the throne of both the Holy Roman and Spanish empires. Spain owns a portion of the Low Countries. Despite the Swedish victories, France remains surrounded by Habsburg lands. Strategically this situation leaves France with no barrier between ourselves and the Habsburg lands, and extremely vulnerable to attack from the north, south and west. His Majesty rightly considers this situation to be intolerable. To insure the safety of the realm, some years ago he ordered His Eminence to take measures to weaken the power of the Habsburg dynasty."

"The empire is very powerful though one or another of the princes is always causing trouble," I said.

"True, and we have tried our best to exploit these divisions, but here is something you don't know. After the Swedish king defeated the emperor in Pomerania, the cardinal conceived a brilliant stratagem, and with His Majesty's consent, he sent me to meet with the Swedes at Stettin. I was able to negotiate an agreement to provide money to finance the Swedish Protestant army's campaign against the Emperor Ferdinand in Germany. The cardinal believed that an alliance with Sweden would serve to distract the emperor.

One million livres a year was a small price to pay to keep both
Ferdinand and the Swedish army busy and away from our borders.
But, as you know, the Swedish king was killed at Lutzen, leaving
France with no counterweight against the Habsburg ambitions."

"France, allied with Protestant Sweden? I would never have
thought..."

The friar's eyes smoldered beneath his heavy brows. "Aye,
no one did. That was the genius of it, but now the emperor, King
Phillip of Spain, and certain of the German Catholic princes have
made a pact with the devil. Their ungodly plan is to invade France in
concert from the west and south. The realm is in grave danger."

"Your Excellency, I had no idea."

"There are other dangers as well. Cardinal Richelieu has many
enemies among our own nobility. These men are traitors. Some
even seek to overthrow the king. They are ruthless and will stop
at nothing to gain power. Luckily the cardinal has His Majesty's
complete support. The cardinal is a great man, Jean-Baptiste. If we
lose him I fear we will lose France."

I was quite shaken by Père Joseph's words. "Your Excellency,
I thank you for your confidence. Whatever you and His Eminence
wish me to do I will do."

Once again the Capuchin's feverish eyes bored into me. "Well
spoken, my son, well spoken. I told His Eminence that you could
be depended upon. The cardinal wishes you to undertake a mission
to Germany. You are a resourceful young man. You speak German;
you are well known and have many friends at the court in Vienna.
What would be more natural than for you to return to the court
after your travels in Persia to visit, to bring presents for your friends
and perhaps sell the odd jewel? I understand that you are quite the
raconteur. Your presence will create a stir, important people will be
curious, and you will receive many invitations. No one will suspect
you." He paused for a moment.

"You will keep your ears open. We are particularly interested in
the doings of Wallenstein, the upstart Duke of Friedland. Have you
met the man?"

"I sat at table with him once at a dinner given by the viceroy, but

I cannot claim to *know* him. He was the emperor's generalissimo, and he enjoys a fearsome reputation at court as a military commander. He was dismissed by the emperor, was he not, after the meeting of the imperial diet at Regensburg just before I left for Constantinople?"

"Yes, exactly. The Catholic electors demanded his ouster, but he has returned. We have had secret contacts with Wallenstein; he is once again Ferdinand's generalissimo. The man claims that he wishes to negotiate a peace between France and the empire, but we believe that he is playing some sort of game of his own. We have seen to it that Wallenstein's machinations have become known in Vienna. Emperor Ferdinand now distrusts him; his reinstatement has brought him even more power and the emperor fears him. This is not good news. He is the most able commander in the empire, and we must watch him as a mongoose watches a snake."

"Well then, Your Excellency, I will be your spy, though I have had no experience at such business. Is that to be my mission?"

"Yes, that and more. We also wish you to reconnect with and draw out your friend Colonel Butler, who is now a general and in command of the emperor's troop in the town of Eger. We desire to know where his loyalties and those of the officer corps lie. Wallenstein may be attempting to subvert the emperor's army for his own purposes. We suspect he may be planning to make himself king of Bohemia."

"Forgive me, but, how is that important, Your Excellency?"

Père Joseph regarded me sternly. "There are some things, my son, that you are better off not knowing. For now we simply wish to know the officer corps's point of view. Our intentions will become clear in time. I will say only this: knowing which bait to use makes it easier to catch a fish."

"My apologies, Your Excellency, it was curiosity only."

His Excellency nodded. "In this sort of business, my son, it is better to stifle one's curiosity. Let me be candid. There is always a chance that you will be discovered and if discovered, interrogated. The means used for obtaining information from spies are often unpleasant, you understand, my son. What you do not know you cannot reveal."

"I understand, Your Excellency. When do you wish me to leave?"

"As soon as possible, within a week!"

A week was a very short time in which to prepare but that was the least of my concerns. I would have to speak to Pierre and because my mission was secret, I could not tell him its exact nature, where I was going, and when I might return. I did not know myself. Then there was my countess. Noelle had been planning a dinner party for three days hence at which I was to be guest of honor. I was relieved that the party could go forward as planned.

Pierre knew of my summons to the palais and showed little surprise at my imminent departure. I thought that curious. He listened gravely to my apologies and vague explanation of confidential and urgent business, winked, clapped me on the back, wished me luck, and said that my position at Torreles would be waiting for me upon my return.

Father Joseph issued one last instruction before he dismissed me: "You are not to come back to the palais. The comings and goings here are carefully watched. You have been seen here twice," he said. "Another visit would draw attention and that we wish to avoid. This is for your own protection, do you understand?"

I bowed.

"You will be contacted in due course, though not by me. We will not speak again," he said. When and by whom I would be contacted Père Joseph would not say, only that my contact would make an observation. Let me see if I can remember exactly, ah yes! "The Paris season seems particularly cool this year." To which I was to reply in these exact words: "We can only hope for an early spring." It all seemed rather overdone, but as His Excellency was rather a humorless fellow, I kept my observations to myself.

Chapter 11

The Dinner Party

Noelle was convinced that her dinner party would be my entrée into polite society. She became obsessed with every detail of the preparations and chattered on prettily about the menu, the guests, and the decorations.

"It will be perfect, Jean-Baptiste. I am inviting only my richest and most amusing friends."

"I fear I will seem a dull bird amidst so many peacocks," I said.

"Nonsense, mon cher, you will be the handsomest man at the fête."

"But, my clothes!"

"Hmm, yes, I take your point. Surely you have something… exotic, something with an Oriental flair."

I mentioned the Persian costume I had worn on my promenade at the Palais Royal. Noelle insisted that I try it on.

"Perfect," she laughed merrily and clapped her hands. "You look like a Persian prince, so imposing and that turban, so droll!" She circled around me. "Hmm, something is missing! Wait a moment!" She opened the doors to her armoire and poked around. "Yes here it is." She brought out a beautiful peacock feather and insisted that I tuck it into my turban. "Let me see! Turn around! Yes, now it is absolutely perfect."

The affair went off on schedule. It was, she said, a small affair limited to forty guests. This was the number that could be seated comfortably around her dining table. The room was ablaze with candlelight. The guests included several barons, three baronesses, a count, an assortment of marquises, a bishop, and several monsignors. There were more women than men.

The menu included four courses and dessert. The table was covered with a cloth of fine linen of suitable length so that a guest might use his portion as a napkin. For the first course a large tureen of oille, a stew of spiced pigeon, was set as the center of the table. It was wonderful feast. The entrees included filet of duck, partridge in cabbage, and fillet of beef with cucumber and galantine of chicken. At the second course, the centerpiece was three quarters of veal to which was added six hens and eight rabbits and two kinds of salads. For our third course we had a center plate of partridge pie with plats moyens of vegetables, fruits and hors d'oeuvres of fried sheep's testicles and slices of roast spread with kidneys, onions, and cheese. The wine was good and plentiful.

One of the guests, a visiting English marquise, was of such robust girth that she required three normal places at table to accommodate her. She did not sit—she docked like a man-o-war entering a berth. I sat between Noelle and the 'man-o-war,' who stank and spoke horrible French. Unfortunately, she soon ferreted out the fact that I spoke English.

"Monsieur Tavernier," she simpered, turning as she pressed against my arm with one of her gigantic bosoms and smiled. "I am so pleased to make your acquaintance. You must tell me simply everything about Persia."

I bowed. "But of course, my lady. What do you wish to know?"

"First, you must tell me about the ladies of the court." She raised her eyes and leered. A hand groped my thigh. "Do they flirt with the gentlemen at table?"

"The women are not allowed to sit with the gentlemen at table, madame; they are confined to the seraglio."

"The seraglio. Yes, I have heard of such places, houses of debauchery without doubt." Her eyes grew bright, her chest heaved, and her breath quickened. She slurped some wine from her glass and leaned closer. "Is it true, Monsieur Tavernier, that captured Christian women are kept in these seraglios as slaves and ravished daily?"

"Yes, madame, I believe so, though perhaps not on a daily basis."

"Truly", she leered at me. "I should like to visit one of these seraglios."

She stank and drank, and the more she drank, the more amorous she became. I barely tasted the food because it was necessary to keep one hand in my lap to fend off the marquise. My attempts to alert Noelle of the woman's lechery fell flat. Noelle only smiled and made cow eyes.

Parisians love to eat, and they love to talk. A dinner party gives them the opportunity to do both at the same time. A bluff young fellow with yellow mustaches, the second son of a duke, sat at my right. He was dressed in the uniform of a king's lancer.

"Tell me, monsieur, what is your sense of the Persian steel? Are they good fighting men?"

"They seem brave enough, Colonel."

A fat older woman, I think she was a baroness, shouted across the table. "Fighting men, hah! I have heard that all the Persian soldiers are gelded, that they are all eunuchs—is that not so, Monsieur Tavernier?"

"Some, madame, but only among the Turks, and they are called Janissaries. Eunuchs are the keepers of the harems."

On the other side of the table, a well dressed gentleman was engaged in a heated argument with a cleric.

"In Persia a man may have as many wives as he wishes," he said.

"That is against God's law." the cleric retorted.

"Violates common sense as well," said the lancer.

Noelle introduced me just before dessert was served. I rose to speak. This proved to be a mistake as it left my lower extremities completely undefended. I kept my talk brief and answered questions.

"Tell us, monsieur, about your costume. Is that the type of thing the better sort of Persian men wear at table?" One of the ladies asked.

"It is, madame, though they do not sit at table. They sit upon cushions set on the floor."

"Truly, how odd."

"It is not so difficult once you get used to it. As I was telling our English guest, the women do not eat with the men. They are confined to the harem."

During my talk, the groping attentions of the English marquise and my obvious discomfort elicited knowing looks and short bursts of laughter from around the table. Several of the guests watched with barely concealed amusement.

"Perhaps the English should adopt this custom," one of the guests suggested laughing.

Just at that moment, the marquise, who was by now quite drunk and not paying the slightest attention, grasped me in a particularly sensitive place. I flinched violently, upsetting the brimming goblet that she had just raised to her lips with her other hand, sending the contents gurgling down between her breasts and cascading like a crimson waterfall down the front of her gown.

Gales of laughter washed over the table. The marquise hooted and grasped the tablecloth pulling a half-filled soup tureen into her lap and causing even more laughter. She jumped to her feet, tipping over her chair, which crashed into her footman, propelling the unfortunate man backwards into a pedestal that supported a large vase. The vase hit the floor with a report like a cannon and exploded into a million pieces. The guests were now almost falling out of their own chairs. The marquise, her dignity ruffled, completely ignored the unfortunate servant who lay sprawled on the floor. She drew herself up, staggered, and strode angrily from the room amidst applause and a storm of laughter.

Noelle remained composed, smiling sweetly as if nothing were happening. She rose gracefully from her chair—the signal that the formal dinner had ended. She took my arm and together we led the party from the dining room into the chateau's main salon, leaving the servants to clean up the mess.

"What a disaster," I whispered as we made our way to the main salon.

Noelle squeezed my arm. "But no, chéri," she whispered, "it was perfect. A wonderful performance. Such a raconteur! They were all charmed and that awful Englishwoman—it was all I could do to keep a straight face."

"But your beautiful vase, the dinner…."

"La, my love, I would have sacrificed ten vases for the look on her face as the wine poured down her bosoms, Jean-Baptiste. I could barely contain myself, and you played your role perfectly, standing there, so innocent! It was better than the latest farce, so droll!"

I was not feeling at all droll—in fact the very opposite of droll. "But madame la marquise! She is your guest. She is very angry."

"That harridan?" she gave my arm another squeeze. "Forget her. She is no one! I only invited her as a favor to a friend. She dare not say anything nor dare she show her face anywhere in polite society for that matter. Mark my words, she will pack up and flee to London as quickly as she can and with her ample tail tucked between her stumpy legs. This will be the talk of the season, and you, mon chéri, are a great success."

"Oh, my dear, I almost forgot. There is a gentleman, a Monsieur Chenault, who has been waiting patiently to speak with you. You see, there he is by the window seat, the handsome blonde haired gentleman. Be a good boy and find out what he wants while I gather the rest of the herd and move them towards the door. I shall make your excuses. I hope you are not tired. She smiled another of her wicked smiles and, with a flick of her fan and a rustle of silk, moved off.

Chapter 12

The Spy

wo days later I was on the road to Vienna with the handsome young man from Noelle's party. There were eight men in our party: Monsieur (now Frère) Chenault was dressed in a priest's cassock. Chenault was a tall slender young man, slightly stooped at the shoulders. He had fine blond hair and an impish face that dimpled when he smiled. The other members of our party were six hard-eyed, tight-lipped young gentlemen who affected to be merchants but possessed little in the way of trade goods. They were, however, well armed with sword and musket and, from their bearing, obviously military men. I was the only one dressed as myself. As part of my instructions from Père Joseph, Monsieur Chenault was to provide me with an introduction into the world of espionage and, I suspected, to act as my minder.

After an unusually warm autumn, the weather had turned cold. Luckily there had been little rain, the snow had yet to come, and the roads were hard and dry. As we rode into Germany we began to see signs of war. Large swaths of territory had been destroyed, farms and crops looted, castles and villages burned out. We met with a group of several dozen peasants just outside the still smoking remains of a farm village, their pitiful belongings piled into handcarts. One man stood barefoot along the roadside, charred rags barely covering his body, a rake over his shoulder; another carried a scythe.

Just outside another village, we rode slowly by a small group; there were no men in evidence, just women and children. The poor souls cringed at the sight of a mounted rider; one young girl made bold by hunger stepped in front of my horse and stared up at me with wide haunted eyes—big eyes that might have been beautiful but for the fear and pain I saw in them. She extended a stick-like arm and tiny hand. A cold drizzle had extinguished the fires, and the acrid smell of burnt wood permeated the air. A gaunt looking mule could be seen off in the middle of a field cropping the burnt grass.

The sight of the starving children wrung my soul. I unwrapped a food bag that had been supplied by the inn where we had stayed the previous night, which I had tied to the pommel of my saddle.

Chenault reigned in alongside me. "Monsieur, why do you stop? We must make time, and there is nothing we can do here."

"I can give them a little food." I reached down and held out a half loaf of black bread and gestured to a thin grimy whey-faced woman who seemed to be the mother. The woman lurched forward, grabbed the bread and backed away. Her hollow eyes stared up at me with a mixture that was equal parts suspicion, fear, and gratitude.

"It's the brigands that these people have most to fear," Chenault said, "Many are deserters from one army or another. The strong survive."

"And the children?"

Chenault shrugged, and then smiled. "You have a good heart, my dear fellow. He rummaged in his own borracho, brought forth a piece of cheese, and tossed it to the nearest urchin. "Now come, we must be away. We cannot put food in the mouth of every starving peasant in Bavaria." He urged his horse forward, trotted a few yards then turned back to see if I was following. He was right—there was nothing more to be done. I urged my own mount into a canter and followed him down the road.

Our road passed by Nuremberg. The countryside had been entirely torn apart by the siege of three years before during which the Swedish king, Gustavus Adolphus, had been confronted by Imperial troops under Wallenstein. The bare earth and the remains of trenches and redoubts were still much in evidence. Everywhere it seemed we found starving children. We encountered a young boy dressed in filthy rags, his fingernails black and bleeding from scratching at the half frozen ground. I threw him what was left in my satchel, a half eaten apple, and we rode on.

As we neared the city of Regensburg, we heard the distant boom of cannon, and as we reached the outskirts, the sweetish stench of unburied corpses filled the air. Duke Bernard of Weimar, acting for the Protestant League, France's ally, had brought an army of eighteen regiments and many squadrons of horse and invested the town. The papists, who had themselves seized the town a few months before and disarmed its Protestant citizens, were now taking a pounding by the duke's artillery.

Closer to the camp we encountered a squad of the duke's pikemen, blocking the road. Unlike many of the soldiers we had seen who were indifferently dressed with little or no armor, these men were dressed alike in uniforms of brown wool knee breeches and jerkins and outfitted in steel corselets and helmets that resembled an upended soup bowl.

All the men were dirty and their uniforms were covered in filth. Each carried a sixteen foot pike and a short sword girded at the waist with a broad leather belt. They were formed up in a disciplined column, three abreast with their spears pointed to the sky. At the sergeant's command, "Port your pikes," the troop halted and slammed the butt end of their weapons into the ground.

Armed only with his short sword, the sergeant stepped forward and put up his hand.

"Halt! And state your business."

Monsieur Chenault, who had wisely shed his monk's robe that very morning for the garments of a well-heeled traveler, dismounted and removed a tooled leather case from his saddlebag from which he extracted a rolled parchment. He walked over and presented it with a flourish to the sergeant.

"Here you are, my good man," he said. He then folded his arms, affecting an air of impatience as if he fully expected the sergeant to read the document and allow us to pass without delay.

The sergeant, a short fat peasant with a dirty face and bulbous nose, scratched his beard and made a show of examining the document, turning the parchment this way and that and peering suspiciously at Chenault. It was clear after a moment that the man could not read.

"Come, come, my good fellow, we haven't got all day." Chenault spoke perfectly accented German. "As you can see, our papers are in perfect order."

"Just a moment, my lord," the sergeant replied. "I'm afraid that my eyes are not what they used to be, what with this smoke and all. I'm going to have to turn this over to my officer."

"But surely, my good man, you can see that this is a safe conduct pass signed by His Majesty, Louis XIII of France. Here, you see," Chenault said walking up and taking the parchment from the sergeant's hand. He turned it around and pointed at the embossed gold seal. "Here! This is the seal of King Louis himself."

"King Louis of France, d'ya say? You lads are a long way from France. We work for Duke Bernard. You'll have to come along with us."

I had no idea that Monsieur Chenault was such a good actor. He played the role of the indignant aristocrat to perfection. If I wasn't a bit unnerved by the prospect of being run through with a pike, I might have enjoyed the exchange.

"My good fellow, King Louis is a sworn ally of your duke, and His Grace will not thank you for detaining His Majesty's representatives."

The sergeant thought a moment and then shook his head slowly side to side. "That is as may be, gentlemen, but orders is orders, and my orders are to arrest anyone who don't have a pass signed by Duke Bernard himself and bring em' to me officer."

We had reached an impasse. Chenault was determined to move on, and the sergeant was just as determined that we appear before his superior. Less than twenty paces separated our two parties. The soldiers lined the road behind the sergeant with pikes raised. Just behind me our men formed up, all six abreast across the road prepared, should Chenault give the word, to force the issue. The horses shied and reared. I unbuttoned my coat so that I might reach my own pistol.

Chenault tried again. "Sergeant, we are on the king's business. Our pass is valid. I order you to step aside."

The sergeant took two steps back, drew himself up to his full height, and repeated his order:

"You will all have to come with us. Squad, charge your pikes for horse and draw your swords!"

At the command each pikeman took a long step forward, his right foot leaving his left in place, dropping his weight, and at the same time lowering his lance and wedging the butt end of his weapon into the dirt just in front of his left insole. A forest of sharp steel bristled three feet from my horse's breast.

"Monsieur Chenault," I called out in French. "Monsieur, we are overmatched. This is a battle that we cannot win."

The captain turned and looked up at me with a rueful smile. "Yes," he said calmly surveying the bristling steel and stroking his chin, "I take your point." He smiled his impish smile, turned toward the massed soldiers, and bowed solemnly. "Of course you are right, sergeant; orders are orders and must be obeyed. We, my friends and I, are at your service. By all means, let us meet with your officer."

Everyone relaxed, and we formed a column with six soldiers in front and six formed up behind, and we picked our way slowly into the Protestant encampment.

We stopped in front of a peasant's hut. The sergeant entered and reemerged with a young subaltern who studied our pass for a few moments and ordered our escort to take us directly to Duke Bernard.

We found the duke's camp set up in front of the moat that ringed the city walls. We dismounted and were herded into a group and surrounded by the duke's guards. Men bustled about setting up camp for the night. No move was made to search us or to take our weapons. Was this a good sign? We had not yet been branded as enemies. After we had cooled our heels for about an hour, a haughty young officer appeared. "What is your business?" he demanded.

Officialdom is the same everywhere; first we are compelled under threat to come before the duke; an hour later we were being asked why we had come.

"Captain Jean-Jacques Chenault at your service, monsieur. My friends and I are traveling on the business of His Majesty Louis XIII of France with a safe conduct signed by His Eminence Cardinal Richelieu. And you are, monsieur?"

"My name is of no consequence, monsieur. You are not in France. Your so-called safe conduct pass means nothing here. What business is this you speak of? Are you spies?"

Chenault bowed and handed over the leather case, ignoring the young ensign's arrogance. "Our documents, monsieur!"

It was getting late. Campfires had begun to spring up through the camp like fireflies in early summer, though the November air was becoming quite chilly. The ensign studied our documents intently for some minutes.

"This document says nothing of your business, Messieurs, only the usual generalities and request for safe passage. It does bear the signature of Cardinal Richelieu, but Duke Bernard of Saxe-Weimar does not take orders from French cardinals.

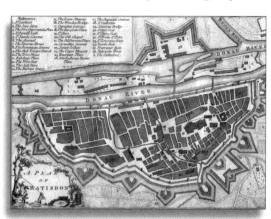

Figure 7: The city of Regensburg, from a 17th Century engraving.

Again, I must ask you, what is your business in Bavaria?"

"Our business, monsieur, is confidential. Are you not aware that France is an ally of your duke? We seek the Marquis de Feuquières, His Majesty's representative to the Protestant League at Heilbronn."

This was the first I had heard of any business with the marquis. I wondered if Chenault was, perhaps, making things up as he went along, but the German officer's tone softened somewhat. "I know nothing of political alliances, but the Marquis de Feuquières is here in the camp as the duke's guest."

Chenault pressed on: "Then if you will be kind enough, monsieur, to let the marquis know that we are here. I believe we can put away this talk of spies. He will not thank you, my friend, for keeping his emissaries waiting."

The officer nodded. "You will excuse me, gentlemen." He bowed stiffly and hurried off.

I accosted our leader. "Captain Chenault, what is going on? Are we indeed supposed to be seeking the Sieur Feuquières? I understood that our destination was Vienna, not Heilbronn? What if this fellow decides we are spies?"

Chenault favored me with one of his dimpled smiles. He was clearly enjoying this game, whatever it was. "Well, in that case, I suppose we shall all hang." He laughed. "Patience, my dear fellow, patience. All will be revealed, and soon, I promise. I say, what a piece of good luck, the marquis being here in camp."

"You mean you know him. We are seeking him?"

"Well, yes and no. Stumbling on this battle may be a piece of good luck and as we are here!" He shrugged then smiled. "I am well acquainted with the marquis, and he will vouch for us with the duke."

"And if he does not?"

"Oh, he will, never fear. We are, so to speak, related."

At that moment the German officer returned somewhat breathless, bowed to Chenault, and handed back the leather case. "The marquis has vouched for all of you, gentlemen. He is in his tent. If the other gentlemen will kindly wait here, refreshment will be provided. Captain, if you will follow me, I am to take you to his lordship immediately."

Chenault bowed and motioning me to accompany him, we were escorted to a large tent of the sort used by nobles in the field. A guard pulled aside the flap. When the marquis saw Chenault, his eyes lit up with pleasure. He was a short fat man, almost completely bald, dressed as for court with velvet trunks and a long jerkin with slashed sleeves. He threw open his arms and greeted our captain with a bear hug and kisses on both cheeks. Finally, Chenault turned to me.

"Monsieur Jean-Baptiste Tavernier, may I have the honor of introducing my brother, the Marquis de Feuquières."

My face must have registered some surprise because both men broke out in laughter.

Once we had purged ourselves of our merriment, the marquis ordered food and wine, bade us sit down on stools around his desk and made us aware of the current situation.

"Well, gentlemen, as you can see, Duke Bernard is doing quite well. Regensburg is tottering. Between us, the documents of surrender will be signed tomorrow morning."

"That is good news, surely," I ventured.

"Indeed it is," said the marquis. "At this point anything that weakens the Habsburgs is in the interest of France and good news indeed."

"I propose a toast. Bumpers, gentlemen," said Chenault raising his goblet. "Confusion to the emperor."

"Confusion to the emperor!" We drank.

Chenault refilled our glasses. "What of the emperor's army and our friend General Wallenstein?" he asked.

The marquis put down his glass. "That is the most curious thing. Wallenstein has put the imperial army into winter quarters in Bohemia about a hundred miles from here. He could have reinforced the garrison here and broken the siege any time he chose. The emperor, in fact, ordered him to do so. But he has made no move. He seems content to remain where he is. He has sent several envoys to both sides with offers of alliance."

"So naturally no one trusts him," Chenault said.

"Precisely. We have no idea what the man's real game is. Some believe that Duke Wallenstein has imperial ambitions of his own," the marquis said.

"Unseat the emperor—surely he is not so mad as that. Perhaps he is simply trying to hedge his bets in case the Emperor Ferdinand relieves him again," Chenault said.

"Charming idea, brother. I wish I knew."

Captain Chenault lifted his glass once again. "Perhaps he doesn't know himself."

The possibility of detaching General Wallenstein, the emperor's most capable field commander, and bringing him into alliance held great charm for the marquis. Such a coup would irreparably weaken the Habsburgs and would certainly bring the marquis a dukedom. Wallenstein was after something, but what that something was remained unclear. Perhaps, as Chenault suggested, the man did not know himself.

Before the sun was up the following morning we were on the road to Vienna.

With Richelieu's authority, the marquis had renewed the Treaty of Bärwalde. Catholic France had once again become a guarantor of the Protestant League of Heilbronn and its Swedish allies and was paying funds to continue the war directly into its treasury. France was firmly committed to the Protestant princes of northern Germany. In my youth and naiveté I thought this a good thing. Perhaps this alliance would mean that Protestants and Catholics would finally begin to live together in peace, but that was before I grew older and began to truly understand the arrogance of kings and the stubborn ignorance of priests.

Vienna was awash in rumor. News of the Protestant victory at Regensburg was the talk of the city. The Viennese could not understand how Duke Bernard had plucked the city from right under Wallenstein's nose. All knew of the half-hearted feint the generalissimo had made at the town just before we arrived in Duke Bernard's camp. Wallenstein had seriously damaged his reputation as a peerless warrior. Many in the capital believed that he had turned traitor and believed the rumor that he was trying to make himself a king.

Official Vienna was nervous. The city had been the Habsburg

capital for two hundred years. Many city dwellers worked for the Imperial court. Others supplied goods or services or benefited from its largess in other ways. The empire was a vast undertaking and though few saw it as seriously in jeopardy, events that threatened it were not taken lightly.

Wallenstein had many enemies at court. Some still saw him as a savior of the empire. Others, particularly the Spanish Habsburgs and the Catholic princes, saw him as a threat.

Wallenstein had created a standing army independent of the princes. Fearing that this army might be used against them, they had demanded his ouster at the Imperial Diet of 1630. The emperor, never much a negotiator, wanted his son elected king of the Romans, which required the approval of the princes who were the electors. He foolishly complied with the princes' demands without first securing a quid pro quo and left the diet empty handed and without his generalissimo.

A few months later when the Swedes invaded, Emperor Ferdinand, in a panic, offered to reinstate Wallenstein as his generalissimo. Bitter over his dismissal, Wallenstein exacted a high price. He demanded virtually unlimited powers and the Duchy of Mecklenburg. The emperor agreed and Wallenstein was reinstated in December of 1631. He immediately raised an army and met Gustavus Adolphus and his Swedes at Lutzen. Lutzen had been technically a defeat, but the Swedish King was killed in the battle. Wallenstein was now rid of his enemy and in possession of the most powerful army in the empire.

Rumors were abroad that after this latest debacle, the emperor would, once again, relieve Wallenstein. But would Wallenstein give up his command? One of my well placed friends told me that Ferdinand hesitated because he feared that it would force the duke into open rebellion. Would the army follow the emperor or the duke? Many assumed it would be Wallenstein, but it was whispered in the capital that some of his leading commanders were unwilling to follow their general into treason against the empire. These officers, it seemed, were keeping the imperial court informed of the progress of Wallenstein's conspiracy.

After a few weeks of spying, I was eager to report my findings to Captain Chenault, who once again had assumed his monk's robe and as Père Chenault was quartered along with his six acolytes at a Capuchin monastery within the city walls. I rushed to the monastery only to find the captain lolling about his commodious cell drinking wine with his companions.

"Jean-Baptiste!" Chenault threw open his arms and enveloped me in a bear hug. "How are you, my dear fellow? A goblet of wine? Sit down, sit down!"

I settled myself and told him my news, most of which he already knew. He did, however, have news for me.

"I have an important assignment for you." He was not smiling. I felt a cold breath run up my spine.

"Yes, Captain."

"As you have heard, there appears to be a conspiracy against our friend, General Wallenstein, among his own commanders. We do not know precisely its extent or seriousness, but names have been mentioned, including a certain Irish mercenary general named Butler, who is currently in command of a detachment of Wallenstein's troops holding the city of Eger. You are acquainted with this man, I believe?"

"Yes, I served under him for a short time in Pomerania in 1630, and I know his wife." Captain Chenault had obviously been briefed by Père Joseph.

Chenault nodded. "We need to know if what we hear rumored is true, and if so, just who is involved in which conspiracy, and who is with and who is against Duke Wallenstein. We need to aid his enemies if they seem to have the least possibility of success. While the emperor dithers here in Vienna, Wallenstein is actively seeking allies. So far as we know, he is settled in winter quarters at Pilsen, but once spring comes, he will either have to employ or disband his army. The men he has recruited fight for pay. They will not stay with Wallenstein if they see no opportunity for plunder."

"But surely he will first have to fight Duke Bernard."

"True, and Duke Bernard is our friend. He did very well at Regensburg, but, frankly, he is no match for Wallenstein. The Duke of Friedland may be less than trustworthy, but no one doubts his abilities. He is a brilliant field commander."

"Who will there be left to fight?"

"Exactly the point, my good fellow!" I was relieved to see the impish grin. "Wallenstein is like a hungry wolf. He must find meat for his pack. If he remains loyal to the emperor, he must turn his attention to France. We do not believe he will willingly relinquish command again or give up his army. He has too many enemies to retire gracefully to his estates."

"And France may be in jeopardy?"

Chenault put his arm around my shoulders. "Is in jeopardy, Jean-Baptiste. I believe you will make a political operative yet!" The Captain spoke lightly, but the grin had disappeared and his eyes bored into mine. "Wallenstein must be stopped, permanently neutralized, if you take my meaning. He is a danger to France. Not to put too fine a point on it, Jean-Baptiste, the Duke of Friedland must die."

Chapter 13

The Assassins

The full import of this business slapped me across the face. My throat became so dry I could barely swallow. The game was turning deadly. I was up to my neck in it, and there was no turning back. I was now part of a plan to assassinate one of the most powerful men in Europe.

I took a deep breath. "What would you have me do, Captain?"

Chenault clapped me on the back. The grin returned. "Don't look so serious, Jean-Baptiste. We don't expect you to do the dirty deed yourself." The men laughed and raised their glasses. "Tomorrow, we leave Vienna. You will go to Eger and renew your acquaintance with General Butler. Feel him out. This Butler is a Catholic, I believe, and we need to know if he and his fellows will remain loyal to the emperor or throw in their lot with Wallenstein."

The captain took my glass and filled it. "This Wallenstein is quite the buccaneer. Never met the fellow, but one cannot help but admire him. Comes from nowhere and now a duke twice over. Gives one hope for the future, actually!" He raised his glass. "To General Wallenstein, Duke of Friedland and Mecklenburg. Pity really, but he's got to go."

The early morning air was cool and crisp with the first scent of real winter. The cathedral rose like a ghost out of the early morning fog, and our horses' hooves echoed off the cobblestones as we rode out through the city gates. The party was one short. Jacques, one of the hard young men, had remained in Vienna. We took the road north to Bohemia.

It would take a week, at the least, to ride to Eger, which was near Prague. Chenault and his party would accompany me as far as Prague. Roads in this part of the empire were dangerous. Brigands and highwaymen, many of them unpaid soldiers and deserters from various armies, were reported to infest the roads. Two of the captain's men were assigned as my minders and would accompany me to Eger.

The previous night, Chenault had come to my room with a pair of saddlebags over his shoulder. "We will be leaving rather early tomorrow morning, dear boy, and I wanted to give you this tonight so as not to interrupt your beauty sleep," he grinned and hefted the bags. They made a familiar sound as he placed them on the writing table.

"What you see before you, dear boy, are four hundred sixteen lovely newly minted golden louis, exactly 10,000 livres in gold."

"What in the world …?"

Chenault threw back his head and laughed. "Gold, dear boy. Gold to grease the wheels of treason! You are authorized to use this money, if you see fit, to, ah, assure the loyalty of certain military officers with whom you may come in contact. Ten thousand should be enough to buy a whole pack of Irish mercenaries, what!"

"Captain Chenault, I do not like this!"

"Don't fret, dear boy. Probably it will never come up, but if it does it pays to be prepared. Oh, and by the way," the captain put his hand on my shoulder, leaned over, and spoke close to my ear, "be sure to keep accurate accounts. The ministry absolutely requires it. All in a day's work, I'm afraid. Ta ta!"

"What are you asking, Captain? First, I offer a man a bribe, then I ask for a receipt?"

Chenault opened the door, gave me a bit of a wave, walked out, and closed the door behind him, leaving me fuming.

We rode into Eger about midday, one week to the day after leaving Vienna. I left my "servants" at a local inn and proceeded to the military headquarters at Eger Castle, which perched on a riverbank at the edge of the town. The castle is a very old structure, built of stone with thick high walls, a square tower, a drawbridge, and the remains of a moat.

General Butler greeted me with surprise and delight. His normally florid face turned even redder, and his mutton chops bristled with pleasure.

"Jean-Baptiste, my old friend, what a pleasure to see you! What a surprise. How in the world did you know I was here in this God forsaken place?"

I looked about me at the cold gray walls; old German castles can be grim especially in winter. "My dear Colonel, or should I say General, may I give you joy of your promotion! As to finding you, nothing could have been easier. I bring you holiday greetings from your friends in Vienna."

"Thank you, my friend. But tell me, what brings you to Bohemia? When last I heard, you were on your way to Constantinople."

"That is a long story."

"Excellent, the longer the better, and you shall tell it all from beginning to end, even if it takes this whole dreary winter," he said, heartily shaking my hand. "Tonight we shall have a dinner in your honor. My wife will not be with us," he said with a meaningful look. "She has returned home. It's just as well. War is no place for a woman."

I kept my story simple. I was in Vienna on business, made enquiries and heard that he was now commandant at Eger. I said that I wished to repay his many kindnesses to me, and I presented him with a gift for his wife, which I had brought from Persia.

The dinner started off as a jolly affair. It was a soldier's meal, rather plain, a joint of beef, peas, and coarse brown bread. Toasts were offered in the hearty local ale, and I was prevailed upon to tell something of my travels in Persia. After that, the talk turned to the war and the political situation in the empire. The officers were anxious to hear the latest news from Vienna, but most of what I had heard they already knew, and they were disturbed by what they had heard.

Colonel Gordon, the executive officer, was a compact baldheaded Scot with a thick red moustaches and bristling muttonchops, much like his commanding officer. He was a careful man with a natural loyalty to his superiors. He was skeptical of the rumors. "This is not the first time General Wallenstein has been accused of disloyalty, is it now? After all the battles he has won."

Others were less sure. Captain Devereaux, a brash young man with brooding eyes, spoke up: "I understand why some question Wallenstein's loyalty. If my colonel will forgive me, how are we to judge his actions during the siege at Regensburg? He led the army to within a day's march of the city and then retired. Why? Why did he not attack Duke Bernard? He had the men; he could have easily raised the siege and driven the Protestant army out of Bavaria. Then he released the captured Swedish officers on parole for practically no ransom at all."

Devereaux shook his head, his black brows knitted like twin storm clouds above his dark eyes, "It makes no sense." This brought murmurs of agreement from around the table.

General Butler was surprisingly liberal. He allowed his subordinates to speak their minds. He listened carefully but said little. Finally, after the other officers had excused themselves, I asked him his opinion.

"As you are my friend, Jean-Baptiste, I will tell you that I do not know what to think. Armies feed on rumors. I have never myself heard Wallenstein utter a single word that bespoke of treason, and I know that he has many enemies, men who will do or say anything to bring him down. Still he has not been the same since the emperor dismissed him. He was bitter over that, as well he should have been. Wallenstein is my commander, but my oath is to the emperor, not to the duke. Should he prove disloyal, I am honor bound to support the emperor."

"Even if you think the emperor is in error?"

"Even so! I am a mercenary, 'tis true, and I serve for pay, but I am no jackal who will tear at any meat that comes within range of his teeth. If Ferdinand gives an order I shall obey it. Perhaps you think me foolish, all this talk of honor; perhaps I should be more practical?"

"No, my friend, I think you are an honorable man, and an honorable man could act in no other way."

The general nodded briefly, and we bade each other goodnight. He had invited me to take lodging at the castle, but I excused myself saying that I had to attend to my baggage and servants in town. The truth was lodging at the castle would subject my companions and me to too much casual scrutiny.

I now knew the general's mind. His first loyalty lay with the emperor. If the emperor ordered it, he would arrest Wallenstein, but he was no assassin. I was relieved. Captain Chenault would be disappointed. He hoped that I would recruit him. The idea of being a spy and working for my country had aroused my patriotism, and Chenault had a talent for making it all seem like a game, but this was no game, and I profoundly wished that I had not gotten myself involved. I went to bed with an uneasy mind and slept poorly.

Two days later an orderly brought me an urgent message requesting that I wait upon General Butler as soon as possible. I left that moment and accompanied the soldier to the castle. I found General Butler hurriedly packing his saddlebags.

"Ah, Jean-Baptiste, thank you for coming at such short notice. I received orders this morning. General Wallenstein has summoned all the senior officers to his camp at Pilsen for a council of war. I must leave immediately. Gordon will take charge while I am gone. I thought that you might find it amusing to accompany me and perhaps meet General Wallenstein. If not, I should return within the week. The camp is two days ride. Frankly, I would value having you along, and a dealer in gems might make some important contacts," he added hopefully.

man, General." I rushed back to the inn to inform the men.

An invitation to reconnoiter Wallenstein's camp was an unlooked for opportunity. My two companions were enthusiastic. Marcel, the senior man, elected to remain behind. He would bring the news to Chenault, seek additional instructions, and return to Eger to await our return. Jules, the younger, would accompany me and serve as valet and general factotum. We were on the road in a bit over an hour.

The imperial army lay spread across a wide meadowland set between two rivers. The camp had been hastily constructed. The soldiers had erected makeshift shelters of every description—tents, thatched wooden shacks, covered wagons and sod—in short, anything to help keep out the winter cold. Wagons loaded down with provisions came from all points on the compass and detachments of foragers marched here and there with heavy sacks over their shoulders. Other soldiers huddled in small groups, like ragged beggars warming their hands at the smoky campfires that dotted the landscape.

Wallenstein had commandeered a large chateau with a number of barns and outbuildings. As we dismounted at the chateau's main entrance, grooms appeared and took charge of our horses.

General Butler was recognized. The young orderly snapped to attention, then escorted us through the double doors into a large well-appointed ante room where several clerks sat at desks piled high with papers, busily scratching away with their quills. After a short wait we were led into the duke's presence. General Wallenstein had taken over the chateau's dining room. It was paneled in a light wood with gold leaf decorating the ceiling, the style typical of a German country house. The duke sat at the far end of the long dining table, sufficient for twenty or more.

He stood up, came forward with a smile, and embraced General Butler.

"Walter, so good of you to come. You have been missed. When did you arrive?"

"We only just arrived, Your Grace. May I name my particular friend, Herr Jean-Baptiste Tavernier?"

I bowed. "An honor, Your Grace."

"Herr Tavernier is a prodigious traveler, my lord. Served in my regiment for a short time in the Stettin campaign and then spent the best part of two years in Constantinople and Persia."

Wallenstein fastened his black eyes on me. He was a slender man with a long thin face, prominent nose, and high forehead with a widow's peak. He had red hair, but his goatee and moustaches were jet black. He offered his hand. "I envy you, Mein Herr. I have always wished to see Constantinople. You look somewhat familiar, and your German is excellent. How do you come to speak it so well?"

"Your Grace has an excellent memory. We were introduced one night at table years ago when I was in the service of the Viceroy of Hungary."

Figure 8: Albert von Wallenstein, Duke of Friedland and Mecklenburg from a 17th Century engraving.

The duke's eyes narrowed. "I see. So you served at court? I never forget a face, Mein Herr." He then turned on his heel and spoke in low tones to General Butler for a few moments. At that point a breathless orderly appeared with dispatches that required the duke's immediate attention. The duke excused himself, mentioning a meeting for senior officers to be held on the morrow. His cold eyes caught mine for a brief second, and he nodded curtly. We were dismissed.

Once we were settled in our rooms, General Butler excused himself and rushed off on business of his own, suggesting that we meet for dinner that evening. Jules and I took the opportunity to stroll around and reconnoiter the camp. Small detachments of men, including some who were obviously high ranking officers, could be seen riding in from every direction. Something very important was in the offing.

I returned to the room around sunset and found General Butler in close conversation with another officer.

"Ah, there you are, Jean-Baptiste," the general beamed. "May I name Colonel Walter Leslie? Colonel, my good friend, Jean-Baptiste Tavernier?" The general clapped the colonel on the back and continued in English: "Colonel Leslie is a Scotsman, and, as we know, the Scots speak a barbarous language that no one can understand but themselves. So we will speak English if you don't mind, Jean-Baptiste."

"Of course. A pleasure, Colonel."

The colonel was a tall slender man with prominent cheek bones and deeply set eyes. He seemed slightly ruffled by General Butler's rough humor: "Enchanté, monsieur."

I smiled. "You speak French, Colonel."

"French," retorted the general. "Not a bit of it." He threw his arm around Leslie's shoulders. "Why, the English barely speak English. He learned that bit of French in a Paris brothel."

The colonel smiled, rolled his eyes, and bowed.

"Colonel Leslie speaks excellent French, Walter, but as I am out of practice, I would welcome the chance to speak English for a while."

Butler nodded and continued. "Leslie is on the duke's personal staff. You will forgive me, my friend, but I have been summoned to dine with the headquarters staff and the other commanders from whom I hope to extract the truth about tomorrow's agenda. I have arranged for you to eat at the officer's mess."

After a few more pleasantries the colonel excused himself. As soon as he left the general's bonhomie vanished. Uttering a long sigh, he sank down on the edge of his bed.

"Walter, you seem troubled."

"I am. Something is very wrong here, Jean-Baptiste. Everyone I speak with has a different story. I know for a fact that a delegation has come from the emperor in Vienna. The emperor's cousin, Ferdinand, the cardinal-infante of Spain, is moving north with an army. The rumor is that the delegation is here to demand that Wallenstein cooperate with the Spanish."

"What of Wallenstein himself?"

"General Wallenstein believes that as generalissimo, the cardinal's army should come under his command. He knows that the Spanish will never accept this. They hate Wallenstein and the cardinal-infante is too proud to accept a position subordinate to anyone. The Spanish are instead demanding that Wallenstein supply them with an additional six thousand cavalry. Wallenstein believes this demand to be a violation of his agreement with Emperor Ferdinand, an attempt to weaken his position. He is right and can be very stubborn. There is also talk that he will be dismissed."

"What then?"

"What indeed! Wallenstein built this army. He picked each of its commanders. Another dismissal would be a grave insult. Do not put your trust in the word of princes, as they say. I do not know. The emperor is the emperor. There is even some loose talk that His Grace is planning to rebel and join the Protestants."

"What is Colonel Leslie's opinion?"

"Leslie, he has an opinion like everyone else, but he doesn't really know. Of late he has been much caressed by His Grace, but he is not part of the inner circle. There are only three: Ilio, Terzky and Kinsky. They are Wallenstein's confidants, the only ones who truly know his mind."

"So we wait?"

The general looked over at me. His face was haggard and lined with worry. "Oh, how I long for a good clean battle, Jean-Baptiste. These political machinations fairly sicken me. We wait, yes. Leslie says that tomorrow will tell the tale. All the senior commanders were summoned and all but Gallas, Colloredo, and Altringer are here."

"What will Leslie do should Wallenstein defy the emperor?"

"I am not sure. He is torn. He owes the duke a great deal, but Leslie will not support treason, of that I am certain."

Following the senior officers' meeting the next evening General Butler returned to our rooms in a state of extreme agitation. Leslie was with him. He threw his gloves onto the bed.

"Walter, how did the meeting go?"

Butler sighed and sat down. "Well, Jean-Baptiste, it would seem that we have all signed our death warrants."

"Aren't you being just a bit dramatic, General?" Leslie asked.

Butler glared at Leslie. "It was neatly done. Oh very neatly done! We all gathered in the main room of the chateau. Field Marshal Ilio convened the meeting. This was to be, as Ilio put it, 'a council of war.'"

Butler rose and began pacing. The emperor's representatives had made a series of demands. They desired that Wallenstein immediately invest Regensburg, and that he detach six thousand horses to ride south and join the army of the Spanish cardinal infante. Short of that, the emperor has threatened to dismiss him.

"Field Marshall Ilio was very angry, and his talk of the stupidity of the court and the insults to our commander was well received. What field officer does not believe that all courtiers are milksops and fools?

"Ilio began 'General Wallenstein has decided to resign rather than accept the humiliation of dismissal. The question is,' he asked, and this is when the drama began 'will we, the army allow our great general to be taken from us?'"

"What happened then?"

"Oh, there was a general uproar, of course. Everyone began shouting at once. None of us wished the general to resign. So at Ilio's suggestion, we sent a delegation of officers to entreat Wallenstein to remain at the head of the army. Wallenstein played the prima donna to perfection. At first he resisted, but after some coaxing he agreed to remain only if we unanimously agreed to support him and signed a declaration pledging our loyalty to him personally."

Leslie cut in: "General Butler, I don't think…"

Butler glared him into silence. "This is serious business, Jean-Baptiste; to sign our names to a letter defying the emperor's orders is treason pure and simple. It could cost all of us our heads."

"Did all the officers agree?"

"Yes, we did! After a few more glasses and much wrangling, yes we did! All the officers agreed to sign the pledge provided that the letter included the words: 'As long as Wallenstein shall employ the army in the emperor's service.'"

"And that was it?"

"No, this is where things began to get interesting. While the document was being prepared, Ilio put on a lavish dinner. There was a great deal of drinking. Two hours later the document appeared and was passed around the table. Everyone began to sign, but before it reached our end of the table, Count Piccolini, who does not drink, spoke out. He noticed that the required words had not been included. This caused a new uproar and some of us refused to sign. Then Count Terzky rose and angrily chastised us, calling us villains and worse, traitors. I also signed, Jean-Baptiste. While the count had been speaking a number of the duke's guards had entered and fanned out along the sides of the chamber. They also blocked the door. Terzky's intent was clear. Had I refused, I would not have left that meeting alive!"

Leslie made a face. "Walter, please do not overreact. We agreed only to support the duke if he remains loyal to the emperor."

"Really, Leslie, where did you read that? We have signed a document personally pledging our loyalty to Duke Albert von Wallenstein above all others, even the emperor. That is treason, nothing less! We shall be branded as rebels. It was very well planned, all of it. Did you hear Ilio and Terzky—while the duke remained coyly hidden away like a virgin before her first meeting with her betrothed?"

Leslie smiled grimly. "It was neatly done, right enough."

"What a pack of fools we were!" Butler shook his head sadly. "You can be sure that a full report of that meeting, together with a list of all the officers present, is on its way to Vienna. The question is what do we do now?"

"First of all, it is important that we not lose our heads," Leslie said.

"Is that to be taken literally?"

Leslie laughed. "I believe, General, you know exactly what I mean. Perhaps, another letter, assuring His Majesty of our loyalty, explaining our position more clearly!"

"More clearly? Dig our graves deeper, you mean. It will be a cold day in hell, Colonel, before I sign another letter?"

"What will you do now?"

Leslie looked grave. "I don't know what to say at this moment. I need time to think, and then we will come up with a plan. For now, Walter, you should return to your regiment. I will reconnoiter here. Once the excitement dies down, and our colleagues realize just how adroitly they have been manipulated, there will be second thoughts—you may depend upon that. Go back to your regiment, Walter. You can do nothing here. I will contact you as soon as I know something useful."

We took Leslie's advice and left for Eger the following morning. I did not trust him, but in the end I was very glad that Leslie was on our side.

The next several weeks passed uneventfully. I stayed on giving as an excuse my dislike of winter travel. I was now completely in the confidence of my friend, the general.

One evening I returned from the castle to my lodgings to find Captain Chenault awaiting me.

"Jean-Baptiste, I have wonderful news! Emperor Ferdinand has issued a secret order, stripping Wallenstein of his command and replacing him with General Gallas."

"This is nothing new, Captain. We have been hearing variations of this rumor for weeks."

"Yes, but the order has now been issued. I have it on impeccable authority, dear boy. The order is secret because the emperor fears that the army will support the duke and that Wallenstein will move against him. The Duke of Friedland is to be arrested and brought before His Majesty for questioning. According to the order, if he resists, he may be killed. The emperor has ordered that he be brought to him dead or alive."

"My God, and there is no possible mistake?"

"None. I have brought an official copy of the document, replete with the emperor's seal. I rode through Pilsen. The rumor is that the duke was preparing to gather his remaining loyalists and retreat to Eger.

"What, Wallenstein coming here, to Eger!, You are certain of this?"

"Yes, Jean-Baptiste. He is already on the move with a force of cavalry, and he should be here within a day, two at the most." He rubbed his palms together. "Now there's a bit of luck! It appears that we shall soon be in the thick of it."

"Does General Butler know?"

"If he does not, he will soon enough. Jules tells me that you have made the acquaintance of a Colonel Leslie. Tell me something of this fellow Leslie. I hear he is in with the duke and is considered to be one of his closest supporters."

I related all that had transpired at Pilsen.

"So, it appears that your Colonel Leslie is playing both sides of the fence. I wonder on which side he will come down. He is, apparently, traveling as part of the duke's suite. Interesting, very interesting! You have done well, dear boy, surprisingly so. I believe you have a talent for this business. Now all that remains is for me to pay a visit to General Butler."

"Visit General Butler? You, on what pretext?

"Pretext? You wound me, my dear fellow. Why as a courier bearing orders from the Holy Roman Emperor, Ferdinand II.

"But you are a Frenchman."

"Yes, and he is an Irishman." Chenault looked at me sourly. "You know very well Jean-Baptiste, that there are men of all nationalities involved in this war. Besides, I grew up in Germany, and I am fluent in the language, certainly fluent enough to fool an Irish mercenary, I do assure you. But I see no reason to lie unnecessarily. The fewer lies the better. A good thing to remember, my friend. Too many lies can easily trip you up. It is difficult to remember what lie you told to whom. So it is a good idea to mostly tell the truth."

"But…!"

"Do not worry, my dear fellow. You will be kept out of it. We have never met. I am the emperor's messenger. I have the emperor's order bearing the Imperial seal. That should be enough."

"May I ask how in the world you managed to obtain that

document?"

"Of course you may ask anything you like, dear boy," the captain said smiling wolfishly.

Chenault left to seek an interview with General Butler. Two hours later I received a messenger from the general summoning me to the castle. I found him in his office pacing nervously. He related the details of his meeting with the emperor's messenger. Apparently Chenault's ruse had worked. He had sent out a scout to make contact with the duke's party and report back. The general had insisted that Chenault accept the castle's hospitality. Chenault was now a guest with a guard at his door.

"Do you know what that messenger fellow told me? What sort of name is Chenault anyway? Doesn't sound German? He said that Leslie was traveling with the duke. The emperor's order gives amnesty to everyone who signed the declaration at Pilsen, excepting Ilio and Terzky, and places the army under the command of Gallas."

"But, Walter, that is good news, surely."

"Perhaps, but what of Leslie? What is the man about? He is my friend, Jean-Baptiste, but he can be most exasperating. He knows my mind. Is he with Wallenstein? Am I to be arrested?"

"No, Walter, I am sure you are safe. I do not know Leslie very well, but I doubt that he will be found on the losing side if he can help it."

The general stopped pacing, looked at me, and laughed ruefully. "You are a shrewd judge of men, my friend, and you are right. Whatever happens, Leslie will land on his feet, never fear. I must consult Gordon."

"Is it wise, do you think, to arrest the emperor's messenger?"

"Arrest? I have not arrested him. He is my honored guest, and it won't hurt him to cool his heels here as my guest for a day or two until we can sort this all out. I dislike extremely getting you into the middle of this thing, Jean-Baptiste, but you know all the facts and I value your advice."

I bowed.

The next morning I went for my usual walk to find a regiment of horse camped just outside the castle walls. The Duke of Friedland had arrived at Eger. I consulted with Chenault's men, who were quite agitated over the captain's failure to return from his mission. I explained, and we agreed that I should go to the castle to reconnoiter.

I arrived at the gate to find that the guard had been trebled. I recognized none of the men. A captain eyed me suspiciously. Finally one of Butler's men, an ensign, was summoned. He vouched for me, and I was given leave to enter under escort.

The door outside the general's office was guarded by two sentries. Walter immediately came out, put his hand on my shoulder, and showed me inside where I found Lieutenant-Colonel Gordon, Colonel Leslie, Wallenstein, and three other officers who were unknown to me.

"Your Grace will remember my friend, Monsieur Tavernier."

I bowed.

The duke's black eyes caught mine. He sniffed.

"Ah yes, the merchant, the dealer in pearls," he nodded curtly, and then turned to the general. "General Butler, we will speak at length later. I will leave Leslie here with you to work out the details."

Then with his suite and guards like pilot fish clinging to a shark, Duke Wallenstein swept from the room.

General Butler closed the door firmly, walked back to his desk, dropped into his chair, and stared at Leslie. "Well, Colonel?"

"Walter, perhaps we should discuss this in private."

I made to leave. "Perhaps I should return later?"

"No, Jean-Baptiste, please stay. You, too, Gordon. I apologize for the duke's behavior. Adversity seems not to have improved his manners. Colonel, Colonel Gordon is my right hand and Monsieur Tavernier is my particular friend. I rely on his opinion."

Leslie looked uncomfortable. "Of course, Walter, as you wish."

The general folded his hands. "Well?"

"May I sit down?"

"Of course. Jean-Baptiste. Gordon, please bring chairs. Sit over here."

Leslie, Gordon, and I pulled up chairs at the other side of the general's desk.

We all waited. Leslie took a breath. "All right, here it is. You know that the emperor has issued an order removing the duke from his command and ordering his arrest."

The general nodded.

"Well, our duke has been very busy. As soon as he realized that he was to be arrested, he sent word to Duke Bernard and to Oxenstiern, the Swedish Chancellor. His plan is to rendezvous here with Duke Bernard, who is on the march with four thousand men and should reach the city within three days. He then will turn Eger over to the Protestants and put together a new army in direct opposition to the emperor. He has pledges from Oxenstiern for an additional six thousand troops to be placed under his personal command."

"Duke Bernard is coming to Eger?"

"Lord, what cheek," said Gordon.

"Was this his plan all along?" the general asked.

"Not sure actually, but I think he is improvising as he goes. He only recently began confiding his plans to me, after Gallas deserted. Ironic really! I believe this was one of several alternatives, but the Swedes and the Protestants wouldn't trust him until the emperor put a price on his head."

Gordon looked narrowly at Leslie. "If I may say so, Colonel, you seem uncommonly well informed about the duke's plans."

"As to that, Major, I am part of the headquarters staff. It is my job to be informed," Leslie said airily.

"Well, he is not going to turn over Eger to anyone, certainly not to the Protestants, not while I am in command," said Butler. "The emperor's order is that he is to be captured along with Ilio and Terzky and brought to Vienna. Is that not so, Leslie?" Thanks to Chenault, Butler already knew the contents of the order; I could see he was testing Leslie, deciding whether to trust him.

"I believe so. I have not seen the actual order, but that, in essence, is the gist of what the broadsides that were distributed to the troops say."

Gordon eyed Leslie. "We cannot take him captive with a regiment camped outside the walls and four thousand Protestants knocking at our door."

Leslie stood up. "Of course not. We will have to kill him and soon. Without the head, the reptile dies."

The cold-blooded tone of Leslie's announcement set my teeth on edge. The room was silent. Walter Butler sat back in his chair and gazed fixedly at Leslie for a few moments, and then he spoke.

"Leslie's right! Holding him prisoner won't work. It's too dangerous. Alive, he has too many supporters. They will rally to him. Wallenstein is a traitor. We'll have to kill him—Ilio and Terzky and Kinsky as well."

I was shocked. "All of them, Walter? Surely just the duke. The rest could be imprisoned and…"

Butler shook his head. "No, Jean-Baptiste, I'm afraid it must be all. Let us not forget, gentlemen, this snake has several smaller heads. With those four dead, the plot will melt away like a spring frost.

Leslie smiled. "True enough. Terzky's officers are loyal. They will not accept his imprisonment. They must be presented with a *fait accompli*."

"Yes, and with the Duke Bernard due here any day, we will need those men to defend the city. Gordon, call a guard, one of our boys. Ask that fellow Chenault, the emperor's messenger, to join us and summon Devereaux as well."

Leslie jumped to his feet. "Messenger? Hold a moment! This is the first I have heard of a messenger. Who is he, and when did he arrive?"

Butler smiled thinly and leaned back in his chair. "A messenger arrived from Vienna yesterday with the emperor's order. Sorry, Leslie, but you came here with the duke, and I had to be sure where you stood. He is an adjutant, a captain on the imperial general staff and comes directly from Emperor Ferdinand. He has offered his services and seems a likely enough chap. We will present him with the situation and give him the opportunity to prove himself. But, first, let us see how he reacts."

"I see," Leslie said looking from one of us to the other then back at Butler. "What is the man's name? Chenault did you say? I have never heard of him, but I can hardly claim to know everyone on the general staff. What if he disagrees?"

"If he has just come from Vienna, I would like to hear what he has to say," put in Gordon.

"Yes, Colonel, so would I. The emperor's order is pretty clear. If he has a better idea, I would like to hear it. Otherwise, he is our guest and shall remain so until the deed is done. After that he shall serve as our witness," said Butler.

It was fascinating to see just how easily the plot came together. Chenault was in his element. To everyone's surprise—except yours truly—he enthusiastically seconded the plan to kill Wallenstein. The rest were lifelong military men, and decisive action came naturally to them.

We were planning to assassinate a legend. Perhaps a dozen loyal, battle hardened men were needed, men who would not flinch at murder. Gordon knew the men best; that would be his job. The grim faced Captain Devereux would be in command of the squad. Chenault and his two men were detailed to neutralize the duke's guards and prevent anyone from entering the room. I volunteered to aid Chenault.

"Now we must decide when and where?" said Gordon.

"Tomorrow is Count Kinsky's birthday," said Leslie.

"Perfect," said Chenault, his eyes twinkling. "May I suggest a dinner party?"

The plan itself was simple. Supper and an entertainment would be announced for tomorrow evening in honor of the count's birthday.

It would be a small party, senior officers only—just the duke and his suite—Kinsky of course, Field Marshal Ilio, Count Terzky, plus Leslie, Gordon, Butler, and Devereaux. Good food, good fellowship, and plenty of wine to lull the senses. Then, at the right moment, the trap would be sprung.

It was quite late by the time I returned to the inn. Chenault had been placed on parole. It was thought best that he not be seen at the castle. He was almost beside himself with excitement.

"Can you believe it, Jean-Baptiste? It will be the most complete thing. We will be rid of Wallenstein, and his own men will do the dirty work for us."

"You hope."

Chenault slapped me on the back. "Indeed I do, my dear fellow. Tomorrow we shall all be witnesses to history."

I found it difficult to sleep. I did not relish my role. The idea of spying on Walter Butler troubled me, and I could hear a murmur of voices from the adjoining room. Chenault and his men talked through most of the night. Jules was not pleased to be out of the action. He was dispatched to carry a message to Chenault's brother, the marquis, whom we assumed was traveling with Duke Bernard.

The next day there was much activity in the town. Wallenstein had taken up residence in a house just across the square from the inn. It was a house I passed early every morning on my walks about the countryside. Wallenstein had a well deserved reputation as a cruel and quixotic man. Wherever he took up residence he had a standing order that all the dogs and cats in the neighborhood were to be killed. Men scurried about carrying out his orders. The dead animals had been thrown into a pile on the street in front of the duke's house.

The morning air was cold and crisp, the sky bright, and I badly needed to clear my head. I turned away from the carnage and set off in the opposite direction, circled around the town and, keeping the river at my right hand, eventually arrived at the castle. After the events of the day before, things seemingly had returned to normal. I had no trouble gaining entry. One of the young Irish dragoons saluted me with a smile and escorted me to the general's office where I found Butler, Leslie, and Gordon in deep conversation.

Thus far, all had proceeded according to plan. The invitation had been offered and accepted, and the affair was to begin shortly after sundown. My role was to be a minor one. Despite Walter Butler's objections, I had insisted on doing my part.

I was to stand guard in the passageway that connected the castle's great hall to the courtyard where it was expected that some of the duke's guards would be stationed. The passage had been built as a service entrance, quite accessible but narrow with room for only one man to pass at a time. Gordon felt that one man could easily hold the entrance. I would be able to hear everything, and I was fairly confident of my skill with a rapier. Still it had been a long time since I wielded a sword in combat. I prayed that none of the duke's guards was a pikeman.

Late that afternoon we gathered in a large chamber in the bowels of the castle. Butler, Gordon, Leslie, and Devereaux, who was to command the soldiers, had picked a squad of tough, battle tested veterans, all Catholics and all drawn from Butler's own regiment of Irish dragoons. These men had been shown the emperor's order and made aware of the duke's treachery. They were outraged at Wallenstein's duplicity and prepared for action.

The senior officers, as is the custom, would carry their dress swords. Devereaux's squad would be armed with swords and halberds. Two would carry crossbows. Pistols were forbidden; they would make too much noise. We dared not alert Terzky's cavalry before the deed was done. After the executions they would be called in to read the emperor's proclamation and would be informed of the duke's treason. General Butler, as ranking officer, would then take command. He would integrate Terzky's men into his own regiment and prepare to defend the city against the army of the Duke of Saxe-Weimer.

Just before dusk I received a summons to come to the castle at once. I found Gordon, Leslie, and Butler conferring anxiously in the general's office. The general rose as I entered.

"I came as quickly as I could. What news?"

"The worst possible. Word has just come from Wallenstein. He is indisposed, sent his regrets, and so forth. He will not attend the banquet."

"Could it be he suspects something," I asked.

"Not unless somebody talked," said Leslie.

Gordon leapt to his feet, knocking over his chair and glared red-faced at Leslie. "May I ask what that is supposed to mean, Colonel? Are you suggesting that one of us is an informer?"

Leslie rose nimbly to his feet. His hand dropped to his sword hilt. General Butler quickly stepped between the two men. "Colonel Gordon, I am sure Colonel Leslie meant nothing of the kind."

"Exactly. I simply meant that if the duke was aware of our plan, someone must have told him. Other than those in this room there are several others who know the details."

"True enough," said the general. "But if Wallenstein knew about it, he would have done more than decline a dinner invitation—of that you may be sure."

"He seemed well enough yesterday," said Gordon. He remained on his feet glaring at Leslie.

"Come, gentlemen, please! Sit down. Gordon! Leslie! I think we are all a bit on edge. I do not believe Wallenstein suspects anything, and the duke's absence may work to our advantage. The men may hesitate to attack the man they consider their generalissimo, but once Kinsky, Terzky, and Ilio are dead they will be committed. We will simply have to deal with first things first."

After a bit more discussion, General Butler's solution was adopted and I returned to the inn.

The fête was held in the castle's great room, a cavernous space rather longer than wide with a vaulted walk-in hearth at each end and high ceilings with heavy carved beams of aged blackened oak. Forged iron candelabra cast an intricate web of shadows over the table.

The dinner went off on time. From my station in the passageway I was able to peer through a peephole in the door and observe the proceedings. The duke's intimates seemed to be very relaxed for men who were about to commit the foulest sort of treason against a monarch that they were sworn to and had served for so many years. Terzky in particular was quite jolly and seemed determined to enjoy an evening that he perceived to be in his honor.

The long narrow table occupied the center of the room. Steaming platters of venison, stuffed pigeon, roast duck, capons, sausages, salads, and pitchers of wine loaded down the scarred slab from end to end. Fires had been laid in the hearths and tended since early morning. The room was filled with the scent of burning fruitwood and comfortably warm despite the winter chill.

Butler was affable enough, but Gordon went stiffly through the motions of welcoming the guests, playing his role poorly. Leslie, every inch the courtier, was gracious, laughed easily, and flawlessly played the boon companion. I did not trust Leslie, and what I observed that night made me trust him less. In the end it was Leslie who would profit the most from the business.

Devereaux sat to the left of Kinsky and remained stone faced throughout the evening, speaking seldom and only when spoken to. Just as the dessert was being served, Kinsky, who was by this time deep in his cups, rose unsteadily to his feet and lifted his glass. The rest of the table rose in concert, glasses in hand. Devereaux, who had drunk little, reluctantly hauled himself to his feet.

"I wish," Kinsky said, "to propose a toast to our honored duke, the greatest general in all Europe. May God protect him, and may he soon ascend to the purple."

Devereaux slammed his goblet on the table. "What does Count Kinsky mean," he demanded, "by proposing such a toast? Is it the duke's intention to displace the emperor to whom we have all sworn our oaths? This, sir, is treason, and it cannot be countenanced." He stalked over to Kinsky and without another word drew his sword and ran the startled count through the body.

The door opposite mine flew open and a dozen armed soldiers burst into the hall, shouting their support for the emperor. Gordon and Butler leapt to their feet and drew their swords. Kinsky was down, his life's blood pouring out onto the floor. Devereaux vaulted the table and made for Ilio, who shrank back and despite his drunken state managed to draw his own rapier.

Gordon turned to his right and challenged the still befuddled Terzky. "Will you fight, traitor, or shall I cut you down as you stand?" Terzky wavered for a moment, then drew his rapier with a drunken flourish and commenced to duel with Gordon.

The soldiers, most of whom were armed with halberds, ringed the group as their officers engaged the traitors. While the others were engaged, Terzky's adjutant, Neumann, momentarily forgotten, saw an opportunity to escape and made for the door behind which I was standing. He threw the door open, and his eyes widened with surprise seeing me blocking the corridor with a drawn sword. The next surprise was mine. Neumann let out a bellow, lowered his head like a maddened bull, charged forward, knocked my blade aside, and butted me full in the stomach. I found myself sprawled out on my back. By the time I regained my feet, Neumann had reached the end of the corridor and was beating on the locked door with the pommel of his dagger.

I grabbed my sword and ran after Neumann. The captain turned at bay, shifted his dagger to his left hand and drew his sword. His movement came just a bit too late. My momentum carried me through his guard. It was a very foolish move, but I was angry and embarrassed, and this time I was the lucky one. Neumann was not prepared for a left-handed swordsman. I slashed left and cut open his sword arm. His weapon dropped, clattering to the stone floor. Without thinking, I lunged forward and pierced the right side of his breast with the point of my blade. His eyes widened as I jerked my sword from his flesh. As I turned and ran back up the corridor, I could hear the awful gurgling sound of a man drowning in his own blood.

I burst into the great room, sword at the ready, and was disappointed to find that the action was almost over. Gordon had made short work of the drunken Terzky. Ilio, who was an excellent swordsman, was the only one of the traitors still standing. He had wounded three of Butler's men and taken several wounds himself. He fought on with his back against the wall, blood running down his face and arms, thrusting and parrying skillfully with his rapier while several soldiers ranged about him like wolves circling a wounded bear, keeping carefully out of range of his claws.

Ilio kept up a constant stream of abuse directed at Gordon whom he felt had betrayed him. He challenged the Scotsman to fight him man to man. Gordon, his face red and his muttonchops bristling in anger, had shaken off Butler who was holding him back and was about to answer Ilio's challenge when Ilio over-reached himself and one of the soldiers buried the spike of his halberd in the soft flesh under his ribcage. Ilio's eyes flashed wide, and he crashed across the table gushing blood, scattering the crockery as he fell.

Then it was quiet. The fight has lasted barely a quarter of an hour. The table had been upturned, and food, wine and broken dishes were scattered everywhere. Gordon stood panting, holding his right arm that dripped blood from where he had taken a sword thrust through his bicep. Devereaux kneeled and matter-of-factly checked each of the fallen men in turn to make sure they were not breathing. The enlisted men stood quietly looking about themselves, not quite sure what to do. The silence lasted but a few moments. General Butler knew better than to allow any time for reflection or regret. He began issuing orders and putting the men to work. He placed guards at each door and ordered the bodies to be removed to the cooling room in the castle cellar. Captain Chenault quietly entered the room and reported that two of the guards had been killed and three taken prisoner. The prisoners were being taken to cells in the castle's donjon.

The first part of the plan had gone well. No one had escaped to sound the alarm. The general detailed several men to raise the drawbridges and issued orders that his regiment be called out to patrol the city. Butler turned to Devereaux.

"Captain, gather your men. You know what to do!"

Devereaux snapped to attention and saluted. He picked six soldiers, being careful to select only those who had been bloodied in the fight and set off. I was not a member of this party, but later he gave me a full account of what happened. Devereaux and his squad of soldiers had little trouble gaining access to Wallenstein's quarters. He was well known to the two generalissimo's guards and was simply waved through by the two men standing by his door, who assumed that the captain had urgent dispatches for the duke. One guard started to object that the duke had just retired, but a sword slice across his throat cut short the protest.

Devereaux threw open the door and stalked into the duke's bedchamber. Wallenstein stood by his bed in his dressing gown and nightcap. The bedchamber was small and dark. Two lamps lit the interior. As his men crowded into the chamber behind him, Captain Devereaux shouted, "Viva l'Empereur" and drew his rapier.

Wallenstein jumped onto the center of the bed. "What is the meaning of this? What is your business here, Captain Devereaux?"

"My business, sir, is to execute a traitor."

"You forget yourself, Captain; you are speaking to your commanding general."

"I am speaking, sir, to a traitor to the empire with a price on his head."

"And you presume to come here and arrest me?"

"Your plan is to turn over this city and this regiment to the emperor's enemies. Do you deny it?"

The duke had begun to regain his composure, though I am told that he was a ridiculous sight standing in the center of his bed with his nightshirt flapping about his bare legs.

"My plans?" he answered. "My plans, sir, are not the business of a captain of infantry," he said in a scathing tone. "You will do as you are ordered, and I order you and your men to put down your weapons now, return to your barracks, and place yourself under house arrest. General Butler will deal with you in the morning."

"No, My Lord Duke, not likely. I am here at General Butler's orders. Sergeant!"

"Captain, I demand to be taken to General Butler."

The sergeant, a stout, hard-bitten veteran, stepped forward while the rest of the soldiers clustered around Devereaux, halberds bristling.

The duke now fully realized the depths of his dilemma. He said not another word but stood proudly in the middle of the bed with his hands at his sides making no attempt to defend himself. At a nod from Devereaux, the sergeant dropped his halberd and thrust the point straight into the general's gut, wounding him mortally. Wallenstein sighed, fell backward, and slid off the bed, his blood spreading like coal oil across the floorboards.

Devereaux stepped forward, picked his mark carefully, and thrust his sword point into the general's chest, piercing his heart. He pulled out his sword, nodded once as if acknowledging a job well done, turned, and stalked from the chamber, sword in hand, spurs jingling, followed by his men. So ended the career of a truly remarkable man, one of the greatest generals of the age. Albert von Wallenstein, Duke of Friedland, Duke of Mecklenburg, lay tangled in his bloody sleeping gown, cut down in a provincial Bohemian town by his own soldiers.

Some hours after Devereaux reported to General Butler, I returned to the inn and snatched a few hours sleep. Chenault's hand shaking my shoulder extracted me from the depths of a blood soaked dream just after dawn. He sat on the side of the bed.

"Well, it appears that we have done it," Chenault said with a tired smile. "I have just come from the fortress; Butler and Leslie have matters in hand."

"What of Terzky's regiment?"

"Meek as new born lambs! Did I not say so, Jean-Baptiste? It is the *most* complete thing. The general assembled the regiments, stood up, had the emperor's order read, and then put them to work. Quite the lad, your General Butler!"

I nodded, more relieved than happy.

"And you have done well, my friend. You have done your king a great service. Cardinal Richelieu will be very pleased. I shall mention your role prominently in my dispatches, of that you may be sure."

"Thank you."

"No thanks necessary, dear boy. You did well, very well. We leave for Vienna in two hours. My brother is there, and I must make my report. He will be amazed." Chenault smiled wolfishly. "Best get packed, Jean-Baptiste. The Protestants will be at the gates by this evening."

"First, I must call and say goodbye to General Butler."

I found the general in his office surrounded by his officers. He was able to spare but a moment to speak with me. I made the excuse that my business required that I return to Paris. I had been invited to accompany Captain Chenault and his party. He said he was sorry to see me go, but that it was best as the outcome of the confrontation with Duke Bernard was uncertain at best. Civilians would not be safe, he said, should the Protestants retake the city.

Even in the dead of winter with the frigid weather and gray skies, it was good to be back in Paris. My first task was to report to the cardinal. Upon my arrival at the palais, I was immediately ushered into his private office where I found Richelieu and

Father Joseph eagerly awaiting my news. The cardinal seemed thinner about the face, and his eyes, as a result, more sunken and prominent. "Ah, there you are, my son. You are most welcome. We have heard the good news and may I congratulate you."

"Your Eminence, I fear you give me far too much credit. I owe a great deal to the indefatigable Captain Chenault."

The cardinal smiled at this reference. "No false modesty now, my son. Chenault is a likely young man, to be sure, but your part in this business has been crucial to its success. Do you not agree, Joseph?" Though Captain Chenault had remained in Germany to finish up some business, his report had obviously preceded me, and the Red Cardinal had many sources of information.

The Gray Eminence nodded solemnly. "I do, Your Eminence."

"There you see, my son, even Joseph agrees."

I left the palace with many assurances from both men of future preference. I was now in high favor with the cardinal and the future looked bright. Noelle who was, as always, exceptionally well informed, welcomed me home as a conquering hero, and as the Count de Rochambeau was not in evidence, I received the accolades due a conquering hero in the privacy of the countess's bedchamber.

Blessed Pierre was the most circumspect of men. He also welcomed me back with open arms, and I was grateful that he did not ask too many questions. I resumed my work at Torreles.

My duties took up much of my time as Pierre began to rely on me more and more. Working with Master Dulac, I became more and more comfortable with rough diamonds, judging their worth and deciding how best to facet them. At the end of my third year, Monsieur Dulac began to pay me the compliment of asking my opinion before making a final decision about cleaving and cutting the rough stones.

2nd Voyage

(1638-1643)

Chapter 14

Return to Persia

One night I had a dream. In it, there was a man in his middle years, portly and well dressed, with a long graying beard. He was sitting by the hearth smoking his pipe, surrounded by a large number of noisy children who joined hands, formed a circle, and, like harpies, danced around him. They climbed onto his lap and pulled at his ears and beard. One, a little girl with a dirty face and snotty nose, sat in his lap and wiped her nose on his waistcoat. I recall feeling sympathy for this poor man until I closely examined his face and realized that the man I was seeing was myself! It was a portent and a warning. I woke in a cold sweat and with a firm resolve; I would leave for India within the year.

I began my preparations. I would need capital. The profits from my first trip had dwindled. When I mentioned my plan to Pierre, he was clearly disappointed.

"So you are leaving just as I was getting used to having you around."

"Pierre, I have been here for the best part of five years, and, as you know, India has always been my goal. If I do not leave now, I never will, and thanks to you, Pierre, I am as ready as I am likely to be."

"Tell me your plans?"

"First Persia. I have business in Isfahan and Mashhad. I received a letter from Bharton, and I shall try to meet with him and perhaps, through his contacts, acquire some pearls. I am hoping he can arrange an audience with the shah."

"I see. I will invest, of course, and I leave it to you what to buy with my money."

"Thank you, cousin. I will do my best. I am in need of capital."

Pierre's eyes sparkled. "Well as to that, I have a plan."

"What a surprise. Well, out with it."

"We offer shares in your voyage to some of our best clients."

"Shares? I am to become a stock company? And in return?"

"The investors tender their money in advance, of course. We price the shares at 1,000 livres each. In return we give them first pick of the merchandise you bring back at half the normal price."

"If I come back, you mean. Pierre, isn't that a bit of a risk? I have never set foot in India. Who knows what I will bring back and what prices I will have to pay?"

"Cousin, cousin!" Pierre put his arm around my shoulder. "You must have more faith in yourself. Of course you will come back. You forget the profit margins you made on the pearls and turquoise you brought back from Persia. Mon Dieu, I shall never forget the profits you wrung out of me, your own blood. If you do half as well as you did on your first trip, we shall make a fortune." He gave my shoulders a squeeze. "Believe me, it will work. You know the men I am thinking of: Toussaint, d'Aubigne—men like that can rarely resist a wager, and what is a wager without risk?"

Pierre was right, of course. His stock issue did appeal to the sporting nature of some of Torreles' clients, and we raised a not inconsiderable sum.

My plans had not progressed very far when I received a

summons to wait upon Cardinal Richelieu at the palace.

"My son, we hear that you are planning to leave on a trip to India," the cardinal said as I nervously completed my bow. "I do hope you were not planning to leave without saying goodbye!"

I was surprised and flattered that the first minister of France would be aware of my activities, but that was Richelieu. His spies were everywhere, and he retained himself in power by always being one step ahead of his enemies and indeed of his friends.

"No, Your Eminence, of course not, I…"

"The cardinal smiled indulgently and raised his hand. "Just a bit of a joke, my son. Sit down, sit down, and tell us of your plans."

Richelieu turned to his aide. "This is the man, Giulio, of whom I have spoken. Jean-Baptiste Tavernier, may I introduce my protégé, Jules Mazarin. Monsieur Tavernier was of great help to us with the Wallenstein problem."

Mazarin was no more than two or three years older than I. He was tall, taller than the cardinal, and of a handsome visage, dark eyes, a long nose, full lips, and pointed chin. He sported a dark rakish moustache and a slender beard in the same style as Richelieu's. He stood and offered his hand.

We took chairs around a small table. "My plans, Eminence? Truly, I have just begun to make my plans. My goal is India. As you know, I have been working for my cousin, Pierre, at Torreles for several years to prepare myself to be a gem merchant, and I believe that I am finally ready."

"Yes, and I am sure that you are. You are a very resourceful fellow as you have proven on more than one occasion. So tell me, how may I be of service to you?"

"Your Eminence, I would never presume."

"Presume, not a bit of it! I told you France was grateful, and you could rely upon our patronage when the time came that you needed help, and this is clearly the time. So money and passports—I take it you will need both?"

"Yes, Your Eminence."

"As I expected! I have already spoken to His Majesty on your behalf, and you shall have a letter of introduction signed in his own hand."

"Your Eminence, I don't know what to say!"

Richelieu raised his hand in dismissal. "Then say nothing. Now there is something I wish to show you." The cardinal seated himself on the other side of the desk. "I have begun a project," he said clasping his hands. "It has been my ambition to build a collection of plates, a complete set of liturgical vessels. One moment!" He snapped his fingers and a servant appeared. "Jacques, the red case!" The servant rushed out and quickly reappeared with a large cylindrical case bound in scarlet Morocco leather. He slid a role of parchments from the case and handed them to Richelieu.

Richelieu motioned to Mazarin: "Look here. Move your chair closer, Giulio. I believe you will find this of interest." The Cardinal unrolled the scrolls, which spilled over the edges of the table. The first was a plan of a massive golden crucifix. As he began to explain the drawing, his whole demeanor changed. It was the first time I had seen this normally cool, taciturn man excited!

"Here you see, Monsieur Tavernier, it is to have a background of tortoiseshell with enameled lilies here and here in honor of the king." He lovingly smoothed the parchment with the palms of his hands. "The plan calls for the use of several hundred small diamonds. You see—here, here and here the crown of thorns, the loin cloth, and the halo, all will be made of diamonds," he said, his finger darting from place to place pointing out various parts of the design. "Seven hundred ninety-two diamonds, to be precise."

"Your Eminence," I said awed, "this is truly magnificent!"

The cardinal beamed. He looked from me to Mazarin, who nodded his head in wonder. "Yes, is it not? And this is but the beginning. Here, let me show you. He unrolled scroll after scroll and smoothed out each upon the table. There was an enameled golden chalice with an openwork base, medallions portraying the four evangelists, a cup encrusted with diamonds, a pair of candlesticks with three enameled cherubs supporting each stem, and a statue of the Virgin holding the baby Jesus, her blue mantle studded with rose-cut diamonds.

"This will be the most magnificent set ever created, and it will go to the crown upon my death. It shall be my legacy. I shall leave it to France so that she will remember me. Jean-Baptiste, I wish you to have the honor of aiding me. What do you say? All in all, the goldsmiths tell me, I shall need nine thousand diamonds."

Mazarin then spoke in his oddly accented French: "Your Eminence has His Majesty's esteem and gratitude, and surely history will remember Your Eminence as a great statesman."

Richelieu slowly shook his head and smiled his thin smile. "The king is God's anointed, and it is our duty to serve him. But if you will take my advice, Giulio, you will not rely overly much on the favor of princes, for their memories are short. Who knows how history will remember a simple priest who did his duty as God gave him the light to see it. As for books, I rescued no damsels. I slew no dragons. More likely I will play the villain in some romance."

Mazarin made to reply, but Richelieu raised his hand for silence and turned back to me. "This is a thing I can do, and here is my commission. I shall provide you with 100,000 livres in gold on account to acquire diamonds in India. My secretary will provide you with a list of approximate sizes."

I left the Palace Richelieu in a transport of joy.

My father gaped and stared in disbelief. "One hundred thousand livres, God in heaven!" My brother shook his head. I don't think they truly believed me until I showed them the draft with the Cardinal's seal.

"Yes, father, but there is more. With Pierre's money and the subscriptions I shall have over 200,000."

My mother's eyes brimmed with tears. "You should stay at home with your family. Pierre has offered you a partnership, and it's time that you found a wife."

"Daniel must go with him," My father said matter of factly.

My brother had been a problem for my parents. He showed neither aptitude nor any interest in the map maker's trade, so my father had apprenticed him to a saddle maker. But after his first year, the master declined to keep him saying that Daniel was not serious. He spent too much of his time in the company of young men and seemed not to care for anything other than ogling the young ladies and playing cards with his friends. Still he was an honest lad with an open manner and a smile that charmed everyone who met him.

My mother glared at her husband. "You know how I feel about that, husband! First your son plagues the life out of me and now you."

"You know I'm right, Mother. The boy will only get himself into trouble if he stays in Paris, and with all that money, Jean-Baptiste will need him. He will need someone he can trust."

Daniel looked from one to the other of our parents expectantly. He was a powerfully built young fellow. He had our father's blue eyes—if anything a brighter blue.

"But what of my two boys? First Jean-Baptiste and now Daniel. I will never see either of my babies again?"

"Oh shush, woman, stop your blubbering. Didn't Jean-Baptiste go all the way to Persia and come home again? He will take care of Daniel."

"Oh, I give up!" she said burying her face in her hands.

Daniel grabbed our mother, swept her off her feet, and danced her about the room. He soon had her crying stopped. "Oh, let go of me, you brute," she said laughing and beating her tiny fists against his chest. "Just make sure that you pay attention to your older brother."

"I will, Mother, never fear. I shall do everything that Jean-Baptiste tells me."

"A likely story."

"No, truly, I swear to God." He let her go and held up his right hand. A dimpled smile spread like warm jam across his handsome face.

"Daniel, I'll thank you not to blaspheme," Mother said, tugging at her skirts. "Are we Romans to be holding our hand up to God?"

Daniel endeavored to look contrite, but I too had my doubts about my brother keeping his pledge. Daniel was barely twenty years old. He was taller than I and thinner, with dark hair and a smooth face and, as yet, no sign of a beard.

I put my brother to work with a list of supplies. Bharton had told me that Indian nobles were particularly fond of enameled work at which our Limoges workshops are unsurpassed. I acquired a stock of finely crafted enameled gold jewelry as trade goods. I also purchased a number of West Indian pearls at a very good price from a Portuguese Jew. These were beautiful, very large, pear-shaped and baroque pearls, larger than any I had seen in the Persian Gulf. These pearls inclined toward yellow and so were difficult to sell in Europe.

We would require several servants and hostlers. When we reached Persia, I hoped to re-employ Danush, but I would need several others to see to loading and unloading the beasts, guarding my goods, and attending my person. Daniel set to work interviewing men who wished employment. I found that though he was disinclined toward physical labor, he was exceptionally good at judging the worth of servants and had a real talent for supervising the work of others—not excluding myself.

Daniel also found a young surgeon by the name of Alain Dellon who wished to travel and see the world. I interviewed him. He was well spoken and seemed a likely enough fellow.

Just before we set out, I then sent Daniel ahead to Marseilles to secure passage on a vessel bound for Constantinople, Alexandretta, or Aleppo. A week later, the rest of our party set off to Marseilles by road with a string of packhorses loaded down with goods. My hope was to join either the Holland or English fleet that sails in the fall from Marseilles and Leghorn.

No sooner had we reached the inn where we planned to meet when Daniel burst in. "Ah, Jean-Baptiste, you are finally here. Have you been to the docks?"

"It is good to see you, too, brother." Daniel's hair was windblown and his face, ruddy. The salt air obviously agreed with him. "No, we have been ten days on the road and only just arrived. I came straight to the inn. What news have you?"

"The fleet has not yet arrived, but I have found us a ship."

"A single ship?"

"Yes, brother, a Holland barque, but she is well armed—forty-five guns—and bound for Alexandretta."

"Will the captain wait for the fleet?"

"He will not. You have arrived just in time. He is in a tearing hurry. He wishes to sail on the morning tide day after tomorrow."

"What is he like, the captain?"

"Typical Dutchman, short, bald, sow belly, and a face like a prune."

"Sounds like a handsome lad."

"Aye, brother, he is that!" Daniel said with a laugh.

I caught the sharp tang of salt as we emerged from the sheltered street onto the cobblestoned quay. The waterfront was a short walk. Several ships were anchored stern-to against the quay: a Dutch Cog, a Venetian galley, and two others. The barque was tied broadside to the pier. Stevedores filed, like a column of ants, up and down the gangway, shouldering heavy bales of cargo bound for Alexandretta. Above our heads the gulls dipped and wheeled, their laughter echoing off the granite-faced warehouses that lined the quay.

I spotted the captain. Daniel's description had been accurate. He stood with legs apart, his hands on his hips, abusing the stevedores who were mostly black Algerians and hardly understood a word of French.

"You are Monsieur Tavernier," he said looking me up and down.

"I am."

He nodded and wiped his thick lips with his sleeve. "I thought so. We sail the day after tomorrow at dawn—mind, on the morning tide. Passengers may load their goods tomorrow. I have already shown your brother your cabin. It will do for two. It ain't nothing fancy."

I nodded. "Thank you, Captain. We will be ready."

He nodded curtly and gestured toward one of the stevedores. "Avast there, you butter fingered lubber, or I'll have the hide off ya!"

We spent the next day loading our goods and set sail from Marseilles bound for Malta and Alexandretta on the 13th of September, 1638.

The port of Alexandretta is in a pocket shaped inlet, and the village lies just to the south. It is a small pile of houses on a hillside, mostly occupied by Greeks. It was founded by Alexander on the spot where he defeated the Persian army under Darius. Aleppo is inland and Alexandretta is the closest port, which is the only reason why anyone bothers traveling there. After making arrangements to rent horses for the three day trek inland, we spent the night at an inn. Early the next morning we packed up and set out for Aleppo, the first stage of our journey into Persia.

After six weeks in Aleppo waiting for the annual caravan to be organized, we finally set off on Christmas day, part of a caravan of six hundred camels and four hundred men. I was anxious to get to Isfahan, but we went first to Mashhad, Basra, and, most importantly, to Shiraz. This may seem a circuitous route, but not to a merchant looking for opportunities to buy.

Chapter 15

Isfahan

After a brief stop at Basra, a port on the Arabian Gulf just south of the island of Bahrain, we reached Mashhad in April, and I left the caravan and went to Nishapur where I was reunited with the faithful Danush. It was touching to see how much he had missed me. I missed him, too. We both managed to break down into tears. He was no longer the scrawny, dirty boy I had met six years before. He had matured into a young man, put on flesh and dignity, and dressed like the small but successful merchant that he had become. He proudly showed me his house. He had also acquired a wife and a cook and two young children. He insisted that I stay with him. There was barely room, but I have stayed in much worse places, and I could not say no. That evening his wife put on a feast: mezze, spring lamb, three kinds of pilaf and a sherbet made with rosewater.

After the meal, while his wife cleaned up the remains and put the children to bed, Danush brought out a bubble pipe. As the shadows lengthened toward evening and the fragrant smoke curled up toward the ceiling, we leaned back on our cushions and talked of old times and new prospects.

"Aga, you are in luck. My brothers have just brought me a parcel of turquoise. Tomorrow you will see them, and you will have first pick."

"Good, I had hoped to find a parcel, but then I must leave—we must leave if you wish to go with me. I have eighty-five camels, half loaded with a prime shipment of wine from Shiraz, and I am anxious to get to Isfahan while the market is still good."

"Very wise, aga. I will be ready, but tell me where do we go? Back to Bahrain?"

I laughed. "So I see you still wish to travel?"

"Oh, yes, aga. This city is driving me crazy. Nothing ever happens here. Like you, your servant wishes to see the wide world."

"What about your wife and children?"

Danush rolled his eyes. "With your permission, aga, I will bring them as far as Isfahan. They have relatives there, and they will be fine until we return."

"Well then, first Isfahan, then we go to Surat, to the kingdom of the Great Mogul."

"India!" Danush's mouth dropped open. Forgive me, aga, did you say India? I have always wished to see India. We go by ship, then?"

"Yes, first back to Shiraz, then by ship from Bander Abassi."

"India! I can hardly believe it. Aga, may I ask, what is your plan?"

"I plan to buy diamonds and other precious gems!"

"Y, Allah," Danush's eyes sparkled with greed; he looked around to see if anyone was in earshot. "Diamonds?" he whispered.

I nodded.

"Diamonds! By the beard of the Prophet, may peace be upon Him, diamonds! Forgive me, do you know about diamonds, aga?"

"I have learned something of them. Enough I think for a start, and I will learn more."

Three weeks later we arrived in the Persian capital. Isfahan together with its suburbs is more than twice the size of Paris, and the population is ten times greater than our capital. The city has one hundred sixty-two mosques, forty-eight colleges, and twelve cemeteries. It is situated in the middle of a broad, fertile plain that spreads fifteen leagues in each direction. The plain is planted with all manner of trees and crops, sufficient to feed the entire population of the city. There are no villages, just tiny clusters of houses, used by those who work the land, and plain-tree shaded channels that have been dug to provide irrigation.

Between seven and eight o'clock each morning it is the custom of the citizens of Isfahan to repair to the coffee houses where they smoke tobacco and gossip with friends.

The first Shah Abbās noted that the coffee houses provided a place for his subjects to talk about the government. Fearing sedition he decreed that in each coffee house there should be a mullah to recite points of law, passages from the Koran, and sometimes poetry. The men must be guarded in their talk for as the old saying goes:

> *"Be careful of the back of a mule, the front of a woman, and all sides of a mullah."*

Thus they must be attentive to the mullah, particularly when he quotes from the Holy Koran. Still a good deal of business is conducted in the coffee houses.

Chapter 16

Madame Twelve-Tomans

One morning Danush and I were walking in an easterly direction across the Meidan toward the Hasanad Gate. A chill winter wind blew across the square. We passed the noisy bazaar named the Sellers of Pomegranates and continued by a fine palace belonging to the shah, which had been converted for the use of Armenian jewelers and diamond cutters. We turned down one of the narrow alleys between the gem cutter's bazaar and the goldsmith's quarter.

Half way down the alley we found our way blocked by three very large, rough looking men dressed in workmen's clothes. Danush shouted at them in Persian, demanding that they clear the way, but they simply stood silently shoulder-to-shoulder making it impossible for us to proceed. I turned to retrace my steps and found another group of men blocking our retreat. Reflexively, my left hand groped for my sword hilt before I realized that I had none. In Persia, merchants are not permitted to carry swords. One wiry looking fellow, a head shorter than his comrades, followed the motion with his eyes, then stepped forward with a mocking smile and addressed me in Portuguese.

"Senhor, your pardon, my, er…master wishes to speak with you. Please, allow us to escort you!"

"What, who are you, and what do you mean by this impertinence? 'Escort me,' escort me where? Who are you, and who is your master? If he wishes to speak with me, he may call upon me like a gentleman."

The man's smile broadened; a livid scar passed from just under his right eye to the tip of his chin. "Senhor, you seem to me to be a practical man. Look around you," he said opening his vest with one hand. I could see a dagger tucked into the sash at his waist. "We have no wish to injure you, but my master is one who does not like to be kept waiting, and I will do what I must."

"Tell me then, just who is this master of yours?"

"Senhor, my apologies. I have been instructed not to tell you. I can only repeat," he hissed, "if you come quietly, you will not be harmed in any way. Now, please, señhor," he said gesturing toward the end of the alley.

"What of my servant?"

"He is wanted as well."

I looked at Danush who was standing quietly by my side. He eyed me with a look of terror.

I hoped that someone might come down the alley, and I tried to stall for time, but the leader of the ruffians was becoming impatient. He stood sideways, his dark hooded eyes darting nervously from one end of the passage to the other. His hand went to his knife hilt. "Enough talk, senhor. You will come with us, now!"

There was nothing for it. The leader gestured and we turned, walked to the end of the alley, turned right, and crossed the main street just behind the royal mosque. We ducked into another alley, passed a large caravanserai built by the son of the chief magistrate during the reign of Abbās the First and, just past the crossroads of Mizra Mo'in, found ourselves at the rear entrance of a stately mansion.

Beckoning us to walk ahead, the chief of our abductors steered us up a path and through the entranceway. Several of the ruffians melted away as we passed through a kitchen, down a hallway, and into a large elegant parlor with high vaulted ceilings.

The leader of the group smiled and bowed. "Your servant will be safe with me. What my master wishes to say is for your ears alone." He gestured to Danush, who looked like a woman about to be attacked by the vapors. "Go with him, Danush. I will be with you presently."

"See that no harm comes to him, fellow," I said. The man smiled, bowed, motioned for Danush to precede him, and backed out of the room, closing the large double doors and leaving me alone.

I had only a few moments to take in the room. A fine crystal chandelier hung from the center vault. One wall was completely mirrored. The floor was marble, covered with Kerman carpets of the finest wool worked with gold. A French chiffonnier was set against one wall; a pair of European chairs, upholstered with embroidered silk, faced a matching couch that was set along the other.

The doors swung open and the most beautiful woman I had ever seen stepped into the room. She was a goddess in silk with a narrow face, high cheekbones, full sculpted vermilion lips, dark almond eyes, and glossy black hair that cascaded like a silk waterfall over her shoulders. She wore baggy pants of water green gossamer silk fastened at the ankles. Over this was a traditional pirhan, a richly embroidered scarlet over-shirt opened to the navel and dropping down to the knees. On her feet were the daintiest slippers of dark green felt embroidered with gold threads. Her smile lit up her face, and in that instant my anger melted away.

"Monsieur Jean-Baptiste Tavernier, I believe," she said in perfectly accented French. She stepped up to me and offered her hand. "My name is Madeleine de Goisse. I am the mistress of this house, but you perhaps have heard of me under a different name. I am called Madame Twelve-Tomans."

I was shocked. Madame Twelve-Tomans was the most famous courtesan in all of Persia. Rumor had it that she bore this name because twelve tomans was the sum that it cost a man to spend a single night in her company. Twelve tomans was a small fortune, but it was said that those who had sampled her charms swore it was worth that and more. It was also rumored that she was the mistress of the nazir, the keeper of the shah's household and one of the most powerful officials of the court.

I bowed over her hand and touched it to my lips. She had long tapered fingers and nails painted the same color as her lips. "Forgive me, madame. I have heard your name many times, of course, but I must say I expected someone of your reputation to be er... somewhat older."

"So, monsieur," she said, her lips forming into a pout, "you thought me a hag?"

"No, madame, never that. Please forgive me. It is just that everyone has heard your name, so naturally I assumed…"

"That I had been around for some time. Là monsieur," she said with a shy smile, "I see that you are as diplomatic as you are handsome. So I forgive you."

The absurdity of this whole scene suddenly struck me, and I found myself laughing. "This conversation is ridiculous, madame. I have been kidnapped in broad daylight by a band of ruffians and brought here, and now I find myself apologizing to my abductor, one of the most famous women in all of Persia, who is also apparently French."

She looked into my eyes and smiled. "Life is strange, is it not, monsieur?"

"Ha, ha! It is, indeed, madame, and now if you will be kind enough to tell me why I was brought here?"

She stepped closer. The warmth of her body and her scent, jasmine I think it was, made me giddy.

"Please forgive me, monsieur, for the somewhat unorthodox manner by which you were brought here and allow me to make it up to you. I mean you no harm, and my reasons for acting as I have will become clear in due time, I promise. But please, you are my honored guest. May I offer you some refreshment?"

Well, there I was, unhurt except for my dignity, and having a conversation with a beautiful young woman. I decided to make the most of the situation. "I am at your service, madame," I said.

She smiled coyly and curtseyed. "Boujour, monsieur." She

clapped her hands and two servants appeared with large silver trays laden with fruit and sweetmeats. Another held a beautifully chased silver wine jug and two goblets of similar workmanship. We sat together on the couch, and the servant poured wine.

"Monsieur Tavernier, I have not been quite honest with you. I am not really Madame Twelve-Tomans, or at least I am not the first woman of that name. The real Madame Twelve-Tomans in my mother, Geneviève de Goisse. Twenty-five years ago my mother's ship was captured by Barbary pirates. She was traveling from Marseilles to Constantinople with her husband, the private secretary to the Count de Arc, who was at that time ambassador to the Turks. All the men on board, including her husband, were put to the sword, and she was enslaved and carried off to Aleppo where she was sold to a merchant, who sold her to a brothel owner in Isfahan.

"The brothel owner was a shrewd man. He saw that she was something special and that he could get a much better return from his purchase if he marketed her charms with care. The Persians, as you know, worship white skin. He bought her a beautiful wardrobe and set her up in a magnificent apartment."

"Truly an amazing story, mademoiselle!"

She eyed me uncertainly over the rim of her goblet for a moment, then took a sip and went on: "You must not judge my mother too harshly, monsieur. She is a proud woman, but she had few choices and she did what she had to, to survive. She created something of a sensation. The brothel owner offered her to only the best connected and wealthiest of his clients at a very high price."

"Very soon she came to the attention of a very high official of the court. The man offered to buy her, but the brothel owner resisted. The price offered was very high, but truth to tell, the whore master had fallen in love with my mother and did not wish to part with her."

"So what did he do?"

"He set her free."

"Freed her?"

She smiled wistfully. "Yes, monsieur. Indeed, you see, he had little choice. The official was very powerful. He could easily have ruined him, shut him down—even have him killed. Despite his love for my mother, he could not marry her. He already had a family, and besides she was an infidel. By giving my mother her freedom, he allowed her to set up on her own. He remained a silent partner, of course."

"And the official?"

"For a while, she was his mistress. But that couldn't last. She was twenty years old. In this country at that age a woman is practically an old maid. The affair went on for several years, and the man was very generous. He gave her this chateau so that he would have a place to escape the intrigues and formality of the court. My mother was a spirited woman, who spoke her mind and this fascinated him. They remain friends, and he still protects us. By the time he grew tired of her, she had accumulated some wealth, paid off her partner, and became Madame Twelve-Tomans."

"He gave her this palace?"

"Yes, monsieur!"

"But isn't this is one of the shah's…?"

Madeleine did not respond. She just looked me in the eyes and smiled, and her eyes glittered. The sun, filtering through the jalousied window, cast a linear pattern of sun and shade onto the carpet at my feet.

I raised my head. "I see. So, mademoiselle, may I ask what service the beautiful daughter of Madame Twelve-Tomans requires of me?"

"That is simple, monsieur. I wish you to help me make my escape to France."

"Escape, mademoiselle? Do you mean to say that you are a captive here?"

Tears filled her eyes. "Monsieur, my mother is very ill, and she will soon die, and with her death I will lose the shah's protection. Oh, not entirely. He wishes to provide for me by arranging a marriage to an old man, one of his favorites. In this way he believes he will secure my future."

Oh, she was a minx, this one! How many men are there that can resist a beautiful woman's tears. "But surely, mademoiselle, is that so bad—a good marriage, children, a good life?"

She shook her head and wiped the tears away with the back of her hand and pinioned me with those beautiful dark eyes.

"A good life? In this country? Surely you jest, monsieur. In this country a woman is little more than a piece of furniture. She owns nothing. She is nothing. For the rest of my life to be locked up behind the walls of an old man's seraglio, a baby factory, guarded by fat eunuchs? No friends, not even allowed to go out without guards and a sack over my head? You call that a good life?

She stood up, her head high with a defiant glare in her eyes. "Well, monsieur, I do not. I would rather die!"

I stood up and gingerly placed my hand on her shoulder. "Please, mademoiselle, don't upset yourself. Come, sit down, and let us talk. You said you needed my help. Tell me, what exactly may I do for you?"

She slumped against me, buried her head on my breast, and began to sob. I sat her down on the couch next to me and let her cry herself out. Finally she lifted her head and dabbed at her tears with her handkerchief. She blew her nose.

"I am sorry, monsieur. Please forgive me," she said, a tiny smile playing under her red-rimmed eyes. "I did not mean to carry on so. It is just that I want to go home, to France. I have never seen her, but my mother has told me all about her. In France a woman can be free—well, perhaps not free, not like a man—but she can have respect, and she can have choices."

"What is it that prevents you from leaving?"

She sighed. "Two things, monsieur: First, my mother. She is, as I said, very ill and I cannot leave her. The second is money. I will go to France in style as a great lady, not as a pauper."

"To do that, mademoiselle, requires money—a great deal of money. But something tells me that you have thought of that."

She giggled and regarded me with a shy look. "A plan. Yes, monsieur, I have—that is my mother has. She has been planning my escape for many years. And that, monsieur, is why I had, I mean, why I invited you to come."

I had no idea what I might be getting myself into. The half-caste daughter of the Persian king! My problem was, the woman was completely irresistible.

"Yes, mademoiselle, and a charming invitation it was. So, again how may I be of service?"

"That I will tell you soon enough, but come," she said brightening. She took my arm. "First I wish you to meet my mother, the real Madame Twelve-Tomans. And enough of this formality. We shall be friends, and I shall call you Jean, and you shall call me Madeleine."

She showed me through the door into the foyer. It contained a wide staircase. We went up into a long hallway, and then down the hall to a closed door. She knocked softly. "Mother," she whispered into the door, "it is Madeleine; I have brought a friend to meet you."

The room was dark; the heavy drapes had been drawn across the window to keep out the bright mid-day light. It was furnished like a room in a French chateau. Madame lay on a canopied bed with the covers drawn up to her chin. In the half-light I could see that she was not an old woman, though she looked pale. Her skin was thin and almost translucent, and her voice was soft like a reed. With her daughter's help she raised herself up on her pillows, smiled, and offered her hand.

"Monsieur Tavernier, how good of you to come."

"It is a pleasure to meet the famous Madame Twelve-Tomans."

She smiled and her dark eyes twinkled. "Infamous, you mean. You should not believe everything you hear, monsieur!"

"I have heard many stories of the beauty and charm of Madame Twelve-Tomans, but now that I have met you, I can see that the stories do not tell half the truth."

"Ha, ha. You are a naughty man." She waggled her finger at me. "Have a care, daughter, this one is a charmer. Tell me, monsieur, is it true what everyone says, that you have the eye of a devi? "

"You should not believe everything that you hear, madame."

"I shall remember that, monsieur." She patted the edge of the bed. "Come, sit here, and let us talk for a while, I rarely have the chance these days to spend time with a handsome young man."

I sat down as she bade me.

"Tell me something of your plans."

For the next half hour I enjoyed one of the most pleasant conversations I have ever had with a woman. Madame was quite charming, and after a few minutes I was completely under her spell. She asked many questions about my life and my ambitions. I could see that this effort took a great deal out of her. Even in her reduced state I could well imagine why the most powerful man in Persia had fallen in love with her. Finally Madeleine brushed aside her mother's protestations that she was feeling *perfectly fine* and insisted that she stop talking and rest. Just before we left, her mother drew Madeleine toward her and whispered a few words into her ear. Madeleine then tucked her in, took my arm, and ushered me out of the room.

"Madeleine, your mother is a remarkable woman."

"Thank you Jean-Baptiste. She liked you very much and more importantly she approves of you," she said as she gently pushed closed the bedroom door.

"Is there a chance that she will recover?"

Madeleine looked at me with moist eyes. "Oh, I do hope so, Jean. I pray to the blessed Virgin for this every night, but the doctors tell me she will not. You know how they talk, the humors and so forth. They bleed her, and it does no good, and then they purge her and... It has been months now and she gets no better. She no longer eats very much. She tells me she has no appetite. But, please, come this way, there is something I wish to show you."

At the other end of the hall we came to a small wooden door reinforced with iron straps that she opened using a heavy key. Beyond the door we entered a dark tiny room entirely lined with whitewashed brick. The room had several shelves built into the wall and a small table with two chairs. Madeleine lit two lamps, drew a large inlaid wooden chest from a shelf, and placed it on the table. She bade me sit and began lifting chamois bags from the chest. Each bag contained a jewel. She carefully removed each and laid it down lovingly on the table. "This," she said, "is my legacy."

I was dazzled. The first bag contained a waist length, cotière strand of finely matched oriental pearls. She picked up the strand, dropped it over her head, leaned back, cocked her hip, and smiled provocatively.

"May I offer you some refreshment, monsieur?"

The pearls were large white gems, each twenty grains or more and as perfectly round as I have ever seen, with a satiny luster and translucent pinkish water. And how they came alive against the silky texture of her skin! She laid out two other strands of similar quality, one a choker and the other opera length.

There were several pendants executed in the old style, pierced gold filigree work with delicate champlevé enameling. All of the enamel work had been executed in European workshops, probably in France. There was a particularly charming enameled, pendant watch. On its reverse side there was a large cabochon sapphire weighing perhaps twenty Florentine carats, set in a bezel, and surrounded by seven others, set thread-in-bead. On the lid was set another sapphire. Madeleine clasped it to her neck and opened it. Inside the lid was a series of square plaques enameled with images of birds and insects.

Many of the jewels were executed in the new style, which favored the use of large gems. Persians love colored gemstones. There were rubies and oriental sapphires from Ava and Ceylon, emeralds and topazes imported from the New World. The gems were superb. Madeleine modeled them. She was by turns smiling and coquettish, then somber, then haughty and regal, depending upon the mood the jewel evoked.

The jewels were fit to be a gift to a king as they surely had been. I recall one large pendant set with flawless diamonds of particularly clear and crisp water, such as are found in the mines at Kollür.

Finally I sat back, fully sated by the beauty of what I saw. "Magnificent, Madeleine, a dowry fit for a princess."

"These were each gifts to my mother from my father. But I am sure you have guessed as much already."

I nodded.

"The question is, Jean, will you sell them for me? It makes me very sad, but I cannot keep them. I will need the money. In Persia the king owns everything. When an official—even a high official of the court—dies, his fortune returns to the crown, and his widow keeps only her jewelry. This house—it is not really ours—it belongs to my father, I mean His Majesty, the shah. It will be reclaimed upon my mother's death."

"Madeleine, we have just met; you hardly know me. You are proposing to trust me with a collection that is worth a fortune."

She smiled and nodded. "Yes, but you see, Jean, you have been carefully investigated. We—my mother and I—have made inquiries, believe me. You have an excellent reputation, and today, your meeting with my mother was the last step. So, listen carefully, Jean-Baptiste Tavernier, here is our proposition. We believe you are a man of honor, and I will give you the collection to sell on our behalf. They must not be sold in Persia. If any of the jewels found their way back to the shah, if that were to happen, our plans would be exposed and all would be lost. So you must take them with you to India and sell them quietly. First, we agree to a set price, and we split that between us—half for you and half for me. If you decide to lower the price for whatever reason, that is your business. My profit remains the same. Is that agreeable?"

"Well, yes, of course, but you are too generous."

"No, as the merchants say, we wish you to be happy with your profit, and I wish you to invest the portion of the profits you hold for me, if the opportunity presents itself. You will return to Isfahan and bring me my share of what you have sold, and we will decide what to do with anything that is left."

"Madeleine, this will be my first voyage to India. I expect to be in that country for at least two years. That is quite a long time. Forgive me for asking, but what will you do if your mother… if she does not get well?"

"You mean should she die before you return?"

"Well, yes, or if something should happen to me."

"You may speak to me plainly, Jean-Baptiste. This is business, and I am hardly a hothouse flower. In that eventuality I shall take myself to a nunnery."

"You will what?"

"Oh Jean" she said, laughing, "The look on your face, so precious. What I mean is my mother has made arrangements with Father Girard. He is my confessor. My mother was very strict and insisted that I be properly brought up in the Catholic faith, though between us, the teachings have raised many questions in my mind that the priest seems unable to answer.

"Father Girard has arranged for me to be taken in by the sisters at a small monastery near Aleppo. I will be allowed a period of mourning, perhaps a year. Then if the shah presses me, I will enter the convent as a novice, and I should be safe. Otherwise I shall be forced to marry. But do not tarry too long, my friend," she said waving a lovely forefinger beneath my nose, "else I will be forced to take the veil in truth. So as you see, Monsieur Jean-Baptiste Tavernier, you have my future in your hands, and you may go on your voyage secure in the knowledge that if you should meet with ill fortune, there will be someone to make a novena and pray for your rotten soul."

Now it was my turn to laugh. What a strange mix of vulnerability, worldliness, defiance, and charm. She did not think the way a woman is supposed to think. Her ideas were scandalous. Did she really believe that she could flaunt society? I did not know. I did not know it then, but my relationship with Madeleine de Goisse would be anything but dull.

"You have ready money?"

"Yes, Jean, never fear. As I told you, my mother has been planning this for many years. I have friends and sufficient money to get to Aleppo or even to France were that necessary, but the bulk of my legacy I am entrusting to you.

"Then, mademoiselle, I shall give you a letter of credit addressed to the Šahrimanian family. I believe you have heard of them. It will be to my very good friend, Bharton. If you need money before I return, just give the letter to him and he will advance you 5,000 louis d'or."

Her eyed widened. "Five thousand louis! The Šahrimanian family. Yes, of course, I have heard of them. Who has not? They are the richest merchants in Julfa. You are in business with them? I am impressed, Jean-Baptiste."

"It is but a down payment on the value of your jewels. Listen carefully, Madeleine, I will also give you the name of an honest Armenian moneychanger in Aleppo. Should you decide to leave, you must convert your Persian silver to gold, preferably German or Venetian ducats or golden louis—they are the best. Inquire among the merchants. They will know the rate. At all costs, avoid the Indian money changers. They are worse than the Jews. I will also give you a letter and the address of my cousin in Paris."

"Yes, I understand. I will do as you say. Now it is getting late. We shall soon open for business, and I must make arrangements for you to leave without being seen. I do not wish to be overly dramatic. At this time of day, your presence might excite some curiosity, and I think it is not in our interest to draw attention to your presence here."

Madeleine led me to the kitchen where I found Danush, stuffing his face and tickling the chin of a large Persian woman, obviously the cook. The chief of our abductors was also there, leaning against the wall with his arms crossed and a bemused look on his face. Danush leapt to his feet.

"Aga, do not worry. Your servant is here. I refused to leave without you."

Madeleine laughed. "So this is Danush. You see, I return him to you, well fed and none the worse for wear. Jean, this is Achmed. You met earlier, I believe. Achmed has been in my mother's service for many years. We grew up together. He is devoted to me, and I would trust him with my life. He understands," she said looking pointedly at him, "that you are a trusted friend. He will be the liaison between us." The man rubbed his hand across his scarred face, smiled his wicked, amused smile, and bowed. I found myself wondering where he had met the knife that lent his visage such a sinister aspect.

We slipped out the way we came, this time without an escort.

"Well Danush," I said, "you seemed to be getting along quite well with that cut throat Achmed, and how is it the mademoiselle knew your name?"

"Aga, Achmed is my wife's cousin." Danush said with a sheepish look.

"What?"

He grabbed my sleeve. "You must forgive me, aga; I did not know this myself until Achmed told me."

"So the mystery is solved. That is how Mademoiselle de Goisse knew so much about me and my business. Your wife has been talking to her cousin."

Chapter 17

A Taste of Paradise

everal days later Achmed brought me a note from Madeleine. It was an invitation to attend an "event" though no particulars as to what sort of event were given, and when I asked Achmed, he shrugged. This made me very curious, and to be honest, Madeleine had been much in my thoughts.

When I arrived at the chateau, the sun was well set, and this time I entered through the front door as instructed. I expected Madeleine, but I was greeted by two lovely young women dressed in costumes that seemed to come directly out of a fable. One had brown eyes; the other's eyes were a shimmering green. The dark-eyed one was Persian; the green-eyed beauty had light brown hair and was probably Circassian, from that region north of Turkey, known for its white skinned beauties. Each wore her hair long and had on a revealing short vest or jacket of bright blue silk and a matching scanty undergarment under a pair of gossamer thin white silk drawers that left little to the imagination. I asked for Madeleine, but they seemed not to understand.

The two beauties bowed and, each taking me by an arm, led me down a staircase into a beautifully appointed dressing room lit by candles set in sconces along the wall. The setting was a lovely garden. A silk dressing gown hung on a hook attached to the wall next to a screen embroidered with an erotic scene. Several beautiful large-eyed *houris*, as the Mussulmans describe the virgins who will attend them in Paradise, happily cavorted with a naked man by a stream.

By their gestures the two young women made it clear they wished me to disrobe and put on the dressing gown. This was obviously part of the *event* that Madeleine had written about. I allowed myself to be persuaded. I stepped behind the screen, disrobed, and emerged dressed in silk. The green-eyed one took my hand and led me through a second door into a large tiled chamber. Set in the floor was a wide stone staircase that descended into a steaming pool.

The pool, its surface covered with rose petals, was round and large enough to easily hold ten men in comfort. Plants and small trees were set in pots along the walls. The walls themselves were cleverly painted with large plants and trees in such realism I felt I had entered a lush garden.

I was led to a long divan where I took my ease. Then another similarly dressed young lady entered through an archway at the far end of the chamber carrying a cup and pitcher set on a silver tray. The cup was filled with sorbet. I tasted the cool fragrant liquid, which had an odd sweetish taste. I drained it, and the cup was immediately refilled from the chased silver pitcher. Meanwhile the two houris were busy sprinkling rose petals and pouring fragrant oils into the water.

After preparing my bath, the two girls removed their garments and hung them on a peg set in the wall. At first, I averted my eyes though it was impossible not to look at the fascinating green-eyed Circassian. She had high firm pear-shaped breasts ending in a nipple the color of a rosebud. The two ladies turned to me and, ignoring my protests, slipped my robe over my head leaving me completely naked. Then smiling and giggling merrily at my obvious discomfort, each took a hand and drew me down the marble stairs into the pool.

If I close my eyes, I can still smell the delicate aroma of roses and feel the caress of warm water as it enveloped my body. The two ladies bade me sit on a shelf that followed the edge of the pool and began to wash my hair and body. I leaned my head back. The ceiling was high domed and painted azure blue like the summer sky, with puffy white clouds and a delicately painted rainbow that passed from one side of the dome to the other.

The evening took on the aspect of a dream. The world appeared as if viewed through a silken veil. Flowers became more fragrant, colors more vivid; somewhere in the distance I could hear the trilling of a flute. My head fell back against a soft bosom and gazed at the ceiling as soothing hands worked over the muscles of my body. The painted sky slowly came alive, clouds floated lazily across it, and the delicate colors of rainbow seemed to deepen and glow.

When I next became aware of my surroundings, I was again dressed in the silk gown, sitting by a marble fountain in a walled garden, such as is found in the homes of wealthy Persians. How I got there, I had no idea, nor did I particularly care. The fountain was carved in the shape of a series of shells with water spilling gently from smaller to larger shells until it flowed into a large pool set at the fountain's base. Fruitwood burned in the several iron braziers set on tripods that surrounded the fountain and warmed the air. A full moon had risen and stood overhead. The gurgling water was like an enchanting melody.

What had become of my two lovely companions? From my left came the sound of whispering silk. I turned to discover another beauty. She was dressed all in red. A veil masked her face. She stood gazing at me with liquid, dark brown eyes. Those were eyes that I recognized.

I started to ask a question, but she raised her finger to her lips, took my hand, and led me along a path between carefully manicured arbor vitae bushes, through an archway into a luxuriously appointed tent hung with silk curtains and rare tapestries like the abode of a desert sheik. Tallow burning in brass lamps cast a flickering light through the dim interior. Thick rugs were piled up as bedding in the center of the room.

The woman turned to me and our eyes joined. She slowly raised her hands, and her veil fell away. She took two half-filled crystal glasses from a small table and handed me one. We touched the rims in a silent toast, and I watched her red lips part and her lovely throat contract as she slowly drank the amber liquid. I drank and again entered a dream, this time with the woman I had desired since our first meeting.

I woke up late the next morning groggy and alone. I looked for Madeleine, but all that was left of her was the impression on the pillow where her head had lain. I buried my face in it and inhaled her scent. The green eyed beauty from the night before stood over me with a goblet of cool sherbet made with rose water. When I asked for Madeleine, she shook her head, giggled, and made signs that she did not understand.

My clothes appeared, and before I knew it I was dressed and politely ushered out the door. I found myself blinking like an owl in the bright morning sun. I returned to my lodgings, fell on my bed, and slept like a dead man. When I awoke it was evening. I felt dreadful. Desire burned like a fever, and my vitals ached with longing. God help me, I was in love with a courtesan.

I had now been in Persia for over a year, I had concluded my business, and I was restless. It was already March; the monsoon would turn against me by mid-April. If I was to get to India that year, I had to leave immediately. Still, I was indecisive; I could not make up my mind to go.

Finally I asked my perceptive friend Bharton. His response was, as usual, to the point.

"Go," he said.

"But, the shah!"

"Jean-Baptiste, my friend, I ask you candidly, is it really the shah you are waiting to see? How long are you planning to wait? Very soon the monsoon will turn, and you will be forced to spend half a year in Persia, or you must take the route overland through Kandahar. I have just come from there, and I tell you the route is too dangerous. The great mogul is preparing to send an army to retake the city from the shah, and the Afghans are attacking merchant caravans."

Early one morning Achmed showed up at my lodgings bearing a letter. I put it to my nose – it bore her scent. I tore it open. It was short. Madeleine apologized for not being able to see me. She was anxious that we meet before I left for India. When did I plan to leave? Achmed would wait for my answer.

Well, that was that. Everyone, it seemed, was anxious for me to be on my way – my brother, Danush, and Monsieur Dellon as well. My brother and the young physician had become fast friends and spent much of their time exploring the city's delights together. Danush had the trip organized for several weeks, and he was growing tired of feeding the camels. I made my decision and penned a response. I would leave for the Indies two days hence.

Achmed reappeared with another note barely two hours later. I must on no account come to the chateau. Madeleine feared she was being watched. She would come to my lodgings the next evening.

If I expected another rendezvous like our first night together, I was to be disappointed. Madeleine arrived by palanquin, after dark, escorted by Achmed and several of his men. Achmed entered first, nodded to me, looked carefully about the room, then posted himself by the door.

Madeleine entered followed by two of her guards carrying two leather satchels. I took her hands in greeting. "Madeleine, I have missed you. What is wrong? You seem agitated."

"Oh Jean-Baptiste, I am sorry," Her eyes darted like a bird about the room. "I think I am being watched."

"By whom?"

She glanced toward Achmed, then looked me in the eyes but did not speak.

"But, why?"

She pressed her finger to her lips, then turned toward the door. "Achmed, I wish to speak with monsieur alone. Please go outside and shut the door."

The man made a quick bow. His eyes caught mine. "Do not be afraid, mistress. I will be just outside." He ushered out the two guards, turned, and pulled the door closed.

Madeleine half turned away, then turned back, and wrung her

hands. "I do not know what to think, Jean-Baptiste. I am afraid. That is why I came at night, and I dare not stay long."

She produced an inventory of her jewels. It was written in an elegant hand, in French. Each piece was carefully described and priced. Her prices were fair and accurate. We each signed both copies, and I slipped my copy into my waistband.

With our business concluded Madeleine took my hands in hers. "I am sorry, Jean-Baptiste, that we did not have more time together, but I promise when you return, we shall get to know one another better."

"But Madeleine, what about the other night, I thought…!"

"The other night?"

"Yes, my love, that wonderful, magical night in your garden, so beautiful, so like a dream!"

She smiled into my eyes. "Like a dream? Perhaps it was a dream. Persia can be a magical place, but dreams are just that, dreams. They are not real. Dreams give us a glimpse sometimes into the world of our desires, but it is only in that other world that dreams come true."

"Madeleine, what are you saying, that our night together meant nothing to you?"

She reached up and cupped my face between her hands. "No, Jean-Baptiste. I too had a dream. I tuck my dreams into a little jeweled box in a corner of my mind where I keep them safe and cherish them, and sometimes when I am alone, I open the box and remember. Tuck yours away and sometimes at night when your spirits are low, open your little jeweled box and think of me."

"I am sorry, Jean, I dare not stay! Bon voyage, Jean-Baptiste Tavernier. Bon voyage and bonne chance. My fate is in your hands." She smiled, stood on her tiptoes and kissed me firmly on the lips, then turned, and walked through the door. Just before she mounted her vehicle, she turned back, smiled, and waved. My hand froze in midair. She had already disappeared into the curtained interior. I watched glumly as her bearers hoisted the palanquin, moved off, and were swallowed by the night. The next morning at dawn I took the road for Bander Abbãs.

We traveled by horse with our goods loaded upon camels. We made good time covering the 75 leagues between Isfahan to Bander Abassi in twenty days.

My brother Daniel rode ahead and was able to procure passage on a dhow with an English crew taking on cargo for Surat. I was proud of my brother. While we were in Isfahan, he had spent much of his time with the Capuchins. He wished to learn to speak Persian. One of the friars lent him a Persian dictionary, and he had it copied. He worked hard and discovered a gift. His spoken Persian was already better than mine.

About six days south of Shiraz, there is an inn called Kaffer. If you leave the main caravan road and take the right hand road by the river about a league and a half south of the inn, you come to one of the most beautiful valleys in all of Persia. The valley is called Dadivan.   Its floor is about five leagues in circuit and is planted with orange and lemon trees. The trees are old and broad with trunks so thick that two men can barely join hands around them. They grow as high as our walnut trees. You pitch your tents in the cool shade beneath these trees. The rest of the plain is sown with rice and wheat. A river teeming with fish – pike, carp, barbells and crayfish – crosses the valley. I have traveled to this valley several times just to divert myself.

Chapter 18

The Kingdom of The Great Mogul

 he date was April 15, 1640, and a blood red sun peeked from behind the dunes across the strait as we won our anchor and set sail.

Figure 9: Late 16th Century engraving of the old Portuguese fort at Hormuz at the Persian port of Bander Abassi.

The captain set a course south-southeast, keeping to the deepest part of the channel, passing the Portuguese lighthouse and leaving the dusty little island of Larec to larboard. Finally I was on my way to fulfilling the dreams of my youth. Though I sailed in and out of this port many times during the ensuing years, I recall that morning vividly.

We made a quick passage with the wind astern for the entire voyage. If you wish to enter the lands of the great mogul by sea, you must call at Surat. This is the only port in the empire. First your vessel must steer for Dui and Port St. Jean and drop anchor at Suwali, a port controlled by the English, located four leagues from the city.

In those days, Swally Hole, as the English called it, was little more than a harbor.

From the seaside we could see a great many tents, some quite large, pitched all along the rock strewn shore. The emperor, who at that time was Shah Jahan, forbade the merchant companies from building permanent factories for fear they might be turned into armed fortresses.

Once ashore we were forced to run a gauntlet of native merchants, porters, dancing girls, hucksters, and thieves. They set up a horrible din, yelling, playing cymbals, beating drums, pushing and shoving, and doing all in their power to attract our attention.

I abandoned all civility. Placing my servants in the lead to break trail, we pushed and prodded our way through the crowd. We entered one of the huts provided for travelers by the British East India Company, had a small meal, then proceeded to rent bullock carts to carry us to Surat. The distance by road is about ten English miles.

Along the road to the city we passed a number of tombs of English officials who had perished in the service of the company. Europeans find the climate of India unhealthy. The average life span in Surat is two monsoons.

After a hot ride we reached the muddy banks of the Tapti River which laps along the city walls. We found a company barge tied up on our side of the river at a small but solid dock.

"This way, your honor." A short, grizzled, white-bearded sailorman, obviously the barge captain, accosted us, jerking his thumb over his shoulder in the direction of his craft.

"Pack your gear toward the middle of the barky, if you please, your honor. We wouldn't want to capsize us!"

He gestured toward a cluster of longshoreman standing on the quay. "Bear a hand there. Bear a hand."

"Not over there, you miserable wog," he shouted, directing a kick to the hind quarters of one of the half naked bearers. The old man winked and tipped his hat.

"Which you got to keep a weather eye on these foreign buggers, begging your pardon, your honor." He turned and ambled back onto his small vessel to supervise the loading.

The barge was a commodious affair, a large raft made of hewn beams with room enough for ourselves and all our baggage. It was attached by a system of block and tackle to the other shore.

"Avast, there, you grass-combing buggers." The old captain shook his cudgel good naturedly at the half-naked urchins who jumped on board, laughing, playing Hide and Seek, diving and cavorting like seals in the tea-colored river water.

The voyage was short. I slipped the old sailor a piece of silver and a few odd coppers for his men. He tipped his hat and directed us to the end of the wharf where we found bullock carts for hire, which took us to the customs house where our luggage was examined.

Gold and silver may be imported into India, but it must be melted down and reminted into golden rupees. This is the only currency recognized in all lands under the rule of the great mogul. The conversion is arranged at the customs house. The master of the mint, an official called the Darogha, handles the transaction. If you are bringing in gold coins, rose nobles or German ducats are the best choice. I brought mostly new ducats. Old or worn coins are discounted one percent. I watched the weighing carefully. While this was going on, other petty officials rifled my luggage. In such situations it is necessary to have eyes on both sides of your head. I found myself engaged in a tug of war with one surly fellow who took a liking to my silver looking glass. A gift to the Darogha of two gold ducats is normally sufficient to smooth out all difficulties.

I had a letter of introduction from the British East India Company's factor in Bander Abbās, and I met a young writer of the company, Appleby by name, who volunteered to guide me to the

English factory.

The young official proudly pointed out the main features of the place. He was a likely enough looking young fellow, thin, fair skinned, and eager. You can always tell a European's rank by the size of his retinue. A writer is on the lowest rung of company officialdom, with a single bare-chested Hindoo servant walking behind him, holding an umbrella to keep off the sun.

"Here, do you see, sir? The offices are on the ground floor. I work just there," he said, pointing to an open arched doorway.

"On the other side of the garden, just there," he pointed with his finger. "Do you see, with the double doors? Those are the godowns, where the goods are stored before shipment, and just above, you see, the roofed verandah running all round the building? The higher ups have their offices up there. We have a lovely chapel up there as well, and the dining hall for the staff."

"How is the food?"

"Oh, excellent, sir, once you get used to the local style of cooking. Cook makes a thundering good curry. There are guest rooms on the upper floor as well. That's where you will be lodging, sir, I'll wager."

My first morning in Surat, I was awakened by an incredible din. I dressed quickly and walked out onto the verandah. The scene below came straight from the *Inferno*. Below, the courtyard was awash in half-naked, brown bodies. I had overslept; it was just after 10:00 AM, when the factory doors opened. The sun was already wickedly hot and bright. This was my first experience with Banian cotton traders. These men are the worst. If anyone offers them the least argument, they make a scene. Each one of them was loudly proclaiming the quality of his goods and demanding attention. The factory officials did their best, but they could bring no discipline to the crowd.

Some of the Hindoos carried samples; others piled bales of goods along the walks and on top of the flowerbeds. One dark wizened old fellow, dressed in little more than a turban and a dhoti, a sort of diaper that covered his lower parts, had cornered and was berating a fat merchant twice his size, who had tried to cut the line. He was shouting and gesturing wildly, no doubt making some reference to the fat man's mother. To hear these men bellow, you would have thought that someone had butchered one of their sacred cows.

Until noon when the gates are closed for dinner, the company officials are nominally in charge, but since they do not speak the language of the country, most of the negotiations are handled by native brokers. The brokers are paid two to three percent, but they make much more. In fact, the company men are almost totally at their mercy. The gates reopen at four, and business goes on until six in the evening, when the brokers are hustled out, and the gates are closed for the night.

During the quiet afternoon hours, I called upon the president of the company, one William Fremlin, a tall, thin, bespeckled gentleman, who kindly invited me to take tea with him and his second in command. The president looked more like a clerk than a merchant adventurer, but the members of the company treated him with great deference, more like a lord than a head merchant.

We were served tea on the shaded balcony overlooking the garden that was now empty except for an occasional servant moving silently along the garden pathways and a quantity of butterflies that flitted about, serving the blossoms. After all the morning's hubbub, it seemed unnaturally quiet. The air hung about us like a wet rag and not a leaf stirred. We sat in rattan chairs around a low table. The taste of the tea put me in mind of Noelle. Over the years since, I had become quite devoted to this beverage.

"Tell me, Monsieur Tavernier, what business is it that brings you to Surat?" the president asked.

"I have come to buy gemstones, Your Excellency. I am particularly interested in diamonds."

The president's eyes narrowed with interest. He leaned forward and spoke softly. "Diamonds? I say, that is interesting, monsieur. Perhaps you would join me this evening for dinner, and we can discuss this business further?"

I bowed.

"Very good. I shall look forward to it. And, monsieur," he said with a significant look, "if you will take my advice, you will not advertise your business or your purposes too widely."

While the main body of company officials gather in the large communal dining hall on the second floor of the factory, the president has his own quarters and dines in splendor. I found Mr. Fremlin alone except for his house servants. The rooms glowed in the suffused warmth of polished hardwoods. Candles burned in silver sconces set into paneled walls. Tall casement windows opened out onto a balcony. They had been thrown open in the vain hope of catching a breeze, but the long muslin draperies hung limp in the moist air. A banquet fit for a dozen or more guests had been laid out, and the table gleamed with polished silver.

The president made every attempt to be amiable, though playing the host did not come easily to him. He was by nature a rather stiff, formal gentleman. I was the only guest, and though I was quite flattered by the attention of such an important official, it struck me as curious that he would expend so much of his time cultivating the acquaintance of an unknown quantity, who was a foreigner to boot.

The president urged me to partake of the magnificence, but I noticed that he served himself little of the banquet, preferring a small portion of a cold vegetable collation to the normal English fare of mutton and beef.

He noted that I watched him, and his face took on a severe look. "If you will take my advice, monsieur, you will be very careful in the articles of food. Europeans in the Indies eat too much meat, sir, too much by half! It lies in the stomach and rots! Everything rots in this cursed climate. Causes an imbalance of the body's humors! Many of my colleagues, I am afraid, insist on digging their graves with their teeth."

I told him that I was much of the same mind and that I hoped he would not think me rude if I joined him.

"Not at all, sir," he said, with a curt nod.

After we had dined, we spent some time discussing trade in the Indies and the latest news from Europe over a bottle of very fine Bordeaux. The English at that time were having a great deal of trouble with the Dutch attacking English ships. The president asked me several questions about my travels and experience, and about diamonds. He seemed somewhat agitated, as if he wished to ask something of me but was not sure how best to proceed. Finally, he made his request.

"Monsieur Tavernier, I have a little money put by. I wonder, would it be an imposition to ask you to purchase a parcel of diamonds on my behalf?"

"Never in life, sir. I would consider it an honor and I thank you, but are there not any number of men with more experience than I at your disposal?"

He paused, pursed his lips, and studied me for a moment over the rim of his glasses. He was balding in a manner that resembled a monk's tonsure, except for some very long strands that he had carefully combed in an attempt to cover the bald spot.

"No, monsieur, there are not! That is to say, none of my factors have any experience with diamonds – not the sort of experience that you have, and, if I may speak candidly, sir, this is a confidential matter, a highly confidential matter. If I were to approach one of my own factors, why he would talk, the creature!" He spread his hands. "So you see, I need the services of an experienced man, sir, and one who knows how to mind his tongue."

I was new to the Indies and did not yet – as the mariners say – know the lay of the land. As I later found out, men recruited by the English company serve in India for a period of five years. Salaries are low, and each employee must post a bond against his good behavior. Writers receive £10 and senior factors £40 per year, plus victuals and lodging. The president himself receives just £500 per year, along with his living expenses and servants. Positions with the company are much sought after, despite the low wages because officials of the company are allowed to indulge in private trade between oriental ports but are absolutely prohibited from trading on their own account between the Indies and Europe. It is much the same with the Dutch.

A judicious trader can make as much as one hundred percent on imports of lacquer ware, porcelain, and other commodities between China and Surat, but the largest profits are to be had by carrying goods to Europe. Though it is forbidden, company officials are always on the lookout for ways to profitably employ their capital on the return voyage. Diamonds are ideal for this purpose. In London, shipping manifests and the belongings of returning employees are carefully checked, but gems are easily hidden in a waistcoat pocket. I have made many friends and some little profit buying diamonds on behalf of officials of both the English and Dutch companies. How they chose to dispose of the gems afterwards was no affair of mine.

Despite my ignorance in matters of trade in India, I did know that making a friend of the president of the British East India Company would be to my advantage. "I would be honored, Monsieur Fremlin, to act as your agent."

For the first time that evening the English president smiled. In fact he beamed and clapped me on the back. "You are very good, sir, very good indeed, and may I say that if there is anything I can do to assist you, anything at all, you must tell me at once. I am at your service."

Chapter 19

The Diamond Mines of Golconda

t is my custom before I trade in a commodity to visit its source. It gives me a certain perspective. Most traders never visit the mines. They content themselves with buying in the diamond market in Goa or at Agra.

To travel with honor in India you must have a retinue. At Mr. Fremlin's suggestion, I hired thirty armed guards and about ten servants, in addition to Danush, my brother, the doctor, and the men I had brought with me from Persia. We used oxen for transport. Neither horses nor camels are used in India because of the heat. A single ox can carry about one hundred seventy five pounds of goods. We hired fifty for carrying and several more for riding. A carriage would have been more comfortable, but during the monsoon season, the roads turn to mud, and carriages are worse than useless.

Rammalakota is the town adjacent to the diamond fields. I arrived at the end of the dry season. The mining area and the town were coated with a brown dust. A gritty film sticks to your body, and you always feel dirty. There were fewer stones available, the heavy rains often wash the diamonds out of their hiding places, so there are more available at the end of the monsoon season.

The Rammalakota fields have been hacked out of raw jungle. The ground is made up mostly of sandstone with rocks and boulders. Thin veins no more than a finger's width run through the sandstone. The diamonds are found in these veins and must be pried out by men using long thin crowbars. Larger crowbars are used to break open the veins, but these often cause the gems to fracture. The diamond merchants in the town are idolaters of the caste of Banians. These are the people who ruled the country before the Moguls came.

After securing lodgings, I left my servants to guard my gold and called on the provincial governor. He was short and wiry, with black eyes and no beard. As with the king at that time, he was a Mussulman of the sect of Ali. He embraced me and called for refreshment.

"May I ask if you have come to buy diamonds?"

"Yes, Excellency," I said bowing. "That is my purpose."

"Excellent. I shall assign you four of my own servants to guard your gold." The governor clapped his hands twice. "Do not fear," he said smiling affably as two large bearded men with naked tulwars tied in their waistbands entered and bowed first to him, then to me. "These men are completely reliable, and in any case I shall take full responsibility. So eat, drink, come and go as you please. Only remember that two percent of the value of your purchases is due the king."

Despite my excitement, I slept well that night. The next morning I awoke early to the earthy smell of rotting frangipani and coconut oil. Danush had already poked his nose into every nook and cranny and befriended the cook. He brought me a cup of bitter tea and a banana leaf with a steaming portion of dal from the inn's kitchen.

I left Danush to keep an eye on the two guards and took two of my Banian servants and my interpreter and seated myself under a large umbrella-shaped banyan tree in the main square of the town to await events. Like magic, a noisy throng of young boys appeared from nowhere with parcels of diamonds and soon surrounded me, jostling and shouting like a tribe of bees gathered around a flower. The Banians are very shrewd. Before a buyer has been in town for an hour, they know what he wishes to buy and how much gold he has brought with him, down to the last golden rupee.

One runny-nosed urchin, no older than ten, wearing a ragged turban and a tiny cloth around his middle, plucked at my sleeve and, with a soulful look, thrust a parcel of diamonds under my nose.

"You buy, you buy," he loudly demanded in Portuguese at the same time clasping his hands together in an attitude of prayer.

His soulful look turned to reproach when I waved him away. I had no intention of buying under such circumstances. I formed my guards into a protective phalanx while my interpreter directed the brokers to bring their parcels to my lodgings that afternoon. When I had located a sufficient number of parcels, I fled back to my rooms, ate a good meal, and took a nap.

By the afternoon rumor had done its work: a large crowd of dealers were gathered outside my door. Danush managed to procure a table and a real chair and set them up in my chamber with a window at my back. He stationed himself and one of the guards in a small anteroom to insure that only one man at a time was admitted. Buying gems you must control the pace of the business. If the buyer is not in control the seller will be.

I spent the balance of that day and several more, working until the light failed, examining parcel after parcel of rough diamonds. Those that interested me I put aside. By custom dealers will leave parcels with a buyer for seven days so that he may consider the stones at his leisure.

The composing of these parcels is an art form at which these Banians excel. I smiled as I recalled the lesson Danush had given me one hot dusty morning in Nishapur. One obsequious young fellow stuck a dirty hand into his tattered waistband and brought forth a parcel. He undid the knot and handed it over. It contained thirteen diamonds weighing about four carats each. It was in fact three parcels in one. The first portion contained three perfectly formed crystals, each of fine water with few imperfections. These were the *eyes* of the parcel, and they flashed those eyes. Each would cut a fine gem of perhaps two carats.

The second portion was made up of four stones of fair quality, not of perfect form but useful. Because of their shapes they would yield stones between one and one and one half carats. The third portion was the worst, five gems of such poor shape and with so many flaws that they were hardly worth the cutting. Oddly, the stones always look better together, the poorer stones gathering luster from the finer.

The dealer stood before me in front of the table shifting back and forth on the balls of his feet.

I turned to my interpreter: "Tell the fellow that I do not need all these stones. Ask him if I may take my choice."

The man knew a bit of Portuguese; he shook his head.

I closed the parcel and slid it across the table.

A thin hand paused over the lump of cloth. The dealer shifted his weight side to side, looked sidelong at me and spoke.

"He says he will consider allowing your pick but you must show him the stones that you have selected." My interpreter said.

"Tell him no!"

He understood me and stared down sullenly at the table: "He says you may pick at one hundred rupees per rati, but you must take at least eight gems." Rati is the unit of weight used at the diamond fields. It is equal to seven-eights of a French carat.

I kept my hands folded in front of me, looked into the man's eyes, and slowly shook my head. "I will pay sixty, and only if I may pick what I like."

The dealer shifted back and forth and spread the parcel on the table. He directed a stream of Hindi at my interpreter, all the while gesturing and, at one point, holding one of the finer stones up to the light. "He says that he offers these stones to you at a special price. He knows your reputation, and he knows better than to try to fool you. He says you may pick at ninety rupees, but you must take eight or more stones."

"Tell him I know a man who is a great judge of diamonds. He would not use this parcel to line his fishpond. I will take five at sixty."

The interpreter sighed. "The dealer says eighty is his best price, and you must pick eight stones. He wishes to know the name of this great man of whom you speak."

"His father."

The dealer stepped back and stared at me.

Danush and my interpreter laughed.

Danush bent down and whispered in my ear: "Do not waste time with this man, aga. He is a fool."

"Tell him there are other dealers waiting. I will pay his price but only if I can select the stones that I desire."

Finally the man gave in and allowed me to select the stones I liked. I selected the four. The man looked at me in disgust. After much talk, I was able to buy them for an additional fifteen rupees per rati.

This was my first trip to Rammalakota, and I was still an unknown quantity. I knew from my experiences in Persia that my first buy would be crucial. If I paid too high, all the asking prices would be high. If I offered too low, I would lose respect and the important dealers would withhold their finer gems.

During my stay in Rammalakota I returned twice to the town square to show the flag, so to speak, and let the dealers know that I was still buying. Each time a crowd of brokers surrounded me. On one occasion a rather dour Banian in his middle years sat down quietly without a word and waited patiently to speak to me. The man was shoeless and dressed in nothing but a calico dhoti. He wore a miserable handkerchief on his head that served to keep off the sun. I learned early in my travels, it is a mistake to put too much stock in appearances. A beggar's attire may conceal a gem worth the price of a kingdom.

I greeted the man civilly, and he told me that he had some rubies he wished to sell. He drew several rags of cloth from his waistband and showed me a small parcel containing about a score of ruby rings. The gems were small, but I remembered that a lady in Isfahan had asked me to find her a ruby ring. The man's attitude told me that he had other things to show but would only do so in private. He spoke Portuguese so I beckoned him to come along with me to my inner room.

Once we were alone I looked over the rubies and purchased one of the rings. I paid a quarter more than it was worth to encourage him because I believed that he had something more interesting to sell. He raised both hands like a woman posed before a mirror, carefully unwrapped his head cloth, plucked a scrap of cloth from his hair, and handed it to me. Inside was a diamond cabochon of the first water with a slight flaw in one side that could be easily removed. It shimmered like satin in the afternoon sun. At 48 ½ carats, a diamond of this size was the first I had seen for sale.

I took a deep breath: "What is your price?"

The man started to speak, then hesitated and his eyes filled with tears.

"Great lord, my eldest son has been sick for several weeks with a malady of the stomach. The Brahmans have said prayers and the local doctors have prescribed herbal mixtures, but none of this has any effect, and my son's condition grows worse. I fear he will soon die." He wrung his hands, and tears poured down his cheeks.

"I am sorry to hear of your son's illness."

"Lord, I have heard that you have brought a Frankish doctor with you. Will you allow him to examine my son?"

I do not consider myself a particularly religious man, but as a Christian I believe it is my duty to be charitable toward those in distress and to uphold the tenets of the true religion as an example to the heathen.

"Be at peace, my friend. Dr. Dellon and I will be at your house this evening."

Upon hearing my reply, the Banian fell to his knees crying and attempting to kiss my feet in gratitude. I took the man by the hands and raised him to his feet and tried my best to calm him. After he was quiet, I asked him his name and directions to his dwelling. The man, whose name was Hiresh, bowed his way out of the room and went on his way, mumbling some idolatrous blessing.

That evening just as the sun set, M. Dellon and I called at the Banian's home. The house was located in the neighborhood where the merchants reside. In India, each caste has its own area within the town and someone of a higher caste will not even enter the dwelling of a lower caste person. It was a simple dwelling built of sticks slathered over with mud with a thatched roof. To look at the place you would never believe that this man was in possession of a diamond worth a fortune. The ground around the hut was bare with the exception of a small vegetable plot and a large plain tree that spread like an umbrella at the back of the house. The yard had been recently swept and watered. The house was larger than most such houses, having three rooms and a small outbuilding – more like a lean-to – that served as a kitchen.

As we neared the door, we heard two voices, one male, the other female, having a loud argument. The merchant met us at the door, bowed, and politely invited us in. He looked distressed. He was dressed somewhat better than when I had met him, still bare-chested but in a sparkling white dhoti. He introduced us to his wife, who barely nodded, then fled from the room. From what little I could make out the woman had been upbraiding her husband for inviting infidels into her home.

Smiling and bowing, the merchant showed us to his son's bedside. The boy was young, perhaps fourteen, lying on the floor on a rough palette that served as a bed in the Indies. He was thin and pale with feverish eyes and a face glazed with sweat.

"This is my son, doctor. He is not able to keep down any sort of solid food."

Dellon nodded. "If I may be left along with the patient," he said raising his eyebrows. Dellon kneeled and bent his skeletal frame over the patient. He was a pleasant but ill formed fellow with rounded shoulders. He had a scholar's complexion, white like the belly of a fish that had now been burned to an equally disagreeable red hue.

The father nodded, bowed, and backed through the door. I followed him into the central room. It was almost bare, just a few sticks of furniture and several tallow lamps set into niches along the walls. We squatted in the center of the room. The wife brought in a tray with earthen bowls of hot sweet tea. With a poisonous look at her husband, she lay the tray down between us. We gazed at each other, sipped silently, and waited for M. Dellon's diagnosis.

Several times during the course of our voyage, I had the opportunity to discourse at some length with M. Dellon. He was a follower of the Englishman Francis Bacon. He had little use for the received wisdom of the ancients. He believed that knowledge must be taken directly from nature. With the observation of many particulars, conclusions, which he called *hypothesizes,* could be drawn.

About a quarter of an hour later, Dr. Dellon emerged from the boy's room and, with a sigh, squatted beside us. He smiled at the merchant. "It is a sort of ague," he said, "and simply cured. The herbs that the Hindoo doctors have given the boy have not helped; in fact, they have made him much worse."

"I will mix a decoction as soon as I return to my rooms and send it over with the interpreter. He will give you exact instructions on how it is to be administered. I will return tomorrow evening to look in on the boy."

Though the Banian understood Portuguese and a smattering of French, I do not know how much of Dellon's talk he understood. Enough apparently. The merchant began to bob his head and smile, and his eyes lit up with hope.

The next evening when we returned to the Banian's home, the merchant and his wife greeted us at the door. She was dressed in a red silk sari. Her attitude had completely changed. She was all smiles, bowing and doing all she could to make us feel welcome. The parents administered the medicine just as they had been instructed. Overnight there had been a dramatic change. The fever was gone. The boy now felt well enough to sit up and eat and could even rise to relieve himself, though he was still weak from hunger.

Two days later the Banian came to my lodgings with the large diamond.

"I have come to thank you, lord, for the life of my son. Here is the diamond. Please take it. My son is worth a thousand times more to me than any gem."

This stone was worth 75,000 livres, and I must confess that I was sorely tempted to accept the Banian's gift. I am not particularly religious, and I am not sure to this day what held me back. Perhaps it is that I believe, as the Bible says, that a man does reap what he sows.

I took his hand. "My friend, I did what my religious beliefs require of me. I am pleased to hear your son has recovered, but it was the doctor's doing, not mine. A diamond such as this cost a great deal of money, and I will pay you a fair price, but I cannot accept it as a gift for doing my duty as God commands it."

The Banian stared at me open mouthed for several seconds. "Lord, I have known several Franks but none so honorable as you. Do all those of your sect act in this way?"

"No, my friend, we are men like any other, and all sinners in God's eyes."

He nodded his head and gazed at me for a moment, thinking. "Yes. It is the same with us. We have a duty to do what is right simply because it is right. We call it dharma. But, it is difficult to avoid the temptations of this life. You are a great soul, lord. May your actions bring you great merit in the next life. I am in your debt and your slave, forever. Whatever you need, simply ask. If it is in my power, it shall be yours. Since you will not accept this diamond as a gift, you shall buy it for the price that I paid. I will accept no profit."

"Hiresh Dhawan," I said, "I have no need of a slave, but I can always use the friendship of an honest man."

The Banian smiled and bowed. "It shall be as you command, lord. You shall be my dear friend and a friend of all my family."

Hiresh Dhawan was indeed an honest man. That day began a relationship that was to last over twenty years. It was a friendship that would repay me many times the value of that single diamond.

My new factor was very well connected. He found me a good many excellent stones. His prices were always fair, and though I insisted that he take a commission, I don't believe he ever did. I worked with him and his son on several buying trips to the mines at Rammalakota and Kollür. But it was some twenty years later that my relationship with Hiresh Dhawan was to bear the greatest fruit.

I spent the better part of two years in India and made a second trip to Golconda in early 1642. This was the occasion of one of my greatest regrets. My factor was able to show me the largest diamond I had ever seen in the hands of a merchant.

It was a long flat gem known as the Great Table that weighed 242 5/16 carats. It far surpassed the weight of the largest diamond in Europe, the Florentine, a 138 carat yellow diamond owned by the grand Duke of Tuscany. I saw this diamond in 1657. It is a beautiful gem, but its water inclines toward the yellow, whereas the Table had a delicate rose tint. The asking price was 500,000 rupees, which was about 750,000 livres in our money. I had nowhere near the capital needed to buy the gem. The owner allowed me to make a lead model of it and send it to my friend at the English factory in Surat. Monsieur Fremlin wrote back offering 400,000 rupees, but the owner would not consider it. At the time I convinced myself that this was the gem that I had dreamed about, and I was with child to have it, but it was not to be. I was very disappointed, but I lacked both the stature and contacts. I believe I could have bought the diamond for 450,000 rupees.

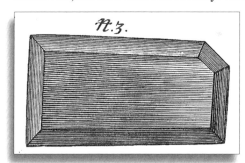

Figure 10: Tavernier's drawing of The Great Table, a 242 carat gem offered to him in 1642. This gem was eventually recut into the diamond we know today as the Darya-i-Noh (Ocean of Light)

Chapter 20

A Lover's Return

On November 1642, the monsoon winds being favorable, I departed from Surat aboard an English merchantman and arrived in Bander Abbās on the 10th of January, 1643. I proceeded directly to Isfahan with no more than a brief stopover in Shiraz to replenish my supply of that city's excellent wine. Madeleine de Goisse had been much in my mind, and after two years in India, I was anxious to see her again. I went immediately to her house and found it deserted. From the look of it, she had been absent for some time. Fearing the worse I went to the home of my friend Bharton. He was traveling, but I was given several letters that had been sent in his care, including one from Madeleine.

My Dearest Jean-Baptiste,

By the time you read this letter I shall be gone. Mother died last spring. She never really got any better, and she suffered so that when she finally died, it was a blessing.

*I was allowed but two months mourning for my
dear mother before "my guardian" became insistent
that I marry the man he had chosen for me. I tried to
hold him off, thinking that you would soon come, but it
was no use.*

*My position here is impossible. I live in fear!
Any day now he will have me bundled off to the
seraglio. I shall flee, my darling, and await you at our
rendezvous. I am sure that you remember. I will take
Achmed and a few of my trusted servants and leave
this very night. I have a little money. I pray that you
receive this letter. Come quickly!*

Madeleine

The letter was three months old, but the message was clear
enough. The words *my darling* echoed and re-echoed in my mind.
There was not a moment to be lost. I made plans to follow her.
Luckily I fell in with a group of European merchants forming a small
caravan going north.

At the Carmelite monastery I called on the abbot, Father Paul
Simon, a white haired gentleman, who informed me – not without
a touch of asperity that went ill with his saintly demeanor – that
Mademoiselle de Goisse had indeed lodged at the convent but
had not entered to novitiate, not at all. Rather the lady had pulled
up stakes shortly after she arrived and moved together with her
entourage, to Jadaydah, the city's Christian suburb located just
north of the wall where she had set herself up in a house.

The sharp staccato of my horse's hooves echoed off the paving
stones as I made my way through the warren of narrow streets with
my horse's reins in one hand and a lantern in the other, looking for
a bronze knocker in the shape of a dolphin that marked Madeleine's
house. The streets were paved with gray cobbles, polished
smooth by the tread of so many feet that they made reflections in
the puddles of light cast by the lanterns set in niches above the
doorways. The directions given me by the disgruntled priest were
of little help. The walls of the houses were the same: dressed gray
blocks, spaced close, one upon the other, with only narrow dark
alleys between. It was early evening and I was beginning to lose

patience. I was tired: I had been in the saddle since dawn.

Finally I found the door. I knocked and a few moments later a suspicious eye gleamed through the keyhole, the heavy door swung open, and there stood the faithful Achmed with the same piratical gleam in his eye. Some distance behind him I could hear that unmistakable bubbling laugh.

For a moment Madeleine stared as if she had seen a ghost, then dropped her apron, and ran into my arms. "Jean, Jean how good it is to see you."

For a moment I stood there and held her. After a few moments she shook herself free and held me at arm's length.

"Let me look at you. You look well, Jean. India obviously agreed with you – you are as brown as a Hindoo."

"And you are more beautiful than ever."

"Flatterer!" She pirouetted out of my embrace. "Come, you must be hungry. Achmed bring wine! Let us drink, and then I will show you my house."

The house was laid out in the Persian manner with a central garden patio, but like many Aleppine houses, the design was more in the crusader style with the garden patio paved in alternating gray and black limestone blocks. A square graceless stone fountain sat in the exact center. The garden was walled in on two sides by adjacent houses. An iron stairway ornamented with beautifully wrought leaves and tendrils led to the sleeping apartments on the second floor.

Dinner was sumptuous. The local woman that Madeleine had hired as her cook laid out small dishes of mezze, piquant flavored appetizers, on a round table set on the patio. Then there was kibbe, a dish made of ground lamb and cracked wheat, stuffed vegetables and muhammara, a spicy paste eaten like hummus but made with a local hot pepper, pomegranate juice, and ground walnuts. These were followed by a kebab in a sauce of stewed fresh cherries, called kababbi-karaz. I added a fine Shiraz and a sweet Muscat as a dessert wine. I ate with good appetite while Madeleine peppered me with questions about India.

"Your house is beautiful, Madeleine, but why did you leave the monastery? The good father was very put out."

"Good father, indeed, the old lecher. He mooned around for almost a week before he began making suggestions. You would not believe it, Jean. The horrid old fool expected me to lie with him!"

"What? I wondered why he acted so strangely. Practically slammed the door in my face! I will kill him."

Madeleine put her hand on my arm. "No Jean, he is not worth it. I gave him a piece of my mind you can be sure. You will not believe it but the disgusting reprobate tried to convince me that it was all in service to our Lord. You should have seen his face when I told him I would have Achmed cut his heart out. That put the fear of the Lord into him, upon my word."

"I have met several such men of God."

"Men of God, indeed! I left the same day. Achmed would have killed him. You have no idea how protective he is, and he is the very devil himself with a knife."

"Where is Achmed now?"

"Ha, ha, don't worry Jean. Achmed likes you."

Madeleine was too well bred to ask about her own business, but I was soon able to put her mind at rest. She laughed and clapped her hands with glee when I told her the price I had been able to get for her jewels, and her lovely eyes danced with greed when I told her that I had reinvested part of the proceeds in a parcel of diamonds. We sat companionably late into the warm, clear night, drinking wine and listening to the night sounds. An idea had been forming in my mind since the last night we were together.

"What are your plans?"

"Oh, Jean, now that you have made me a rich woman, I must go to Paris. Will you take me? I do so long to see Paris."

I laughed. "You still wish to go to Paris. It can be a difficult city for a single woman alone without protection."

Her eyes flashed. "You mean without a man! As to that, I have looked after myself for some time now." And more softly, "You will be with me, will you not?"

"Yes, of course, I will take you, but Madeleine what I am trying to say is that you mean a great deal to me. Ever since I met you, I have felt this way, and in the past two years I have had much time to think and my thoughts have often been about you and now I am sure. Madeleine, I love you. Please, marry me!"

She gazed at me with soft eyes. I was about to further press my suit, but she put a finger against my lips. "Shhh! Jean, your proposal is very flattering, and I am probably a fool not to jump at it, but please understand, Jean, I am not yet ready to marry."

"I think we could be happy, Madeleine. I did very well in India and my prospects…"

"Yes, can you doubt that I believe in you," she said taking my hand. "Oh, Jean, if I were to marry anyone it would be you." She squeezed my hand, "Please don't be upset with me. Say you understand."

"Madeleine, I am sorry. I am trying but I don't understand. I thought you would want what other women want – a home, children?"

She turned and looked away. "I have never wanted what other women want. Perhaps it was the way I was raised. I want the same things you want, to be free to pursue my dreams. To be married, to have children, someday, I suppose. I am not sure." She turned back and looked at me. "You find it difficult to understand because you have always known what you wanted. I know what you have told me – how you dreamed while still a young boy that you would travel and see the world and buy and sell magnificent gems? And now, look at you; you are living your dream. I do so admire you for that."

"But, Madeleine, be practical. You are a woman!"

"A woman, yes, of course!" She raised her chin and tossed her head, her voice filled with tears. "I am a woman, and because of that I am allowed to have no dreams other than those that men think proper. Excuse me but spending my days in a squalid shack surrounded by bawling babes with shitty bottoms is not my idea of paradise."

"That is not what I meant. I don't care about children. I only care about you. We could travel, see the world. I love you. I want us to be together."

She took my hand once again and squeezed gently. "Look at me, Jean-Baptiste Tavernier. My name is Madeleine de Goisse. Who am I? – The bastard daughter of a French courtesan and a Persian king. I am like my poor dead mother. I am my own woman, and I will tell you one thing: I will be no man's chattel."

"Then what, Madeleine?"

She hesitated for a moment, then looked into my eyes, smiled, then looked off into the distance. "Since I was a little girl, Jean, my mother told me tales of Paris, always Paris, the beautiful chateaux, the court, fine ladies dressed in silk riding in gilded carriages. That was her dream for me and that will do for a start. Jean surely you, of all people, can understand why I must do this?" She turned and took hold of my hands and looked deeply into my eyes. "Please say that you understand and that we can still be friends. Oh please, I could not bear it if I lost you."

Well, of course, what else could I say? And so it was decided. We would travel to Paris. I held her and said I understood. What else could I say? I had never met a woman like Madeleine de Goisse. She did not seem to want what other women wanted, but Paris was a long way off, and I would have plenty of time, I decided, to press my suit.

Chapter 21

Rome and Paris

We took ship at Alexandretta and four weeks later dropped anchor in Naples. From there we went overland to Rome. Madeleine had always wanted to see the Eternal City, and it was my pleasure to show it to her. Urban VIII was Pope, and Rome was the cultural capital of Europe. We went everywhere, saw everything. With Madeleine on my arm, Rome took on a fairy tale quality.

I called upon the Pope's nephew, Cardinal Antonio Barberini, and found that the letter of introduction Giulio Mazarini had kindly provided me had become a magic charm. Many changes had taken place in France during my five years absence. Cardinal Richelieu, Father Joseph, and His Majesty, Louis XIII, were all dead. The young Roman diplomat, created Cardinal Mazarin by Richelieu, had become first minister of France and chief advisor to Ann of Austria, the king's widow, now queen regent.

Mazarin had sought the patronage of the Barberini family when he was a young man, and this connection brought him to the attention of the pope who was the cardinal's brother. Cardinal Barberini received us at his Palazzo, a magnificent marble structure built in the heart of Rome.

Madeleine exercised her charm, and the cardinal was enchanted. We borrowed her mother's story, and I introduced her as a French gentlewoman whom I had ransomed from Moorish pirates. At a stopover in Malta, I hired a forbidding looking older Maltese widow to act as Madeleine's "aunt" and chaperone. Cardinal Barberini saw to it that we were introduced to the cream of Roman society. Everyone wished to hear of our adventures; we were received everywhere and I made several sales. Madeleine spent much of her time shopping for a suitable European wardrobe.

"European clothes, Jean-Baptiste. They remind me of your European morals – hypocritical! You truss a woman up like a roasting chicken and force her body into shapes that nature never intended."

"Do you mean that our morals are unnatural?" I walked up behind her, wrapped my arms around her, and pressed up close.

She slipped from my grasp. "No, silly goose, they are like you, ridiculous."

Madeleine much preferred the Persian clothes she was used to and always wore them when we were alone. Although she claimed to dislike western fashion, she put half the dress, shoe, and hat makers of Rome to work creating a wardrobe.

"If you hate the fashion, why then are you spending a fortune outfitting yourself?"

She pirouetted in front of the mirror. "How do I look?" she asked while critically eyeing her reflection in the glass.

"Like a duchess!"

"Good. That is exactly how I wish to look. People believe what they see. If I am to be taken as a great lady, I must look like a great lady."

Rome was lovely and profitable, but Paris was our goal, and after five years I was anxious to get home. If we lingered too long the cold weather would set in and neither of us wished to subject ourselves to winter travel. So after a month and a half in Rome, we bid the

Eternal City a fond goodbye, made our way back to Naples, and took ship for Marseilles. Madeleine de Goisse was about to enter Paris, and the city would never be the same.

We reached the city in October of 1643. Madeleine was intent on an introduction into Parisian society, and I agreed to help her. I could think of no one better to advise us than my old friend Noelle, the Countess Rochambeau.

"Jean-Baptiste, my dear friend, what joy! How long has it been?" Noelle grasped my shoulders and held me at arm's length. "Let me look at you. It must be five years!" Noelle had changed very little since the last time I had seen her. Perhaps a little worn about the eyes but full of life. We had parted as friends.

"Noelle, Countess Rochambeau, may I have the honor to introduce my friend Madeleine de Goisse? Madeleine, this is the Countess Rochambeau of whom I have often spoken."

Madeleine curtsied, "my lady."

Noelle took Madeleine's hands. "Charming, absolutely charming. Come, come, my dear, let us not stand on ceremony; I am pleased to make your acquaintance." She looked at me and raised an eyebrow. "Your *friend*, did you say Jean Baptiste? How many men in Paris would give all they possess for so beautiful and charming a friend? Come, sit down, my dears, you must tell me everything."

We were ushered into the sitting room where Noelle and I had spent our first afternoon together – it seemed so many years ago. A servant brought tea, and we spent the afternoon recounting our adventures. As I had hoped, the two women got on splendidly. Noelle sat open mouthed, her eyes widened as Madeleine told her story, and clapped her hands gleefully as Madeleine described her escape from the amorous intentions of the wicked old priest.

"And Jean-Baptiste rode in on a white horse like a knight out of the romances and rescued you. How wonderful," she exclaimed, eyes shining. "Tell me, my dear, de Goisse is an ancient name. Do you have relatives in Paris? Where will you stay, and what will you do now?"

Madeleine lowered her eyes and shook her head sadly. "My mother had very little family, and she was captured and taken to Persia twenty-five years ago. She never spoke to me of any relatives."

"I see, how sad. Well, in that case, you must stay here with me, child."

"Here, in this beautiful chateau?" Madeleine shook her head. "Thank you, madame, you are very kind, but I couldn't possibly. You need not worry. I am used to looking after myself."

"I am sure you are, my dear, but this is Paris, and I assure you that having you would be no trouble, no trouble at all. Jean Baptiste!"

I shrugged helplessly. "Noelle, we have taken rooms at an inn…"

Noelle took Madeleine by the hands and smiled into her eyes. "I won't hear of it. You certainly cannot stay with Jean Baptiste," she said glaring at me. "Rooms indeed. Think of her reputation. It simply won't do! You must talk to her, Jean-Baptiste!"

She turned back to Madeleine. "It will be no trouble, I do assure you, and I will see that you are introduced to all the right people. My friends, your story, it is like a fairy tale. My friends will adore you, and you will be the toast of the season."

Madeleine looked at me, her eyes alight. What more was there to say? It had been decided. Noelle sent me off with instructions to arrange for Madeleine's servants and luggage to be brought to the chateau that evening.

Madeleine took my hand and saw me to the door. "Isn't she wonderful? My dear, Jean, how can I thank you for all you have done?" She looked up at me with liquid eyes.

I raised my hand to her cheek. "You are well on your way, Madeleine. Noelle will see to that. Please remember that these last months we have spent together have been a joy to me. We make a wonderful team, you and I. Please reconsider my proposal!"

Madeleine shook her head slowly. "My dear sweet, Jean, we have spoken of this so many times. I too have enjoyed the time we have spent together. It has been a wonderful adventure. Please don't spoil it. Rome, and now Paris, so much is new. I…I need time to think. Won't you give me a little time?"

I slid my finger gently across her cheek. "Of course, my darling, please forgive me. I do not mean to be a bore. It is only that, can't you see, I love you, and I want us to be together, always."

I left the chateau that afternoon feeling uneasy and downhearted. Oh, I was grateful to Noelle because I knew that Madeleine was in good hands, but for the past four months Madeleine had been all mine, and I knew in my heart that all that was about to change.

Chapter 22

The Power Brokers

y first order of business was to pay a call on Cardinal Mazarin. Early the next morning I left my card at the Palais Cardinal. With Cardinal Richelieu dead, I was concerned about his commission. I had purchased, on his behalf, a quantity of diamonds that exceeded the funds he had advanced. I need not have worried. I received a note from Cardinal Mazarin asking me to call upon him late that afternoon.

The cardinal rose smiling. "Monsieur Tavernier, what a pleasant surprise! It is good to see you again." Mazarin greeted me in the same office where I had my first interview with Cardinal Richelieu.

"Thank you for remembering me, Eminence. May I offer my condolences on the death of Cardinal Richelieu. I know you were very close."

Mazarin walked from behind his desk and offered his hand. He had a strong grip, and I was once again struck by his appearance. He was tall and strikingly handsome. I had already heard the rumor that he was the queen's lover.

"Thank you, monsieur. I have been blessed, and, yes, the death of His Eminence, the cardinal-duke, was sad, very sad. He was a great man and a good friend. But, come, let us not dwell upon the past; tell me, monsieur, how long has it been?"

"Five years."

"Truly," he shook his head slowly side to side, "Five years! So much has happened, so much has changed. But come, sit down, and give me an account of yourself. Did you manage a visit to Rome?"

The cardinal listened attentively, his eyes never straying from my face as I gave him a brief account of my stay in Rome and what little I knew of the political situation in the Vatican. I conveyed Cardinal Barberini's best wishes.

"All Rome sings your praises, Eminence."

"How kind. Tell me, your trip to the Indies, it was successful?"

"It was, Your Eminence."

"And, what of the diamonds you were to obtain for Cardinal Richelieu?"

"I have all of the gems required!"

His face brightened. "Really, so many? Very good, monsieur. I promised His Eminence that I would complete his bequest. It was his dying wish. You have brought them with you?"

"Actually, I have more, and no, Eminence, I do not have them with me. I keep them under guard. You may examine them whenever you wish."

"Yes, of course, one cannot walk the streets with a bag of diamonds." The cardinal smiled, but his face showed disappointment. "Well, this is good news. I could use some diversion. We must arrange to see them. Tomorrow evening. Unfortunately, I have pressing business this evening, but tomorrow…. I will arrange to have the goldsmiths present as well."

The next evening I returned to the palace with two of my servants and my stock. Mazarin and the two goldsmiths Messrs. Dujardin and Courtois were also present. I had met these two gentlemen briefly before I left for the Indies. One other man was present.

"Monsieur Jean-Baptiste Tavernier, may I name my secretary and homme de confiance, Monsieur Jean-Baptiste Colbert. Mazarin placed his arm on his secretary's shoulder. "Colbert has my complete confidence, and you may direct any and all inquires to me through him."

I bowed. Colbert nodded his head gravely. In these same rooms, five years before, Cardinal Richelieu had introduced me to Mazarin. That evening I met Mazarin's successor.

He was a dark man, dark eyes – brooding eyes – black eyebrows and hair. His dress was also black and without ornamentation of any kind. He had a long face and a long Gallic nose with a slight bump at the center. He seldom smiled.

I laid the small leather pouches on a baize-covered table brought in for the purpose. Candles had been placed all around the table. I doubt that the two craftsmen had ever seen so many diamonds in one place. They gasped with delight as I poured glittering mounds of gems on the green cloth. They sparkled in the candlelight like thousands of tiny stars.

The cardinal watched with a hungry gleam in his eye. I noticed that his hand shook slightly as he bent his tall frame and picked up one of the larger gems.

"Marvelous, marvelous, monsieur," he said picking up one after another and examining them close to the flame. Colbert is this not a beautiful gem?" he asked and placed it in his secretary's hand.

"Truly beautiful, Your Eminence," Colbert said. He put the stone back on the table. He dutifully examined each of the stones that Mazarin placed in his hand.

The goldsmiths went methodically through the parcels. They held the gems to the light, passed them back and forth, and talked quietly. Finally they bowed and pronounced themselves well satisfied.

Mazarin beamed. "Thank you, gentlemen," he said rising. The craftsmen bolted to their feet and bowed themselves from the room.

Mazarin sat back down and turned to me. He eyed the leather

bag that stood unopened. "Very good, my son. You have carried out your commission in exemplary fashion. Tell me, are these all of your treasures?"

"It is a pleasure to serve Your Eminence. I did bring along a few of the finer things – rubies, pearls, and larger diamonds. I did not know if you would be interested, and I know that you are very busy, but if you can spare the time, I would be honored to show you."

"By all means, Monsieur Tavernier!" Cardinal Mazarin clapped his hands and laughed. "I am at your service. We have all the time in the world."

For the next hour I showed the two officials my best stock. A light went on in the cardinal's eyes as he picked through the pearls. He chose a particularly large egg shaped oriental gem, took it between his thumb and forefinger, and held it to the light. "There, do you see, Colbert, the delicate pink glow so ethereal? It seems to cling to the surface like the blush on a baby's cheek or that of a beautiful woman, eh?"

Colbert sat with his hands folded in his lap. He nodded and smiled slightly. "Yes, Eminence, a remarkable gem, truly beautiful."

The cardinal glanced at his secretary and then at me, and smiled sourly. "There you see, Tavernier. Colbert is a marvelous businessman, but he has little appreciation for the finer things."

Colbert shrugged. "I do appreciate the value, Your Eminence."

The Cardinal laughed. "You see, it is as I said." He rolled the pearl in his palm and gazed at it.

"I have seen many pearls, but this is the first I have had time to study. It seems to glow with life. And you say it was found in the Persian Gulf."

"Off the island of Bahrain, Eminence."

"It is difficult to believe, Monsieur Tavernier, that a thing so beautiful can come from such a lowly thing as an oyster. Surely God's hand is at work here."

"It surely is, Your Eminence!"

Cardinal Mazarin became particularly devoted to large diamonds. By the end of his life he had acquired a magnificent collection that came to be called the Mazarins. When he died, he left his collection, together with the bulk of his estate, to His Majesty Louis XIV. I flatter myself that I helped to set his feet upon that road. That evening he purchased several of my largest diamonds and the pearl. I learned later that he had the pearl set in a pendant and presented it to the queen-regent, Anne of Austria.

The next morning I strolled, unannounced, into Torreles. Pierre was on the floor. His jaw dropped open at the sight of me. He rushed over and wrapped his arms around me in a bear hug.

"Jean-Baptiste, cousin, I thought you were a ghost. When did you get back? It has been a year since your last letter. I have been very worried. Where have you been?"

By this time the whole staff was crowded around us laughing and touching, everyone talking at once. I greeted everyone in turn and answered a lot of questions.

"All right, give Jean-Baptiste a little room. Everyone shoo now, back to work." Pierre grabbed my arm and dragged me into his office.

Pierre seated himself behind his desk. "Now," he said rubbing his hands together, "what have you brought me from the Indies?"

"No 'how are you, Jean-Baptiste'? How are you feeling, Jean-Baptiste?"

"Yes, yes, of course, cousin, I want to hear about all that," he said gesturing impatiently with his hands. "How are you feeling?" He squinted at me. "You look a bit peeked, tired I'll wager from your long voyage? You must tell me everything; hold nothing back, and that will give you something to talk about," he grinned, "while you are showing me the merchandise." I laid the gems out one at a time, and we talked away the afternoon.

"Mon Dieu!" Pierre sat back in his chair like a man sated from a feast and gazed across the parcels filling the top of his desk. "I can scarcely believe it. You have made a killing! What quality and such prices! My blood fairly boils when I think what those greedy Armenians and Venetians have been charging us all these years!"

"So you are satisfied with your investment?"

"Satisfied? Satisfied! I would jump across this desk and kiss you, but I am not that sort of fellow. That citron diamond, mon Dieu! I know just who to show it to and the rubies! And that sapphire – why it is the size of a pigeon's egg, and I know just the pigeon…. But never mind, it's getting late. Let us lock up your goods and then we go. First dinner, and you must tell me more about the diamond mines of Golconda."

By the following afternoon I had eliminated most of my debts, my pocket was jingling with golden Louis, and I still had a respectable stock. To celebrate, I decided to pay a call at the Chateau Rochambeau. Neither Madeleine nor Noelle was at home.

The next months went by quickly. Business went well. I called at the chateau several times, but it seemed that Noelle and Madeleine were not able to receive me. Noelle's husband, the Count, had returned from one of his many absences. My former relationship with Noelle was no secret, and I felt awkward calling with him in residence. Meanwhile, Madeleine was causing something of a stir in Paris society. I began to hear her name mentioned. She was seen at a certain ball beautifully dressed, dancing with a prince or as a guest at a fête on the arm of a duke.

Finally I lost patience. I still had a portion of Madeleine's jewels, several I had sold and a few pieces that would require some adjustment if they were to be sold at all. One morning I left my card at the chateau with a note that I must see Madeleine on an urgent matter of business. When I returned that afternoon, I was quickly ushered into the formal parlor. Madeleine swept into the room dressed in blue silk. Her eyes were alight with excitement.

"Lovely dress."

"Oh, you think so?" She tossed her head and pirouetted, laughing. Then she took hold of my hands. "Congratulate me, Jean Baptiste. I am engaged!"

"You are what?"

"Engaged! Now, Jean, don't pout. It has all happened so quickly, I can hardly catch my breath. I am to be a marquise!"

"What, who?"

"The Marquis de Chamboulet. Noelle introduced us."

"Of course, Noelle. The Marquis de Chamboulet! Surely you

don't mean... the man is a dotard! He must be nearly 90!"

Madeleine stamped her foot. "That is unkind and unworthy of you, Jean-Baptiste Tavernier!"

"Unkind? He is old enough to be your grandfather. You ran away from one old man in Persia, and now you have run into the arms of another? Madeleine, will you now pretend that you expected me to be happy about this. Have you conveniently forgotten how I feel about you? You have been in Paris barely three months and now a Marquise. I see that I have been a fool. All the talk about being confused and needing time. A title and a fortune, that is what you really needed and wanted. I should have known! You might, at least, have been honest with me."

"Jean, I am sorry that you are angry. I know how much I owe you, and I hoped you would understand and be happy for me."

"I had hoped that we would be happy together."

She sighed. "A woman must look to her future, Jean Baptiste; with the marquis my future is assured. I shall have position. Could you give me that?"

"I love you, Madeleine."

"Love, oh please! Must you men always talk of love? Love, love, love! What is love, a temporary infatuation? Men flit like bees from one flower to another. But for a woman, marriage is a serious business."

"Yes, and I have been a fool. I wonder how your marquis would feel if he knew who and what you really are."

She looked me straight in the eye with her fists clenched and her hands on her hips. "Jean Baptiste, that is truly unworthy of you. This is how you would show your love for me?"

What a pathetic creature I was. Love had unmanned me. Despite everything, I could not bear her anger. "No, forgive me please, Madeleine. I spoke out of anger. I did not mean it."

Her face softened. She took me by both hands and looked up into my eyes. "Oh, Jean, please do try to understand. There has been too much uncertainty in my life. I need security, a stable place to set my feet. You are an adventurer, a free spirit…The marquis is older, it is true, but he is wise and very understanding. He knows that a young woman has certain needs. I do care for you. We could still see each other."

"I have done very well, Madeleine, and I will do better. Pierre would gladly make me a partner. He said so only last week. We could settle down, I have the money. You could have a house in Paris."

"Settle down, yes, but for how long? How long would it be before you felt the need to travel again, a year, two? And how long would you be gone, three years, five? What would I do in the meantime, sit alone in a drafty old house waiting for you? I know very well that love will not keep a man from being what he is destined to be, and you have a destiny, Jean Baptiste Tavernier, a great destiny I believe."

"So, what do you propose, my lady? You marry another man, and I become what, your lover? Will you keep me?"

"Yes, and I will buy you silk hankies. Oh, Jean, don't be silly! I will hardly be 'keeping' you. I am simply offering you an arrangement, one of mutual, ah, benefit." She flashed her most be-guiling smile. "Why not, for all love? What a truly exasperating man you are, upon my word. Any other man would positively leap at the opportunity. What is it that men say – you needn't buy the cow; you will have the milk for free!"

The Marquis de Chamboulet had a well-deserved reputation as a drunk, a gambler, and a rake. I could have pointed that out to Madeleine, but to what purpose? It would only seem like sour grapes. For my part I was disgusted and heartsick, and rather than moon around Paris like a lovesick fool, I determined to sell my remaining goods, take my profit, and set sail for Persia and India.

3rd Voyage

(1643-1649)

Chapter 23

Voyage to Batavia

 y third voyage commenced December 6, 1643. I followed my usual route by ship to Alexandretta, then overland to Aleppo, then Isfahan where I stayed for the best part of a year. I then took ship from Bander Abbās and arrived in Surat in early January of 1645.

I went to Raolconda and also to the mines at Kollūr and to other parts of India where my business took me, most of which I have already described. I had several letters from my brother Daniel begging me to visit him in Batavia. I had not seen him for more than six years, and I had never been to the Dutch East Indies, so I decided to make a voyage to Batavia. I took ship from Mingrella on April 14, 1648 bound for Batavia.

I saw a well-made, familiar looking young man waving at me as our boat reached the wharf.

"Jean-Baptiste," he called, waving his arms over his head.

As soon as I set foot on the dock, Daniel took me up in a bear hug, nearly crushing my ribs. "Brother, it is so good to see you," he said smiling broadly. My father's blue eyes and even white teeth gleamed in his tanned face.

Daniel had been living on the island of Java since 1642. Once he finished his clerkship with the Dutch company, he bought a small trading vessel and moved from the Dutch settlement at Batavia and took up residence in Bantam, a small sultanate at the extreme west end of the island.

"Daniel, I am amazed. How did you know I would be on this ship?"

"Ha, ha! As to that, I received your letter, and I have met each ship that has come in the past month. Besides, brother, you are a famous man, and your comings and goings are remarked upon. The captain of a Dutch ship that arrived last week told me that he had seen you at Pointe de Galle, and he knew the name of the ship you sailed on."

"You have put on weight and muscle, too, by the looks of you."

"Yes, brother, and so have you. You look like a rich burgher," he said, pointing to my expanding paunch. "But, come; let us get

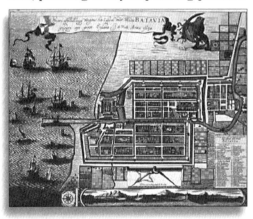

Figure 11: Batavia Harbor from a 1681 engraving.

out of this sun. I have arranged lodgings for you at the best hotel in Batavia. Have your servants gather up your luggage. The boat is waiting."

I left Danush and my servants to supervise the unloading of my goods and stepped into a long-tailed, native dragon boat. Danush had begun acting listless of late. He tired easily and he looked liverish. I wondered if it was a mistake to bring him to this fever-ridden city.

The boatman cast off. The sights and sounds of Batavia soon engulfed us. Twin wharves jut straight out into the harbor.

Between them a canal leads toward the center of the town. Batavia is a city built on trade; it radiates commerce as the sun radiates heat. Ramshackle wooden buildings and small wharves stacked with bales of goods and tall godowns, built in the Dutch style with sloping roofs and stuffed full with all the riches of the Indies, line the shore. Reed thin coolies, their naked backs burned black by the tropical sun, moved about like ants in thin lines, unloading barges and carrying huge bales of goods.

"You can see that the Dutch have adopted the Portuguese customs."

"What do you mean, Daniel?"

"You see the one standing under the umbrella, over by the wharf just behind the palm tree, shading his lily white skin?"

"Yes."

"The Dutch here in Batavia are quite the dandies. They strut about like gamecocks with their retinues of servants. Their style of dress is a bit less colorful than the Portuguese, but their pretensions are not." He laughed. "Really quite amusing! Even the overseers, who boss the work gangs, must have two servants and affect a sunshade.

"Can you conquer the Orient, do you think, from beneath an umbrella?"

Daniel laughed heartily, then looked into my eyes. His face had broadened and lost some of its youthful beauty, but he was, if anything, more handsome. He wore his dark hair down to his collar, and it had developed a bit of a curl. Like many sailors, he had a web of wrinkles around his eyes from squinting into the sun.

"Tell me, Jean, I am your brother, and you need not play the confidential agent with me. Why have you come?"

"You think me secretive?"

"Secretive, of course you are, Jean-Baptiste. You are a veritable clam, a man of mystery, even to your own brothers. Why does Europe's most famous merchant traveler come to Batavia?"

"Hmm. I came to see you and this famous city."

"No other reason?"

"None! Well, you never know where you might find an opportunity for profit!"

Daniel embraced me. He was a few inches shorter. "Well while you are here, perhaps I might put you in the way of an opportunity or two. We must go to Bantam. I will introduce you to the sultan." We held each other at arm's length. It had been a long time, too long. Daniel looked at me meaningfully. "He is a good fellow and, by the way, has a passion for gemstones, particularly diamonds."

"The Devil you say! In that case we absolutely must meet him, mustn't we?"

Balancing on a narrow platform at the stern, the boatman sculled with his single oar propelling us slowly along. We passed the castle the Dutch had built to defend the city. It is constructed of heavy stone blocks with walls that slope inward up to the battlements. The fort is an island surrounded by canals. Opposite the castle there are no warehouses. The land has been kept clear and is low. Tall pines stood motionless in clusters along the opposite bank.

"Daniel, are these to be our lodgings?"

"Ha, ha! No, I just thought you would like to see the fort, and we are not far out of our way."

"Formidable!"

"Yes, I thought you would like to see it so you may report to your friend in the ministry that the Dutch are here to stay."

"It seems you know a great deal about my business."

"I know the family gossip. Notes from the duke-cardinal, summons to the palace, and so forth."

"Yes, between us, brother, I have been an informal envoy, a confidential informant, first for Cardinal Richelieu, and now I serve His Eminence, Cardinal Mazarin."

"I am not surprised to hear that. I had thought you were involved in something along those lines. Jean-Baptiste, when will France form a merchant company of its own? There are riches aplenty, enough for all."

"I have spoken of this several times with Colbert, Cardinal

Mazarin's secretary. The idea is dear to his heart."

Daniel's eyed widened. "You know Colbert? I have heard of him. They say he will be the next first minister. Perhaps the next time you speak with him, you might mention your brother's name. I could be very useful in Bantam. I am in very well with the sultan."

"You may depend upon it."

Our craft bumped up against a stone wharf. Beyond it was a broad cobble stoned avenue, and across from that, the governor's palace, a small two-story chateau built in the colonial style with a colonnaded porch shading the first floor. It was still quite early in the day, and a few couples promenaded the avenue. Servants kept them well shaded.

"We disembark here. Our lodgings are over yonder," he said pointing off to the left. "You will like it, Jean, I think – a real Dutch inn like the ones in Antwerp."

"With real Dutch beer?"

"English actually, brought in from the British factory in Bantam City. The Dutch don't control the whole island. Not yet. I like the English beer better. The governor-general has recently taken against it because it is made in Birmingham, and now we must smuggle it by him. Come along."

Daniel was right; the inn was charming, decorated in the Dutch style. We might indeed have been in Antwerp except for the heat. The summer monsoon would soon begin and the air hung limp as a wet rag. We sat on the shaded verandah and talked over a pint of excellent English beer.

"I expect you will hear presently from the governor-general."

"Really? It appears, brother Daniel, that you are very well informed. Do you know something I do not?"

"Only that, nothing more. I have no details."

"Well I do have some business with that gentleman. I have a letter from the commander of the Dutch factory at Vengurla."

As if on cue, one of the governor's guards dressed in full livery walked through the door, presented himself, and asked if I were Monsieur Tavernier. When I answered in the affirmative, he presented me with an invitation to dine with his master, Governor-General Cornelius Van der Lijn on the 25th, just two days away.

"Most honored, His Excellency's servant," I replied and scribbled my acceptance on the back of the invitation. The guard bowed, turned on his heel, and left.

Daniel smiled across the table: "I don't believe I have ever seen such a splendid uniform – all that silver and the yellow silk. Were we sitting in the sun I fear that the magnificence would have blinded me. He must have been an admiral at least."

"A corporal, I believe, ha, ha! Dear brother, Daniel, I had forgotten about that rapier-tongue of yours and how much I missed it."

Two nights later I was treated, at dinner, to a convocation of the most important Dutch officials. Besides Governor-General Van der Lijn, the guests included his second in command, the Director-General François Caron, two other councilors, the major, the advocate fiscal, and their wives. We ate in the palace dining room that was also decorated in the Dutch style, with a long oval table and heavy carved wooden chairs. The dinner was quite convivial. The officials were most interested to hear news of Europe. Since I had been in Asia for four and a half years, there was little new that I could tell them.

After the meal the governor-general asked me to accompany him to his office. The general was a tall man, rather plain faced, with a moustache, a tiny chin beard, and a haughty manner. We spoke in Dutch for a few minutes about unimportant things. Then the talk took a serious turn.

"Herr Tavernier, may I ask you why you have come to Batavia?"

"Why of course you may, Governor-General. I have come to visit my brother, to see your city, and, at the request of the chief of your factory in Vengurla, to do your company a service as you can see from the letter in your hand."

"And, that is all?" the general demanded coldly.

"Yes!"

"Herr Tavernier, let me speak bluntly; we know something of your activities on behalf of some of the officials of this company."

"What activities are you speaking of, Herr Van der Lijn?" I did not like the man's tone.

You are acquainted with the former commander of our factory at Bander Abbās?"

"You mean Herr Constant?"

"Just so."

"Yes, I have known him for some years."

"The council is investigating Commander Constant. There have been charges that while he was chief of the factory at Bander Abbās he was engaged in private trade."

"And what does this have to do with me?"

"The council intends to call you as a witness."

"A witness to what precisely, general? Commander Constant is an official of your company. I know him, yes, but I know nothing of his business affairs."

"We – that is to say – the council is in possession of certain facts that contradict what you say," the general said sternly.

My blood was rising though I did my best to remain calm. "Are you calling me a liar? You are forgetting, general, that I am not an employee of the Dutch East India Company. I am a subject of His Majesty, the King of France."

The governor-general raised his hands in a supplicating gesture. "Please, Herr Tavernier, no one is impugning your word. The council merely wishes to secure your cooperation in its investigation."

"My cooperation? What sort of cooperation, General Van de Lijn? You are looking for a spy? Commander Constant is an old friend, and I am not a spy."

"A few questions."

"Very well, general. It has always been my custom to cooperate with my hosts to the highest extent possible. Let us see what tomorrow brings."

What the next day brought was a meeting of the full council of the Indies, the governing body of the Dutch East India Company in Asia. The council met in the palace. I knew several of the gentlemen present. Caron, the director-general, acted as the council president and brought the meeting to order. He got right to the point: "What, Herr Tavernier, can you tell us about Commander Constant's business activities while he was commander of the factory in Bander Abbās?"

"Very little."

This response occasioned some whispered conversation between the committee chairman and the advocate fiscal. The advocate spoke: "Herr Tavernier, we have information that Commander Constant engaged in private trade while he was head of the factory and that you procured on his behalf a parcel of diamonds for 16,000 rupees."

Upon hearing this I had to laugh at the utter hypocrisy of these officials. I knew that I could put an end to this proceeding any time that I liked and my attitude, I fear, ruffled the feathers of some of the rarer birds present.

"Herr Tavernier, we do not consider this a laughing matter," Caron said.

"Really? You say that Herr Constant engaged in private trade to the amount of 16,000 rupees as if this is a significant sum. I know, and so do you, that any number of the company's servants," I said, looking from one man to another "have made far greater sums. Virtually every official of the company stationed in Asia, not excluding members of this council, engages in private trade, trade that costs your company perhaps 1,600,000 livres a year in lost profits."

Several of the council members shifted uneasily in their seats as I spoke. "As to my own activities, they are private, and may I remind you, gentlemen, that as a private individual and a citizen of France, I am not subject to your rules and regulations?"

"Herr Tavernier," the chairman said icily, "may I remind you that you are in Batavia and are therefore subject to the authority of this council."

"Remind me all you like," I retorted with equal sternness. "Do your worst. I enjoy the protection of His Majesty, King Louis XIV, who will certainly resent this treatment. I repeat, I am not subject to the rules of your company."

The advocate fiscal rose and gave a long disjointed speech, in effect demanding that I either answer the council's questions or be placed under arrest. In the end the council dismissed me, with four days to think about what they had asked of me and to return prepared to answer any and all questions truthfully. They ordered the advocate fiscal to prepare in writing a series of questions so that I might have time to prepare my answers.

The four days came and went, and I heard nothing further. Eight days later one of the council members, a friend of mine, came to my lodging and spoke to me urging me to come forward that morning with detailed answers to all the council's questions. He feared that if I refused the council would have me arrested and thrown into prison.

It was past time to end the charade; quite early next morning I paid a call on General Van der Lijn. One of the servants showed me into the general's office and asked me to wait. After a few minutes the general arrived, still wearing his nightgown and cap. "Herr Tavernier, please forgive my appearance, but I was unwilling to have you wait while I dressed. What may I do for you?"

"You may put an end to this absurd investigation immediately!"

The Dutch official drew himself up like a tall Bantam cock. He had a high forehead and small close-set, beady eyes. Upon hearing my demand, they widened and seemed to start from his head. "Why, how dare you come here at this hour and make such a demand?"

"Governor-general, Herr Constant and I have been friends for many years, and I know a good deal about his affairs including the details of several investments that he made on behalf of yourself and two other members of your council."

The General stared at me, his eyes grew brighter and his face turned red.

"For example, Commander Constant gave me 44,000 rupees to procure a parcel of diamonds on your behalf. Perhaps you have forgotten? I also know that he invested monies that you sent him on a cargo of goods from Sironj that were shipped to Bander Abbās on the company account and thus avoided the freight and customs when it arrived at the port. I do not know why you have chosen to persecute Herr Constant for crimes that you and several members have been a party to, but if the council insists that I answer these impertinent questions, I shall tell all I know. Do you wish me to go on?"

He raised his hand to stop me. "Please, Mein Herr, I have heard enough!"

"Very good, sir. Then you will do me the courtesy of calling off your minions. I have been in Batavia now for several weeks and although I came here partly to do your company a service, I have been the subject of constant harassment. I am tired of it, sir."

The general motioned me toward a chair. "Please sit down."

"Thank you, no, general. I prefer to stand. Now what is your answer?"

"Herr Tavernier, you must understand my position. We are both men of the world, are we not? We understand these things, but the council received an official complaint and several of the councilors… well, Commander Constant has enemies and these men insisted on an investigation."

"You are the governor-general, Herr Van der Lijn!"

He shook his head impatiently. "Yes, of course, but for me to interfere in such a matter would seem odd, and it might focus suspicion on me. Back home, the company directors have become very sensitive in the matter of private trade, and I am responsible to them. Before you arrived in Batavia, there was no evidence of any sort, and in time the whole matter would have been dropped."

"And, now?"

"I will see to it, I promise you. I will speak with Herr Caron, this morning. You will hear no more about it. May I count upon your continued discretion?"

Less than three years later, François Caron, the same man who was making all the fuss, would find himself indicted by the council for private trading and would be forced to sail to Holland and defend himself before the company directors. In 1664, Caron would be recruited by Colbert and become governor-general of the French East India Company.

Chapter 24

The King of Bantam

ith this unpleasantness out of the way I decided to yield to my brother's desire that I visit Bantam. The city is a mere fourteen leagues from Batavia. If the wind is favorable, you can sail there in a single tide.

Daniel had a good relationship with the Dutch East India Company. He was much caressed by the general and the council. He had even been allowed to fit out a fourteen-gun brig and trade on his own account, so long as he did not deal in spices.

Daniel made several trading voyages to Siam, Cochinchina, and Tonkin. These voyages must have been very successful because the moneylenders who provide the capital for such ventures receive 100% return on their investment, and Daniel had been able to pay them back and still realize a tidy profit. My brother had a gift for languages. He spoke fluent Dutch, Persian, and Malay, the language that is the lingua franca in this part of Asia. He had some business with the English company at Bantam, where he had met and become friends with the sultan.

We set sail that evening with a breeze like a hot breath off the land. The shoreline ghosted past in the light of the rising moon, a series of darkening shapes held together by the palm-treed skyline. Below decks the heat was insufferable. Daniel had our dinner served on deck. I tasted each of the sauces that the cook assembled on a hatch cover. The combination of flavors turned my mouth into a battlefield, with one side at war with the other and my tongue unfortunately hung between.

After dinner with the deck lanterns shrouded, we stood together at the rail, talking and drinking wine. The wine helped to cool my tongue.

"Brother, this wine is ambrosia! Shiraz, do you want more? My friend Sultan Agung is much devoted to good wine, a little too devoted if the truth be known."

Earthy smells drifted out on the land breeze. I closed my eyes and breathed deeply. I wore a light Indian cotton shirt, but in that heat it stuck fast to my skin. I bought the cloth in Baroda and had the shirts made in Agra. The Agra tailors are the best in all the lands of the Great Moghul. Daniel wore a sarong with his rapier strapped to his waist. We both wore sandals.

"Jean," he laughed, "in the articles of clothing, at least, I see we think alike."

"Yes, but you know how the Dutch and the English, too, for that matter, raise their noses and sniff the air at the thought of 'going native.'"

"Yes, while they dress in wool like proper fools and sweat like pigs. Wearing European clothes and high leather boots in the Indies is a form of madness!"

"Agreed, brother! Much of what we Europeans do in these countries is madness. The Dutch massacre the English. The English make war on the Portuguese. The Portuguese are finished in Asia. They have fouled their nest, and the native princes hate them."

Daniel crossed his arms in back of his head, arched his back, and stretched luxuriously. He was muscular and lithe as a cat. "The Portuguese padres say that God wants us to bring salvation to the heathen at any cost."

"Yes, the Spanish talk the same sort of rot."

He turned from the rail and looked at me. "How do they justify this as Christians?"

"The justification is fairly straight forward in their eyes," I said and slapped a mosquito. "Slavery in this life is a small price to pay – they say – for salvation in Christ."

Daniel cleared his throat, shook his head slowly, and spit down into the dark water. "Jesus Christ," he said and looked off toward the black shrouded shore.

At dawn we sighted the town. The smell of wood and breakfast and other things not so pleasant drifted out on the dying breeze.

Daniel brought the ship to anchor. Then we let all but four of the crew go ashore, set a guard, and slept through most of the daylight hours. I woke just before sunset and spent some time studying the harbor. Across the dark oily water, the town appeared to be a ramshackle affair, built entirely of wood. Swamps ringed the harbor and clouds of mosquitoes hovered near the shore. My brother appeared at dusk.

"Here is what I suggest, brother," he said yawning. "The sultan has been pestering me about you for months. I am to bring you to him as his guest. You have some set jewels, I hope?"

"About 60,000 livres worth, mostly diamond rings, some with rubies. I brought only a few things. I have an emerald, an old mine stone."

"Is it from India? I have heard that Indian emeralds are very beautiful."

"No, Daniel, between us, the dealers talk of India, but the emeralds come from the mountains of Tartary and from the Spanish New World. They are a true green with few imperfections, and the water is very pure. Tomorrow when the light is good, I will show you."

He nodded. "How large is this emerald?"

"Ten and one quarter French carats."

"My God. It must be worth by itself 60,000 livres."

"Yes, that and more!"

"You have done well, brother!"

"Yes, it is time to go home. One more voyage, perhaps two, and I will be a rich man. You must join me, Daniel. I can use a good man, and I will see that you get rich as well."

"Then what will you do?"

"Why retire to my chateau, let my beard grow, and live long and well."

"Then I will take over your business affairs?"

"Nothing would please me more."

"That is a handsome offer, Jean. I feel very much inclined. There is so much you can teach me, and two are better than one. But let me think about it. For the present, let us call upon the sultan this evening; he sleeps mostly during the day. Bring the jewels as well."

"You have heard the story of the Reynaud Brothers?"

"No, but tell it, brother, if it is a good one. I have always loved your stories."

"The story is very long and complicated. I will give you a short account if you will order the dinner. I spent half this afternoon on the seat of ease. So please, ask the cook to go easy on the chilies."

"I will, ha, ha! He is Malay and they are a bit heavy handed in the article of chili. Tell me the story."

"The brothers Reynaud were reasonably prosperous small merchants, not unlike myself during my first two voyages. They worked hard and were each worth, perhaps, 50,000 livres. They visited the sultan of Aachen. He was a stubby little fellow. He particularly liked a group of rings that the younger Reynaud priced at 18,000 livres, but the sultan refused to pay more than 15,000 for them.

"What happened?"

The younger Reynaud returned to his lodgings. A day or two later the sultan sent a messenger urging the younger brother to return and to bring his jewels with him. The man returned and had an audience with the sultan, who paid him his price. Then M. Reynaud left the presence of the sultan and was never seen again.

He was apparently butchered in the palace, and his body disposed of, no one really knows."

"Well, what say I go ahead and inquire as to when Sultan Agung will receive you."

"Perhaps that would be better. In any case, it is best that I not put myself forward or seem too eager."

"You need not worry on that score, brother. As I told you, the sultan is my friend."

"I believe the Reynaud brothers considered the Sultan of Aachen a friend as well."

Daniel laughed and ordered the boat lowered. Several of the crewmen rowed him ashore. About two hours later a delegation came in an official looking boat with a canopy gesturing for me to accompany them. They were dressed in the costume of the country, but Daniel was not among the group, which gave me pause, but in the end I went with them.

The sultan's palace was built in a square about forty feet by forty feet with large pillars at each corner. The floor was covered with a mat woven of bark that keeps off the fleas. The roof was thatched with pond fronds. The sultan had with him a guard of two thousand retainers, who sat in ranks under the shade of palm trees. I was relieved to see Daniel was in attendance.

I saluted Prince Agung and presented him with several gifts. He was seated on the floor in the Oriental fashion on a small Persian carpet, dressed in a single piece of calico that wrapped about his waist and fell to his knees. He wore a sort of handkerchief tied at three corners on his head. Two slaves sat behind him and fanned him with long handled fans, tipped with peacock feathers.

An old woman with a face like a dried prune sat behind the sultan's right shoulder. Using a mortar and pestle of solid gold, she crushed betel leaves and ground them with a mixture of areca nuts and seed pearls. Betel is a drug used throughout Asia. It creates a mild euphoria and turns the teeth black. The grinding finished, the old woman formed a quid in her hand and touched the sultan's back. He opened his mouth and received the quid like a baby bird being fed by its mother.

His Highness was affable enough. He seemed pleased with my gifts. "Senhor Tavernier, your brother has told me much about you." He spoke decent Dutch but with an odd accent and he slurred his words. The prince had lost all of his teeth as a result of betel chewing.

I bowed.

"Have you brought your jewels?" the sultan asked.

"Yes, Your Highness." I showed him the rings I had with me. He summoned two old black women who took them into the harem to show his wives. This was not a rich kingdom. They entered through a miserable door behind the throne. The walls of the women's enclosure were made of logs plastered with a mixture of earth and cow dung. None of the rings came back, and I took that to be a sign that I should stick to my price.

The sultan clapped his hands and ordered sherbet. It was served up cold in silver goblets and flavored with lotus blossoms. He did not bargain over my price and paid me on the spot. I had paid only 3,000 livres for the rings so I made a good profit. My brother and I then took leave of the sultan. I promised to return the next afternoon. He wished to show me a Turkish style dagger he was having made. He sent us on our way in his own palanquin with a guard of honor.

"Jean, I believe Sultan Agung liked you. I am sorry that I did not come back with the party, but His Highness insisted that I remain and drink with him while his men went to fetch you," he said as we jostled along the path to the shore.

"Beware the friendship of princes."

"Sounds portentous. Is that meant as a warning? Well, I am sure you are right. His Highness is an excitable fellow. We often play cards, and I make sure that I lose. On my last visit he had his vizier trampled by the royal elephants."

"Really, why?"

"The man displeased him in some way. I believe he failed to extract sufficient taxes from the people to pay the sultan's debts."

"Then his fate was well deserved."

"Ha, ha! Yes, exactly right. When the elephants were through all that was left of the vizier was a red stain."

"That should serve as a lesson to the next vizier."

The sultan's palanquin deposited us at the harbor. There was no wind and the sea lapped gently against the shore. We found our Malay boat crew squatting in a circle around a small fire on the sand; their brown backs gleamed in the waning moonlight. They were eating rice and swatting mosquitoes. Daniel's crew was mostly from the eastern side of the island. Daniel treated them well, and they were much devoted to him. They seemed relieved to see us. We bantered back and forth while the crew rowed us across the harbor to our anchorage.

The next afternoon we set out again for the sultan's palace. We found him seated as before.

"Senhor Tavernier, I have a dagger that was a gift of the queen of Tonquin. As you can see, it has been made with bezels. I wish to buy a quantity of diamonds to fit into these settings." A servant placed the dagger in my hands.

"Your Highness, I fear that I cannot do as you command. Normally, the goldsmith makes the bezels to fit the diamonds. If I was at Golconda it might be possible to find suitable gems, but here, I fear there are not enough diamonds in all of Java…" I said in a tone that I hoped would convey the hopelessness of the effort.

The sultan looked annoyed. Monarchs are not used to the word "no." Kings surround themselves with courtiers to do all they can to never use the word, regardless of the hopelessness of the task. In the end I agreed to take the dagger with me.

We sailed back to Batavia where we stayed for the better part of three weeks, enough time to prove to the king that I had tried to fulfill his commission. There is little to do in Batavia but gamble and drink. I had developed a form of leprosy; the officials of the Dutch company avoided me as if I was diseased. It was so hot during the daylight hours that I could not even take my usual morning walk. Exercise is impossible until the sun sets and the evening breeze brings some respite from the heat.

After amusing ourselves in this fashion for twenty days, we sailed back to Bantam. I brought the dagger and some jewels which the sultan had not seen. We anchored and the next morning, Daniel and I, accompanied by a Dutch surgeon who was attending one of the sultan's wives, were walking toward the palace talking companionably. The road was flanked by the river on one side and a large garden enclosed by a shoulder high log palisade on the other.

"Odd, this road is normally quite busy this time of day," Daniel remarked.

"Yes, it does seem quiet compared to yesterday."

"Perhaps the villagers are attending some sort of native ceremony," the doctor said.

We were walking abreast, and my brother was walking a few steps ahead. Just then a spear shot out from a crack between the logs and passed just in front of the surgeon and me.

By reflex I grabbed hold of the spear shaft. I looked through the fence, but could not see our attacker clearly; he was partly hidden behind the fence. I had only the impression of broken teeth, wild eyes, and a matted beard. The surgeon recovered himself and grabbed hold. Together we wrenched the spear from the unseen hands behind the wall.

Daniel had turned and drawn his sword, and once he saw that we were not hurt, he stepped up on a knotted branch and vaulted over the palisade. After he gained his balance, my brother did not hesitate; his polished blade leapt forward like an adder's tongue and buried itself in the madman's throat. Our would-be murderer collapsed into a heap of filthy calico.

I clamored gracelessly over the fence. Daniel stood as if in a trance, staring down at the dead man, his chest rising and falling rapidly as if he had just run a footrace.

I grasped his shoulder. "Well done, Daniel. Well done!"

Daniel gazed at the ground and slowly shook his head. "What is wrong with these beggars?"

"What is wrong? Religion probably! Once when I was in Surat, a fakir – a madman dressed just like this one – attacked a mob of Dutch sailors and killed twelve before he was shot to death by an officer. You only did what you had to do. You saved all of our lives, Daniel."

I looked down at vacant haunted eyes that stared up toward the heavens. The madman had long coarse hair woven into snake-like locks. Blood from a severed artery leaked from the wound and began to puddle, forming a grizzly halo around his head. The body had already begun to draw flies.

Almost at once, a mob of idolaters issued from their hiding places like crabs out of a hole. The road had been empty. Suddenly it was filled with people who surrounded us, holding hands, chanting and dancing. Several grabbed at Daniel's hands and kissed them to thank him for removing this man who had already killed eleven people and was terrorizing the whole neighborhood. Daniel looked about vacantly and hardly acknowledged the people, killing a man had affected him so.

We left the dead fakir and continued on our way toward the palace with our escort. The crowd sang, clashed symbols and danced about making all sorts of racket. When we reached the palace compound, several of the sultan's guards, alarmed by the large crowd and all the noise, rushed forward with their swords drawn. Once they understood what was happening, they put away their swords and eventually convinced the people to leave.

Sultan Agung stood up smiling in greeting as we entered the courtyard.

"Daniel, my friend, you have done me a great service!" he said in his halting Dutch. He clapped Daniel on the shoulder and smiled a toothless smile. "Come, sit. You too, Senhor Tavernier. We must have a drink to celebrate."

Daniel smiled, shook his head, but said nothing. I seated him on the raised platform next to the sultan and put a drink in his hand.

The sultan looked at Daniel, then, at me and frowned. He had obviously begun drinking early.

"Why so glum, my friend?"

Daniel raised his head and looked up at the king. "I take no joy from killing, Your Majesty."

"But you have saved many lives. This man was mad."

Daniel nodded.

"The man you killed had just returned from the Hajj. The

mullahs call such men saints, but this one was mad! These are poor men. They return from Mecca filled with foolishness and begin killing anyone – idolaters, those not of our sect, those who cross their path. I sent my guards to kill him, but my men are superstitious. They fear the mullahs so they disobey my orders. It is a great problem."

"You see, brother," I said, putting my hand on his shoulder, "it is as I said – a religious fanatic. If you had not killed him, many others would have died."

After a few drinks, Daniel seemed to come back to himself. Over the course of the afternoon, I showed His Majesty a parcel of rubies that he immediately purchased, and I returned his dagger, apologizing for not being able to find the diamonds needed. He handed it to a servant and said no more about it.

Daniel looked pale. I set it down to his recent experience, but during our return voyage from Bantam, I found Daniel shivering in his cabin. "Daniel you look like a ghost. What is troubling you?"

"Not sure, brother," he said, his teeth chattering. "I have been feeling a bit out of sorts since we set sail. It will pass."

"Do you have a fever?"

"I felt hot earlier, and now I feel frozen. I drank too much with the sultan." He smiled wanly. I hoped that he was right, but I had seen these symptoms before. By the time we dropped anchor in Batavia, the symptoms had grown worse. Daniel was feverish and was shivering uncontrollably. I ordered a palanquin and had him taken to my quarters.

I had the servants put him to bed. His eyes looked liverish, and dark hair spread in damp strings across his forehead. "How do you feel?"

"I am not sure. Lord, this room is like a furnace. I need water."

"Try to sleep."

"I will. Could I please have some water?" he said and passed out.

The week passed by slowly. One minute he would be burning up, the next we would be piling blankets on him to keep him warm. Then he became delirious.

I did not get much sleep and spent most of my time taking care of him. Finally I lay down and snatched a couple of hours sleep between vigils at his bedside.

I opened my eyes and found Danush shaking me. "Aga, aga, come quickly. Your brother is awake." I got up and rushed into Daniel's room where I found him sitting up in bed. One of the servants was feeding him hot broth.

"Greetings, Jean," he said, smiling weakly between spoonfuls of the hot liquid. "Lord, but I feel weak as a newborn babe. How long have I been out of it?" His face looked pale and pinched. He had not been able to hold down anything solid in many days.

"A long time, Daniel. I was very worried. How do you feel?"

"Capital, brother, capital! And I'm hungry as a bear. How does a man go about getting something to eat around here?"

A surge of joy ran through me. Daniel sounded like himself again. All would be well. Two hours later the fever returned, worse than before. He lapsed into a delirium and never spoke again. Ten days from the day he had his first symptoms, my brother Daniel was dead.

Daniel's death affected me more than I believed possible. We had made such plans. My father had been ailing before I left Paris and had probably died but that was different. It was expected – he had lived his life. Daniel's life had barely begun. I had long ago given up expecting life to be fair, but when my brother died, a dark cavern opened beneath my feet, and I found myself staring into the darkness. Perhaps it was because he was so young. It was not his time and I felt death's hot, black breath on the back of my neck. Old as I may be, I shall not welcome the Reaper.

Chapter 25

The Perfidious Dutch

To add insult to injury, in order to bury my brother, I was obliged to follow the strange customs the rapacious Dutch have invented in order to make a profit from a person's death. First, there is a fee for professional mourners who go to pray at the burial – the more prayers, the more honorable the internment. If one mourner is engaged, the fee is 2 écus, but if two are engaged, you must pay 4 écus to each.

The price increases dramatically with each added mourner. I wanted my brother to be buried with honor, so in ignorance of this pleasant custom, I hired six mourners. When it came to payment I was astonished that each demanded 6 écus or 48 livres.

The pall, which is placed on the bier, is purchased from the hospital. There are four choices: the commonest is of cloth; three others are of velvet, one plain, one with a fringe, and the last with fringe and tassels. The price is between 5 and 30 écus. I paid 20 for the one that was placed on my brother's bier.

This was not the end; there were other expenses. Mourning is thirsty work. A cask of wine must be provided to refresh the mourners at 200 piastres; likewise food: 26 écus for three hams and some ox tongues and more for pastries. It is customary to provide a gratuity for the bearers. This costs 20 écus; the gravesite was 100 écus for internment in the church. The entire affair cost 1,233 livres of French money, a fantastic sum! If you will take my advice, you will do all you can to prevent yourself dying in any country owned by the Dutch.

My thoughts turned more and more to Paris and Madeleine, who, to be honest, was always first in my thoughts. I was more than ready to leave Java, but my friends the Dutch were not yet through with me. I attempted to secure passage on a Dutch ship bound for Surat or to Bengal or Hormuz so that I might visit the diamond mines one last time before I sailed home, but the governor-general refused me passage.

I was left no choice but to cool my heels in Batavia or sail to Europe. So I sold the remainder of my jewels and started looking about for an investment that would allow me to employ my capital profitably on the voyage to Europe. A friend suggested that I purchase *rekenings*. Employees of the Dutch company are paid only a portion of their wages while they are in Asia. To discourage former employees from remaining in the Indies and setting up on their own, they are given a voucher called a rekening for back wages payable in Antwerp. Former officials who decide to stay in the Indies sell these rekenings at a substantial discount to anyone sailing home.

I bought a lot of rekenings, worth 11,000 guilders, from a tavern owner at a good discount. By chance a day or two later I met the Dutch advocate fiscal.

"Herr Tavernier, I hear that you are seeking to purchase company vouchers to take back to Europe."

I nodded. The advocate was exceedingly well informed, and I did not trust him.

"What did you have to pay?" he asked. His tiny close-set eyes glittered in the sunlight.

I had paid 82% of value and I told him so.

"That is rather dear. I know of two parcels that can be purchased at a cheaper rate if you are interested."

I said that I was, and with the advocate's assistance I bought two parcels amounting to some 6,000 guilders at a rate of 79% of the face value.

Five or six days later I was still looking for investments to use the rest of my capital when I ran into the advocate fiscal again as he was leaving the governor general's palace. I saluted him.

"Herr Tavernier, have you been able to secure any additional rekenings?"

"Other than those I purchased through your kind offices, I have not. There seem to be no more available."

"Herr Tavernier, it grieves me to have to tell you this, but the general and the council have ordered me to require anyone who purchased these vouchers to return them to those to whom they were issued."

I was shocked. "Return the rekenings? For what reason?"

"My apologies, Mein Herr, but the governor general and the council have decided they must protect the rights of our employees. The governor feels they should not be forced to give up such a large percentage of their wages."

"Well, Herr Advocate, this is most irregular. If the governor general is so concerned, why doesn't he simply pay these men what they are owed? You may tell His Excellency I am willing to return the rekenings, provided my money is repaid at the same time. I sent them to Bantam with the rest of my baggage, and I will now have to go back to Bantam to retrieve them. I intend to travel to England with the English president, who has kindly offered me passage."

At six o'clock that evening, one of the governor-general's halberdiers came to my lodgings with a message that the general wished to see me. I immediately went to the palace and was conducted to the large hall where I found the governor-general together with the director-general and most of the council.

"Herr Tavernier, would you kindly tell me why you have not obeyed my order to hand over your rekenings to the advocate fiscal?"

"Governor Van der Lijn, this order is outrageous. I purchased a quantity of these vouchers with the help of your own advocate fiscal who, no doubt, received a commission on the transaction. Now I am told by this same official that I must return what I have purchased with no guarantee that my money will be refunded. I came to Batavia in the first place partly to do your company a service. Since I have arrived I have been harassed. First this nonsense about Commander Constant and now you demand that I turn over what I have purchased and paid for. I warn you that I have many friends who will resent this treatment of me and complain of it to your states general."

"Herr Tavernier, you have not been singled out. The company directors are quite up in arms over private trade in any form. New instructions from Antwerp arrived with the fleet. These vouchers are issued to pay our people who are returning to Europe. Our directors have strictly prohibited trading in them. So I ask you again, where are the rekenings?"

"As I explained to the official who is standing next to you, I cannot hand over what I do not have. I sent them with my luggage to Bantam. I have been offered passage on a ship to England."

"You intend, then, to go to Europe?"

"I do!"

This was a cause of some whispered conversation between the governor-general and several members of the council.

"Herr Tavernier, since you desire to go to Europe, our vessels are as good as the English, and we will treat you as well. So may I offer you free passage on one of the company ships?"

After all the trouble the Dutch had caused me, this kindness took me back a little, but I knew what the Dutch officials had in mind. A friend had told me in confidence that the general's plan was to ship me back to Europe to prevent my returning to India. He feared that some of the members of his own council would commission me to purchase parcels of diamonds on their behalf. In fact, several members of the council had approached me with just this object in mind.

After some hesitation and with as good grace as I could muster, I accepted the Dutch offer. I was afraid that if I did not I would not be allowed to leave Batavia.

"Very good, Herr Tavernier. You may select any vessel in the fleet, and I will see that you are provided with a private cabin. If you will take my advice, you will go with the vice-admiral." He gave me a sly smile. "I believe several of your friends will be returning to Holland on his ship."

"Thank you, General Van der Lijn. I am sure that I shall take your advice."

"There is only one condition, Herr Tavernier. You must place all the rekenings that you have purchased in the council's hands. Otherwise you will not be permitted to leave Batavia."

"And, my capital?"

"When you are about to leave, I shall give you a written order from the council to be paid by the company when you reach Holland."

I delayed turning over the rekenings for as long as I could, thinking, this too might pass, but the governor-general proved to be unbending. Several company officials who had refused to turn over rekenings they had purchased were arrested and thrown in jail. I requested permission to go to Bantam to retrieve the rekenings, though they had been with me all the time. This request was refused. The Dutch correctly believed that if I were allowed to go to the English factory, I would not return to Batavia. I then demanded to see the general's order, but this was not forthcoming. Finally, at the urging of several friends who told me that the general intended to have me arrested, I turned over the rekenings to the advocate fiscal.

The date came to set sail, and, as I feared, the promised reimbursement order did not appear. When I asked the advocate about it, he assured me an order would be sent and it would be in Holland when my ship arrived. Well, the order was not in Holland when I arrived, and it took two years and a lawsuit to obtain the return of half of my capital, but that is another story.

Chapter 26

The Cape
of Storms

On the 14th of October of 1648, as the sun rose into a cloudless sky and with a stiff northwest breeze, my ship, *Les Provinces,* sailed from Batavia some twenty-four days behind the main fleet. We were lucky to clear the Straits of Sunda where the wind ordinarily comes from the south at that time of the year. The southwest monsoon arrived shortly after we cleared the straits. With a steady twenty-knot breeze, *Les*

Figure 12: View of Capetown harbor with Table Mountain in the background from a 17th Century engraving.

Provinces stayed on a starboard tack for the entire voyage.

Day followed lazy day and each was sunny. I often woke just before dawn and climbed up on deck to view the sunrise. The sea color, at that latitude – pewter in the false dawn – changes to a brilliant blue as the sun peeks over the horizon. I love the sight of the sun's reflection, scintillating off the sea like a thousand tiny diamonds. At night I lay in my bunk and was rocked to sleep, listening to the creak and groan of the ship and the voice of the wind in the rigging.

Fifty-five days out of Batavia, we sighted Table Mountain. I then learned why the Portuguese call this place the *Cabo das Tormentas,* the Cape of Storms. For six days we stood offshore tacking the ship endlessly against an offshore wind while we waited for it to turn and the heavy surf to subside.

The Dutch have built a small fort at the mouth of the bay and a tiny settlement a league inland. It was all very informal because the Dutch had not yet laid claim to the place, which they did two years later. It is good country, pleasant in winter. European vegetables grow readily. Many of our crew had come down with the scurvy, and green stuff is the only cure.

The temperature at this time of the year averages about seventy degrees. A strong wind called the Cape Doctor blows constantly from the southeast. The harbor faces south, and there is little protection from the east so it can be dangerous in the summer months. The port is called Table Bay because of the massive flat-topped mountain that looms up above the plain several miles inland. The air in the morning is light and sweet like chilled champagne.

The native people are called *Kaffirs* or *Hottentots* by the Dutch; they call themselves *Khoi.* They have black skin like all the inhabitants of the southern part of Africa. When a ship comes in, the natives come down to the shore to trade. They are cattle herders. I can still recall my first glimpse of these people; they were unlike any I had ever seen.

When we first arrived, four women came on board carrying several young ostriches to cook for our sick. The women were short and thin with fat bellies, flat noses, and protruding lips. They wore a skin cape called a *kaross* and a girdle of skins round their middle that in no way hid their private parts.

We remained at the cape for twenty days. I made several excursions into the countryside, often with a young Dutch soldier named Van Scoy, a boyish, fair-haired young fellow who was stationed at the fort and was familiar with the country.

One day we came upon a group of Kaffir men lounging around a small fire, smoking and passing around pipes while their cattle grazed. Men and women always carried a tobacco pouch filled with a smoke weed they call *dagga*. Van Scoy saluted them. He spoke a bit of their unusual language. They make clicking noises with their tongues, which serve them as words.

The Khoi motioned to us to sit and join them. My young Dutch friend was apparently well known to these people, and unlike most Dutch, he was an affable, curious young man. The Khoi seemed at ease with him. We sat down with them on a grassy slope next to a stream. A pipe was passed. The odor was familiar: they were smoking the leaves of the hemp plant that the Indian's call *bhang*. In India, I smoked this herb several times and found it a pleasant diversion.

One old man gestured in my direction and said something to Van Scoy. The old man's skin was shiny with grease which gave off an odor of rotting flesh. He wore a lion skin kaross.

"Forgive me, Herr Tavernier, this old man asks why you have come to this country."

I leaned back, exhaled the smoke, and gazed up at the sky. The sky was bigger here and vivid blue. Thick white clouds rolled across the broad plain from the south and a gentle wind rippled the grass.

"Tell him that I am a merchant and the ship is taking me home to my country."

"I am sorry; I do not know how to say that, there is no word in their language for merchant. He asks if you are rich, how many wives do you have, and how many cattle?"

"I have no wife and no cattle."

The old fellow looked at me sternly; his face was wrinkled like a dried coconut.

"The old man says he is sorry for you."

"Sorry for me, why? I have better things to do than pick the cow shit from between my toes, and no woman tells me what to do."

Van Scoy translated. The old man laughed and shook his finger at me.

"He says he has never heard of such a thing. He asks how you build your houses if you have no dung and if you have no wife to do the work."

The old Kaffir wore a peaked leather cap like a jester, his gap-toothed smile struck me funny, and his laugh was infectious. A thick bank of clouds crested the mountain.

"Tell him that I too am a herder. I herd diamonds, rubies and pearls."

"He does not know what these are. He asks can you show him."

Why not, I thought. For security, I always carried my finer goods on my person. I drew a small pouch of rough diamonds from my waistcoat and handed several to the Kaffir. His friends gathered around him. They spent several minutes making clicking noises and examining the stones. Then the old man turned to the soldier, handed back the diamonds, and spoke for several minutes.

"Of what good are such things? They are not good to eat. You cannot use them to build your house or cover your body in winter. He says that he too is a great traveler. He has been to the north, to the dry lands where there is not enough water, and the cattle starve. He has seen pebbles like these. The children sometimes play with them. They are of no value."

"Tell him," I said to the young soldier, "that his women also wear beads, glass, and copper, and that his people trade meat for them. Of what use are these beads? Tell him that the women in Europe desire diamonds to adorn themselves and will do most anything to get them."

The pipe was passed. Regiments of clouds marched across the deep blue sky.

"It is a new thing, this wearing of beads," the old man said. "Before the Dutch came, our women would wear the entrails of pigs around their necks for decoration and wrap them around their legs to make leggings to keep off the briars. It made the women smell good. Then if they got hungry, the entrails could be eaten. You cannot eat the copper beads." The old Kaffir shrugged. "This is a great pity, but the women demand them so what can a man do?"

"It is exactly the same for us," I said.

I stretched out on the warm grass. Nearby I watched a young Khoi herdsman do an extraordinary thing. He was accosting a cow. The man held its tail in the air and appeared to have his lips glued to the cow's nether parts.

"What is that man doing?" I asked my guide. "Is he attempting to have relations with that cow?"

"No, though it certainly looks odd," Van Scoy choked back a fit of laughter. "The cow will not drop her milk, and he is blowing air into her vagina to encourage her."

"Disgusting! The cow seems quite agitated."

"Yes, you will notice that he first tied the cow's back legs together so that she cannot kick him."

I laid my head back and watched the cloud battalions. I thought about the old Kaffir's story. I am sure he was mistaken about what he saw. What a strange idea? Imagine, naked children with barely enough to eat playing games with diamonds!

Finally after gorging themselves on green stuff, the sick men were well enough to resume the voyage. We upped anchor and sailed out of Table Bay at dawn on the 13th of January, 1649. We sailed northwest stopping for a few weeks at St. Helena, an island off the east coast of Africa to revictual. After we left St.Helena, we sailed due west to pick up the favorable current off the Brazils and continued to Europe.

Chapter 27

The Duke's Mistress

My ship docked at Antwerp. I traveled overland to Paris in early July of 1649, after spending a frustrating month in Holland attempting to collect my money from the officials of the Dutch East India Company. They claimed to know nothing of any order to reimburse me for the vouchers confiscated by the director general in Batavia. The best they could offer was passage on an Indiaman returning to Asia. They suggested that I might collect my money in Batavia. I had not seen my home in six years. I gave up for the moment, acquired about two dozen mules and borrowed a dozen experienced guards from a diamond dealer of my acquaintance, secured a good horse for myself, and took the road for Paris.

I returned to my parent's house to find that my father had died just after I left Batavia, and my mother was ill and failing. My brother Gabriel was caring for her. It seemed all those I loved were dead or dying.

The room was dark; a shade had been drawn over the window to keep out the light. I could barely make out my mother as she lay, covers up to her chin with her head on a pillow and her hair was covered by a tight fitting sleeping cap. Her eyes flickered open.

"Who, oh, Jean-Baptiste, my boy! You have come home at last."

"Yes, mother, I am here."

"Fluff up the pillows, son, so I can sit up a bit."

She began to struggle to sit up. I reached forward, put a hand behind her head, and tucked in a pillow.

"There now, that's better. Now I can see you." Her cracked lips formed a smile. "Tell me, was your voyage successful? Are you well?"

"Very well, mother. I thank you, and the voyage was successful. Pierre is very pleased."

"Good, that is good! And Daniel, where is my Daniel?"

I had not the heart to tell her the truth. "Daniel is in Batavia, mother. You remember, he is doing very well and he sends you his dear love."

She bit her lip and her eyes seemed to shine vacantly out of holes set deep in her skull. Finally a glimmer of recognition, "Oh yes, I remember now. I had hoped that he would come home before, before I..."

"Shh, mother, do not tire yourself. I am home. We will have a nice long visit." Three days later my mother died.

Chaos reigned in Paris. The streets were filled with trash and barricades, shops were boarded, rumors flew everywhere, and no one seemed to be in charge. Six months before, the queen had taken the little king and fled to St. Germain. A few days after my arrival, I left my father's house and cautiously made my way to the Marais and the chateau of my old friend, the Countess Rochambeau.

Noelle was as vivacious as ever, though a bit worn looking about the eyes and mouth. "Jean-Baptiste, how long has it been? Do you remember the first time we met? You were so young and so shy, such a sweet boy."

"Noelle, it has been six years, and you are as lovely as ever. How do you do it?"

"Flatterer!" she said, tossing her head. "Such talk will get you everywhere. As to the city, these peasants have ruined the entire season. Never mind. The queen will soon return, and when she does, the parliament and the rest of the riff-raff will be put in its place."

It was a sunny summer afternoon. The servants brought tea, and we reminisced for a while about old friends and the latest gossip. Then she stood, took both my hands and looked deep into my eyes. "Enough of politics. Come, I have missed you. Let us go to my bedchamber; I have something to show you. Later we will talk."

Noelle's bedroom was much as I remembered it.

"Here," she said, turning her back, "help me out of these lacings."

I did as I was told. She had put on flesh over the years. Her skin once soft and silky as an ermine pelt had perhaps coarsened a bit. Her bodice slipped off onto the floor. I ran my hands across her shoulders, cupped her soft breasts, and felt her warmth suffuse through my hands. She leaned back against me and sighed. I buried my face in her hair.

The afternoon stretched toward evening, and the room grew dark. Noelle rose, pulled on her dressing gown and walked slowly about the chamber, lighting candles. The play of warm light and shadow set off her face to perfection.

"There, that's better. She sat down next to me on the bed, leaned over, cupped my cheek, and softly kissed my mouth. "Now, Jean-Baptiste, when do you plan to ask what you really came here to find out?"

"Noelle, what do you mean?"

She looked me full in the face and smiled.

"Am I so transparent?"

The smile turned indulgent. "Why, of course you are, dear boy."

"Dear boy? Noelle, I am forty-five years old!"

"Yes, and I am…well never mind. Shall I tell you the news?"

"Please!"

"Madeleine married her marquis a few months after you left Paris. At first things went quite well. Madeleine's charm and exotic beauty and the count's ancient name proved a perfect social combination in our insular little world. Madeleine was the toast of Paris society. The couple was seen everywhere."

"She is happy, then."

"To tell you the truth Jean-Baptiste, I rarely see her. Oh, at parties, of course, before all this nonsense started, to exchange pleasantries. At first she was caught up in the social whirl, but now I think she avoids me. She is embarrassed though she really needn't be. I would be seen publicly with her. When you reach a certain age you cease to care. My true friends would understand and for the rest…"

"I take it there is more to the story."

"Yes, less than a year after the marriage, rumors began to circulate. The marquis is an ardent gambler, though not a very successful one. Debts began to mount, bills were left unpaid. Dear boy, a gentleman may cheat the baker or the butcher, but he pays his gambling debts; it is a matter of honor. So the money dried up and with it the invitations. The latest thing I hear is that Madeleine has been seen in the company of a new man, a very powerful man, a man to whom the marquis owed a great deal of money. The rumor is that she has become his mistress."

"Who?"

"Gaston d'Orléans."

"What! Surely this is a cruel joke."

"You know better."

"Gaston, Duke of Orleans, Prince of the blood, the king's uncle and the next in line for the throne should Louis die without issue!"

Noelle nodded, "Just so, Jean-Baptiste. The inimitable "monsieur" himself."

"But Noelle, the Duke d'Orléans is a… that is to say… he prefers…"

"Boys! Yes, young boys, or so they say, but he has a wife and children. Perhaps he is a man of more catholic tastes."

I could not help but laugh, "Noelle, that was unworthy of you."

"Yes, I will burn for it, no doubt, but our duke is a very foolish man. First he plotted against his brother, the king, and Richelieu, and now that both are dead, he plots against Mazarin. He aided Her Majesty and our boy king to escape from Paris, but he also flirts with the rebels. I believe he still hopes to be king or regent at the least. Just now he is in St. Germain with my husband and the rest of the court, keeping his eye firmly fixed on Mazarin."

"I must go to Madeleine and warn her!"

"How gallant! Yes. I believe you must, but be careful, Jean-Baptiste. That man is like a plague; Gaston d'Orléans will destroy himself and any who stand too close. Mark my words. I fear for Madeleine. She must break free of him. Perhaps she will listen to you. She loves you, you know."

"Loves me? She chooses an interesting way to show it."

"Oh, you men. So naïve about so many things! A woman cannot afford such romantic nonsense. The beauty that you men worship lasts for only an instant. Once that is gone, what has a woman got? She made a brilliant marriage, or so we all thought at the time. She had a title, her position was secure, and if you had been more, ah, flexible…"

"Now, you sound just like Madeleine. I loved her and wished to marry her."

"Loved? How long has it been, this last voyage, six years, seven?"

I looked away.

"What will you do now?" she asked gently.

"I shall go to see her and warn her."

"Good! Go, go now! Tell her what I said, and, Jean-Baptiste," she said placing her hand gently on my arm, "be careful. The streets are not safe, and tell Madeleine I miss her and give her my dear love."

It was already dark when I left the Rochambeau palace. I decided to go immediately and pay a call on Madeleine. Her chateau was close by, and I knew the quarter well enough to avoid most of the trouble, but Madeleine's lane had only one entrance. I cut through an alley that brought me out on the Rue de Pas de la Mule near the Place des Vosges. Her street, a narrow cul-de-sac, ran at right angles to it. The night was clear, and the moon near enough to full that I could make out a barricade across the head of the lane. As I walked toward it, I saw a small group of figures loitering around a fire just in front of it. I was not surprised – one faction or another controlled nearly every street. Scruffy bands of ruffians manned barricades and extorted tolls from all those who wished to pass.

The shadow of a man detached itself from the group around the fire and came towards me. "Halt, who goes there?"

I pulled up my breeches, adjusted the two pistols tucked into my belt, and buttoned my coat over them so they would not be seen. "A citizen of Paris and a loyal subject of His Majesty, Louis XIV," I responded boldly.

"Advance and be recognized." This was really too much. These fellows had obviously been soldiers at one time or another and knew the sentry's language.

As I got closer it was as I thought. They were a motley looking crew gathered around a fire. A tall man stepped out to meet me with the lantern held aloft. He was unshaven and dressed in bits and pieces of a dragoon's uniform: a waistcoat with tattered pants and broken, leather calf-length boots that looked much too large for him. He carried a heavy looking cudgel in his right hand and attempted an official demeanor:

"Who are you, monsieur? State your business"

I have learned in the course of my many travels that it is never advisable to show weakness in front of such creatures, so I spoke with authority. I stated my name. "I have business at the residence of the Marquis de Chamboulet. Kindly stand aside and let me pass."

The tall man stepped closer and studied my face. "Stand aside, is it? Well now, monsieur whoever you are, we have strict orders, see, to keep the peace in this part of the quarter. I don't remember ever seeing you before. How do I know that you have business at the chateau?" He stepped back and raised his cudgel and rested it on his shoulder.

The man was not to be easily bullied, and although I had my

pistols, I was badly outnumbered. My situation was becoming more dangerous with each passing moment. It seemed prudent to adopt another tack.

"I have business at the chateau," I said in a softer tone. "I will write a note, captain. Send one of your men, and the marquise herself will vouch for me."

The man drew himself up straight. The term captain appealed to his vanity. "Well, I don't know. I have me orders."

"Here," I said, taking a card from my waistcoat pocket, "take this, and please, captain, allow me to give you something for your trouble. I stepped forward and placed the card and a Golden Louis into his outstretched hand.

He hefted the coin, bit it, studied for a moment in the lamplight, and then slipped it into a pouch at his waist.

"Never mind." He turned and, shouting to the men behind him, "This here is a gentleman. I've seen him before, and I will vouch for him. Open up there. Here you, Pierre," he ordered pointing with his cudgel, "grab that there lantern and escort this gentleman to the chateau." He turned back to me, bowed, and stepped aside.

"What about the orders." A voice responded sullenly.

I felt a twinge in my stomach and slipped my hand into my waistcoat.

He caught the movement, eyed me for a moment, and then turned toward the voice. "Is that you, Patapouf?"

"I don't want to get in no trouble, that's all." The voice came back. "You remember what that lord fellow said, Jean, and you remember what he said he would do if we didn't keep to his orders."

Another voice cut in. "He's talking true, Jean. You know it."

"And you remembers who he put in charge." The captain shouted.

"Captain," I whispered and handed him another golden Louis.

"Now see here. The gentleman here wants to hire us to keep away the ruffians, and all you got to do, Pierre, is take him down to the chateau – just down there, and he give me a gold Louis for us to share."

"What about the orders?"

Pierre stepped forward. "Here, give me the lantern. Shut up, Patapouf!" he shouted. The captain laughed and handed him the lantern.

"This way, your honor," the man called Pierre said. He turned and started down the lane.

We carefully picked our way through the piles of debris. A rat scurried over my foot, then turned, and squeaked indignantly. The garbage had not been collected in several months, and the night smelled of rot and piss. The streets were becoming a sty. We got close to the chateau. A squad of dragoons dressed in the livery of the Duke d'Orléans stood guard at the gate. My guide stopped, motioned me forward, then turned and, without a word, hurried off back the way we had come.

Torches burned in stanchions on either side of the ornamental gates and cast flickering shadows on the marble façade and the red and blue uniforms of the guards. I hailed the guard. He leveled his musket.

"Advance and be recognized!"

I expected more trouble but there was none. The guard summoned his sergeant, and I presented my card. The sergeant sent in one of his men, who returned immediately, saluted, and ushered me through a pair of massive, carved wooden doors.

"Jean-Baptiste, is it really you?" Madeleine rushed toward me in a rustle of expensive silk, took my hands, and looked me full in the face. The entrance hall was long and dark, and her voice echoed. "I could not believe it when the guard handed me your card." Here she was with that dazzling smile that I had seen so often in my dreams. I forgot everything I planned to say in a rush of feeling.

"My dear marquise, how very good of you to receive me," I said, bowing formally.

"Là, Jean-Baptiste," she said beaming, "such formality between two old friends."

"It is good to see you, Madeleine, you look…you are as beautiful as ever."

She colored slightly and smiled. "And you, Jean, you are looking well, a bit travel worn, perhaps? How long have you been back in Paris? Why have you not come to see me before this?"

"As to that, I have been back for less than a week. I have just come from Noelle; she told me where to find you."

Madeleine bristled slightly. "And a good deal more besides, I'll warrant."

"Madeleine, Noelle is a true friend; she is very worried about you. She sends her dear love."

"Indeed? Come, Jean-Baptiste," she said taking me by the hand. The servants will bring refreshments. You look like you could use a brandy. Let us talk awhile as we did in the old days."

She led me to a small, beautifully decorated sitting room off the main hall. A liveried servant silently glided about the room, lighting candles and setting a crystal decanter on the table. Then we were alone, sitting together on a small silk embroidered sofa, and one brandy became two. I had forgotten how much I enjoyed just talking with Madeleine.

"I almost forgot. I have brought you a gift." I drew the pendant from a hidden pocket and held it out, dangling from a thin golden chain. The ruby glowed like a hot coal in the candlelight. Madeleine clapped her hands with glee. She took it and held it toward the light. "Oh, Jean, it is beautiful, so beautiful."

"Like the pigeon's blood. I bought it in Masulipatam. It is small, but when I first saw the stone I knew it must be yours. It glows like your spirit, Madeleine."

She turned slightly, and I fastened the chain to her neck. The glowing red gem slid down between her breasts. Tears filled her eyes. Her smile trembled. "Oh Jean, I have missed you so. You have no idea how lonely it is in this drafty old mausoleum. The sun never shines here. It is always cold."

"But, Madeleine, you have your position and your title to keep you warm." I regretted my words as soon as they left my mouth.

Madeleine stiffened a bit and then shrugged. "Let's not fight, Jean. Are you are still angry with me!'

"I still love you."

"I hurt you. I did not mean to. I am sorry."

"And now?"

"What do you mean?"

"Listen, Madeleine, it is not too late. Your situation here… surely this is not what you want. We could go away together, leave Paris, and go back to Persia. You have never been to India. You would love India, Madeleine, and we could be together."

"What has Noelle told you?" she asked, looking away.

"I know about your husband, the debts, your situation. It is obvious. The duke's men are on guard outside your door."

She shook her head and smiled. "Jean-Baptiste, you truly are a romantic, but what you suggest is impossible."

"Why, Madeleine? You are not the cause of any of this. What sort of a man uses his wife's favors to pay off his gambling debts? If your husband was any sort of man at all, this could not, would not have happened. Will you stay here and allow this man to turn you into, into…?"

Her eyes flashed, "Into a whore?"

"No, Madeleine, I did not mean…"

"Of course, you did. That is exactly what you meant! What is it with you men? A woman is either a Madonna or a whore. Well, if I am a whore, at least I am an honest whore. What you are suggesting is that I give up everything and go traveling the world with you. What an absurd notion! Have you thought about what that would mean, for me? You are the great traveler. What will I be? We could not marry as long as my husband is alive. I would be a vagabond with no place to call home. I will certainly never be able to show my face in Paris, nor will you for that matter. Here I have position. I am the Marquise de Chamboulet. If I go with you, what will I be then? I can already hear the whispering, 'Have you met Tavernier's little bit? Quite the slut, I hear!'"

"As to that, I see no problem. I shall challenge him. You will be free to marry me once he is dead."

"Oh, yes, of course. Challenge him. He would laugh at you. He is a marquis, and you are what, a jeweler? He would have you arrested."

"Madeleine, it is important to know who you are. You and I were born commoners, and to them we will always be commoners. These aristocrats will never truly accept you into their society."

She eyed me coldly. "You think not? Everything and everyone has a price, my friend. That is the first lesson a whore learns, didn't you know? It was the first thing my mother taught me. It is the same everywhere, here or in Persia. To survive, the old noble families pimp their daughters for ready money. At court the favorite game is musical beds, and it is not played strictly for pleasure. The duke is a powerful man. I like my silks, Jean-Baptiste, and I much prefer this chateau to a mud hut. If I must bed the uncle of the king of France occasionally to pay for it, then so be it."

"He is also a dangerous man, Madeleine. Some say he plots to become king."

"Do they?" Madeline smiled wistfully. "Mistress of the king of France. Now that would be something!"

"Shhh, Madeleine, not so loud. Yes, quite something until they slip the noose around your pretty throat. Such things are not to be joked about. Treason is serious business. What of your husband?"

"Là, Jean-Baptiste, do you truly think me a conspirator? I know nothing of plots, treasonous or otherwise. The duke does not confide in me, nor, so far as I know, in my husband. Really, my dear, no one takes my husband seriously. The duke enjoys beating him at cards, and I am only a woman."

"Women have been separated from their heads for much less. Have a care Madeleine."

"Why, Jean-Baptiste," she said laughing, "I believe you are trying to frighten me?"

"Frighten you, no. I care for you Madeleine. I came here to warn you. At any rate, I give up; I fear I will never understand you."

"Of course not, my dear Jean-Baptiste." She reached over and touched my arm. "Of course not, or at least I hope not, but that does not mean that we cannot still be friends and allies."

"No," I said, petulantly.

She leaned over, and her lips brushed mine. Then she stood up and held out her hand. "Come, my love, it has been a long time since we have been together, and you have had a long day. I can see it in your eyes. Stay the night with me. It is much too dangerous to be on the streets."

"But Madeleine, the duke's guards!"

"The guards, oh, you need not worry about them. The captain is in love with my maid Shadeh. Surely you remember Shadeh, Jean! We have an understanding, the captain and I."

"Every man has his price?" Certainly I remembered the green-eyed Circassian houri whom I had first met in Isfahan and who had given me a foretaste of paradise.

Madeleine's dark eyes sparkled in the candlelight. She giggled. "Exactly," she said tugging on my hand.

What is a man to do? I woke early the next morning content but exhausted. Madeleine was asleep; she lay on her stomach, breathing softly with her lovely face buried in a satin pillow and her glossy black tresses spread like a fan across her shoulders. I lay quietly for a while on my back with my hands behind my head, stared up at the ceiling, and considered my options.

Life is strange, is it not? I lay in bed next to one of the kingdom's most beautiful women, who willingly shared her charms and in return demanded nothing whatever from me. How many men would have paid a fortune for such a privilege? But you may say, she was a fallen woman, a courtesan who dispensed her favors for gold. The world is not kind to such women, but show me a good woman, a church going woman, who bestows her favors without exacting the heavy price of marriage and constant attendance until the end of your life.

Chapter 28

Cardinal of the Queen's Bedchamber

By the end of August, the Fronde was over. The barricades came down, and the queen, the little king, and the court, including Cardinal Mazarin, returned to Paris. This was a great relief to most of His Majesty's subjects. I had business with Cardinal Mazarin, and I called upon him the first week in September.

"Ah, Tavernier, good of you to come." The cardinal smiled and extended his hand. He was dressed in a simple red vestment and wore his cap of office. "You must forgive my keeping you waiting. There has been so much to catch up with since I returned from St. Germain. I trust you have not yet sold everything."

I bowed, then shook his hand. "Not at all, Your Eminence. I acquired several larger diamonds in India that I have kept aside until I had the honor of showing them to you." In fact I had sold a number of my finer gems, but it is never a good idea to let a client, particularly one as powerful as Cardinal Mazarin, believe that the goods you are showing him have been rejected by other clients.

He nodded graciously. "Very good. I wish also to hear about your travels. I believe that trade with the Indies possesses great potential for France."

"I could not agree more, Your Eminence. I have given a detailed report to your secretary."

"Oh, yes, Colbert mentioned that. Very considerate of you, and you may be assured that I shall read it over carefully as soon as I get a moment. In the meantime," he said vigorously rubbing his hands together, "what have you brought to show me?"

I laid out four diamonds, each over ten carats. The cardinal preferred larger gems, but he did not like the Indian style of cutting. Diamonds cut in the lands of the Great Moghul are cut to maintain maximum weight.   Each stone he acquired he had refashioned to bring out the gem's rainbow of brilliance. Over the years, the cardinal became an aficionado and built a magnificent collection of large diamonds. Working with his diamond cutters, he invented a new cutting style that bears the name "Mazarin Cut" in his honor.

The cardinal carefully examined each stone, viewing it from every angle while holding it to the light. Finally he looked up from his desk, smiled, and rang a little bell to summon a servant. "Magnificent! If you do not mind, monsieur, I would like to have Monsieur Pitau, the king's diamond cutter, examine them."

I bowed. "Of course, Your Eminence."

He smiled and sat back in his chair. "So, monsieur, you purchased these gems in India?"

"Yes, my lord, three of the stones, excepting the largest, are from a mine called Kollür in the Kingdom of Golconda. The largest is from Rammalakota, another mine about seven day's journey from the first."

"And where is that located?"

"In the northeast, Your Eminence, about four weeks travel from the Great Mogul's capital at Agra."

"My God, to think such places really exist. It sounds like a fairy tale. Tell me more about the diamonds that are found there."

"What do you wish to know?"

The cardinal leaned closer. "Between you and me, monsieur, I have an opportunity to acquire the Sancy. As you know it weighs 55 carats, and it is the largest white diamond to be found anywhere in the courts of Europe, but I have always wondered, are there larger gems to be found in India?"

"Oh yes, Your Eminence, there are at least two that weigh in excess of two hundred carats. The largest is called the Great Mogul; it was given to Shah Jahan by the Emir Jumla. It weighs just under 260 carats. The other, the Great Table is above 250 carats. I attempted to buy it during my first voyage but, alas, I lacked the funds.

The cardinal placed his hand on my forearm; his eyes alight with greed. "Monsieur, should another opportunity present itself, I would be most interested in acquiring a fine diamond of that size. Would either of the stones you mentioned be for sale, and at what price?"

"I do not know the whereabouts of the Table. As for the Great Mogul, I doubt that the mogul – that is Shah Jahan – would part with it. He too is a great lover of jewels. As to the price, Eminence, Shah Jahan considers that this diamond is worth all the gold in the world."

"All the gold in the world, you say, Really! Well, yes, that would be a bit steep. Tell me what is this man, Shah Jahan, like? Is he a big man, a warrior?

"No, my lord, were Shah Jahan standing in this room, you would tower over him. He is short and slender. They say he is fearless in battle and very devout."

"You have met him?"

"I have had that honor, Your Eminence."

"He is a Mussulman."

"Yes, of the sect of Ali."

"There is more than one?"

"Yes, the Persians are of one sect, the Moguls of the other."

"How large is the capital?"

"Both Paris and Vienna could be easily contained within its walls. Agra is more than ten miles wide and as many long. For twenty years Shah Jahan has been building a magnificent marble mausoleum, the Taj Mahal. It is the tomb for his dead queen, and it is one of the great wonders of the world."

The cardinal's eyes opened wide in astonishment. "Surely not greater than St. Peter's?"

"Larger, yes, Your Eminence, though the Sistine is very beautiful."

"Monsieur, we must speak more of this. Perhaps you would honor me with your presence at dinner, say the evening after next? Nothing formal. Colbert will join us as well. He is very keen over opportunities for trade and will be astonished by your tales of India. In the meantime I am interested in your two largest diamonds. I will have Master Pitau look at them, and I will give you an answer the same night.

"Now, forgive me, but I must return to my duties. The court has been back in Paris less than a month, and there is much to do. One last thing, monsieur, I tell you this because of my confidence in you. During this late unpleasantness, Her Majesty found it necessary to pledge some of the crown jewels to pay our troops. It might be embarrassing were it to become known that I was considering a purchase at this time."

"You may rely on my discretion, my lord. If anyone hears of this, it will not be from my lips."

The dinner started off well enough. The cardinal was a charming man and took pride at playing the host. He had learned, somehow, that I am much devoted to fine wine. He brought forth some excellent French and German vintages and insisted that we try each one. As we drank, he discoursed about the wine, the grapes, and the soil where they grew.

We sat at a table in a sitting room next to his formal office.

Colbert spoke little; he seemed to endure rather than enjoy the wine.

"A glass of wine with you, my lord," I said, raising my glass.

Colbert looked up startled, raised his glass, nodded, then gamely drank off the remainder and placed the glass firmly on the table. "Can you tell me, Monsieur Tavernier, what is the yearly value of the trade between the English and the Hollanders and the Indies?"

"That is a difficult question, my lord. Both the English and the Hollanders are very close with that sort of information."

"An estimate then. Would you venture to say it is in the millions?"

"Oh, without question, my lord. Several millions, certainly."

Colbert and Mazarin exchanged glances across the table.

Mazarin rose, walked around the table, put one hand on Colbert's shoulder, and poured more wine into his glass. "My good friend here believes that the key to the greatness of France is to be found in the East. Unfortunately, at this time we have more problems than we can handle. We cannot afford to spend our gold on foreign adventures."

"I must agree with Lord Colbert, Your Eminence. There are great opportunities to be found in the Indies and fortunes to be made. The English and the Dutch are busily making treaties and building forts. The longer we wait, the more solidly they will be entrenched and the more difficult it will be to establish ourselves."

Colbert smiled warmly. "Your Eminence, perhaps we could make a small start with Monsieur Tavernier."

The cardinal laughed. "Not one, but two enthusiasts! I see that I am outnumbered. I warn you, Jean-Baptiste, do not listen to Colbert. He will try to get you involved in one of his many schemes."

"My lords, I am completely at your service."

"Yes, Jean-Baptiste, I remember well your response to Cardinal Richelieu when he asked if you believed you would take on that adventure in Germany. He told me the story. His Eminence was somewhat taken aback by your forthrightness."

"I meant no disrespect to Cardinal Richelieu."

"Yes, the Cardinal was well aware of that. I may tell you that Cardinal Richelieu held you in the highest esteem. He was … we were all very grateful for your service during that difficult time with Wallenstein."

I bowed, quite moved by Mazarin's words.

"However, we are still at war. The Habsburgs still surround France. Colbert is worried, aren't you, my lord? But he needn't be. We will win, never fear. It is only a matter of time."

"May I ask, Your Eminence, how you can be so certain?"

The cardinal smiled distractedly. "Simple arithmetic, really! In the end it comes down to numbers. The population of Spain is ten millions; the Empire and the Low Countries perhaps another ten millions. France has fifty millions. Even were the Habsburg's not a family of inbred fools, with a strong king on the throne, we must win."

"We will win more quickly if we have enough gold," Colbert said. "Look at what the Hollanders and the English have done with their small populations and the huge profits they have made in trade! With all our millions, we dare not challenge them at sea."

Mazarin sighed. "You are right, my friend, we must improve our navy, but all in good time. First, we must strengthen our borders against the Habsburgs and secure the throne for our young king. Once that is done, we shall have the time to turn our attention to India."

I was about to raise a question when a knock came at the door. The door flew open, and there stood a beautiful sandy haired young boy of barely ten years in his nightshirt, accompanied by a nurse. It was the king!

We all rose and bowed low. "Your Majesty!"

The young man studiously returned our bow and addressed Mazarin: "My lord, I have come to say goodnight. Nurse didn't want me to come, but I told her, I am the king, and I wish to say goodnight to my first minister." He grinned.

"I am honored, Your Majesty."

"Now, Uncle Jules, will you give me a horsy ride? Nurse says she will give me a ride, but she is much too gentle. You are a much better horsy."

"Yes, Your Majesty, but as you can see, just now I am busy, perhaps tomorrow. May I introduce one of your loyal subjects, Monsieur Tavernier? He is a diamond merchant and a great traveler. He has just come from India."

The boy strode up to me. "A pleasure, Monsieur Tavernier," he said looking me straight in the eye. "You have been to India? I am very interested in India. You must come and tell me about India sometime."

I hardly knew what to say. I bowed. "It would be an honor, Your Majesty. I am at your service."

"Good, I will speak to Uncle Jules, and you will come and visit me and tell me all about India. But now I must go to bed." He took a step closer and lowered his voice: "Nurse insists that I go to bed early. A king must get his sleep, you know."

The cardinal picked him up and kissed him on both cheeks. "Good night, my liege." he said and put him down.

Without another word, the king turned, took his nurse's hand, and walked out of the room.

I stood gaping. Mazarin clapped me on the back. "So now you are a friend and advisor of the king," he said with a smile. "It seems I must arrange an audience."

"So poised, for one so young," I said, astonished. "How old is His Majesty?"

"Yes, you see it, do you? He is young, barely ten, but there is steel in him. Louis will be a great king, mark my words. Come; sit down. A glass of wine with you, monsieur."

4th Voyage

(1651-1655)

Chapter 29

The Forbidden Land

I thought it was all over, the Fronde, the tempest that took its name from the slings used by the Paris mob to smash the windows of the great houses, but it was only a lull between a small upheaval and a much greater one. Mazarin's return proved to be temporary. He was the most hated man in France. His continuance of Richelieu's war against the Habsburg's had beggared the kingdom. It was rumored that he was the queen's lover, and the Paris wags began calling him "The cardinal of the queen's bedchamber." Three princes of the blood, the Prince of Condé, his brother, and the Duke of Orleans, began to plot his overthrow.

The Prince of Condé and his sister the Duchesse de Longueville schemed openly against Mazarin. In early January the cardinal struck back. He ordered the arrest of Condé and his brother, and the barricades went up once again in the streets of Paris. Under pressure from the Paris mob and the Duke of Orleans, the queen was forced to release the two princes less than a month later, and Mazarin wisely exited Paris and exiled himself to Brühl.

I had one more interview with Colbert, who gave me passports signed by Mazarin and the queen and I took the road to Marseilles on June 18th in the year 1651 and booked passage from Marseilles on the good ship St. Crispine. From Marseilles I worked my way through Persia, and on July 2, 1652, I reached the Indian city of Masulipatam.

Masulipatam is a fairly large city of detached wooden houses built on an island that can be reached by a long wooden causeway. It is known mainly for being the finest port on the Bay of Bengal. There is a small market in this city where a merchant might buy the blood red rubies of Ava. It is also just two hundred miles from the diamond mines at Golconda. I badly wanted to buy some fine rubies and perhaps arrange to visit the mines, but there were few stones and fewer traders. Most of the gems available were not worth the prices asked, and none ever claimed to have visited the mines. The way, I was told, was impassable, jungle-infested with awful fevers that no European could survive.

I am always skeptical of such statements. During the course of my travels, whenever I have asked another dealer about conditions in the countries where the gems were found, I have invariably received a similar answer. The dealer shakes his head sadly and, in the most emphatic terms, tells me of the impassable terrain, the bellicose nature of the inhabitants, and the utter impossibility of buying anything at a profit. This invariably leads to the suggestion that I buy from him at a very good price. Had I believed such talk, I would never have ventured beyond the suburbs of Paris and, like most men, would have ended my days tucked snugly in my bed without ever pursuing my dreams.

As luck would have it, during my visit to the town I encountered a Portuguese ruby trader named Pedro Ortiz. He was a short, swarthy man with a broad face, dark eyes, flaring nostrils, and a paunch that spilled over the front of his trousers. After a good deal of haggling, I managed to acquire three stones at a reasonable price.

The Portuguese was a very likeable fellow and fond of good drink, with a particular weakness for the wines of Shiraz. That city is on the road between Isfahan and Bander Abbās, and I always purchase a stock of wine on my way from Persia to India. I made him a present of several bottles. When I returned to conclude our business the next day, he insisted that I must be his guest at dinner that evening.

Now this Portuguese had, as the English say, "gone native." He lived with a Banian woman in a cluster of native shacks on the bank of the river that surrounded the city. The shack, woven of sticks with mud slathered between, had a thatch roof and was open on the side facing the river to catch the night breezes coming off the water. He had been cast out by his countrymen for taking an idolater to wife, and he was childishly grateful to have a European for company. The Portuguese in India are very proud of their pure blood and they are great hypocrites. Many a newly minted "dom" would take a native girl as mistress but would publicly condemn honest liaisons between their countrymen and native women.

On this particular evening he lured me to his house to sample his wife's *bacalao*, a stew that the Spanish and Portuguese make from salted codfish and to which I am particularly devoted. There are no codfish in the Indies, but Ortiz swore that she had found a fish that, when dried and salted, ate better than cod. Knowing his capacity for drink, I brought along a dozen bottles.

We sat back in two rickety bamboo chairs set just outside the open hut on the bank overlooking the river. Night comes quickly in the tropics, the sun soon dropped below the horizon and the sounds of the night replaced the day-bred sounds of river commerce. The moon had not yet risen, and the stars stood out brightly against the inky firmament. A pleasant breeze blew in from the river, carrying with it the pungent scent of wood smoke and spices.

The Portuguese brought out part of a bottle of sugarcane liquor from the Brazils, called *cachaça*. This is an odious concoction that had more than once played me false. To be polite, I ventured a sip and handed back the bottle with the explanation that it had a very bad effect on my stomach. Ortiz nodded, grinned, threw his head back, and drained the bottle in three long swallows. "Ah," he sighed, wiped his mouth with the back of his hand, and tossed the bottle to the ground. The woman, who I took to be his wife, labored wordlessly at the open hearth and produced a bacalao that was the best I ever tasted.

As the evening wore on and the wine began to lubricate his tongue, Ortiz began telling me stories of his life in the Indies. At one point as he seemed well into his cups, I mentioned my desire to travel to the ruby mines that I had heard were near Ava in the kingdom of Pegù. I hoped he might have some advice as to how I might proceed.

His eyes glittered in the firelight, and I braced myself for the usual talk of the dangers and difficulties of such a trip.

"Senhor Tavernier," he said his voice slightly slurred, "I think perhaps that you are trying to get me drunk." He was correct more or less, but I started to object. He raised his hand in dismissal.

"Do not worry, my friend, many have tried, but none have succeeded. Ortiz knows," he said placing his index finger alongside his nose, "it is business. You have treated me fairly, and you are a gentleman. You pay your bills. As I wish to be your friend, I will not lie to you. To visit the mines is difficult but not impossible. They are located in a deep valley, and I myself traveled to this valley many years ago."

A slight thrill ran through me. "Have you indeed, Dom Pedro?"

I said, hoping to sound as impressed by this exploit as indeed I was. But was his claim true or just a drunken boast? "I had never heard of a European visiting the ruby mines."

The Portuguese grinned, winked, upended the wine bottle, and wiped his mouth. "Well, I have done it, my friend, and I will tell you that I was not the first. The bottle stands by you, Senhor, and it is empty. If you will open another, I will tell you a tale that will amaze you." He grinned again. "Story telling is thirsty work."

Figure 13: The Inquisition at Goa; the torturing of the idolaters from a 16th Century engraving.

Clearly, I was about to hear something. Would it be the truth or a fairytale? Gem dealers are mighty tellers of tales. I pulled out the cork and handed over the bottle.

Ortiz raised the bottle in a salute then took a swallow. "I have not always been, Senhor, as you see me now," he began. "I came to India as a young man and like all young men I believed that the world was there for me to take. All I had to do was to reach out and grasp it. I worked my passage on a ship from Lisbon bearing cargo for our colony at Goa. I landed with enough gold to last me for a few months. As I cast about looking for a way to make my fortune, I met an old Hindoo.

"He was a scrawny old *cabron* who walked about half naked. A dealer in rubies. At this time I knew nothing of such things. This Idolater showed me his stock, and you, I am sure, know what I mean. I found these stones fascinating, so small, like glowing red coals, so beautiful! Here, I thought, is the key to my fortune. The Hindoo wished to sell his goods to Europeans, but he dare not show his face in Goa. The Holy Office – the Inquisition – was in full cry. They were imprisoning idolaters and Mussulmans, and forcing them to convert to the true religion.

"So I have heard."

"Yes? Have you seen it, Senhor, the Inquisition? Those who would not convert were first tortured and then, if they persisted in their errors, were burned at the stake. I personally witnessed an auto da fé in 1607 at which twenty were burnt by the river on the Campo Sancto Lazaro. Twenty, Senhor! It was the third act of faith in as many years. This was most unusual. Ordinarily there is only one in five years, but this grand inquisitor, Senhor, he was a true zealot.

"So you see if the Hindoo wished to sell his goods inside the colony, he needed a Christian to represent him. Before this, under the former inquisitor, he had done good business. So I agreed to work with him, and he became my master. I would receive a commission on each ruby that I sold, and I also made him promise that he would teach me about the gems. It was necessary; otherwise how could I sell them?

"I did very well. There were many diamond merchants in the

city but few with rubies, and my master had the finest stones. We worked together for about a year. I made a great deal of money for him and a little for myself as well.

"I made him keep his promise to teach me about the stones. At first he was annoyed by my questions, but he saw that I was sincere and shared his passion. He eventually took a liking to me and began to teach. He was an odd old man with a face like a chicken and a chest like a chicken, too. You know, Senhor, no meat on him at all. He lived alone. His house had a dirt floor and no furniture, just a rug for him to sleep on. He kept to himself and seemed to have no friends, just an old woman who cooked for him."

Ortiz took another long pull from the bottle. "After a while the Hindoo also began talking about Pegù and Ava and spoke with great longing about a valley called Mogôk, where, he said, the rubies were found. He told me that he had been married and had several children, but they were all dead. One day my master announced that he was going to the mines. We had sold most of his best stones, he said, and we would need to buy new stock. He was old, a bit lame and needed me to go with him. Of course I agreed, who would not. We would take ship from Goa to Masulipatam and from this port seek passage on a ship east across the Gulf of Bengal to Dagôn – some call it Rangoon – the city at the mouth of the great river in the kingdom of Pegù that leads north into the interior and to the ruby mines of Ava.

"It may interest you to know, Senhor, that even in the early years of this century my people had established a trading post at Dagôn, though none had been allowed to travel up river to Ava, the city nearest the mines. It is a journey of thirty days, and the king forbids all foreigners from traveling there."

"Why didn't you Portuguese just sail your ships up the river and demand entrance under threat of your cannon?"

"Ha, ha, a good question, Senhor," he said waggling his finger at me. He took a long pull on the bottle. "Ah, that is better, my throat it was getting dry. We Portuguese did a lot of that in the old days, but the river is too shallow for a caravel. You must travel by the native craft, and they are too light to carry cannon. So how was Pedro Ortiz to travel to these mines? Well, Senhor, it was then that the idolater gave me a surprise. I had told you that he was a Hindoo because that is what I believed. In those days, Senhor, I could not tell one infidel from another. Then he told me he was not a Hindoo at all, though he followed the same filthy religion; he was a Shan."

"A Shan, Dom Pedro?"

"Yes, the Shan are an ancient people, the same people who for hundreds of years had ruled Mogôk or the Valley of the Serpents as some call it, where the mines are located. The old man had been born in Mogôk, and he wished to return to his home."

"But, you?"

"Ha, ha, Senhor, this is the most beautiful part. I would accompany my master dressed as a fellow tribesman. I am of small stature and with my broad face and nose, he told me, I could easily pass for one of his race, that is, unless I opened my mouth. But the sly old devil had a plan for that, too. To disguise my accent I would play the role of a deaf mute. Ha, ha, imagine me deaf and dumb, pointing, making faces, grunting like a pig to make myself understood. An amusing idea, no!"

"Indeed yes, but it worked?"

"Ha, ha, yes, I will tell you, we took ship south for Point Galle and the east coast. Luck was with us; as soon as we rounded the point we caught the beginnings of the southwest monsoon and a fair wind all the way up the Coromandel. We arrived here in this stinking town in mid July. The luck of the Virgin was with us, and we found passage on a native dhow taking on cargo bound for Dagôn. The steady winds of the monsoon made for an easy passage, and we sighted the golden spires of the town just sixteen days after we raised our anchor."

Ortiz paused and raised the bottle to his lips, then, remembering his manners he handed it to me.

I took a short drink then passed the bottle back. "It seems, Dom Pedro, as if you had a fairly easy time of it."

The man favored me with a sour smile. "Yes, we made it to Dagôn easily enough. The captain timed the monsoon perfectly. He was a fine fellow, a Portuguese renagado like me, ha, ha, with an Arab brother-in-law, so what do you expect? But, Senhor, the journey was far from over. We now faced a journey of no less than two hundred leagues up river to the country of Ava."

"The river is called the Irrawaddy, which means 'the mother of all rivers' in the language of the country. It is broad; in some places so broad that standing on one bank, you cannot see the other side. Much shipping moves up and down the river.

"We ate rice, rice, rice traveling up the river, the entire length of the river. The voyage required two weeks. When we stayed in Ava, we ate rice. When we returned, we ate rice traveling down the river. Sometimes we would have a little fish or chicken or mutton. But I tell you, Senhor, I had a belly full of rice. What I would have given for a good mutton curry, never mind a joint of beef. That is what is wrong with the people in these countries. It is no wonder that we conquered them. They are too small and too feeble to fight from not having meat to eat. In my country we understand this; a man must have meat."

Ortiz continued along these lines through the early evening hours and into the night. The more he drank, the more talkative he became. Drink addled his brain so that his narrative wandered from his early youth to his more recent exploits, neither of which was of much interest to me. It also became clear that his romance with the bottle had cut short a promising career as he had accomplished little of note since parting company with his master. He told me the story of the entire voyage, his arrival at Ava, which is the name of the capital city as well as the kingdom. He went into great detail about his exploits there and his trip by boat and donkey into the mountains to Capelin, the main village where the miners brought the rubies to be traded.

Towards dawn Ortiz's account guttered out like a spent candle. He curled up like an old flea bitten cat on the bare ground in front of his shack and began to snore. I was exhausted, but I had learned enough. I resolved to make the trip myself, just as soon as I regained my wits.

Chapter 30

The
Emir Jumla

ver the next few days, I conceived a plan. I would be the first Frenchman to visit and buy gems at the ruby mines of Ava. Pedro Ortiz claimed that he had been the first westerner to visit the mines in fifty years. I would be the first Frank. I could not disguise myself, as he had done, so I would require another stratagem. The Portuguese ruby dealer had given me a crucial piece of information that inspired the beginnings of a plan. He told me that the king normally kept his court in the city of Ava during the wet season.

My plan relied upon a simple but stringent requirement of court etiquette. Unless he wished to offer insult, a king must personally receive a royal ambassador and accept his credentials. I would outfit a ship and sail boldly to the port of Dagôn, posing as the official ambassador of the king of France, confront the appropriate officials and demand to present my credentials to the king at Ava.

I had the passport secured by Mazarin and signed by the queen regent. It was an impressive document, written on the finest velum and sealed with the arms of His Majesty. This document named me an ambassador, though calling myself an official envoy to the king stretched the truth; however, it would serve. More was needed. I must look the part of a king's emissary. I would require all the trappings, including an impressively outfitted military escort. I decided to apply to the Emir Jumla, who was, at that time, still the chief general of the king of Golconda. He had captured the city of Gandikot from the nabob the year before and was kept busy maintaining an army of twenty thousand men on the plains outside that city.

The emir was a man who loved fine gems. He was one of the most intelligent of princes. Before entering service with the king, the Emir Jumla had been a very successful diamond merchant. In fact, at times he acted more like a merchant than a prince.

"So, Senhor Tavernier, I see we meet again. Come, sit down. I wish to hear of your adventures since out last meeting." The emir smiled graciously. He was tall for an Asian, with a swarthy complexion and a broad nose. He wore long pointed moustaches and a full beard that showed flecks of gray. He ordered the servants to bring wine.

The emir was particularly interested in my impressions of the diamond mines at Kollür. While overseer of the king of Golconda's mines, he had spent time at Kollür. This is the mine where the Great Mogul's diamond, the largest and most valuable diamond in the world, was found. Emir Jumla had acquired that gem and a few years later presented it to Shah Jahan, the father of the current emperor. The emir was a thoughtful man and enjoyed hearing a good story.

"My lord, have you heard of the fighting monkeys on the road from Pulicat to Gandikot?"

"Fighting monkeys, you say? No, I have heard nothing of them. I am afraid most of my time is taken up by the business of the army and the government. I envy you, Senhor. You travel as you wish, do your business, and enjoy your life."

"Envy me, Excellency? I am a simple merchant, and you are the grand vizier and chief of the armies of your king."

"Yes, and I had much more leisure when I was a simple merchant, but enough of my whining. Tell me about the monkeys."

"Well, on our way here, we passed through Pulicat and were well entertained by the governor. When he heard that we were journeying toward Gandikot to see Your Excellency, he suggested that we might divert ourselves by stopping in the woods along the road and making the monkeys fight. Along one section of the road between the villages of Cholavaram and Uttukottai, the road passes through a bamboo forest where the monkeys live."

"Yes, I know this road. I have marched through there with the army. The bamboo groves are so thick that it is impossible to penetrate them."

"True, Your Excellency, the bamboos are very thick. The governor told us of a place we could stop to buy rice. We bought five baskets of rice and placed them open on the road with about forty or fifty paces between and cut a dozen or so thick bamboo poles two feet long and an inch thick and placed them next to each basket. Then we drew off a short distance and waited.

"We did have not long to wait. Small groups of monkeys began to come out of the forest and gather on either side of the road. The monkeys on the left were of a different tribe from those gathered on the right. They spent a good deal of time showing their teeth and making threatening gestures, each doing his best to frighten off the other tribe so that they might feast on the rice in peace.

"After a while the females from one side, who seem bolder than the males, grew tired of the show and approached the baskets. These monkeys, like human mothers, carry their young cradled in their arms. The males from the other side rushed up and started pushing and biting these females in an attempt to drive them off. This made the males of the other tribe furious. They rushed out to protect their females. Each side grabbed the sticks, and a fierce battle ensued.

"It did not last long. The battle ended with the stronger tribe of monkeys driving off the weaker. The defeated monkeys limped off, some bloody with broken heads, others maimed. The winners then ate their fill, graciously allowing the females of the other side to eat with them."

The emir smiled and stroked his beard thoughtfully as I finished. "An amusing tale, my friend. I suppose that the monkeys fight with the sticks because men have taught them?"

"Yes, Excellency, the local villagers consider it great sport."

"Hmm, but, think, perhaps it was the other way around. Perhaps the monkeys taught human beings to fight, and it is not the monkeys acting like human beings but when we go to war, we human beings act like monkeys."

The emir had an odd point of view for a warrior, but he was right. War is, for the most part, stupid – men acting like monkeys – and it interferes with trade. The emir and I had been talking and drinking for several hours. It seemed the right moment to make my request. "Excellency, I wonder if I might ask you a favor?"

The emir sat back against the cushions, gazed at me, and nodded. "If it is in my power. Speak my friend!"

"I am in need of an honor guard."

The emir's eyes narrowed. "An honor guard, Senhor? For what purpose?"

"I am about to mount an embassy to the king of Pegù and Ava, on behalf of my sovereign Louis XIV."

The emir pondered for a moment. "Pegù and Ava, Pegù and Ava," his eyes flashed. "Of course, the ruby mines. An embassy indeed! You are seeking a pretext to visit the ruby mines."

I bowed deeply. "Your Excellency is far too canny for a humble trader, but let me amend that. I am going to try to get to the mines."

The emir waved away the compliment and sat for a moment, stoking his beard. "No foreigner has yet visited those mines. They are reputed to lie in a high mountain valley far to the north."

"I hope to be the first Frank to visit them."

A sly gleam lit up the emir's dark eyes. "Ha, ha, perhaps you shall. An emissary from a friendly king! You are an audacious fellow, I will give you that, and what is written is written. Either you will succeed, or you will fail. But I warn you, Senhor, if you fail you may find your head mounted on a pike above the city gates with the crows pecking at your eyes. I would hate to see that happen, but as they say; venture nothing, gain nothing.”

I bowed.

The emir stroked his beard thoughtfully for a few moments. “I will make you a bargain, my friend. I believe I have just what you need, a squad of men from my own guard, well dressed and well mounted. You shall review them tomorrow and decide, and if you take them, in return you agree that I shall have first pick of the results of your, ah, embassy. How say you?”

“You are most generous, Excellency. I will be honored to give you the first look at my goods.”

The guard’s uniforms were magnificent. A long blue brocaded silk under-tunic hung to their knees; the over-tunic, with epaulettes, fell just below their waists and was richly embellished with black devices on red brocade. A gold inlaid sword belt cinched the waist. The belt buckle and sword hilt gleamed with polished gold. On the head, a Mongol style steel helmet with a horsehair tassel, and on the feet, soft felt, calf length boots, fine enough for the entourage of an ambassador.

Chapter 31

Up the Irrawaddy

I now required a ship. I wished to avoid sailing on an English, Dutch or Portuguese vessel. These countries were jealous of their prerogatives, and I feared that once they knew of my plan, they would do all in their power to thwart it. I solved this problem by booking passage from Masulipatam to Dagôn on a Persian dhow with an Arab captain who knew the ports. The wind was fair for the coast of Pegù, and we completed the voyage in two weeks without a moment's misadventure.

Upon our arrival in Dagôn, I sent Danush ashore dressed like a potentate and accompanied by a translator – also lent to me by the emir – to seek out the governor of the place. I gave Danush a note, written in French and Portuguese explaining my mission and requesting permission to wait upon His Excellency the next afternoon. I prayed that Ortiz had been correct, that the king still followed the custom and had moved his court north.

Danush returned beaming. "Aga, your humble servant has

been successful. The king is not in the city. The governor will receive you tomorrow afternoon. He is called the *meoon* and is the king's brother. Aga, the captain of the guard addressed me as your lordship."

"Well, you are certainly dressed the part. What of His Majesty?"

"I was told he holds court in Ava."

"Excellent, Danush. You have done well. Now please get out of that suit before you ruin it. You will need it tomorrow, and there is much work to do before then."

We spent the rest of that day and half of the next making preparations, polishing leather harnesses and gold buttons. The voyage had been gentle and our horses were in excellent shape. My guardsmen brushed them until their dark coats shone.

The next morning the sun shown and the sky was the color of pure sapphire. We disembarked onto the quay and formed up for the parade. My guardsmen in full regalia, led the way, white silk pennants embroidered with gold fleur de lys streaming from the tips of their lances. The lead guardsmen carried flags embroidered with the French royal arms and edged in gold. The horses, pleased to be released from their confinement, preened and pranced, their coats gleamed in the sun.

Following the guards, six drummers dressed in red and blue silk livery kept time as we marched. Danush wore a blue silk turban and a silver inlaid sword, belted at his waist. I was mounted on a horse with a silver inlaid saddle and bridle, festooned with tiny silver bells that jingled as I rode along. As we marched slowly along the broad avenues of the town, work stopped, heads turned, and people gawked. Things were going as planned. It was important that the people of Dagôn be dazzled. Men in awe rarely ask awkward questions.

A double row of guards lined the walkway leading from the entrance to the palace grounds to the main entrance. On the palace porch, the governor awaited us sitting in an intricately carved chair set upon a raised dais. The palace was built entirely of dark teakwood; the roof was layered in nine sections and peaked like a Chinese hat. A crowd of colorfully dressed nobles, military officers, and dignitaries stood to either side of the dais. I noted several Europeans, Portuguese naval officers from the look of them, scattered amongst the crowd.

The palace grounds were large and beautifully landscaped with beds of flowers, ponds, and groves of acacia and sandalwood trees. I was greeted by an official who informed me of the proper court etiquette. Leaving the guardsmen behind, I approached the dais accompanied by my translator, a servant carrying a small carved sandalwood box and Danush, shading me with an umbrella.

The governor was dressed much less formally than officials of the Mogul court, except for his headgear. His hat resembled a layered cake with its apex in the shape of the male organ. He received me with formal courtesy.

"My lord, it is my duty and pleasure to welcome the ambassador of the king of the Franks," the governor said in his native tongue. I waited for the translation.

I bowed. "I thank Your Excellency and look forward to presenting the felicitations of my sovereign, Louis of France, to His Most Excellent Majesty, the king of Pegù and Ava," I answered in French.

The governor listened to the translation and frowned. "My lord," he replied in good Portuguese, "I regret that this will not be possible, at least not for several months. His Majesty is in residence at his capital at Ava. As His Majesty's representative you may present your credentials to me."

I said nothing and gazed fixedly at the governor.

After several moments, His Excellency fluttered his wings like a nervous chicken and speaking Portuguese, made an elaborate speech to the effect that, to his great and unending regret, foreigners were not allowed to travel inland in his country.

I waited until the governor finished and replied in Portuguese.

"Your Excellency, this is most irregular. It is not possible for me to remain for who knows how long. I have important letters for your king. Protocol requires that I present my sovereign's compliments to His Majesty, in person. Perhaps Your Excellency might consider dispatching a message to His Majesty informing him that the ambassador of the king of France has arrived? In the meantime, may I present Your Excellency with a token of my sovereign's esteem?" I snapped my fingers, the servant stepped forward, dropped to his knees, and presented the governor with the open box. Inside was one of the large baroque pearls I had brought from Europe.

Pearls are much sought in Pegù, and gems of this size are rarely seen. The governor's eyes widened and an astonished murmur of appreciation rose from the assembled courtiers. The governor smiled.

"My lord, I thank you for this sumptuous gift. I shall send word to His Majesty immediately. While we await his royal pleasure, I beg you to accept our humble hospitality. A villa has been prepared on the palace grounds for you and your entourage, and it is my pleasure to invite you to a feast this evening in honor of your king."

I bowed and smiled graciously and was then introduced to several of the court officials and to the Portuguese admiral. He was a stout, pompous fellow with a bulbous nose and a large amount of gold frippery smeared across his chest. He nodded civilly though it was obvious that he was quite discomfited by my arrival. The Portuguese still strutted about as if they owned the Indies, but they lacked the power to do much more than bluster. Their time was over; the English and Hollanders had become the real powers in Asia.

Because of their intolerance and cruelty, the Portuguese were despised. I felt confident that the more they protested my presence, the stronger my position would become. I took the opportunity to make a graceful exit, suggesting to the meoon – for that was the governor's formal title – that after a long journey I was tired and wished to rest before the evening's festivities.

The meoon assigned one of the court officials to guide me to my quarters and to attend to any other services my lordship might require. Well, as I have said before, in the Indies every European is a lord of one sort or another. How this little deception would end was not clear but so far so good. I was in Pegù, a guest of the governor of Dagôn.

The villa was quite spacious with ample grounds, stables for the horses, and sleeping quarters for the servants and guards. The main building, like most of the finer dwellings in the country, was built entirely of dark teak. The inside was cool and dark, even during the brightest part of the day.

The evening's festivities got off to an early start, as is the custom in that part of the world. Torches blazed. A large table was set out under a huge acacia tree on the palace grounds. The table seated forty and included every important personage in the city, including the pompous little Portuguese admiral. I was seated in the place of honor at the governor's right hand. I was pleased to see that the admiral had been seated at the far end, quite out of earshot.

Our host began with a toast extolling the virtues of our king. The drink was palm wine, a thin sour beverage with an unpleasant taste. The governor put himself out to be gracious and, between the many courses, asked me questions about our king and country. He was a dark, handsome fellow, tall and robust for an Asian. He was particularly interested in the state of our military and the armament of the ships in our navy.

The dishes were cleared and a box was placed before the governor. "Have you tried betel, my lord?" The governor asked.

The people of Pegù are the color of mahogany, and the women are comely except that when they smile their teeth are black. This is quite arresting, and it is the result of the habit of chewing betel, practiced everywhere in this kingdom and many other places in the East Indies.

"I have not."

"Then you must try it. You will find the effect most salutary."

Over my years in the Indies, I had been offered this herb many times and managed to avoid it. I am quite proud of my teeth. Despite my advanced age I still have them all, and by avoiding sweets, I have kept them white. However, I was now caught. I did not wish to insult His Excellency. I agreed to try the betel.

The concoction is prepared by taking the betel nut, which is small, black and very hard, crushing it and rolling it up in a heart shaped leaf from the same plant, which is laced with a powder made by grinding seashells.

A servant prepared a quid and presented it. The whole

procedure is disgusting. The betel is not chewed; it is packed into the cheek until it becomes a sodden wad and there it sits. After a while I did begin to feel a sense of well being, but it caused my mouth to fill with crimson colored saliva and my face to turn an unpleasant greenish hue, much to the amusement of the governor who laughed and slapped me on the back. Unless a man wishes to drown, he must spit or swallow. There is no dignified way to rid yourself of the noxious stuff. I was obliged to spit on the ground. Everywhere in Pegù you must take care to avoid splotches of bloody red spittle. And then there is the business of the black teeth.

As I said the women of Pegù are lovely to look at, that is, until they smile. The women's dress is quite distinctive; in Europe it would be considered salacious. Each wears a sort of skirt called a longji, as do the men, but the woman's garment is folded so that the fabric comes together in the front leaving a long slit that shows off their shapely legs and thighs and a good bit more. This manner of dress was decreed by an ancient queen who noticed that the men of the country were much addicted to the "English disease." She believed that if the women exhibited more of their charms, they would entice the men away from buggery.

I was obliged to wait in Dagôn until the governor received word from the king. I was anxious but the wait was by no means unpleasant. The people of Pegù are very friendly, and I diverted myself by getting to know the city and something of the customs of the people. After several weeks, a messenger summoned me to an audience with the governor.

"Ah, My Lord Tavernier, I have excellent news. His Majesty has agreed to receive you. He has ordered me to place a royal galley at your disposal."

"That is good news, Your Excellency. When may I begin the journey?"

"Any time, my friend. Tomorrow if you choose."

I bowed.

"Very well, tonight we feast, and tomorrow you shall be on your way."

The royal galley was long and narrow with a raised stern, its rail gaily decorated with carvings of strange beasts and plants. The bowsprit was fashioned in the shape of a gold leafed dragon with eyes made of magnificent balas rubies each over ten carats. A large square sail was mounted on a mast set toward the bow. The hold was specially equipped to carry the royal horses; our beasts traveled in splendor. I was given the royal cabin that was set amidships.

The Irrawaddy River widens as you sail north. At sunrise, in that season, a thick mist cloaks both banks, and the sound of the dipping oars echoes back at you from the unseen shore. As the mist burns off, the river is quite beautiful. Sometimes you can see the golden dome of a pagoda sparkling in the misty sunlight or a village outlined in purple haze against the shore. At the last hour before sunset, the river turns gold.

Chapter 32

The Royal Court at Ava

arly in the morning of the seventeenth day, we sighted the fabled city of Ava; its gold clad domes broke through the purple mist and stood against the bone-white sky like a vision from a fable. As we sailed closer, I began to make out a high, stuccoed white wall surrounding the city. Several hundred lancers,

Figure 14: The king's palace at Ava from a 17th Century engraving.

soldiers of the honor guard, stood shoulder to shoulder lining both sides of the paved road that led to the open gates of the city. They were magnificently dressed in saffron breeches with green surcoats.

It took some time for our party to disembark and form up. After their long confinement, our horses were restless and difficult to handle. I had dressed myself in a khalat that had been presented to me by Shah Abbās II. The fur-lined hat was a mistake, and despite having two servants constantly fanning me, by the time I reached the city gate, rivulets of sweat streamed down my face. I was greeted by a gorgeously attired official, the grand vizier, who stood next to a magnificently appointed palanquin.

I dismounted, handed the reins to a groom and bowed to the vizier. The vizier was an ancient, whip-thin man. He studiedly returned my bow, smiled a thin-lipped smile, and announced in heavily accented Portuguese: "We welcome the ambassador of the king of the Franks on behalf of the king of Pegù and Ava, Pindale the Great."

I bowed again.

The vizier stepped aside and graciously gestured for me to precede him into the sedan chair. Did I say chair? It was a huge, high-roofed, carved and gilded contraption that required twenty half-naked brown men to lift and carry. Thankfully, it was open on all sides.

The vizier turned to me and smiled. "My lord, you may order your guard to take up positions in front of the palanquin."

It was done, and at a signal from the vizier, the king's honor guard divided into two battalions. Each formed into precisely ordered columns, one before and one behind. We set at a stately pace along the main avenue into the city.

"My lord, we are taking you to your lodgings," the vizier informed me. "You are the king's honored guest, and you must consider this your home for as long as you choose to stay in Ava." A bony finger protruding from the flared silk sleeve of his singlet pointed languidly toward a large teak building set back off the road in a park-like setting. Fifty servants were lined up at the entrance, and all performed a charming ceremonial bow called a *sheko* as our party approached.

The official stepped down from the chair, the silk clad arm rose, and the finger gestured: "Here is your major domo." A stout man, dressed in a working man's costume, detached himself from the line of servants, rushed forward, and fell to his knees. "You have had a long journey, my lord," the vizier said. "If there is anything you need, please inform the captain of the guard. He will see to it." A tall man, obviously the captain, bowed in his turn.

"Your Excellency, please convey my thanks to His Majesty."

The vizier formally returned my bow. "I shall, and if it is convenient, My Lord Tavernier, His Majesty will receive you this evening. Your guards may escort you as far as the palace grounds, but they are not permitted to enter the grounds. A regiment of the king's own palace guard has been detailed to guard the perimeter of the villa." The vizier bowed once more, mounted the palanquin, took one more look around, and clapped his hands. The procession moved off.

It appeared that my deception was working. I had been accepted as my king's ambassador. The presence of the palace guard was of some concern, but I consoled myself in the knowledge that I was totally in the king's power, and if he truly wished to do me harm, there was little that I could do to prevent it. Truth to tell, I was enjoying myself immensely.

King Pindale was a short, boyish looking man, with a pudgy face and a charming smile. He rather reminded me of the jovial fat boy who knows he is too big to be seriously challenged by any of the other boys in the school yard.

His Majesty received me in his largest throne room, one of eight reception rooms in the palace. It was built of teak with a large full porch and multiple columns. A sea of colorful silk silently parted and formed an aisle that led up to where the king sat in a golden chair, set on a dais. I walked slowly up the aisle, preceded by a herald bearing a gold headed staff and bowed as the courtier announced me.

"Your Majesty, I bring you the fraternal love and best wishes of my sovereign, King Louis XIV of France," I said in Portuguese. To my delight he addressed me in the same language:

"You are welcome, my Lord Tavernier. I hope that my brother,

King Louis, is in good health."

"Yes, Your Majesty, our king is a robust man and enjoys perfect health. He begs you will accept these humble gifts as tokens of his great esteem." I motioned my attendants forward with my credentials and the gifts that I had brought with me, set on satin pillows. There were several gifts, a pair of pearl handled pistols inlaid with silver and gold, an enameled pocket watch, and a pair of pearls, altogether worth12,500 livres. My servants placed them at the foot of the throne. Two officials immediately came forward and held the gifts up to His Majesty for his inspection. The king nodded, and the gifts were whisked away.

The very next evening I was guest of honor at a welcome banquet, seated at the king's right hand. The king was quite affable and had an infectious laugh. He asked me many questions about my country. He was particularly interested in our relations with the Portuguese, of whom he seemed wary. I knew from court gossip in Dagôn that these scoundrels were up to their usual tricks and were putting a great deal of pressure on the king to sign an exclusive trading agreement. The king had been putting them off for some time but obviously feared offending them. I was pleased to see that there was no sign of a Portuguese presence in the city.

The two large pearls pleased the king. He was curious as to the source of such large gems. I answered his question, and then not to be upstaged, he began to speak in extravagant terms about the rubies and sapphires of Ava. This was just the turn I had hoped for.

"I have heard, Your Majesty, that the rubies of Ava are famous throughout the world. I beg Your Majesty to forgive my ignorance as I know very little of these matters. Perhaps Your Majesty would be kind enough to instruct me, for I have heard that these gems are indeed magnificent and inferior only to the rubies found on the island of Ceylon."

The king's smile faded, he bristled, and his brown face turned a dark reddish hue. The room became unearthly quiet. The change in the king's countenance was alarming; a knot formed in my stomach, and sweat broke out on my forehead. I feared that my riposte had worked too well. If I knew then what I was soon to learn, I would have proceeded with more caution.

"My dear lord, inferior?" the king asked in a soft voice. "The truth, I assure you, is quite the opposite; the rubies of Ava are the finest in the entire world. Have you ever seen our rubies?"

"No, Your Majesty, I have not had that pleasure. I have seen the gems on the island of Serendib but have never seen the rubies from your own kingdom."

"Aha," he said. His face cleared like the summer sky after a thunderstorm and broke out in a smile. "In that case, my lord, tomorrow you shall inspect our royal collection, the most beautiful rubies our kingdom has to offer. In the evening we shall dine together, and you shall give us your opinion as to which – the rubies of Serendib or the gems of Ava – are the more beautiful."

The next morning a palanquin arrived bearing two officials wearing official robes, the keepers of the king's jewels. The officials spoke no European language, so I brought along my translator. We rode to the palace and the two officials escorted us to the king's treasure room. It was a fairly small, square chamber with a high ceiling and a series of small windows set high up in the walls. The walls were of brick that was plastered and whitewashed, and windows were cunningly arranged to capture the sunlight from all four directions. The windows were set too high and were too small to allow anyone to enter through them into the chamber.

The taller of the two officials invited me to sit. I settled myself on a thick rug in the center of the chamber, and he brought two carved sandalwood chests with sliding drawers. The younger man with the shaved head of a eunuch knelt down and drew out the drawers, one after another, and placed them before me on a pillow of golden silk.

The stones contained in the first chest were all rubies, large and small, some cut, some still in their rough state. Their color was remarkable; some were a true red; others inclined towards the pink.

"These are rubies of the finest quality," the translator told me, pointing to the reddest gems. "They are called *lai-the-yae* in our language, when they show a bit of blue; we call them *kuthway,* or pigeon's blood in your tongue. The second quality, with a bit of orange, is *yeong-twe* or rabbit's blood. The more pink is called *beef blood*." I had, of course, seen rubies from Ava in the past, but these were exceptional, the colors far more vibrant than the rubies of

Serendib.

I was then shown another tray that contained much larger stones – some with crystal shapes not unlike fine diamond crystals – like two perfectly shaped pyramids put together at their bases.

"These are the spinels, or false rubies," my translator explained. "These," he said, pointing to several perfect red crystals, "are called *nat thwe*. The words mean 'cut by the spirits.'"

Once I had seen them all, the taller official nodded to the eunuch who reverently opened a square lacquer box. The gem was taken from the box and presented on a polished brass plate. It was breathtaking, the most beautiful ruby I had ever set eyes upon.

"This is the *Naga Mauk,* the finest ruby in all the world." said the translator reverently. "It is the true pigeon's blood color. There is a saying among my people, Senhor. 'To see the pigeon's blood is to know the face of God.'"

The gem was the size of a small apple, and it weighed a bit over ninety ratis or about eighty Florentine carats. The gem had been found and presented to King Pindale by a rice farmer by the name of Naga Mauk, who came upon the gem while working his field. It had been cut into a high-domed cabochon and set in a gold ring. The color was a pure brilliant red with just a touch of purple, and it glowed like a red hot coal.

I left the king's strong room, sated with the beauty of the king's collection. The officials sent us on our way by palanquin, though I would have much preferred to walk rather than sit in that ungainly machine. As we made our way back towards the villa, the translator looked around nervously then asked in a lowered voice: "Have you heard, my lord, the story of the Naga Mauk ruby?"

"I have not."

The man nodded. "You have seen that His Majesty is much devoted to rubies. By royal decree, all rubies mined in the kingdom that weigh more than seven ratis must be turned over to the royal treasury. When the farmer, Naga Mauk, found the ruby, he did not wish to give it up. He was a poor man with a wife and children to feed, and the gem was worth a fortune. So he divided it along a flaw, almost in half. He gave one half to the king and the other half he entrusted to his brother to sell quietly in the market in the kingdom of Arakan."

"I have heard that such things happen."

"Yes, quite often, and all would have been well, except that sometime after acquiring the ruby, King Pindale gave sanctuary to a certain Chinese emperor who had been deposed by the Moguls. This prince brought with him a large uncut ruby and presented it to the King. When His Majesty examined it, he saw that it fit together with the Naga Mauk, like the piece to a puzzle. The king realized what had happened and was enraged. He ordered the execution of the miner and all of his family, Senhor, down to the seventh generation."

"That seems a cruel fate."

"Indeed it was, my lord. The king's soldiers gathered up the man's family, his parents and all of his children, herded them into a stable and burned it to the ground."

"His whole family burned to death?"

"No, his wife, Daw Nann, escaped death. She was not in the village at the time, but her fate was no less cruel. She stood and watched helplessly as the flames consumed her family. She saw it all from a hill near the town of Kyatpyin. The hill is now called Daw Nann Kyi Taung, 'the hill from where Daw Nann looked down.'"

The entire court was present that evening. I could not help but notice that all talking ceased and the chamber became silent as I made my way to the dais. His Majesty acknowledged my greeting, and, with a straight face, bade me sit, took my hand, and looked into my eyes: "Now that you have seen the rubies of Ava, my lord, tell us your opinion of their quality."

"Your Majesty," I said, and as I spoke I prayed he could not hear the tremor in my voice, "never have I seen rubies so beautiful! You were correct. The rubies of Serendib pale in comparison with the peerless gems of Ava. May I sincerely thank Your Highness for instructing me and allowing me to see your magnificent collection?"

The king's demeanor changed completely. He clapped his hands with glee, all the court cheered, and I took a deep breath. His Majesty motioned to one of his servants who brought forth a small but beautifully carved sandalwood box, which the king presented to me with his own hands. Inside was a large ruby from his collection, one that I had particularly admired, weighing almost six ratis, over seven of our carats. It was an oval gem without flaw and of the finest water. He also presented me with a saffron bag containing several smaller gems along with three blue sapphires, the largest about the size of the upper digit of my thumb, weighing 25 carats, a balas ruby of a slightly pinkish water, and a large bag of uncut tourmalines. This was a magnificent gift. The smaller gems alone would have made for a good profit from my journey.

After the dinner had been cleared, the king dismissed the court and invited me to retire to a small sitting room with a few of his most trusted courtiers.

The king took a drink from his goblet, made a face, leaned over, and asked in a low voice. "Palm wine! Lord above, Senhor, do you, by chance, have anything to drink other than this rancid stuff?"

"Why yes, Your Majesty, I do. May I offer you a borracho of shiraz?"

"Shiraz, did you say shiraz, my lord?" His eyes glittered with lust. "Not a drop of that heavenly wine has passed my lips in ten years or more."

"Well, we must correct that. I shall send a servant …"

He put his hand on my arm. "No, no, not now. Say nothing, my friend. You have no idea how much these greedy courtiers can consume. Tomorrow evening I shall dine alone with you at your villa." He winked. "I am tired of all this ceremony, and, there will be more shiraz for you and for me!"

His Majesty dined at my villa often. The king was a prodigious drinker. He enjoyed shiraz, but he was also quite fond of French wine, brandy, arrack, and just about anything with alcohol, other than palm wine. Together we drank through most of my stock. Drinking seemed to improve His Majesty's temper, and we often talked together late into the night. One night, after a particularly long drinking session, I raised the subject of the valley of rubies.

"You wish to see Mogôk?"

"Yes, Your Majesty. I come from a temperate climate, and the heat is beginning to disoblige the balance of my humors."

"You are not feeling well? Why did you not say so? The weather in the mountains is cool this time of the year, but I warn you, my friend, the road can be dangerous. The mountains are filthy with dacoits, but never fear, I shall send a battalion of my guards to accompany you. How is that?"

I bowed and filled his cup.

He took a sip, lowered his cup, waggled his finger and smiled. "Don't forget my friend; any large rubies you find belong to the king, ha, ha!"

I bowed. "Of course, Your Majesty," I said with a smile. "You have the word of the ambassador of Louis XIV, king of the Franks."

Chapter 33

A Test of Cold Steel

The rising sun has just crested the hill on our left hand. Our boat rounds a bend in the river. The captain gestures toward a small group of huts, clustered by the riverbank, just visible through the gray mist. "Thabeit-Kwin," he announced. Thabeit-Kwin was a tiny village located on the left hand side of the river just twenty leagues from the mountain town of Kyatpyin in Mogôk, the valley of rubies. We were a day upriver from Ava, and my destination was within reach.

I was the first off the boat. I scrambled up the high bank, and Danush and my translator followed. A goat, startled by these apparitions rising from the mist, scampered off into the bushes. Along the path just south of us, a few huts made of plaited bamboo rest in the shade of a large banyan tree. On either side of th path, the waist high brush had dried brittle as fish bones. We walked toward the village. From the shade of a grass-roofed hut a man bestirred himself, rose, and tottered slowly toward us.– He performed an elegant little bow and began speaking. He was a thin old man dressed in faded blue silk, the village headman. My translator bowed and explained who we were and our purpose. We had a few porters, but our party had grown, and we would need more, and mules as well. The headman nodded and led us into his village.

Our party now included fifty of the king's soldiers and was over one hundred strong, but King Pindale warned me that these hills swarm with dacoits, local bandits who accept no man as their master. Our route would lead us over goat trails, over steep mountain passes.

Danush, our guard's captain, the translator, the captain of the king's soldiers, and I stood in the shade of the headman's hut gazing up at the mountains that lay between us and our destination.

"Aga, these mountains remind me of home. The land here is dry," Danush observed shading his eyes.

"Yes," our translator agreed, "but a month from now, perhaps two, the rains will come, and these trails will be thick jungle."

"Then we have chosen a good time."

"Yes, my lord, if we are lucky and the monsoon does not come early. The road to the mines becomes impossible particularly with loaded pack animals."

"And if we are unlucky?"

"Then we must remain in these mountains until the rains moderate, three months perhaps four."

"What is written is written," Danush said.

The translator looked at Danush and shook his shaggy head. He was a short, thin dark man, an idolater, half of the race that lived in India long before the Moguls came. He spent most of the years of his youth in Pegù, the son of an Indian sea captain who married a Shan woman. "Aye, first we must get to Kyat Pyin and hope that their prince, the sabwa, will aid us."

"We have letters from the king and are under his protection, are we not?" I asked.

For the first time the captain of the Burmese soldiers spoke up: "What you say is true, My lord, but the Shan hate us, and the sabwa constantly schemes to throw off the king's yoke. Ten years ago this prince was at war with our king. The king fears that the sabwa is attempting to rebuild his army, and so he refused to allow him to recruit more soldiers. If we were to disappear, the sabwa would blame the dacoits and remind His Majesty of his many requests for more soldiers to suppress the bandits."

The young captain of my Mogul guards straightened his shoulders and grasped the hilt of his sword. He and his men have done little other than parade since we left India, and he was anxious to prove himself. "No bandit can stand against Mogul steel," he says.

I could name one or two who had, but it seemed impolitic to mention it to the captain.

Early the following morning we began the journey up the mountain. It was hot and the dark blue-gray sky was brooding and cloudless. The king's infantry took the lead. I, my servants, and our pack animals had been placed in the center of the column, and our Mogul guardsmen brought up the rear. The trail was rocky and so narrow that we were forced to proceed single file stretching out the column, which made us more vulnerable to attack, but we had little choice. Our first day's travel brought us to a village called Wapyi-daung about ten miles into the hills.

Our next stage led toward a second village called Kyaukebin. It was only six miles, but the trail wound between clusters of large boulders and the climb was difficult. Bandits favored this stretch, and we had to beware of ambush. Before we set out that morning, the headman warned us that a band of dacoits was spotted two days before in the hills above his village.

The morning passed without incident. Looking back down from the mountain, I had a view of the Irrawaddy River snaking across the plain and losing itself at the horizon. The sun was relentless. By mid-afternoon I was exhausted. My mouth was as dry as dung. During my short career as a nobleman, I feared I had gotten soft. I looked back at Danush. He smiled bravely, but I could tell that he was barely able to place one foot in front of the other.

Our party was strung out all over the hillside. My mind told me this is dangerous, but I was too tired to care. We had been walking since early morning with just a short break for the mid-day meal.

It was two hours, perhaps a bit more, before sunset. We were struggling to make it to Kyaukebin village before nightfall. Even with a large party, it was too dangerous to camp along the trail at night, and there was no water.

The attack came out of nowhere. Just ahead of me one of our bearers staggered, clawing at the arrow that sprouted from his throat. His jaws worked up and down soundlessly like a puppet until he pitched forward, sprawling dead on the broken ground. Danush and I drew our swords and looked around. We had lashed our heavy muskets and pistols onto the pack mules ahead of us thinking we could retrieve them quickly at need, but the mules had worked their way a hundred yards further up the trail – it might as well have been a hundred leagues. Bare-chested dacoits materialized out of thin air from both sides of the trail. Musket shots, shouting, and the sound of a cavalry horn echoed off the rugged hillside.

Short swarthy men dressed in baggy trousers came at us with long knives and heavy short swords like scimitars. The first bandit to cross my path walked into an overhand slash from my rapier that sliced him open from shoulder to hip. I set my back against a huge boulder. To my left, Danush had engaged one of the bandits. A huge, almost naked bandit appeared like an apparition from behind a boulder just across the path. Wild-eyed, he charged toward me swinging his scimitar like a hammer. I raised my sword and parried, but the force of his blow buckled my knees and drove me to the ground. My arm was numb and my shoulder was on fire. His huge shape loomed grinning above me. Just as the bandit raised his sword to finish the job, his eyes opened wide in surprise and his mouth formed the letter O. Danush had moved in behind and slashed sideways behind his knees. The bandit crumpled. Now with the man reduced to a manageable size, Danush stepped forward and neatly sliced off his head. My servant grinned as the head bounced off down the trail. The dacoit's body pitched forward into my lap soaking me in a fountain of blood.

I pushed the body off and scrambled to my feet. Two more attackers emerged from the rocks. The first one was quite short. I instinctively performed a classic lunge. The point of my sword slid over the man's raised forearm and pierced his throat. Out of the corner of my left eye, I saw Danush was in trouble. He gamely parried a vicious overhand stroke, but his attacker was stronger and a more practiced swordsman. My servant's attacker stood parallel to me with his right side exposed, the perfect target for a left-handed swordsman. I jerked the point of my blade from my man's throat, sidestepped toward Danush's attacker and just as he was about to penetrate my servant's guard, cut left slashing through the muscles beneath the bandit's ribs. The man fell, blood and steaming offal spilling like a waterfall from his gaping wound.

The attack ended as abruptly as it began. The bandits seemed to melt into the rocks. I looked around to assess the damage. It could have been much worse. From what I could see, eight of the king's men were dead, three wounded. Two pack mules and four horses had been killed and two so badly cut up that they had to be destroyed. I counted eighteen bandits dead along the trail. We left them where they fell, food for the buzzards that had already begun to circle. Our guard's captain came forward, bloody sword in hand. Our rearguard suffered two dead.

We reached our destination at dusk, stopped, and took stock. This village was smaller than the last but better located for defense. To mount an attack, the bandits must cross a small bridge over a narrow defile. Our guard's captain posted two men on each side. We stopped for two days to bind up our wounds and rest. From there the trail wound uphill past a monastery called Swe-u-daung, and then crossed another river. The headman thought we would be safe from here on. We had been tested: the dacoits had paid a bloody butcher's bill and would leave us be.

We climbed steadily. The monastery perched on a high cliff, its golden dome shimmering in the sun. Three days later we crossed a bridge over the Kin River and entered a small village situated alongside it. Rice fields stretched out like a green carpet. Another long day's march and we breasted a mountain ridge. Our destination stretched out before us.

Centered in the meadow clad valley, the town of Kyat Pyin was small and spread between sixteen small lakes that dotted the lowlands. The valley air was cool and bracing after the steaming heat of the lowlands.

Chapter 34

Valley of the Serpents

anush and I called on the sabwa the day after our arrival in the village of Kyat Pyin. This prince keeps a small palace in the center of the town which he uses when he travels here from his capital at Momeik. I recall his name – Sao Yun Pha. He was a plain spoken, grizzled old campaigner. He received me without ceremony, dressed plainly in a cotton lungyi and a simple head cloth. In his youth, he fought and lost a war against the king's father, King Thalun. I found him stretched out in the sun, dozing like an aging lion.

Just as we approached, he jumped to his feet. "Greetings, your lordship, and welcome to my humble valley," he said, smiling through black, broken teeth. "You must be a very important man to have the king's guards to escort you." To my surprise he spoke perfect Portuguese.

I bowed to hide my surprise. This was obviously an old lion whose claws might be blunted but he still retained his eyes and wit. "I thank Your Highness. I have come to see your beautiful mountains and enjoy the brisk mountain air."

"Mountain air, is it?" He cocked his head and looked me over with narrowed eyes. "Bah, take the mountain air is it? If you have come for that, you are the first."

"I have heard many stories about the wonderful rubies to be found in the valley."

The old man smiled slyly. "Rubies, aye, that is more like it. Did you bring gold?"

"I did, Your Highness!"

"Good, good. Then you will get your belly full of rubies, like as not." He rubbed his chin thoughtfully then winked. "You seem a likely enough young fellow." His eyes narrowed. "Have you seen our king's collection?"

"I have had that honor."

"Hmm, then maybe you know what you are about. You know the king's law? He is a harsh one, the Burman king." He placed one finger up next to his nose. "These eyes may be old, but they still see, if you take my meaning. We are very strict in this village about the king's rights."

"I understand."

"Good, then tonight you will come to my villa and eat with me. Just the two of us, you understand."

"I would be honored, Your Highness."

"Yes, I expect you would, and mayhap I might be able to find a few choice bits to show you. I can change your gold as well. No promises now and I must return to my nap. Good day to you, my lord!"

I dined with this old lion several times during my stay in the mountains and like everyone else in Kyat Pyin, he was a gem broker and found me several good rubies.

The next day I got my first glimpse of Mogôk, the legendary Valley of the Serpents. Danush and I, accompanied by our translator, spent several days strolling about sightseeing and letting it be known that we were interested in buying gems.

There are, at most, five thousand people involved in the mining. The work is a family affair. The method for extracting the rubies was quite different from those used to mine diamonds at Rammalakota and Kollür. The Shan miner digs a narrow shaft called a *twinloon* straight down until he reaches the *byôn*, as the miner's call it, the coarse sandy clay layer where the gems are found. The miner then burrows sidewise into the gem gravel like a badger building his nest, sending up bucket after bucket of the byôn to the surface.

Primitive cranes stick up in the air above the shafts like a forest of fishing poles. They are constructed of two bamboo poles, one driven into the ground, the other lashed across it like a child's seesaw. A bucket is tied to one end and a large rock is tied to the other as a counterweight. One miner fills the bucket, another raises the precious gravel to the surface.

Wives and sometimes children squat in the cold streams and rivulets that flow down from the steep tree-clad mountains. Unlike the diamond mines in India, water is in good supply. The women wash the byôn in shallow rattan baskets, swishing back and forth, sluicing away the red mud, their sharp eyes seeking a tell-tale glimmer of fire.

We came upon a young miner working in the bottom of a hole— He was burned brown as the dirt and his thick ropey muscles stood out on a back glistening with sweat. My translator saluted him. He squinted up at us, using his hand to shield his eyes from the hot afternoon sun, favored us with a toothy smile, bowed then bent back to his work.

My translator cupped his hands round his mouth and hailed the fellow.

The miner paused, raised his head and looked up at us questioningly.

"Yes, my friend, I am speaking to you. "Have you found any rubies?"

The young man smiled, scratched his nose, thought for a moment, grinned and held up three fingers.

My servant turned to me, smiled and shrugged helplessly:

"Well then, come up and let us have a look."

Obediently, the young fellow clamored up a wooden ladder made from the thick notched trunk of a single tree. He plucked a nodule of stone from his waistband, held it to the sun, wiped it on his ragged pantaloons and squinted at it. He spat on it, wiped it again and placed it gingerly into my open hand. He bowed, stepped back and smiled shyly.

"I thought he said three?"

"My apologies, aga, the fellow must be simple. Speaking slowly and distinctly, he repeated the question.

The miner stopped, scratched his ear then slid his dirty fingers into his garment, felt around a bit then out they came with two more red pebbles which he proceeded to put through the same process as the first before handing them over.

Finally I had three glowing pebbles in the palm of my hand. The color was very good. I judged that they would cut gems of over two carats each.

"These look interesting. Ask the man to name his price for all." I said.

The two clasped hands, my man unwound his neck cloth and draped it over the clasped hands. The two men gazed into each other's eyes and though they hardly moved and not a word was spoken, it was clear that some sort of communication was taking place. The men smiled, frowned, grunted and grimaced and shuffled their feet. Finally my man nodded, withdrew his hand and signaled to me to walk off with him for a quiet word.

"Lord Tavernier the miner has set a price, he asks…"

"What, he gave you a price, how?

"Just then, we used the hand talk."

"Hand talk you say, that was the most unusual procedure I have ever witnessed. Kindly explain."

My servant bowed. "Please excuse me, lord, I had forgotten that a foreign gentleman might be unfamiliar with our manner of doing business. It is a very old custom. As you observed it allows us to keep our bargaining private. If you will allow me to clasp your hand, my lord. You see we have five fingers and each can be divided in two at the knuckle, so we have the numbers from one to ten."

"Ha, ha, ingenious! You must teach me this hand talk."

"I would be honored, my lord. It is quite simple, with a bit of practice you can easily master the technique."

I named my price and the two men resumed their odd colloquy."

My servant turned back to me. "Aga", he said shaking his shaggy head, "this fellow does not wish to bargain. He says that you are a great lord and he knows that you will pay him a fair price. You may take the stones. He will come to your lodgings tomorrow morning and collect whatever payment you decide to give him."

Danush tugged at my sleeve and rolled his eyes.

"This is foolishness. Tell him that I like his stones and I wish to offer for them, but we must agree on a price" I said.

The translator spoke for quite some time to the young fellow who just stood looking down and shaking his head slowly back and forth.

"Aga, I am sorry, this fellow is quite stubborn! He says that he knows you will not cheat him" the translator said.

Danush shrugged. "Aga, if a chicken chooses to place his own head beneath the knife..!"

"Very well", I said, "tell him to be at our lodgings just after sunrise and I will pay him."

I placed the stones in a small leather bag I carried tucked into my bosom and stalked off mumbling to myself. Surely, the young man was mad, but I turned the matter over in my mind for the rest of the afternoon and into the night.

The sabwa had exchanged some of my gold for lumps of silver *yowetni* or blossom money as they call it in those parts. When I placed the silver pieces in his hand, the young miner looked me in the eye, bowed, grinned and left without a word. In the end I had negotiated for him a far better price than he could ever have obtained for himself.

I rented several small houses to accommodate my retinue and hired a cook and several servants to look after me. The word of our presence spread quickly and by the fourth morning, sellers began to queue up at my gate early each morning to wait patiently in the gray morning mist.

The nights were cold and each evening my servants lit a fire. Snow sometimes appeared on the mountaintops, but the days were warm and sunny. I spent most of my time looking through parcels of rubies, sapphires, and diverse other gems mined in the hills surrounding the valley. I took my midday meals squatting at an outdoor eating shop, slurping the tasty soup, and sitting and talking with the local people. I found this mountain sojourn very much to my liking. In the evenings, Danush and I would sit together on our verandah and enjoy the cool mountain air.

"Aga, may I ask you a question?"

"Yes, of course, Danush. What is it?"

"Do you believe in God?"

"In God! Why, yes, of course. Why do you ask?"

"You are a Nazarene?"

"Yes, Danush, I was raised as a Christian, a Protestant Christian. I am a Huguenot. And you are a Mussulman?"

"Oh yes, aga. I am very devout. I bow towards Mecca, and I say my prayers every day, and someday I shall make the Hajj, the pilgrimage to Mecca."

"Why do you ask if I believe in God?"

"I never see you pray."

"Danush, we Christians do not pray five times a day as devout Mussulmans do. Many Christians pray in private, and usually Christians attend services and pray on Sundays.

"You do not pray on Sundays."

"Well, true enough, but I am not very devout."

"But, you believe in God?"

"Yes, Danush, I believe in a God."

"You believe in more than one God?"

At this I had to laugh. "No, my friend. I believe there is one God, but some men believe that this God has no interest in us and that we need not take much interest in him."

We were sitting outside on a verandah and it was very dark, but I could tell by the tone of his voice that he was becoming quite agitated "Aga! Is this what all Nazarenes believe?"

"No, this is what some philosophers believe. There is an Englishman named Bacon…"

"Bacon, excuse me, aga. This is meat from a pig, is it not?"

"Yes, I mean no. This is also a man's name, an English philosopher, Francis Bacon. I have read his book."

"Odd, a man named after a pig. No believer in the true God would endure such a name. I mean no disrespect, aga. He has written a book so he must be a learned man. What does his book say?"

"It is not only Mr. Bacon, but I have read other books. There is a Frenchman named Descartes."

"And this Frank, he has written a book, also?"

"Yes, Danush. This is very difficult to explain, but these men propose a new way of thinking about God. As Christians we believe we have faith that God exists and that he cares about us, but we cannot know this for sure. All that we know about God is what we have been told by other men. How do we know that what these men have told us is true?"

"This is very interesting, aga. I will confess to you that although I am a faithful believer in the true God, I too have questions the mullah could not answer. When I asked these questions, he became very angry and said I was stupid. When I asked more questions, he beat me."

"Danush, you are not stupid. Perhaps your question was so intelligent that he could not answer it, which made him feel stupid, and for this reason he became angry, and that is why he beat you."

"Do the priests of the Nazarenes behave in this way?"

I smiled to myself. "Oh, yes, quite frequently. You have seen the Inquisition in Goa."

"Yes, aga, I have been with you to Goa twice and everyone fears these priests."

We spent almost two months in the valley and by the end of that time I had spent most of my capital. But I had gold I had left in India, a fabulous stock of rubies, and some large fine sapphires.

After the better part of two months in Mogôk, I returned to Ava and took my leave of King Pindale. The king presented me with yet another fine uncut ruby equal in size to the first. He had been most gracious and expressed a desire to discuss a treaty of friendship with France. I dutifully passed this on to Cardinal Mazarin upon my return to Paris, but, I am afraid, little came of it.

Chapter 35

A Hard Bargain

pon my return to Masulipatam, I started off at once to Gandikot to keep my promise to Emir Jumla. The trip took three days. I found the nabob much as I had left him, taking his ease among his troops.

"Ah, my dear Tavernier, you have returned. I see that you managed to escape with your head."

"Yes, Your Excellency, and I achieved what I set out to do."

"Did you, by God? Sit down!" The emir clapped his hands. "Ali, bring wine! The Frankish lord will eat with me." He turned back to me. "Now begin at the beginning. Hold nothing back. I wish to hear the whole story."

The emir found my account quite amusing and showed great self-possession, but as the meal wore on, I could see that he was becoming impatient to see some of the jewels. I drew out the leather pouch containing a large ruby. The emir opened it and let the ruby fall into his open hand. His eyes widened at the sight of this gem.

"By the beard of the prophet, this is magnificent! I must see it tomorrow in daylight."

"If it please you, my lord, keep the gem with you overnight and examine it at your leisure in the morning light," I said rising. I bowed and took my leave knowing that I had made a sale.

The next day at about noon I waited upon the emir. He had left orders, and I was immediately escorted to a small chamber perched at the top of one of the fort's towers. This chamber was open in all directions. Gandikot's citadel is called Bhuvanagiri. It sits perched on a bare gray rock three hundred feet above the town. From this height, the river that fertilizes the valley gleams like quicksilver, and the rice paddies roll away towards the mountains like an emerald carpet.

The emir was seated at a small wooden table in the center of the room with the ruby set before him on a polished brass tray.

"As you can see I have been studying your ruby. Marvelous color, the finest I have seen, and quite large for a ruby. You saw larger ones in the king's treasury I'll warrant."

"One or two, Your Excellency, but none finer."

"I believe the color shows a bit of orange. What is your opinion?"

"Perhaps a touch, Your Excellency."

"Hmm, I know some prefer a bit of blue. It appears a truer red when set in gold, but I like the way the orange brightens the hue. Six ratis is really quite large for a ruby from Ava. I have seen stones from Serendib that are larger, but none had the color. What is your price, senhor?"

"My lord, you have been dealing in gems for many years. May I ask you a question?"

The emir nodded.

"In your experience, my lord, just how rare is this gem compared to say a diamond of equal size and quality?"

The emir's eyes held mine for a moment, and my heart jumped. I feared that I had offended him. Finally he said, "To be honest, my friend – I think you know this very well – this ruby is a gem of the first water, and it is at least one hundred times rarer than such a diamond."

"Thank you, my lord, for your honesty. We are both aware that a gem such as the one you hold in your hand is something rarely seen. It is so rare that it is difficult to put a price on it."

The emir nodded. "That is true."

"So to compare it to a diamond seems to me to be a reasonable approach. I am much of the same mind as you, my lord. The ruby is one hundred times rarer; therefore, let that be the price."

The emir looked up, his eyes locked on mine. "What? You are asking one hundred times the price of a diamond of the finest water?"

"Yes, my lord."

For a long moment the emir eyes held mine. Then a smile creased his face, and he laughed. "Very neat, senhor, very neat indeed! A clever gambit. You have skewered me like a wild pig squealing at the end of my own lance. You will go far, senhor, very far – that is, if you live. I would suggest that you not try that trick on the emperor. He would separate you from your head." He shook his head. "I have half a mind to do so myself."

"Your Excellency, I…"

The emir raised his hands in a negative gesture. "Just a little joke, my friend. I envy you. I would give much to make that voyage with you once again as a simple merchant. No war, no politics! But, alas, that does not seem to be my fate. Now tell me, senhor," he said, the smile fading from his lips, "we agree that the stone is worth one hundred times the value of a diamond. Will you accept payment in kind, in diamonds?"

It was now my turn to be wary. I hesitated. "Do I understand you correctly, my lord – one hundred diamonds of the finest water weighing at least six ratis each?"

"That is my offer. As it happens, I have recently come into the possession of a large number of diamonds, formerly the property of a certain rajah who kindly, ah, vacated the city, leaving them to me as a token of his esteem." The emir eyed me archly, a slight smile at his lips. "Come, come, my dear Tavernier, a worthy trade and a princely sum in diamonds."

I bowed deeply. "My lord, I know when I have met my match. May I see these gems?"

"But of course." The emir clapped his hands. "Ali, will bring them to us here? You may make your choice. I am interested in your opinion of the lots. There is, however, one other piece of business – the use of my guards in your latest, ah, venture!"

I had come prepared for this and reached into the pocket of my waistcoat and took from it a pouch containing a blue Mogôk sapphire the size and shape of a walnut, flawless and of a fine clear peacock blue water. I slid it from its pouch and rolled it across the table to him.

The emir snatched it up and held it to the light. A sigh of pleasure escaped his lips. He turned to me with a broad smile. "Upon my head, senhor, this is a princely gift! I have never seen finer. It is worth far more than the small service that I rendered you. I can see that you are a man of honor. For this you have my deepest gratitude, and you shall have my personal passport and an escort of my guards whilst you remain in the lands of India."

The servant returned with five heavy leather bags. Two of them were filled with flat stones of indifferent quality, two bags contained large, fine diamonds, and the other was a mixed lot of smaller stones. It took most of the day to sort through the bags and make my choice.

The emir examined my selection. Altogether they weighed a bit more than 700 ratis, or 650 1/4 Venetian carats – a king's ransom. Emir Jumla carefully examined my selection.

"You have chosen well. Are you satisfied?"

"Well satisfied, Your Excellency, and I thank you," I said, meaning it. "It is always a pleasure to do business with an honest man".

The emir smiled. "I have heard that you are the son of a map maker. I too come from a humble family. My father was an oil seller in Isfahan. Henceforth I shall think of you as my good friend. If there is any service that you require, at any time, you may call on me. Now I must ask you to excuse me. I have business that requires my attention. You will dine with me this evening, and we will speak more of the lands of Ava and Pegù."

Several days later I bid goodbye to the emir. I traveled to Surat in an ornate palanquin provided by the emir. Like the diamonds, it had formerly been owned by the king of the Carnatic. My retinue now comprised over one hundred men and two hundred animals. The trip was long and dusty, but it passed without incident. Few dared trifle with a man bearing the passport of the mighty Emir Jumla. I arrived at the city of Surat on the 15th of December in the year 1653.

Chapter 36

War at Sea

I now had a large stock of diamonds, rubies, and divers other jewels. I was anxious to begin my homeward journey and called upon the president of the Dutch Company, who informed me that war had been declared between the Hollanders and the English the year before. No more Dutch ships would be leaving for Persia. I then enquired of the English company and was told the same, however an English fleet was expected from Hormuz any day.

This was bad news indeed. I considered attempting the route from Agra through the wild Afghan mountains to Kandahar, but the war between the forces of the Great Mogul and the Persian shah over control of that city raged on, and the roads were not safe.

While I brooded in Surat, on the 27th of December a Dutch fleet was sighted and arrived in port a few days later. The Dutch East India Company built a series of small Indiamen that looked like innocent traders but were designed also as formidable warships, each carrying thirty guns and sometimes more. The Dutch fleet consisted of three such ships: *Muijen*, *Sluijs*, and *Cabeljau*. I was offered passage on the *Avenhorn,* the fourth ship of the fleet. She had been built in Zeeland in 1650, was 110 feet long at the waterline, and carried 26 guns.

Soon after I boarded, the Dutch admiral received word that the English fleet had arrived off the coast and decided to seek it out and attack.

The admiral, a merchant by the name of van Goens, stocked the three most powerful ships – *Muijen*, *Sluijs*, and *Cabeljau* – with powder and shot, and sent them off under the command of his vice admiral, a man named De Bie, due west toward the island of Diu to seek the four English vessels.

The fleet arrived off the island and, seeing no sign of the English fleet, De Bie decided to send a small sloop toward the island to seek some intelligence. The sloop overhauled a fishing boat and captured an old Mussulman who claimed he had seen the English sailing north. The vice admiral detached the sloop with the prisoner back to Surat to seek further instructions.

I was on deck when the prisoner was brought on board. He was thin to the point of starvation with a gaunt face, hollow, haunted eyes, and only a scrap of rag covering his private parts.

Admiral Van Goens personally questioned the fisherman. The admiral cut a fine figure, standing under an awning on the main deck, tall, slender, and well made with a long oval face, long dark hair and jaunty moustaches. He stared down at the poor wretch and addressed him in Farsi.

"Tell me, fellow, have you told the truth? The English Fleet was sailing north when you sighted them?"

The fisherman stared resolutely at his feet, "I spoke the truth, lord. Why should I lie?"

Van Goens had to step closer to hear the mumbled answer to his enquiries. "Why indeed, but just the same do you swear it?"

"I swear on the beard of the Prophet, lord."

"How many days ago?"

"The moon was a quarter full that night, lord."

Accepting the fisherman's story, Admiral Van Goens ordered my ship, *Avenhorn,* together with a much older yacht, the *Saphier,* to up anchor and proceed to Diu to reinforce the Dutch squadron.

We rendezvoused with De Bie and the rest of the fleet off the island on the 12th of January. From Diu, we sailed north to Sindi where both the Dutch and the English companies maintained small factories at the mouth of the Indus River. Upon our arrival the admiral sent a boat ashore to the Dutch factory to enquire after the English. The Dutch officials informed our admiral that 200 bales of goods were stacked on the quay outside the English factory awaiting the fleet. The rumor was they were expected any day. We therefore decided to anchor and await events.

Our captain, a man by the name of Van Roosendael, was kind enough to invite me to dine with him that evening. He was a serious fellow, as are most Hollanders, tall with a long face and a hooked nose.

We dined on deck. I casually mentioned my experience as an artillery officer with the Duke of Nevers and volunteered to help in any way he might require.

His dark eyes studied me for a long moment. "You can serve a twelve pounder, Herr Tavernier?"

"Yes, I have had some experience with even larger cannon, though I must confess none at all firing from the moving deck of a ship of war."

The captain nodded. "At Mantua, you say? We are merchants, Herr Tavernier. Our fleet carries a full complement, but most of our people have never engaged in battle. Many are youngsters, and we enlisted a number of freed blacks in Batavia. They have no experience and, I fear, little stomach for war."

"I have assigned any man who has actually fired a gun as captain, but we are still short. So if you will oblige me, Mein Herr, you shall captain number three gun. As for your lack of experience, you are correct. Siege warfare is somewhat different, but your lack is easily remedied. Tomorrow we begin gunnery practice. I can allow you, the purser, and three blackamoors for your crew. They have had some dry practice, rattling the guns in and out, though none have actually fired one."

"As you wish. I am at your service, Captain."

The next morning, after the cook had thrown the breakfast slops overboard, the crews assembled on the gun deck at our assigned stations. The gun deck was just beneath the main deck. The port lids sat flush with the ship's planking. From a distance we looked like an unarmed merchantman, fat and ready for the plucking. The ceiling was barely six feet between the beams and the only light came from sunlight filtering through the gaps around the edges of the closed ports and from above through the open hatches. Not a hint of a breeze stirred, and the morning air was filled with the sharp smell of sulfur and saltpeter from the slow matches smoldering in the tubs. It was, in short, a dusty airless coffin.

Captain Van Roosendael ordered the ports opened and walked slowly along the length of the deck, ducking his head and bending his slender frame to avoid the crossbeams. He inspected the guns and adjusted the gun crews.

Under our Captain's baleful eye we went through several dry runs, charging and running the guns in and out. He was a taut commander, and he worked us hard. We all stripped to the waist, and I was soon dripping sweat. A slight breeze came up. We secured the guns, and the *Avenhorn* got under way, setting topsails only for maneuverability. We bore off northwest and when we had gone about a league, the Captain hove to, and we began live practice. A boat was lowered and a target, composed of barrels lashed together on deck by the ship's carpenter, was taken in tow.

With the ports open and the guns run out, the *Avenhorn's* starboard side bristled like a porcupine with a row of stubby black quills. I caught a glimpse of the target about a cable length off, being towed from left to right. At the command, "Charge your guns" the purser, a dour jumped-up little fellow who clearly thought the whole procedure beneath him, placed the powder bag in the cannon's mouth.

"Gently, gently there." I shouted as blackamoor number three grabbed the ramrod and rudely rammed the gunpowder bag down the barrel. I found it difficult to tell the three blackamoors apart. They were freed slaves and all three were burly creatures, so I assigned each a number. Blackamoor number one, a completely bald fellow with bulging arms, tipped in the ball followed by a cotton wad, and number three rammed it into place. I kneeled and while Blackamoor number two, the shortest of the three, levered up the gun with a handspike, I wedged the quoin halfway up the carriage and brought the barrel level with the deck.

With a gesture I ordered my crew to secure the tackles and fall back. Blackamoor number three, a graying old man, smiled uncertainly and gingerly handed over the slow match. I stood sideways with my body arched over the barrel like a bullfighter, blew softly on the match, and awaited the captain's command.

"Fire as she bears!" the captain ordered. I waited until guns one and two fired at the target, and then timing the ship's upward roll, put the match to the pan.

A moment's hesitation, then a spark, and the cannon belched thunder. The three blackamoors' eyes bulged as the gun leapt straight back and came up short against the tackles, just inches from where they stood. The wind was in our face. Smoke filled the gun deck.

We all crowded the gun port. As the smoke cleared, I could make out the target, bobbing up and down in the light swell. The day was uncommonly clear; a few long thin clouds clustered around the horizon. Our ball skipped like a flat stone thrown across a pond. It splashed down about half a cable beyond the target – I had misjudged the ship's roll – a poor showing to be sure. The remaining seven guns boomed out, one following the other. Their balls cut up the water to the left and right, but the target bobbed jauntily in the swells, untouched.

We fired three more broadsides with similar results. On the fourth round, our gun scored a direct hit and blew the target to pieces. This caused much rejoicing among our gun crew. Blackamoor number two did a little dance. Even our little clerk stood up straighter and managed a smile. By this time, night was closing in, and the wind had shifted around, causing the seas to become confused. The captain ordered the cutter to tow out the second target with a lantern attached to the mast, and we blazed away one more time. Our shot narrowly missed and number five gun nicked the target, but no one scored a direct hit. We housed the guns and dropped anchor for the evening.

I was much caressed by Captain Van Roosendael. He invited me once again to share his table at dinner. The purser was also invited to dine. The three blacks were rewarded with a double ration of grog. All through the dinner, the obnoxious purser prattled on about gunnery. Somehow between securing the guns and dinner, he had become a gunnery expert, and the captain, an excessively polite fellow, indulged the little scrub.

The following morning, the sun rose golden over the lush green hills of Gujarat at our backs. The fleet lay at anchor with a stiff topgallant breeze out of the northwest. As the early morning haze began to thin, a commotion broke out aboard the flagship. The flagship's lookout had spotted four sails directly upwind and bearing down on us. They were so far off, at first sighting, that we could not identify them. The captain crossed over from the quarterdeck and gave me his hand.

"Well, Mein Herr, we shall soon be in the thick of it."

"What makes you so sure, Captain, it is the English fleet?"

"The ships are European by the look of them, and what else would they be in these waters?"

Figure 15: Dutch warships from a 17th Century engraving.

By 9:00 o'clock the red-striped cross of St. George was visible at the masthead of the leading ship, removing all doubt. It was the English fleet and they were bearing down on us with ill intent.

By the time we won our anchor and sheeted home our topsails, the four English were upon us bearing down stem-on toward our flagship. They were before the wind, the best point of sale for a square-rigged vessel.

We had the lee shore at our backs. Fortunately we had anchored a league offshore, and there was little danger of being run up on the beach. The English, however, had the weather gauge and could close with us whenever they chose, and we could not make way upwind to meet them. With the wind full in our face, our options were limited to tacking either left or right.

By rushing in to attack without first reconnoitering his situation, the English admiral, a man I later learned bore the name of William Noke, made a grievous error. From far at sea, our ships looked like harmless merchantmen deeply laden with cargo. The English admiral made the mistake of believing what he saw. In fact, his squadron was heavily outgunned.

Welcome, the English flagship, broke to port while the other three English ships went to starboard, flanking *Muijen*. *Welcome* passed so close abeam on the starboard side of *Muijen* that her mizzen shrouds got caught up in our flagship's rigging.

Admiral De Bie now proved himself totally unfit for command. His ship was well manned, yet he threw away the opportunity to grapple and board the English flagship. With a bull-like voice that could be heard clear across the water, he shouted, "Cut the rigging there. "Fend off, fend off!"

Two men slashed at *Welcome's* rigging with cutlasses while several others fended her off with oars. The two ships drifted apart. The English admiral waited until the ships stood about thirty yards apart and then loosed a full broadside at point blank range, holing our flagship at several places along the water line and carrying away her larboard mizzen shrouds.

Admiral De Bie, now with little choice, finally decided to fight:

"Drop your port lids!" he shouted. "Roll out your guns! Fire!"

Muijen cranked out her 15 smashers and poured 180 pounds of iron into the hull of the English ship.

The English Admiral now realized the extent of his mistake. These were no toothless merchantmen. Fearing for his precious cargo of Persian silk and no doubt for his life, he signaled the Dove and hauled his wind. The two ships tucked their tails between their legs and ran downwind, leaving the other two English ships to defend themselves against our four. Aboard Muijen our admiral signaled Sluijs, and together they raised all available sail and made off in pursuit of the two retreating Englishmen.

As *Welcome* and *Dove* made their escape, Captain Van Roosendael prepared to engage *Falcon*, one of the two remaining English ships. The few minutes it took for us to come up on the English ship seemed like an hour. I saw excitement mixed with fear in every eye. As we prepared to pass the *Falcon* to larboard, she luffed up, turned larboard side, too, and fired a broadside. In his eagerness to engage us, her captain misjudged the range. Every ball fell short, plowing up the water in front of us.

"Steady, boys. Stay steady," our captain yelled. "Keep those port lids closed."

Falcon ran in her guns, recharged, gathered way, and, emboldened by our lack of response, sailed in closer, turning into the wind and firing a second broadside. This time the aim was better. I could feel the ship shudder as we took several hits at the waterline. One ball smashed through the number six port upending the gun. Another ball smashed through the hull and whistled by my ear. The twelve pound ball caught blackamoor number two in the chest and bowled him across the deck. Later I found him, or parts of him, in the port scuppers, crumpled up like a bloody rag.

The English had drawn first blood, and this caused a good deal of anger and cursing on *Avenhorn's* gun deck. It pulled us together remarkably. Fear momentarily forgotten, we itched to run out our guns and avenge our shipmates, but the captain held us back until the *Falcon's* captain, who had apparently learned nothing from his admiral's mistake, luffed up once again in preparation to fire, exposing her larboard flank.

We were ready, our hearts burning with vengeance. The English ship lay abeam, virtually motionless, no more than half a cable length off. The captain shouted, "Open the ports! Run out your guns!"

The port lids dropped open with a bang, and we cranked out our guns. We caught the English gun crew leisurely sponging out their guns.

"Fire as the bear." the captain ordered.

The hours of gunnery drill now told the tale. I dropped to one knee and levered up the cannon. Truth to tell we were so close to the English ship not even a blind man could have missed the target. The ship rolled downward. I paused, waited for the upward roll, and touched the match to the pan. Just the slightest hesitation and the cannon belched a sheet of flame. White clouds blew back on us, filling the gun deck with choking smoke. Peering through tears, I watched the ball skip once about twenty yards off the *Falcon's* larboard quarter, then bounce up, and pass straight through the after cabin. Moments later, flames leaped from the ship's aft quarter.

The *Falcon's* gun deck exploded in a full broadside! I ducked instinctively just as a thick splinter of wood passed through my cloak and took off the head of the purser who stood just behind, showering me with blood and brains.

The two ships were now beam to beam. The air was filled with smoke, the gun deck slick with blood. My eyes stung and the taste of gunpowder burned in my throat.

"Grapple them boys," the captain shouted. "One more broadside and we board them in the smoke."

We ran in our guns, sponged, charged, ran them out, and loosed another broadside at point blank range that all but wrecked the English ship. We did not need the grapples. *Falcon,* her rudder blown away, drifted rapidly down upon us. With victory all but certain, discipline on our gun-deck completely broke down. Sailors began jumping up and down, cheering and hugging their mates. The men of the gun crews began crowding the ladders leading to the main deck. Abandoned by my crew, I left my gun and ran up the ladder to the poop just in time to see the two ships collide.

Cutlasses and boarding axes had been served out. Captain Van Roosendael stood legs apart in the ship's waist, surrounded by armed crewmen. I had seen it before. Some men in the heat of battle go a bit mad. The captain's face was red, and his eyes burned with the mad passion of the berserker. The red, white, and blue ensign of the Dutch Company flapped on the flagstaff. The captain caught my eye, laughed, raised his fist, and pointed to the single stern chaser, an eight pounder mounted on the poop. "Grape!" he shouted. "She is loaded with grape. If the English try to board, sweep the deck."

This set off another cheer, and the captain, howling like a madman, drew his sword and leaped over the bulwarks onto the English ship. The rest of the crew poured onto the deck.

Shouting through the noise and confusion, I located the remaining two blackamoors to help fight the deck gun. Grape is a man killer. Iron balls no bigger than a man's thumb are wrapped like a bunch of grapes and packed into the cannon's mouth. When fired, the lethal fruit spreads a murderous hail of metal, mowing down anyone in its path.

From my vantage point on the poop, I had a good view of the deck of the English ship. Our boarding party had scattered all about the deck in little knots, fighting man to man. The encounter was short and bloody. The English had little will to fight, much less to board our vessel. The English captain was overawed. His ship on fire and faced with a howling mob of Dutchmen, blackamoors, and Malays, he threw up his hands and struck his colors.

We did not come off unscathed. After securing the other ship, Captain Van Roosendael was carried back onto the ship, pale and dripping blood. He shouted to the men to bring the English prisoners over into our ship in groups of ten. Some of the English crew volunteered to stay aboard their ship and fight the fire, and, after several hours of hard work, managed to save it.

While we were thus engaged, our sister ship *Saphier* took on *Endeavour,* the only English vessel that remained in the fight. The two ships exchanged several broadsides. Our first mate took command and maneuvered us to assist *Saphier.* We were able to get close enough to fire several broadsides into *Endeavour's* hull and do considerable damage.

Endeavour began taking on water so quickly that her pumps were powerless to stop it. Discipline aboard the English ship broke down. Earlier in the fight, several of the more cowardly members of the crew had gone below and broken into the liquor stores. The rest now joined their shipmates and began to drink the cargo of Shiraz wine that was destined for the English factory at Surat. The *Endeavour's* captain, his crew drunk, his ship sinking by the stern, raised a white flag to the masthead.

The captain of the *Sluijs,* who had been ordered to accompany our flagship in pursuit of the two fleeing English ships, spied *Endeavour's* white flag. She was closest to the *Endeavour.* Ignoring the admiral's order, she dropped her pursuit, veered off, and set out to make *Endeavour* a prize, leaving our flagship in lone pursuit of the two English ships. The *Sluijs* went alongside, set her grapples, and, with her entire crew, boarded the English ship and took possession.

With the exception of Captain Van Roosendael, who two days later died of his wounds, and the crews of *Avenhorn* and *Saphier,* both the Dutch and the English acted in the most shocking manner. It is difficult to see whose conduct was the worse. The crew of the *Sluijs* joined the crew of the *Endeavour* in their drunken revel, and later that afternoon the *Endeavour* rolled over and sank, taking fifty men to the bottom. *Muijen,* with two feet of water in her hold, was too heavily laden to catch the retreating English and eventually broke off the chase. *Welcome* and *Dove* escaped and moored safely at Suvali. After effecting some repairs, my ship, *Avenhorn,* together with the *Cabeljau* and the *Sluijs* set sail for Bander Abbās.

Chapter 37

Mazarin Returns

reached Paris in the early autumn of 1655 and hurried over to Torreles early the first morning after a good night's sleep. The weather was cool and crisp, the streets were clear, the barricades had long since been removed, and Paris, it appeared, had returned to normal. I found Pierre in his office as usual. He had not changed much though the hair beneath his wig had turned a snowy white.

Pierre rose from his chair and we embraced. He held me at arm's length. "Jean-Baptiste, it is good to see you. Let me look at you. You are as brown as a Hindoo nabob. Honestly, you are like a fresh breeze. Things are bound to improve now that you are back."

"Pierre, everything appears to be normal."

His pale eyes narrowed in disbelief. "Normal? Yes, now perhaps. The barricades are gone…finally! You missed two years of chaos: pillaging, burning; armies coming, armies going, Paris under siege. Did you not see the suburbs – the Faubourg Saint Germain nearly in ruins and St. Michel as well?"

"I arrived last night and came straight here this morning; I have not had a chance to reconnoiter."

"Well, all I can say is thank God for the king. Oh, how the people love him! He put the parliament in its place, I will tell you that. You should have seen him, Jean-Baptiste! The coronation two days short of his sixteenth birthday! It was a grand parade. The king in white satin. The whole court dressed in their finest. They rode, bridles jingling along the Rue St. Honoré from the Place Royale to the Châtelet across the Pont au Change, and drew up before the Palace of Justice. Louis was in the center, behind the garde du corps, mounted on a bay charger, hat in hand, bowing to the ladies crowding the windows, dressed like beautiful birds in full plumage, shouting, 'Long live the king!'"

"It must have been a sight."

"Indeed it was. Your pardon," Pierre said, wiping his eyes and blowing his nose in a large silk handkerchief.

"What of the parliament?"

"Well, the parliament of Paris had gotten quite full of itself during the years of the Fronde – making proclamations, claiming authority where they had none, usurping the rights of the crown – that sort of thing. He forbade them to meet. The king walked in on them dressed in his hunting clothes and forbade them."

"But things did not get better."

Pierre wiped his eyes. "No, for a time they got worse. Condé rode out of Paris the day of the coronation, and the Fronde des Princes began. Eventually the Duke of Orleans was drawn into it as well, but when the Spanish invaded, the people and the rebels in the parliament turned against the conspirators. Mazarin returned with an army at his back, defeated the Spanish, and the rest you know."

"You have had a difficult time. How is the family?"

"We were closed for almost half a year, and things looked grim for a while. Sometimes I wonder, Jean-Baptiste…." Pierre got up, opened the door and looked around. The workers had arrived, and the atelier was starting to get busy. He closed the door and lowered his voice. "Sometimes I wonder about all these princes and dukes and so-forth. They are nothing but trouble, strutting about like peacocks. We would be better off without them."

"Some are our very good customers, are they not?"

"Well, yes, certainly, but they are always, you know, prattling on about this jewel and that jewel that they have in their strong rooms. They would buy but, of course, they already have such and such left to them by so and so. Bah!" Pierre waved a hand in dismissal. "Give me a nouveau riche grain merchant, anytime, Jean-Baptiste. There you have a man who doesn't mind spending money. No bowing and scraping, no expectation of credit, no chasing his lordship for overdue payment and having to endure being talked to like a dog for having the temerity to ask."

"Ha, ha! Well, cousin, I must say you make a good case."

"Do I? I am most anxious to see what you have brought me?"

I reached into my doublet and brought out a leather bag containing the ruby that the king of Ava had presented me with and placed it on the desk in front of him. It glowed like a burning ember in the sunlight streaming through his office window.

Pierre's eyes widened. "My God, what magnificence, such splendor!"

His eyes never left the gem while I told him my tale. "What a story. It reminds me of the day we met. You take amazing chances, cousin!" He picked up the stone and rotated it between his fingers, examining it carefully in the sunlight. He eyed me with a grin. "But I believe that this was worth it. How much is it worth, by the way?"

I laughed and shook my finger at him. "Do you not wish to enthuse over the beauty, to savor the color? What do you think we can get for it?"

Pierre held the ruby close to the light and peered closely at it. Then he put it down, took his chin in his hand, and sat for some moments contemplating the gem. "I don't know. I have never seen its like – seventy, perhaps eighty thousand livres? No one in Paris has anything like it and, I would venture to say, there is not another true ruby so fine in all of Europe. If there was I would have heard of it."

"I believe you are right cousin. Let us ask one hundred fifty thousand."

"Truly." Pierre took a deep breath, "Very well, you know better than I. I know a financier, Claude de Guénégaud – you have heard of him, I think? Good customer, who has a chateau in the Marais. It was sacked once during the first Fronde and twice during the second. He has recently developed a taste for portable wealth."

"I have heard the name. By all means, show the ruby to Monsieur Guénégaud, but Pierre, the price is one hundred fifty thousand, and I will accept no less than one hundred thirty. I can get one hundred thousand easily in Persia or in India, perhaps more. The omrahs, particularly the Persians, understand the rarity of such gems and will pay dearly for it."

"Why didn't you sell it in Persia?"

"I wanted to show it to you, and it is important that I have something truly magnificent to show about the city.

Pierre laughed. "You are a showman! Once the word gets out that you are back, there will be a line of footmen standing outside the door, each with a message demanding that countess so and so be the first to see what you have brought home."

"Well then, we must nurture such a legend, must we not?"

"Indeed, yes, but let us get down to business. Word travels quickly. We must have an inventory ready by the day after tomorrow at the latest."

Figure 16: The Jewelry district of Paris at the Quai des Orfèvres viewed from across the Seine. From a 17th Century engraving.

The next day I had business at the Place Dauphine and in the jewelry district at the Quai des Orfèvres. It was a warm, sunny autumn morning. I left my lodgings at the Rue de Balais about 9:00 o'clock in the morning and strolled down the Rue St. Paul to the quay where I hired a boat.

Construction was going on everywhere. Workmen clambered like hungry ants over the staging that sheathed many of the finer houses. The sound of hammers – mason's hammers, carpenter's hammers – filled the streets and echoed off the quays. Paris was rebuilding herself.

All manner of watercraft crisscrossed the river, some heaped with charcoal for heating, others with stone building blocks, barrels still oozing sap on their way to the wine merchants, and pelts on their way to the tanner's quarter. It was harvest time. Regiments of *flettes,* the pigeon-breasted barges that plied the Seine, made their stately progress upriver, loaded with brown mountains of ripened grain and looking like buxom matrons being pulled by teams of horses trudging along the towpaths that flank both sides of the river, their cargo bound for the bread ovens of Paris.

The water taxi dropped me off at the Quai de Conti, just a two minute walk up the narrow stone steps to the street, a quick left and halfway across the Pont Neuf to the entrance to the Place Dauphine. It was just 10:30 in the morning, and the Pont was crowded: a few carriages, but mostly foot traffic. Laborers covered with dust and grime mixed with well-dressed, bourgeois financiers going about their business, and a sprinkling of aristocratic ladies and gentlemen were bound for the fashionable shops which lined the arcade of the Place Dauphine. But I had little time to contemplate the scene. I had an appointment, and I was running late.

Chapter 38

The Duke of Orleans

Since my return, I had made a number of discreet enquires about Madeleine but learned little. As a reward for his constant intrigues against the king, Gaston, Duc d'Orléans, had been exiled to his estates at Blois by Cardinal Mazarin, and from what I could learn, the Marquis and Marquise de Chamboulet were living at the chateau on the duke's largesse. My best source of information, my dear friend Noelle, had, sadly, passed on while I was in India.

As much as I wished to see Madeleine, I had no excuse to call upon her, and to present myself at Blois without an invitation would be awkward. Fate sometimes takes a hand, and to my great surprise, a letter arrived at my lodgings bearing the seal of the Duc d'Orléans. In this letter, the duke said that he knew of my reputation, had heard that I was in Paris, and invited me to wait upon him at what he called his country seat in Blois.

Blois is a very old walled town, founded sometime in the Twelfth

Century. It is located in the Loire Valley about thirty leagues or perhaps one hundred English miles from Paris. It was not without apprehension that I undertook the trip. The duke was officially in disgrace, and so I thought it wise to inform the palace of the summons. Apparently it was not viewed with too much alarm. I received a note from His Eminence asking only that I report anything of interest to Colbert upon my return to Paris.

The duke's letter specifically mentioned his wish to see my jewels, and so I loaded two mules and took a selection of my finest goods, along with six of my servants as guards. It was late September, and the weather was still quite warm. I set out at once, wondering what I would find when I arrived at the duke's chateau.

The road through the Loire valley is always beautiful. The grapes hung heavy on the vine, pregnant with juice. The last night we made camp in a tiny valley by a stream. The night was clear, and the heavens looked like an upturned bowl or a knit cap pulled down over the ears of the world with the stars shining brightly through it. I woke to the sound of my horse cropping the thick grass outside my tent.

I arrived at the Chateau Royal in the late morning after a pleasant few hours' ride over gentle hills carpeted with grass. The duke's chamberlain greeted me. I was gratified that he knew my name and obviously had been told to expect me. The chateau is an imposing structure: five stories high, mostly brick with windows trimmed in marble.

His Grace was out hunting, the chamberlain informed me, and was expected back in the late afternoon. Servants dressed in the duke's familiar blue and yellow livery saw to it that my men and animals were taken care of, and I was conducted to a beautifully appointed bedchamber on the second floor of the mansion.

Large curtained windows looked out on a colonnaded porch that ran the length of the building. I walked along it, and after about ten minutes Madeleine found me. I fear I would have done something inopportune, but a finger placed against her lips alerted me to the possibility that we were being watched.

I made a leg. "My lady!"

I was treated to a brilliant smile. My dear Madeleine did so love the prerogatives of an aristocrat. I thought of my dream, the great diamond. If I ever found it what then would not be possible.

"Oh, Jean, I hoped you would come. How good it is to see you again. I would give you a real kiss, but there are always prying eyes in this drafty old dungeon. How well you look. How are you?"

"And you, Madeleine, are as lovely as ever. It appears that the country air suits you. You are positively blooming."

Madeleine blushed, then laughed merrily. "Flatterer! Jean, I swear, you could charm the hair off a goat." She turned and leaned on the balustrade.

"That depends completely upon the gender of the goat, my dear." In truth Madeleine was in high looks. Viewing her in profile as she stood beside me, leaning on the stone railing looking out over the city, her hair blowing gently in the breeze, I could see that she was no longer the ingénue I had met so many years before in Isfahan, but she still had the figure of a young girl and a complexion that showed barely a crease. Her dark eyes sparkled as mischievously as ever. She wore the ruby pendant I had given her.

She turned to face me with a coquettish smile. "I have told the duke all about you. He is fairly salivating at the opportunity to see your jewels. I trust you have brought your best with you." She sighed. "I do so regret selling my lovely things. The duke knows that you rescued me from Persia and that we are friends but only that."

"Hmm, and your husband, the marquis?"

She frowned. "Oh, fie on that man, Jean-Baptiste. Little do I care what he knows or guesses! He forfeited his rights as a husband long ago, and besides, he is beyond caring. These days he does little but wander aimlessly about the chateau. The duke keeps him on a very short tether. He no longer has any money to gamble away. By dinnertime he will no doubt be drunk. He is most nights. We should have time together since the duke retires early, except for the evenings he plays cards with my husband. We are no longer intimate. The duchess is here, of course, and the children, but we barely speak. It is all so very tedious."

"Ah, the carefree life of the aristocracy…"

Her jaw tightened. "Very amusing, Jean, I see your tongue has not lost its bite." She sighed, "The truth is, my dear, you don't know the half of it. Blois is a million miles from anywhere. I have been cast up on the beach here, like a dead whale, no parties, no theatre, nothing to do. Tell me, what of the court? We hear very little of the goings on in Paris."

She kept those bright eyes fixed upon me as I told her what little I knew of Paris and my tales of Pegù and Ava.

"It's so unfair," she said with a sigh, "I do so envy you your freedom. You men do as you please while we women go nowhere and do nothing but loll about dressed up, with our faces painted like porcelain dolls, and await your pleasure."

"You recall that I invited you…"

"We have been over all that, my friend."

"Have I mentioned the beautiful sunsets off the Coromandel coast?"

"Ha, ha! No, nor shall you. You are an incorrigible rogue, and I have seen enough blistering hot weather, not to mention bloody flux, to last a lifetime. Now a chateau in Paris, winters in Capri, that is another matter."

"Perhaps after one more trip to India."

"Hmm, one more trip! Then perhaps. Just one more! I know you well, Jean-Baptiste, better, perhaps, than you know yourself."

"Someday I might surprise you, Madeleine. I will not be a vagabond forever, and I plan to retire rich."

Just then a footman brought a summons from His Highness. The servant led the way. The sound of our footsteps echoed off the marble floors. Madeleine arched her eyebrows and whispered quietly in my ear: "With luck he will have made a kill. His Grace is always in his best humor after he has slaughtered something."

We found the duke in the chateau's council chamber with its arched ceiling and walls, decorated with the royal fleur de lys. He was a hale and hearty fellow, the sort of man's man who is very comfortable to be around. He was dressed in his mud spattered hunting costume. Several dogs cavorted about his high booted legs.

"Ah, Monsieur Tavernier. Very good of you to come. I see you have found our marquise. I trust she has kept you well entertained in my absence?"

I bowed and Madeleine curtsied by my side. "Indeed, Your Grace, my lady has been the perfect hostess."

The duke raised his eyebrows and looked from one to the other. His laugh came easily and echoed off the chamfered ceiling. "Well, monsieur, I have heard much of you, of your exploits in the Orient and of your adventures with madame, la marquise, in Persia."

I bowed. "I thank Your Highness."

"You will join us for dinner, I trust. Tonight is an occasion," he said rubbing his hands together. "I bagged a nice fat doe. One shot, by God! We shall celebrate and perhaps monsieur will favor us with a tale or two."

By royal standards, dinner was a simple affair. The duchess and her three children were present, as was Madeleine and my rival, the marquis, though to look at him it was difficult to summon much bile. Drink had aged him. He barely acknowledged me, seemed bemused – perhaps already drunk – played with his food, drank glass after glass of wine, and barely said a word through the entire course of the meal. I had expected to be bored by hunting stories, but after a blow by blow account of that afternoon's slaughter and the felling of our dinner – "One shot, by God!" – the duke sat back and played the genial host.

"I have heard, monsieur, that in India they practice a most barbarous custom. I can hardly credit it. They say that when a husband dies, his body is burnt, and his wife is expected to throw herself upon the pyre and burn herself alive."

The duchess pursed her bow-shaped mouth in distaste. "Oh, Gaston don't be ridiculous. They do no such thing. Have a care, monsieur; my lord husband will have his little joke."

"Oh, the stories are true enough, my lady. Self immolation is a custom among the idolaters, the Hindoos, who are the original inhabitants of the country. I have witnessed the practice myself."

"Have you, by God? Extraordinary, upon my word, though

perhaps it is a custom that we should consider adopting in France," the duke said looking meaningfully around the table.

The duchess raised a handkerchief, sniffed, and glared at her husband. One could see that she had been a very pretty woman. Now somewhat overweight, she had not aged well. "You must forgive my husband, Monsieur Tavernier. His Grace is always at his most blood thirsty after a successful hunt. What I do not understand is why the women put up with it?"

"Ha, ha! You will not see my wife tossing herself upon my pyre, of that you can be sure, monsieur," said the duke.

"Not I, but perhaps one of your coterie of strumpets will volunteer," the duchess suggested, gazing pointedly across the table at Madeleine.

"Speaking for myself, I have rarely met a man worthy of a burnt finger," Madeleine responded, meeting the duchess's eyes, a slight smile playing about her lips.

"The Hindoos believe that such a death purchases them great merit in the next life."

"They do not believe in heaven?"

"They believe that a man dies and is reborn many times. In what form he is reborn depends upon his conduct in his previous life."

The duke spoke up: "Come, come Tavernier. I wish to hear the meatier parts."

"But, my lord, the ladies!"

"Oh, do come along now, Tavernier. They have heard worse, I'll wager. Ladies?"

I looked around the table. Madeleine raised her eyebrows and smiled expectantly; the duchess raised her hand. "A moment, if you please, monsieur." It took her about five minutes to gather up her brood and send them off with a servant. She then sat up and folded her hands. I took her level gaze as a signal to begin.

The duke laughed and clapped his hands with glee: "There you see, and now, monsieur, men are not the only ones with a thirst for blood. We are all ears. The story, if you please."

I looked about the table doubtfully, but as I heard no dissension,

I began the tale.

"In India there are three different methods used to commit *sati*, as the practice is called, depending upon the customs in that part of the empire. I have witnessed all three. First, before a woman may burn herself, she must get permission from the governor of the province."

"This is how it is done in the Kingdom of Gujarat. First, a small roofless hut about twelve feet square is built out of reeds near a river. Unless the family is very poor, the reeds are doused with oil so that the fire will burn hot and fast to reduce the poor woman's suffering. The widow comes dancing to the music of flutes dressed as for her wedding, wearing all her jewelry. She places herself in a half-reclining position in the center of the hut with her back resting against a post. A Brahmin priest ties her to the post, and her husband's body is draped over her knees as the priest sits down beside her. The widow sits in that position chewing betel and holding the body for about half an hour, after which the Brahmin gets up and goes outside, and the woman calls upon the priests to set the fire.

"How awful for the widow!" the duchess said.

The marquis mumbled something unintelligible and held out his glass to his servant to be refilled.

"Indeed it is, Your Grace. It is a horrible way to die. The women's screams of agony can be heart wrenching. If the wood is dry and has been liberally wetted with oil, the fire burns quickly, and the woman does not suffer too long. Once the body has been reduced to ashes and the fire cools, the remains are taken up and thrown into the river. The jewels are gathered up and taken away by the Brahmins."

"The priests appropriate the dead widow's jewels?"

"Yes. The jewels belong to the priests by right, and they carefully sift through the ashes to get them."

"How disgusting! If only these poor souls could be brought to the true faith," said the duchess.

The duke laughed. "Do our own priests behave so differently? Cajoling and wheedling, frightening people on their death beds! "

"Don't be ridiculous! That is not the same thing at all. Our Catholic priests seek money to support their good works," Her Grace responded.

"Good works, indeed, bah! Fine wines and gilded carriages and wenches more like. Churchmen in this kingdom live better than the aristocracy. Have you never heard of the Inquisition, my dear?"

The duchess's face reddened. "That is blasphemy. I will not listen to any more of it. Have a care, my lord husband, your soul is at risk." She clapped her hands over her ears.

"You see, monsieur. Just like a woman. My wife does not wish to know the truth, and if someone speaks it, she refuses to listen. Tell me, do these poor unfortunates ever change their minds at the last minute?"

"I have not seen it, Your Grace. Some say that the priests give the widow a strong drug called bhang that is made from the hemp plant. It is made into a tea and renders them almost insensible so that they hardly care what is happening to them."

After the dinner the duke took me aside and asked that I join him in the billiard room and show him some of my goods. I had my servants bring my pack and laid out my finest pieces on the billiard table. The duke walked around the table and selected a few and put them aside. We quickly reached agreement on price.

The room itself was quite formal as were most in the palace. The wallpaper was patterned in red, and the moldings were of dark polished walnut with chamfered ceilings. There was a marble fireplace large enough to walk into with the duke's coat of arms set above it. The evening had turned cool. His Highness took a chair near the fire and offered me one facing him. A liveried servant brought a crystal carafe of brandy and two glasses and placed them on a table set between us.

"I must say, monsieur," he said studying the brandy in the firelight, "your reputation is well deserved. Rarely have I seen such quality – the workmanship and the gems! Our marquise was quite correct when she called you a jeweler par excellence. Now, tell me what you can of the news of Paris?"

"There is little I can tell you, Your Highness. I have only just returned from Asia, and I am not privy to the councils of the great."

The duke raised an eyebrow. "Come now, my dear Tavernier, no false modesty if you please. I happen to know that you are very well thought of in certain official circles. I am familiar with your services in Germany. You continue to advise Mazarin and Colbert on affairs in Persia and India, do you not?"

"Your Grace is very well informed."

"Harrumph! Was well informed, you mean. I know a good deal of history, but I too am no longer privy to the councils of the great, and it is the present situation that interests me. Perhaps you could do me a service. Carry a message?"

"I am at your service, my lord."

"If you find the proper moment and believe me I know that this is a very delicate thing. Well, to be blunt. I would very much like to be brought back into the government. It's not fair. You know I am left to sit here on my backside. Damn it, I could be very useful to Mazarin, you know."

I nodded. "Is that the message, Your Grace?"

His Highness shifted his weight in his chair and nodded. "It is. Will you carry it back to the cardinal?"

"I can, Your Highness."

"And, tell him that I have no plans to challenge His Majesty. Never have. Just a misunderstanding, that is all. Dash it! Just tell him he can depend upon my full support whatever he decides."

"I will convey your message faithfully, my lord."

There was little left to say. We sat companionably and shared another brandy, and then I rose, thanked His Grace, and took my leave. I had spent half the day in the saddle. He called a servant to light my way to my chamber. No sooner had I put my head down when I heard a faint knock at the door. It opened and a lithe shadow flitted like a moth into the chamber over to the bed and slid beneath the covers.

"Brrrr, I do hate these drafty old castles. My feet are like a block of ice. Quickly, Jean, tell. I must know everything. You were closeted with His Grace for quite a long time. What did he want?"

I slid my arm around Madeleine's waist, gathered her into my arms, and kissed her. She wore only a long silk gown. "Well, my lady, what a lovely surprise."

"Umm, Jean, I had forgotten how good a kisser you are. Lord, your hands are freezing! Do you greet all the ladies who slip into your bed in this fashion? I might have been the duchess."

"Madeleine, really!"

"Oh you doubt me? Beware! Her Grace is far from the paragon she pretends to be. She likes you. I could tell, and I know a certain handsome young footman who has been seen tiptoeing from our duchess's chambers early in the morning."

"You are incorrigible."

"I try, Jean, Lord knows, I try. Now tell all. "

"I'd rather another kiss."

"All in good time. You must sing for your supper or…dessert. Now tell!"

Needless to say I did not get to sleep early that evening, but I didn't mind. I awoke late the next morning or should I say early in the afternoon.

5th Voyage

(1657-1662)

Chapter 39

Barbary Pirates

n February of 1657 I left Paris, and on the 25th day of that month took passage from Marseilles on a French ship bound for Malta.

Early on our second morning at sea I woke with a start to the sound of a hundred bare feet pounding across the deck above me. I forgot for a moment where I was but was painfully reminded when my head collided with the overhead. I rolled out of my bunk, threw on a thick woolen cloak, and stumbled out on deck, mumbling curses and rubbing my aching skull.

The sky was a slate gray, the sun was barely up, and the pale orb reflected off a turbulent sea dotted with foam, like dabs of whipped cream on a tart. A single sail was visible downwind, heading toward us from the southwest, an Arab rig by the look of her. The captain was on the quarterdeck huddled in anxious consultation with the pilot. Some of the other passengers were on deck clustered together in worried little knots around the open deck.

"What cheer, Captain?"

The captain's gray eyes focused on mine. He smiled grimly. "You are far from a babe in the woods, Monsieur Tavernier. You can see our situation as well as I. Yon galley is most likely an Algerian pirate. I have ordered a change of course westerly. You see how he changes course to intercept us?"

The captain was right. No sooner had we altered our course than the galley dropped her sails. Oars sprung from her thwarts like the arms of a giant water bug, and she began scuttling upwind with a clear intention to cross our bows. The galley was light and fast, and with the aid of her oars she could move upwind, whereas we could not. Heavily laden as we were with goods and passengers, our only choice was to flee.

"Yes, Captain, but perhaps you might speak to the passengers. Your words may bring them some measure of comfort."

He stared at me as if I were mad. "Comfort? There will be little of that I fear if these godless devils succeed in overhauling us."

"A grim business!"

"Aye, grim indeed, monsieur. I have lost many a friend to these cutthroats. They show little mercy to Christians. If you are rich, you can arrange for ransom. You should be safe enough. These bastards have a great respect for gold. But if you are poor, that is another story. Able-bodied men are chained to an oar, beaten, and starved until they die. Comely women are sold in the slave markets. Christian women bring a good price. The young and old men like me are just thrown overboard. To them it is one less Christian! They take great pleasure in it, the devils."

The captain could not know it, but everything I owned was packed aboard his vessel. There would be little chance of ransom. By this time, the other passengers had come on deck and had gathered around listening.

I asked the obvious question: "What are our chances?"

"If he catches us, little to none, I'm afraid. There are probably eighty well-armed cutthroats aboard the galley against thirty of us. Aye, and these are men that know their bloody business. We have one chance. You see the point yonder? That is Cape Sepet. Beyond it is the town of Toulon. If we can clear the cape on this tack, we should be safe. If we cannot, all is lost. The galley will surely overhaul us. As you can see, it will be a very near thing. If we make it, we will anchor by the fort. He dare not follow us. The fort's big guns will blast him into cord wood if he enters the port."

The passengers were not reassured; they all began to speak at once. One woman began sobbing. Another kneeled down, enfolded her three children in her cloak, and hugged them. Two men began gesturing and arguing loudly.

One woman took hold of the captain's sleeve. Two children clung to her skirts. "Surely, Captain, surely there is something we can do."

"Aye, madame, we can pray, pray for wind. He pulled away his arm and bowed curtly. "Now if you will excuse me, I have work to do and little time to do it."

I signaled to my servants and ordered them to break out the swords and muskets that we had packed away. My personal sword, a plain curved blade with a worn leather pommel and a plain scabbard, I had brought from my cabin. It had been a gift from the Emir Jumla.

I recall that the emir had smiled as he handed me the sword. "Don't be fooled, my friend, by the lack of jewels and fancy fittings. The value of a blade lies in its usefulness in combat. Observe!"

The emir unwound a gossamer thin silk scarf from around his neck and tossed it into the air. It was so light that for a long moment it floated motionless like a cloud in the air. He drew forth the blade and held it edge up beneath the scarf as it slowly settled earthward. Like a whisper, the scarf divided neatly into two and the pieces dropped to the ground.

Pursuer and pursued, we raced across the open sea. *St. Crispine* was a broad beamed craft and, sailing with the breeze at your back, it is always deceptively quiet and even with all sails set, the ship seemed to waddle along. The seas too were running with us. A large swell would slide up under the hull, lift the ship, heave it forward, and then run out from under us, leaving the ship to slide down its retreating back.

The galley slowly gained. Little by little it drew closer until, standing at the stern, I began to make out small details of the faces of men on the galley's bow. What I saw was not reassuring. These were hard men, burnt black by the Mediterranean sun. The ominous sound of a drum beat time for the oarsmen.

The captain stayed on deck gazing at the sails. The sailors stood alert, ready to race up the rigging to make any small adjustment he might require.

A group of the passengers gathered on the poop, formed a circle, and kneeled in prayer. The steady beat of the drum, louder now, ticked off the minutes.

The shoreline was clearly in view. The booming surf pounded against the headland, and the sea sucked about the two huge beetle-backed rocks lying just off shore. A narrow passage came into view. Like a jagged scar it cut a path between the largest boulder and the bare, wind scoured rocks of Cape Sepet.

I joined the captain standing at his lonely post, staring over the starboard rail. "We cannot clear the cape! You see, monsieur," he said pointing toward a narrow passage between the rocks and the rocky shore. "That is our one chance. I have never even thought to try to pass through it, though I have been told it is deep enough. A seafaring man should keep as much water between his ship and the shore as ever he can. My father taught me that, and in forty years I have never lost a ship. It looks deep enough, but who knows." He turned toward the stern. "You see we have beaten him to the strait, but still he crawls up our wake. The bastard hopes to get close enough to steal our wind and once we clear the passage, he will crawl up our backside just outside Toulon."

"Is there anything more to be done?"

"Yes, we will try the stern chasers, though they have not ever been fired before to my knowledge. And, if the Lord be with us, maybe we can slow him down. He will have to fall in line and follow us straight through the cut between those rocky jaws. There is no room to maneuver, so he will make a good target. Perhaps we can stop him if my boys don't blow themselves up trying. Most of them have never fired cannon. Have you had any experience with cannon, Monsieur Tavernier?

Once again I thanked God for my training in Italy. At the captain's bidding, I took charge of the guns.

"These six men will assist you, monsieur. Each of them claims some knowledge of ordinance."

The men had already pried out the tompions. I peered down each barrel. I expected to find rust and pitting, but the barrels had been greased and the tompions well seated. The tackle was still serviceable. Not so the balls. They had been stored as ballast in the hold and were rusty and badly pitted. Round balls were the most accurate. One old man-o-war's mate had begun chipping away the rust. Another crewman had located some rusty chain.

There was a single barrel of powder. I broke it open and spread a handful out on the deck. It was old and had begun to congeal, but with luck it would answer. The galley had come up on us a bit and was directly astern, and by the time we got the cannon loaded, was less than half a league off. The booming drum had grown louder. I could not help but think about the poor devils chained in her hold. In my mind I heard the sharp crack of a whip. Chained as they were, if the pirate went down they would drown like a passel of rats.

With the help of two of the older sailors, we set to work getting the two cannon loaded and primed. We charged each with ball. The chain would come in handy later when the galley got closer. For all her virtue sailing upwind, a galley is light and fragile, like a leaf upon the water and a direct hit could well sink her. We were well within the straight. She had reduced our lead by a third and was less than two cable lengths off, well within range. I decided to lob my shots high with the hope of dropping one onto the deck and perhaps hole her and, with luck, cut up her rigging. I levered the barrel up with a marlinspike to gain elevation.

I nodded and held my breath. One of the crew touched the slow match to the fire hole, and the gun bucked. Shading my eyes I was able to follow the ball's trajectory. It went high and wide and splashed down quite short of the galley's bow. At least the powder was still good.

The pirates found our efforts amusing. Several rushed to the bow, pointing and laughing. One dropped his drawers and wiggled his butt end in our faces.

I corrected the aim and levered the larboard cannon up to gain a bit more elevation. The galley continued to gain. I could now clearly see the pirate's sinister smiling faces. Several more had gathered in front of the foremast to watch the entertainment.

The seaman touched her off. This time the ball pitched higher but came down well off the galley's starboard bow. Two of the seamen had sponged out and reloaded the starboard cannon. I readjusted the angle and fired. The ball went true but splashed down just beyond the galley's stern.

The crew and the passengers, gathered in the waist of the ship, watched intently. Another crewman had joined the work on the pitted balls, and they had two more pretty well rounded. We carefully sponged out the barrels to clear them of any smoldering residue, measured the powder, slid the smoothed balls down the barrels, and rammed the wadding home.

I increased the elevation even more. The galley drums had grown louder. The galley's bow had become crowded as more of the cutthroats gathered to watch the fun. This time I fired the larboard cannon first. The ball lofted up, a black punctuation mark in the cloudless blue sky, and came down just off the galley's beam, smashing an oar. The galley wobbled off course for a few moments and lost a bit of her gain before a new oar was fitted and it resumed its course and speed.

I made a slight adjustment to the port chaser and stepped back. The sailor touched the slow match to the hole. The cannon belched flame, reared up, and leapt back against the restraining tackle. On the galley's deck the cutthroats danced about and made antic gestures. The ball pitched high. It looked as if it were going to splash down well beyond the galley's stern, but angles are deceiving. It dropped straight down, missed the galley's rigging, and smashed through the deck planking dead amidships. The crew and passengers began to cheer.

I studied the galley, waiting, but nothing happened. The drum continued its ominous rhythm and the galley stayed straight on course. The passenger's disappointment was palpable. I set my crew to work sponging and reloading the two chasers. This time I loaded the starboard cannon with chain. The galley was now well within range and the mob on the bow had begun to annoy me, and so I decided to give them something to remember me by. I noticed a change. Had the galley settled lower in the water?

I lowered the elevation of the starboard chaser so that it was parallel with the deck and fired. This time I was on target. The chain cut a bloody swath across her bow. Screams filled the air. At least half the pirate mob was down. One of the beggars had been literally cut in two, and the galley's scuppers ran red. Narrow rivulets of blood snaked down her hull. I jumped over to the port cannon, made a quick adjustment, crossed my fingers, and signaled the sailor to touch the slow match to the pan. The ball lofted straight up, almost out of sight, and then dropped straight down, smashing through the galley's deckhouse.

The rhythm of the oars now broke. Some kept time, others thrashed wildly, smashing into each other, and not a few trailed lifelessly in the water like broken limbs. The galley began to jigger right and left like a giant beetle in its death throes. The drumbeat ceased. Men burst through the hatches, scurrying about the deck like ants after a stick had been poked into the nest. The galley fell back, lost way, and began to wallow helplessly between the swells. Our passengers began to cheer.

A large swell picked up the stern and swung her broadside. We were now well into the narrow passage, and she was sandwiched between the rocks and the shore. Men were leaping into the sea. Another swell broke over her port rail and swamped her. One moment she was there, the next minute she was gone, leaving behind a circle of debris and the heads of several dozen pirates bobbing in the swells. The cries were pitiful.

Our ship's passengers shouted and danced. Some dropped to their knees and thanked God for their deliverance. The captain came up and gripped me by the arm. "Well done, monsieur. Well done!"

We stood at the aft rail staring at the scene. "Thank you, captain, but what of the men?"

He looked at me in surprise. "Those cutthroats? Let 'em drown! Save the hangman the trouble."

"What of our duty as Christians?"

"Well, Monsieur Tavernier, let me ease your mind. Look around you. Even if I wished to, do you think I could bring her about in this passage with seas running as they are? It would be suicide. There is nothing to be done."

Later that afternoon we dropped anchor in Toulon's inner harbor under the protective guns of Fort St. Louis.

I was heartily sick of sea travel, but my business required that I go to either Smyrna or Aleppo. I took ship on an English vessel bound for Tuscany because I knew that most ships that call on Smyrna were out of Leghorn. The passage was without incident, and I arrived two weeks later. I spent a short time in Tuscany and called upon Ferdinand II and was much caressed by the Grand Duke, who was very gracious and entertained me sumptuously. Around the middle of March I took passage on *The Justice*, a Dutch cog out of Leghorn, and arrived in Smyrna early in the month of April.

Chapter 40

Kismet

I completed my fifth voyage and arrived in Paris in the spring of 1662. Paris is my home, and it feels good to come home. But the return was bittersweet. Both my parents were dead. Only my brother Melchior and a cousin of the same name were still alive. Still I shall always love Paris.

The winter that year had been a hard one, and the city seemed to let out a collective sigh as the first buds began to sprout on the trees that line the towpaths along the Seine. Per my usual custom, after I had secured my lodgings and my goods, I took my gems and pearls, together with two of my servants, and sought out my cousin Pierre, whom I found, as usual, presiding over his shop in the arcade of the Palais Royal.

Pierre seemed always the same. He had gained a bit of weight, but otherwise the years weighed lightly on him. The shop was bustling. We sat together in his office as he broadly sketched out the happenings in the city since my last trip.

Pierre sat back in his chair and eyed me with a crooked smile "I am surprised Jean-Baptiste, you have not yet asked for news of the Marquise de Chamboulet."

"Madeleine, you have news of her?"

"Yes, I have some news that will please you, I think. The Marquis de Chamboulet is dead."

Madeleine's husband dead! A million possibilities coursed through my mind. Madeleine, free! "When? How?

"Quietly in his bed. From what I hear it was the drink that finally got him, though he was quite old. He died at the Duke of Orleans's chateau at Blois about a year ago.

"I am surprised he lived so long."

"No one was more surprised than the marquise herself, I'll wager."

Pierre had met Madeleine only once and though he liked her, he did not approve of her. He raised his hand. "Far be it from me to stand in the way of true love. I only speak this way as your cousin, your partner, and your good friend. Had you taken my advice and married a nice Parisian girl, you would have had a son by now to carry on your name."

"Yes, cousin, I am sure you are right, but tell me what have you heard of Madeleine?"

"I have not seen her, but then why would I? I have heard that she is in Paris."

"Do you know where she is living?"

"I do not, but since I see that you are determined, I shall initiate inquires at once. She should not be too hard to find."

I took him by the hand. "That is kind of you, Pierre. I must find her. I am sure the old wastrel has left her without a sou."

Early the next afternoon, a courier arrived at my lodgings with a message from Pierre. He had an address for Madeleine in the Faubourg St Michel. I was to ask for the house of a Mistress Basquiat.

I started off at once. St Michel is one of the new suburbs built outside the city walls and a dangerous place. The streets in the quarter are narrow, and it was difficult to tell where you were because there were few signs. The poor had set up housekeeping in makeshift shacks built with materials scavenged from the ruins of houses destroyed during the Fronde. These habitations partially blocked the streets, and I found myself gingerly picking my way through a maze of wood, stone, rotting garbage, children, dogs, chickens, and laundry flapping in the cool spring breeze.

The sun was warm and little rivulets of sewage had turned the unpaved warren of streets into a sticky, slippery, stinking morass. I met several groups of urchins, dirty ragged little creatures with bold feral eyes. They travel in packs and, like rats, will set upon anyone who appears weak. I had brought along two of my servants, each armed with a cudgel – that and the brace of pistols jutting from my girdle was enough to discourage them.

After asking directions several times, I found myself at the head of a narrow alley.

A grizzled old man with one leg leaned with his back propped up against the corner building staring at the ground.

"Monsieur, can you tell me the address of a Mistress Basquiat?" I asked.

He looked up at me with rheumy, washed out eyes, the color of a cloudy sky, smiled through rotten teeth, and held out his hand. I fished out a copper and dropped it in his open palm. He spat, jerked his head, and pointed down the alley.

"Third on the left!" he croaked, leaned back, and returned to his reverie.

A short way down the narrow alley, I spied a woman in front of a small stone house hanging wet laundry out on poles to dry. Though she had her back to me, had her hair covered by a head cloth, and was dressed in plain peasant's garb, a long skirt, and a coarse woolen doublet, there was something very familiar about her erect carriage, not at all like that of a peasant. My heart began to pound. It could only be Madeleine.

The duke had put her out. A week after they buried her husband, he told her that she would have to leave. The duchess would give him no peace, and she had to go. He gave her 3,000

livres. We sat together by the hearth on a rough wooden bench.
A large iron kettle steamed over the fire. Her loyal Persian maid,
Shadeh, and her husband, Marcel Basquiat, the marquis's former
valet, elected to go with her.

"My Shadeh refused to leave me in spite of the fact that I was
practically penniless and homeless as well. They are such dears.
Can you imagine? – the duke had offered Marcel a position. So early
the next morning Shadeh and Marcel loaded my clothes and the few
sticks of furniture and silver that my dear departed husband had not
managed to sell, and we set out for Paris."

Madeleine rented a chateau and attempted to put on a bold
front, but polite society was not taken in. The French aristocracy is
a close-knit club, and there are few secrets. Old friends turned their
backs or simply would not receive her.

The money dwindled. Shadeh and her husband rented a small
house in St. Michel. They moved in and lived frugally, but what little
money remained was soon gone. Six months after her return to the
city, she told the two servants that she had nothing left with which
to pay them. Shadeh refused to leave her. They took in washing and
did whatever they could, but it was barely enough to keep them
fed. She could get no more credit, and the landlord and the local
merchants were beginning to hound her for payment.

"Oh, Jean-Baptiste, I am so embarrassed that you should see me
like this. Look at me! Look at my hands, all raw and red, and I have
no decent clothes." She buried her face in her hands and wept. I
noticed a tiny glint of gold and red flash, that glowed like a hot
ember at her throat. She still had the ruby I had given her.

I put my arm around her and drew her to me. "I am here now,
Madeleine. I will help, you know that."

She kept her face buried in her hands. "I am so ashamed. You
are my only true friend, and I have treated you abominably."

"Yes, that is true. You have treated me rather badly. By rights I
should leave you to wallow here, like a pig in a trough."

Her head snapped erect, and she glared, but then catching my
smile, she laughed, threw her arms around me, and squeezed me
tight. "Darling Jean-Baptiste, it is so good to see you. Welcome to

my trough." She looked me in the eyes. "Do you think you could loan me 2,000 livres?"

"Aha, now that's the Madeleine I know and love." I handed her my handkerchief. "Two thousand livres, my lady, and may I ask what you have for collateral to secure such a large loan?"

A smile lit up her face and, except for the red-rimmed eyes, reminded me of the beautiful girl I had met so long ago. Her spirit was bent but far from broken. I felt a surge of love.

"Collateral, my dear sir? You have the word of a French noblewoman."

"But, of course. A thousand apologies, my lady. I will have to get it from my lodgings. How would you like the money, in silver or gold? Will golden Louis do?"

"Perfectly, monsieur, and perhaps monsieur would care to stay for dinner?"

I bowed. "Delighted, madame."

Madeleine laughed and clapped her hands. "Shadeh, Marcel, come quickly! We are in funds." The two servants crowded into the room. "You both remember my dear friend, Monsieur Tavernier. Marcel bowed and Shadeh curtsied shyly. "Shadeh, go at once to the butcher, pay our bill, get his fattest goose with an extra liver, and then to the baker.

"Oh, Jean, could you manage a small down payment on the loan?"

I handed Madeleine my purse.

"This will do marvelously!" She pressed two Louis into her maid's hand. "Marcel, charcoal. We must have charcoal. It will be cold tonight. And candles, we must have real beeswax candles at least a dozen, no two. And Shadeh we shall need eggs, cream and butter, and wine. Go to M. Chaumet, pay him the 50 livres we owe, and get six bottles of his best Margaux."

Two hours later the house was abuzz. A linen tablecloth had transformed the rough-hewn table in the center of the room. Candles had replaced the tallow lamps, and a succulent goose turned on a spit over a crackling fire. While Shadeh and Marcel busied themselves at the hearth, Madeleine and I sat across from each other at the table and sipped wine from small clay bowls.

"Jean, I must apologize for not having proper wine glasses."

"Do you remember the goatskin borracho we shared on the road from Aleppo?"

She laughed. "Yes, I had forgotten, but that was Shiraz. The French reds are better, don't you think?"

"I don't know. Goat adds a bit of a tang, don't you think? And goat hair is a sovereign remedy for dropsy."

"Ha, ha. Really Jean-Baptiste, you are incorrigible. Truly I despair of ever making a civilized man of you."

Shadeh proved to be a fine cook. She served up an excellent goose, roasted to a turn, and, wonder of wonders, set it on a bed of pilaf that proved to be as tasty as any I have ever eaten.

The servants finished up their tasks and retired. Madeleine and I sat late into the evening staring into the fire and talking companionably of old times and my tales of India and cities of the kingdom of the Great Mogul. Her hair shone like silk in the candlelight.

I reached out and took her hand and looked her in the eyes. "Madeleine, how long have we known each other?"

Her dark eyes glistened. "Twenty years and a bit more."

"And how many times have I asked you to marry me?"

"Let me see, counting the time you shamelessly suggested that I run away to India with you, not more than four or five."

"Then this shall be the sixth time. Madeleine, will you marry me?"

Tears filled her eyes. "Oh Jean, after all these years. Do you still want me?"

"More than ever, Madeleine."

She wiped her tears away with her fingers, extended her other hand across the table, took hold of both of mine, and looked directly into my eyes. "I don't know what to say."

"Then, say, yes, though I am afraid I have no title to offer you. I know how important that…"

She pressed her fingers to my lips. "I have learned many things since we first met, Jean, and I know how much I have hurt you. A title no longer seems important."

"Truly?"

"Truly, and, yes, Jean-Baptiste Tavernier, if you will have me, I would be honored to become your wife."

I held her hands tightly: "Madeleine, before you commit yourself I must tell you, I have done very well, and you will want for nothing, but I must make one last trip to India and soon. After that, I promise, my days as a traveling merchant will be over."

She squeezed my hands and smiled. "Jean, if I am to be your wife, I must trust your judgment. You have waited for me for more than twenty years. I can wait for you until you return from a single voyage."

Four weeks later we were married. It was a small wedding, just a few relatives and friends. I expected a great deal of planning, but my bride had mellowed over the years and pronounced herself in favor of a quiet ceremony. I insisted upon buying her a trousseau and a proper wedding dress.

"I am not sure what to do. Tell me the truth, Jean, do you like it?" Madeleine said as she stood before a large mirror that took up half of her tiny cottage.

"You look absolutely beautiful, my love."

"Jean, you say that about everything."

"You picked a beautiful fabric, and the dress is already made."

She turned and put her hands on her hips. "So, you don't like it."

"No Madeleine, I do. Truly I do. It is very becoming. I only wish to point out that it's a bit late for second thoughts."

"Well, yes," she said, turning back to the mirror. "I suppose it is, but I think the neckline is scandalous."

I walked up behind her and wrapped my arms around her waist. "Really? I think that is the best part."

"Men! Naturally *you* would think so, but I shall catch pneumonia parading around half undressed. Now unhand me, if you please, monsieur, so I can get out of this rig."

I held her tighter and nuzzled her neck. "Perhaps what is needed is something to cover up some of that neckline."

She leaned back and smiled and the warmth of her suffused into my chest and arms. "Something in white ermine, mayhap?"

"Not exactly." I reached into my pocket and held up a double strand of pearls. She could see them reflected in the mirror. Her mouth fell open and her face reddened.

"Oh, Jean, pearls!" I let go of her waist, swung the pearls around her neck and clasped them. "Voilà! Madame, you see you are warmer already!"

Madeleine's eyes grew large. "Oh, my God, Jean, they are so beautiful. They must have cost a fortune." Her face suffused with color. "Jean, are these my mother's pearls?"

"Yes, my love".

"Where? How"? She turned around and looked up into my face.

"Well, my love, you know that I have been planning this marriage for many years, and pearls are the perfect betrothal gift. Everyone says so. So I thought it best to keep them."

"Oh Jean," she threw her arms around my neck and began to sob. "All these years. I thought all my beautiful jewels were gone. You are the most wonderful man."

"Yes, you showed them to me the first day we met. You tried them on for me. Do you remember?"

"Yes, yes I do. Lord, it seems like ages ago."

When I first announced my plan to marry Madeleine, Pierre was standoffish and disapproving, but there are few men on this earth who could long resist a determined assault by my Madeleine. She turned on her charm and within a week, Pierre became her staunchest supporter and insisted on giving away the bride.

The next year was the happiest of my life. Our rented lodgings were cramped. We needed a house. Madeleine had heard about a small chateau in the Marais. It is my favorite part of the city. She arranged to see it while I was off on other business. When I returned to our lodgings that evening, her eyes were alight with excitement as she told me of her find. She had made an appointment for us to see it the next day.

It was a tall, narrow stone townhouse on a good street with three floors and a Mansard roof. It had a total of twelve rooms with a large well-lit space on the third floor. It had been built by the Duke de Lorraine for his only son's attendance at court, but the son died. In his grief the duke had left it as it was, partially finished. It had a small paneled reception hall with vaulted ceilings and parquet floors, a kitchen and a master bedroom, with south facing glass doors. After we had spoken with the agent, Madeleine conducted her own tour.

"You see, Jean, this will be our bedroom and the adjoining rooms on either side – the smaller one will be my sitting room and here a library for you. We will have cabinets built for your books and curios and look here, Jean, the best part of all!" She opened the bedroom doors, and we walked out on the narrow balcony. It looked out over a small walled courtyard boxed in by stone walls on three sides. Madeleine spread her arms wide. "This will be our own private garden. We will do it in the Persian style with a splendid fountain. I will work on it while you are gone. It will be lovely with the doors open in the spring and summer. What do you think?"

"Can we afford it?"

"Yes. I have spoken to the duke's man of business. I believe he is willing to negotiate, and it is well within the price range you said we could pay."

"It is not the purchase price that worries me. I just hope that the cost of your renovations will not get me thrown into debtor's prison when I return."

"Oh, Jean, I have been so happy these past months that I had almost forgotten. When must you leave?"

"I can put it off until the end of the year but no longer. Young Pierre, my brother's son, is to go with me as far as Persia. He is to stay in Isfahan and learn the Persian language. You remember my friend Bharton, Madeleine. He has promised to educate him in the Armenian fashion. Pierre is to become our factor in Persia. He will be able to do his sums backwards and forwards in half a dozen languages before Bharton is finished with him."

"I had no idea that you had such grand plans."

"Yes, but now it is important that you know, and there is a good deal more, and we must discuss it in detail before I leave. When I was last in Persia, the new shah purchased several of my best Limoges enamels and commissioned several more jewels of the same sort. I promised him that I would bring a French goldsmith and a watchmaker, and you know, my dear, princes are not renowned for their patience. It is important that I remain high in the shah's favor if our plans are to prosper."

She nodded.

"We have formed a trading company. My cousin Pierre, my brother, and I have been planning for some years. Since I am providing most of the capital, we are to hold 55% of the venture, and should anything happen to me, that portion will come to you."

She clutched my sleeve. "Jean, please do not talk like that. Promise that you will come back to me."

"Oh, I shall come back, my love, never fear, but it is important that you understand how I am trying to secure our future."

"How much money is involved?"

"Aside from the 50,000 I have put aside for our expenses and 200,000 in merchandise that Pierre will sell on our behalf, we will have about 400,000 livres invested in the voyage."

"My God, I had no idea we were so rich!"

"Not rich, my dear, comfortable. Perhaps if we are careful – with luck – when I return from this voyage, we shall never want for money again."

It was a warm spring day with a bright sun. We stood holding hands and talking on our balcony framed in the open doors overlooking Madeleine's soon to be Persian garden. There was a light breeze coming from the direction of the Seine. The river was hidden by a solid phalanx of buildings. Off to the east, dark rain clouds were forming, and we could see their shadows moving slowly towards us over a forest of pointed roofs and chimneys.

"Madeleine, have you ever thought of children?"

She turned to me and looked up into my eyes. "Why, Jean, this is the first time you have mentioned children. Is there some special reason?"

"It is something Pierre said to me when I first returned to Paris. He said that I should have married and had a son to carry on my name."

"And you regret that you have no son?"

"No. I had never really thought much about it. I was too busy with my own affairs. Having children is the way a man cheats death and lives on, I suppose. All this business with the trading company brought it to mind again. You have never mentioned children."

"When I was first married, my husband spoke once of having children, but then he never mentioned it again. I confess I was relieved. I know that the priests say that children are part of God's plan and that woman was put on earth to be fruitful and bear as many as she can, but they seem such a nuisance. I grew up in an adult world. There were no children my own age. So I suppose I just never got used to them. Do you think that I am unwomanly, Jean?

I leered at her. "Not that I have noticed, my love."

Madeleine giggled and slapped my arm. "That's not what I mean, you oaf. Seriously, do you think there is something not quite right with me?"

I looked out across the rooftops. "Wrong? No, you seem perfectly fine to me. Perhaps there is something wrong with both of us. We don't think as other people do. We are misfits of a sort, I guess."

A misfit? I have never thought of myself in that way. Do you think that other people just pretend to like children because that is what people expect of them? Are you sure that you will be happy without a son to carry on? I mean, if you really want to have children, Jean, we could try. I am sure I would love a child of yours."

I put my arm around her shoulders and squeezed. "I think most people are miserable and pretend that they are happy. They spend most of their lives doing what is expected of them. People should have children only if they want them. We don't and anyway we are both too old and set in our ways, and I am content just the way things are."

"I think you are right, I have spent most of my life trying to become a great lady because that was what my mother expected of me. That was her dream for me, and I made it my own."

"I was sorry that you had to give up your title to marry me."

"Oh I don't mind, not really. Of course, it's lovely being called marquise and my lady and having one's hand kissed, with everyone bowing and so forth, but in that world a woman is an ornament, and the men treat you as though you haven't a brain in your head. All those foolish parties and soirees, so tiresome! And the gossip! Endless gossip. Some duke would fart, and it would be the highlight of the evening."

"Madeleine!"

"Well, it's true."

"I didn't realize that dukes broke wind?"

"Duchesses too and rather loudly at times."

"And a marquise?"

"Never, but you must remember – I am no longer a marquise!"

"Hmm." The cloud's shadow drew closer. There was a dark mist beneath the cloud. You could smell the rain.

"We are misfits, but we are happy misfits, aren't we, Jean?"

She turned and I folded her into my arms. "Yes, my love, we are very happy misfits."

Madeleine was right about the townhouse. His Grace was quite anxious to sell. I was able to obtain a good price, and for the first time in my life, I had a wife and a home. It felt odd but very satisfying at the same time. Madeleine's excitement was infectious. As soon as we purchased a bed and a few sticks of furniture, we moved into our new home. Unfortunately, I would not be able to enjoy hearth and home for long, and before I left for India, there was much to be done.

Chapter 41

The French East India Company

Colbert rose from behind his desk, came forward, smiled, and took my hand in what was for him an effusive greeting. Mazarin had died two years before, and Colbert was now finance minister and Marquis de Torcy. King Louis had abolished the post of first minister upon the death of Cardinal Mazarin, but Colbert was that, too, in all but name. He had put on flesh in the five years since I had last seen him, but otherwise the same long face and dark eyes, the same signature black clothing. He seemed unchanged.

"Please, monsieur," he said rounding the desk to his chair and pointing to one of two cushioned chairs placed just in front of it. "Sit down. I have read your report twice. Interesting, *very* interesting. I am more convinced than ever of the need for France to vigorously pursue a place in the East Indian trade."

"Thank you, Excellency, and yes, I recall we spoke of this several years ago. It seems France's destiny to make her way into Asia."

Colbert looked up and his eyes studied my face for a moment before he nodded. "monsieur, let me get to the point of my asking you here. We have a very important mission, and we believe that you are the only man capable of carrying it out. Will you help us?"

How does one answer such a question, particularly when posed by the most powerful man in the kingdom? "Of course, my lord," I said. "I am at your service."

"Good, l was sure that was what you would say. But before you agree, let me be candid, monsieur. The mission we have in mind may involve some personal risk."

"What sort of risk?"

"Our plan is to send a fleet to the Indies within the next five years. It would be useful if some of the ground could be prepared beforehand."

"How may I be of service?"

"In the strictest confidence, monsieur, His Majesty has graciously agreed to charter a French East India Company of which he himself will be a major stockholder."

"This is good news." Although I pretended ignorance, the offering was hardly a state secret and it had not gone well. Shares had been very difficult to sell and over time, the king would eventually contribute over four million livres to that ill fated venture.

Colbert made a wry face. "Yes, quite right. Well, we finally have the financing we need, and I am ready, that is to say, His Majesty is prepared to equip a fleet and send it to the Indies, and we wish you to recruit—if that is the right word—partisans, friends, people who would be helpful, able to influence the mogul court in our favor. You know, trade concessions, exemptions from duties, that sort of thing."

"I can certainly identify such people, but let me be candid, Excellency. In India many such *friends* are easily obtainable through purchase."

Colbert smiled thinly and shrugged. "The courts of the Orient are not so different from those of Europe in that respect, I suppose. At any rate, we are prepared to provide you with the necessary funds, in gold."

I met his eyes. "Your plan was to send a fleet. When?"

Colbert looked away. "Hmm, yes. I quite take your point. The timing is difficult. If the fleet were in the harbor with its guns ready, it would be different. I should think it should arrive in the year '65 or '66 at the latest. When had you planned to depart?"

"Very soon, Your Excellency. If the fleet arrives on schedule, I will have between three and four years to make the proper arrangements. I will be able to stay in India until 1666 at the latest, and I will provide whatever support that I can."

Colbert brightened. "Excellent, monsieur. What amount do you think would be necessary to assure a sympathetic ear at the court of the emperor?"

"Two hundred fifty thousand livres I should think."

Colbert stared at me in disbelief. His eyes grew hard. "So much? Why that is a king's ransom!"

"I would set that as a minimum. A great deal more could be spent. Every eunuch at court has the emperor's ear or knows someone who does. There are two men—one is the Great Mogul's uncle, and there is one other, an official high in Aurangzeb's favor, whom I believe could do a great deal to smooth our path. These are great lords, Your Excellency. Each controls territories larger than all of France."

"Truly. It is difficult to imagine. Do you expect trouble from the English and the Hollanders?

"From the English, most certainly. They are well established in Surat and have a good intelligence system. They have been badly knocked about by the Dutch in the Spice Islands. They consider India their fief, and they will be utterly ruthless when it comes to protecting their position."

Colbert nodded. "You know them, then?"

"Yes, I know several of their highest officials, some quite well."

"So be it. I shall see to it that the funds are made available."

I bowed. "Remember, my lord, timing is of the essence. If a

French fleet does not arrive by '67, I will be forced to leave India and return to Paris, and much of what I may be able to accomplish will be lost."

"Yes, of course. Who remembers last year's bribe! I thank you, monsieur. I admire your frankness. We shall do our best. Certainly that should be sufficient time. If it is not . . ." Colbert shrugged. "Which brings me to another point, monsieur; you were aware that Cardinal Mazarin left his entire collection of diamonds to the French crown?"

"Yes, my lord, a truly princely gift."

"Yes, but unfortunately it has only excited His Majesty's appetite. King Louis has decided to build the greatest collection of jewels in the world. He is particularly anxious to obtain the largest and finest diamonds and among my many duties, His Majesty requires that I 'search the world,' in his words, for great jewels to add luster to his crown. As you know, monsieur, I know nothing at all about diamonds. His Eminence had the greatest respect for your knowledge and acumen. I would be grateful if you could help me find something that would please His Majesty."

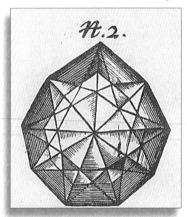

Figure 17: Tavernier's drawing of the Florentine or Tuscan Yellow diamond.

"He has the Sancy."

"Yes, and you would think that a diamond that weighs over 50 carats would be large enough for anyone, would you not? Well, the king is aware that his cousin, the Duke of Tuscany, has one that is much larger."

"Yes, the Tuscan Yellow. So then you would require something larger, meaning over 120 carats."

"Just so, monsieur. Can you supply a diamond of this size and at what cost?"

The finance minister was a man who felt most at home with a column of figures.

"I regret to say, my lord, that there is no diamond of that size available at the moment. To be perfectly candid, I have not seen one for sale in twenty years. Perhaps when I return to India…"

Colbert stroked his chin. "I see. A diamond of that size is truly rare? Suppose one could find such a diamond, monsieur. What should one expect to pay?"

"Difficult to say, my lord. The demand for a fine diamond of that size far exceeds the supply. Fifteen thousand per carat at the least, I should think."

Colbert performed a quick calculation in his head and stared at me dumbstruck. "Monsieur Tavernier, you are talking about 1,500,000 livres. Monsieur Le Cardinal paid less than half of that for the Sancy, and I believe the Florentine cost even less.

"Yes, my lord, a bit over 360,000, I believe, which included the Mirror of Portugal, but you will recall the situation. Queen Henrietta was in dire straits. Her husband, King Charles, had just been executed by Cromwell, and she had spent a great deal of money financing the English cavaliers. So it was something of a forced sale. As for the Florentine, you must consider that the diamond is lemon colored and that it was originally purchased in the rough by the present duke's grand sire. The family has had the stone in its possession for fifty years."

Colbert crossed his arms and regarded me sourly from across the desk. "I must say, you are exceptionally well informed, monsieur. Cardinal Mazarin kept the details of his business dealings very close."

I bowed.

We both sat measuring one another for a few moments, and then Colbert smiled. "Upon my word, monsieur, you do know your business, and I am convinced. I have always admired competence above all things. It is a singular virtue. I believe we shall be able to work together."

"You are very kind, but permit me to say, my lord, that it is you who are well informed. Diamonds have been my business for twenty-five years, yet you know almost as much as I. You may depend upon it. I shall put forth my best efforts on His Majesty's behalf."

Colbert rose from his chair and offered his hand. "Thank you for coming and one thing more, monsieur, you may shortly receive a summons from His Royal Highness, Philippe, Duke of Anjou, the king's younger brother."

I stood up. The king's younger brother? I was confused; the king himself was barely seventeen. I was vaguely aware that he had a younger brother, who would naturally be a duke.

Colbert walked around his desk and extended his hand once again. His lips parted slightly and turned up at the corners, forming one of his thin smiles. "Yes, it would seem, Monsieur Tavernier, that your exploits have penetrated the highest circles of the realm. The duke has heard of you and desires to meet you. He is a curious young man and a great lover of jewels. I believe he wishes to hear about your exploits in India and of the gem mines in particular. He is two years younger than the king and a rather delicate boy. Her Majesty dotes on him. He spends much of his time with the Queen and her ladies."

I could sense from Colbert's manner that he did not altogether approve of this young man. I bowed. "I would be honored to wait upon His Highness."

"I know that you are a busy man, and I thought it best to forewarn you. His Eminence was like a second father to the young prince, and I hope perhaps you may stimulate his interest in more manly pursuits. The summons may come from the Queen, in which case you may have the honor to be received by Her Majesty as well. A useful thing for a purveyor of jewels, I should think."

As Colbert predicted when I returned home, I found a summons from Her Majesty. Madeleine was impressed. Two days later I presented myself at the Louvre.

Chapter 42

Brother of the Sun King

The Louvre Palace was built as a fortification in the Twelfth century, and the city of Paris spread out all around it. It has been added to and subtracted from a good deal over the centuries, and looking at it from the outside always gives me a headache.

I was shown into the salon. It is a room designed to impress, with high vaulted ceilings. The marble floors are covered with rare carpets and the walls, doors, and frames are ornately carved and gilded. We French love gilding. French architects seem to work on the principle: *If it doesn't move, gild it.* I am particularly devoted to the beautifully precise decoration of the Persian style and find our French love of ornamentation for its own sake somewhat gauche.

As I had hoped the queen was present, together with several of her ladies. I bowed low and greeted Her Majesty.

I was expecting a formal audience. Queen Anne received me seated in something more akin to a sewing circle. She and her ladies-in-waiting sat together in a semi-circle, with their embroidery set out. The ladies were dressed in the older fashion in long brocaded gowns with ornately crocheted white lace millstone collars worn over the newly fashionable bare neckline.

Anne of Austria was rather homely. She did not like wigs. She wore her own dark hair, which was thin and without luster. She was not portly, but her face was jowly with a double chin and a large bulbous nose. Perhaps you think me unkind, but I merely report what I saw. Her eyes protruded like those of a frog. She introduced her son.

The young duke was rapier thin. He was a pretty fellow, dressed in dark blue velvet with shoulder length hair, curled so that it fell in ringlets around his crimson mouth and rouged cheeks. It was said that his mother often dressed him as a girl, and when he grew up he often dressed as a woman complete with makeup, wig, and beauty spots. He was darker than the king and had his mother's dark eyes and a very small bow shaped mouth. It was a warm afternoon. He held a silk handkerchief loosely in his right hand. He nodded graciously when we were introduced.

"Monsieur Tavernier, I have heard so much about your travels. Gems are so very fascinating, don't you find?" He smiled airily and fussed with his hair. He seemed perpetually distracted.

I make it a rule never to go before a king or a prince empty handed. I presented His Grace with a small carved teakwood box. Inside there were four compartments lined with silk and in each a perfect gem crystal. There was a diamond crystal from Kollür, a garnet from Mogôk, a long narrow sapphire crystal from the island of Serendib, and a Balas ruby crystal from Ava. None were suitable for cutting. They were not of good water and contained numerous fractures and spots, but His Grace's eyes grew very big when I presented the box and never left my face as I began to explain something about each of these curiosities.

"Ma petite," the Queen interrupted gently, "Monsieur Tavernier is an older gentleman. Perhaps you should take him over to the window where you can see and he can be comfortable."

The duke rolled his eyes. "Yes, Mama."

"And," she said, with a meaningful look, "perhaps you might also offer the gentleman some tea?"

The duke made a face and beckoned to a servant, who brought forward two chairs and called for tea. This was highly irregular. Etiquette requires that one stand in the presence of royalty, but Her Majesty was a kind woman who rarely stood on ceremony.

"Fascinating, is it not, monsieur. Each crystal is so beautifully formed—such symmetry, almost as if they had been made and polished by a skilled craftsman, yet, you say, they are entirely natural? They are found in the earth, just as they are?"

"Just so, Your Grace. Gems are fashioned from crystals. These particular specimens lack the transparency to be of interest for fashioning into gemstones, but they possess a perfect symmetry. Crystals of perfect form are very rare, and the Hindoos love them—they consider them to be manifestations of their gods. The Brahmans—they are a priestly caste—believe that such things have magical properties. The more perfect the form, the more potent the magic. You will notice that the diamond and the Balas ruby are identical in form. Each is shaped like two pyramids bonded together at their bases, and each has eight sides and six corners. This is considered very lucky. They are often used to cure sickness, fevers, and so forth, and have great efficacy—or so I am told."

"Fascinating, I believe there is magic in such things, don't you? Have you seen them used as a cure?"

"I have not had the occasion, Your Grace, though the Indian fakirs swear by them."

"Monsieur Tavernier, thank you very much for your gift. I shall treasure it. May I ask you to show me some of the places where these crystals were found?"

"I am at your service, Your Grace."

The young man clapped his hands, and a servant brought forward a book. It was a beautiful leather bound copy of Abraham Ortelius's atlas the *Theatrum Orbus Terrarum* with the ducal arms of Anjou engraved on a gold plate set into its cover. How ironic. I had never seen a copy of the complete atlas, though, as a boy I had studied these same maps from the handmade copies my father kept in his cabinet. I showed the young prince the routes I had taken and pointed out the locations of the turquoise mines and the pearl fisheries in Persia and of course the diamond mines in the kingdom of Golconda.

The prince looked up at me with shining eyes. "What a grand life you must live, monsieur. I do so wish that I could be like you and travel the world in search of beautiful things."
"Perhaps someday, Your Grace."

"Alas, I fear not," he said, dabbing at his forehead with his hanky. "My physicians and mama—everyone—tells me that my constitution is far too delicate to withstand the rigors of travel. They constantly scold me to guard my health, and then, of course, there is my station. One must do one's duty. I am hardly ever allowed to leave the palace, and besides the queen does so depend upon me. She becomes frantic if I leave her for more than a few hours."

At that moment a courtier entered the hall, bowed, and presented a message to the queen. She read it, rose abruptly and with a nod in my direction swept from the room. The young prince beckoned me forward and whispered into my ear. "Monsieur, I wish to purchase a ruby for my mother. She so adores the color red, and I wish you to advise me. I do not wish the servants to know. They are tattle tales, and, anyway, they cannot keep a secret. I have saved the money myself. Everyone at court made me presents of Louis d'ors at my confirmation, and I wish this to be a surprise." The young prince looked up at me hopefully.

"Your Grace, a fine ruby is very expensive."

"Oh dear, I was afraid of that." His lip trembled, and I was afraid he might cry. Then he smiled bravely. "I have 15,000 livres. Would that be enough?"

I thought a moment. "I believe I may have just the thing."

As is my custom I had one of my servants carry along a selection of my finer goods, just in case. I remembered a lovely ruby of about two and one-half carats that I had bought at the mines and had set in a simple enameled gold band. The stone was easily worth twenty thousand livres, and I had others that would better fit the young man's budget, but the boy's love for his mother touched my heart, and this was to be an investment. If the queen was to have a gem from my stock, I wished it to be a fine one obtained at a very good price.

I found the ring and placed it in his hand. He took it and skipped over to the window and held it up in the light. "Oh, monsieur," he said dancing about with pleasure, "it is just the thing. Such beautiful color! Mama—I mean Her Majesty—will love it. May I take it now? I shall present it to Mama at dinner and have one of my servants bring payment to your lodgings this very evening."

Just to tease him, I rubbed my chin and pretended to consider his offer.

"Monsieur," he said with a look of alarm, "you may depend upon prompt payment. I give you my word as a prince of the blood."

At that moment, an elderly and very agitated servant appeared and bowed. "My Prince, you must not excite yourself so. You know what the doctor says. Your mother, the queen, will be very upset."

"Oh, Edward, don't be such an old woman. As you can see, I am perfectly all right. I just wished to see this wonderful gemstone in good light. Away with you now. Monsieur Tavernier and I wish to speak together—alone!"

"Your Grace…"

The prince stamped his foot: "You heard me, Edward. You will leave us, now!"

The servant bowed reluctantly and withdrew.

"My Lord, I…"

"Oh, do not listen to Edward, monsieur. He has been with me since I was born, and he means well, but he is an old worry-wart. I am perfectly fine, I do assure you."

Meanwhile, Edward did not go far. He stationed himself at the other side of the room where he eyed us with clear disapproval.

"Very well, Your Grace, if you say so. I agree to your offer, but we must seal our agreement. Shall I teach you the secret handclasp that we gem dealers use to complete our business transactions."

"A secret handshake?" The prince laughed a high pitched and girlish laugh. "But of course, monsieur, you must teach it to me, and at once, monsieur, if you please. We must seal our bargain before Mama returns."

"As you wish, my lord, but remember what I am about to reveal is a secret known only to our fraternity, and you must solemnly swear never to reveal it to anyone. Have I your oath?"

The prince placed his hand on his heart and intoned solemnly: "You do. I swear upon my sacred honor."

"Very well." I spit on my palm and extended my hand.

The prince's jaw dropped open. He froze like a deer caught in the light of a bright lantern, and hurriedly hid his hands behind his back. For a moment I thought I had gone too far with this effeminate creature. Then a smile broke out on his face, and he let out his high-pitched laugh.

"Monsieur, I believe you are having me on. Upon my word, I do! How droll, how truly droll!" The prince raised his hand, opened his palm, and spat tentatively upon it, held it out, and we clasped hands.

This is the story of my first meeting with a young man who, as the years went by, would become my patron. In later years he became increasingly foppish and more and more decadent in his habits, but we remained friends.

.

6th
Voyage

(1663-1668)

Chapter 43

Abbās II, Shah of Persia

y sixth voyage was in many ways the most interesting and was certainly the most lucrative. I departed Paris on Nov 27th 1663 with goods worth in the neighborhood of 400,000 livres and took ship from Marseilles for Leghorn on January 10th in the year 1664. I took my young nephew Pierre, the son of my brother Maurice, together with a goldsmith and watchmaker. After a series of difficulties, I finally sailed from Leghorn on the Dutch cog *Justice,* arriving in Smyrna on April 25, 1664. We proceeded by caravan after stopovers in Erivan and Tabriz where the watchmaker unfortunately succumbed to the bloody flux, and I left my nephew in the care of the Capuchins to study the Persian language. I arrived in the Persian capital on December 20, 1664.

The weather had turned cool, and I was glad to finally reach the city. I was anxious to show Shah Abbās several enameled jewels I had had made at his request.

As soon as I was settled, I sent a messenger to inform my friend Bharton and my old servant Danush of my arrival. I then ordered one of my servants to bring clean clothes and went to a steam bath. The months on caravan had burned my face dark as an Arab's, and in my native robes I could pass for one. I peeled off my filthy clothes and my companions at the bath were amazed by the sight of a dark skinned Arab turning into a lily-white Frank.

I lay with the water up to my chin and the back of my head resting against the cool tiles and let my mind wander. Travel by caravan is monotonous. The caravan from Aleppo formed a single line longer than an English mile. With my eyes closed, I could see stretched out before me a seemingly endless procession of a camel's hind quarters. The beast moves with an odd gait. A horse walks like a Christian, but a camel is an awkward brute. The legs on each side of the animal move forward in parallel, producing a rolling motion which leaves the rider feeling as though he is perched on the edge of a precipice and about to be pitched forward onto his head.

When I was a young man, the excitement of new places sustained me, but I had by now made this journey many times. Both the body and the spirit were less and less willing. Still, I had yet to find that great diamond, the one I had dreamed about for all these years. Where was it and would I ever find it?

After my bath I made my way to Bharton's house and found him at home. I was immediately lifted off my feet in a bear hug, which nearly broke my ribs. My old Armenian friend was immensely strong, built like a wine barrel equipped with arms and legs. He seemed much the same, the hawk's face softened by the scraggly beard now, with more than a bit of salt mixed with the pepper, the same hooked nose, and a look that had evolved from bemused to ironic.

He led me to his office and seated me on a long low divan. A servant brought coffee. After the preliminaries were over we began to talk serious business.

"You wish to see the shah? You are in luck this time. You have the most intolerably good luck, friend tavern keeper. There is a new nazir. Do you know Mohammad Ali Beg?"

"I do not."

"Good," he said, slapping me on the back. "I knew you were a man of taste. He is an Armenian renegade, a turn coat."

"Another Armenian has become nazir? I had not heard."

"Like Judas, he sold our lord Jesus Christ, but he got far more than thirty pieces of silver, I will tell you that. He has embraced the false religion."

"He did it for money?"

The look became more ironic "Why, you ask. Why would anyone do such a thing? In a word, power. Money, of course, but power is a more potent drug, and when you have it, wealth soon follows in its train. An Armenian can do many forbidden things in Persia, but he cannot become an officer of the government. This is limited to Muslims. Mohammad Ali Beg is the son of a tailor, and a favorite of another Armenian turncoat, Allāhverdi Khān, the shah's great friend, and Allāhverdi Khān wanted an Armenian to become vizier to consolidate his own power…"

"I have met that gentleman. He was in power when last I met with the shah. Is honest conversion, then, such a bad thing?"

Bharton gave me a hard look. "No, not if it is from the heart, you understand. But this man has no heart. For the Mussulmans, converting one of us is a feather in their caps. It wins them great merit, they think, before their god. He was cajoled, but he was also threatened with death."

"It would seem that he did what he had to."

Bharton's face colored. "Others have been threatened and remained steadfast, have gone to the pyre, you understand, rather than renounce the true savior."

Well in the end, I knew that no Armenian trader would ever allow his personal feelings to come between himself and a lucrative business deal. So despite everything, Bharton sent a letter to Mohammad Ali Beg on my behalf… ah, begging for an audience.

The minute I saw the nazir I understood why Bharton disliked him. He was a short, rotund, oily little man with coarse features which even the richest silks could not disguise. He had about him the sort of arrogance that only a man who has been raised from the gutter can effect toward those less powerful than himself. To those with more power he invariably acts the toady. As you may have guessed, I did not like him either.

He received me in a beautifully appointed chamber in the Persian style, arches within arches and a high vaulted ceiling. The chamber was open on three sides. At the room's center was an octagonal fountain with a delicate jet of water dancing in the mid-morning sun. A small channel ran from the fountain's base outside to a pleasant little garden with a carefully laid out plan of shrubs and tamarind trees.

The nazir sat on a raised dais set against the only wall. The dais was covered with rugs of the type woven in Bhatiari, a cold region, snow-covered in winter, to the southwest of Isfahan. Each rug contained one imperfect thread so that the weaver would not seem to compete with Allah, who alone is perfect. I made my bow.

"Monsieur Tavernier, I see you bear a letter from my very good friend, Bharton, the head of the Šahrimanian family." His mouth smiled and his pig's eyes glittered. "How may I be of service to you?"

I opened my hands, palm up, and bowed once more. Your Excellency, as you can see, I am a merchant, a purveyor of gems and jewels and the finest luxury goods. On my last voyage, His Majesty gave me several designs to execute, and I seek an audience with him so that I may show him the results."

The nazir's dark eyes glittered. "Who has not heard of the famous Monsieur Tavernier?" he said slowly shaking his head. "I regret to say that an audience is difficult, most difficult to arrange. You understand, my dear aga. The shah is very busy." He spread his hands to show his impotence. "Perhaps if you would be good enough to show your merchandise to me, I may be able to persuade His Majesty to spare you a moment at some future time."

I bowed once more. "Your Excellency is most kind." The nazir's pig-eyes followed my hand as I reached into my bag. "Perhaps, Your Excellency, you would accept these small tokens as a gesture of thanks for taking your time to consider my unworthy petition." I placed before him several expensive objects, among them a lovely pocket watch on a gold chain. The watch was finely worked and set with diamonds, the case delicately enameled in dark blue, the color of lapis lazuli. He found the button, the watch cover sprang open, and the watch played a little tune. The pig eyes danced with glee as he held it to his ear.

"Many thanks," the nazir said with a broad smile. The smile faded. He paused for a moment and ran his tongue over his fat lips as if pretending to work out a thorny problem. Then he smiled again. "Upon consideration, it will not be necessary to show me your goods. If you will return tomorrow just after noon, I shall personally petition His Majesty to grant you a moment."

So that was that. I would receive my audience, but it had come very dear. The value of the gifts altogether was almost 20,000 livres. The watch alone had cost nearly 10,000. It turned out to be a good bargain.

The following day the kalantar, the mayor of the Armenians, called with four horses to bring me before the nazir. The sun was warm and framed by a sky of azure blue. We rode over the Allāhverdi Khān Bridge which spans the river between the city and the suburb and along the tree-lined boulevard, Tcharbag, which in Persian means "street of four gardens." We rode along the channel that runs down the center of the avenue. It is flanked on either side by a row of tamarisk trees, and the morning was cool and sweet in their shadow. We rode leisurely along, listening to the flowing water and the song of the birds.

When we arrived at the palace I was pleased to find my old friend Father Raphael du Mans, the superior of the Capuchins. Together we greeted the nazir, who conducted me to a large table covered with a carpet of gold and silver and directed me to lay out the goods I had brought for the shah's inspection.

Once I had arranged my treasures to the nazir's satisfaction, a servant was sent and Shah Abbās II entered the room. He was preceded by two servants whose job it was to pull off his shoes when he enters a room and to put them on again before he departs. The shah was dressed simply with a pair of red and white checked taffeta drawers, like our Gally-Gascoignes—which end at the calf—a short cassock, and a cloak with sleeves edged in sable that fell down to the ground.

As soon as he spied me, he smiled and said to the nazir. "I

recognize this man. He is the Ferenghi, Aga, who sold me several rare jewels about six years ago."

The nazir motioned to me, and I stepped forward. At eight steps I kneeled and banged my head on the carpet as is the custom. I presented His Majesty with the large steel mirror which distorted the image of those who looked into it.

Father Raphael explained the mirror's use.

"I see. Ali," the shah ordered, pointing to one of his servants, a fat eunuch, "come here. Stand before the Ferenghi's glass."

"Ha, ha, Ali. You look like a toad," the shah said, laughing. The eunuch looked as if he was about to cry.

He dismissed the eunuch and ordered several more of his servants to stand before the mirror, one after the other, and doubled up with mirth at the sight of them distorted in the mirror's reflection. "Oh funny, this is very funny," he cried. "I shall have this placed in the harem to amuse my wives."

I brought out the jewels which I had made at his instruction and laid them on the table.

His Majesty's eyes lit up, and he clapped his hands with delight and patted me on the shoulder. "I am pleased. You have done very well. You made these jewels exactly as I wished."

The nazir frowned and nodded.

After that the shah retired, and I packed up my jewels. When I reached my lodgings, I found Danush waiting for me.

"Aga, how long has it been since you left your poor servant? I thought you would never return."

He had put on a great deal of flesh since I last saw him. Truth to tell, Danush was fat as a tick. He had deep lines around his eyes and looked very much the successful middle aged merchant. Still, somewhere inside, I knew, he was the same gangly, half starved urchin I had first met at the rug merchant's shop in Nishapur thirty years before.

"Are you ready to accompany me on another voyage to India?"

"Oh aga, I am so sorry, but I cannot. Please forgive me." His eyes filled with tears. "My wife has said that she will divorce me if I go on another long voyage. Of course, you know, aga, that a woman cannot divorce a man, but what she *can* do—a curse on her entire sex—is much worse."

"How many children do you have now?"

"Six, by the grace of Allah. Six, but only two boys! There are five women in my house. Women are a great curse, aga."

I was disappointed. I had come to rely on Danush and treasure his friendship. The trip would be lonely without him. He would serve me so long as I was in Persia, and that, at least, was something.

The next morning Father Raphael and I were summoned by the nazir. With Father Raphael translating the nazir's secretary wrote down the price of each piece.

"Monsieur Tavernier," the nazir said, "His Majesty wishes to purchase the gemstones you left but will return the pearls." He cocked one eye. "His Majesty suggests that you might get a better price for the pearls in India."

This was a diplomatic way of saying that the price of the pearls was too high. I bowed to the nazir. "Please thank His Majesty for his condescension and guidance."

"I shall and, monsieur, I have the honor to inform you that His Majesty has decided to honor you with the appointment as his "Jeweler in Ordinary," and His Majesty says further that you may ask any favor of His Majesty that you might desire."

I bowed and expressed my gratitude. "Your Excellency. Since His Majesty would honor me with a favor, there are three things that I would ask."

"Yes, monsieur?"

"First, I wish to be exempted from duties within His Majesty's domains, and, second, I would ask that His Majesty graciously extend his protection to my nephew Pierre, who is presently in Tabriz studying your beautiful language at the Capuchin monastery."

"And, the third favor?"

"Only that the shah gives me a patent to allow me to purchase three loads of wine in Shiraz."

The following day I was once again summoned. "Monsieur Tavernier, I have the honor to inform you that his Majesty has granted your wishes and as a mark of his esteem and affection he is pleased to present you with a khalat. Tomorrow the grand treasurer will pay you the sum owed for your jewels."

The presentation of the khalat is a singular honor. When a Persian king wishes to honor a man, he presents him with a sumptuous suit of clothes. The Persian costume consists of several garments, the more complete the ensemble the greater the honor.

The next morning the nazir conducted me to the treasury. The treasurer placed before me 3,460 silver tomans in sealed leather bags. He asked for a fee of 168 tomans.

"Please open the bags and weigh them," I said.

The nazir conveyed this to the treasurer, who spoke only Persian. The grand treasurer's face turned red. A fierce argument broke out between the treasurer and the nazir. The treasurer was a eunuch and much larger than the nazir. He had tiny eyes and protruding lips, and when he was upset his cheeks puffed out, and he looked like an angry blow-fish. The nazir did not even turn a hair.

The nazir turned to me with an amused smile. "Monsieur, the grand treasurer has certified that it is the correct amount. He says that he is your friend and wishes to know why you need to count the money. He says that in Persia friends are trusted."

"Odd, I have never heard of such a saying among the Armenians who all agree are the most astute businessmen in all of Asia. Please tell my friend the treasurer that it is not a matter of trust. Among the Franks we make a distinction between friendship and business. My esteemed father taught me that as a matter of business always to count the money, and I do so to honor his memory."

The nazir bowed. "Well said, monsieur, but you must remember that we are a complex people, and His Excellency is a Persian."

"Yes, I thought so."

The nazir's tiny eyes glittered wickedly. "Your father was a wise man." His voice a whip, the nazir ordered the silver to be counted. Once I had weighed the silver toman by toman, I presented the grand treasurer with half of the amount he had asked.

That afternoon one of the nazir's attendants brought the khalat to my lodgings. It consisted of a vest, tunic, girdle, and bonnet. He also delivered three patents, each written in beautiful flowing script and each sealed with His Majesty's seal confirming the three favors I had requested.

Two mornings later I was summoned once again. I dressed in the khalat and went at once to the palace where I found Father Raphael and two Hollanders. To my surprise, the nazir, with his own hands, draped over my shoulders an exquisite silk cloak in the Persian style with hanging sleeves and faced with the finest sable. It was a magnificent piece of silk worth over 2,400 livres. The nazir then took me by the hand and brought us all before the shah.

In a large chamber set aside for banqueting, His Majesty was seated on a cushion covered with a thick carpet woven with threads of gold. Against his back was another cushion about four feet long with a covering of silk brocade the color of lapis lazuli. A group of fat eunuchs with muskets on their shoulders stood like statues in a half-circle behind him. Just in front of the dais was a small low table with eight or ten dishes of solid gold filled with fruits and sweetmeats and two carafes of the finest Venetian crystal, a cup of gold for the shah to drink from, and a large golden bowl with a gold ladle that was used to serve guests.

We all bowed and banged our foreheads on the floor, which luckily was covered with the finest Kerman carpets. "Bia, bia, (come, come), Raphael," the shah said and motioned the Capuchin to come forward. "If you would drink wine, stay here. If not, be gone."

The priest bowed deeply. "Your Majesty, since you would honor me, I will stay and drink a little."

"Very well, then, take your seat," the shah said.

We all sat down. A troop of musicians carrying lutes, guitars, spinets, and brass flutes filed in, sat down, and began to play. Though it was two hours before noon it was clear that we had been summoned to a drinking party.

Abbās II was a young man, only 32 years old, not exactly fat but soft and fleshy as one might expect of a man raised in the seraglio surrounded by women and eunuchs. His long face was florid from an over fondness for wine. In truth His Majesty, like his father Shah Sefi, had a reputation as a drunk, but a wily one and one who wielded absolute power. His hair was black and his eyes were dark and cold. He wore long pointed mustaches and a narrow chin beard that added to his sinister air. He was a moody man. An affable companion one moment, he could suddenly turn cruel. He was a dangerous man to drink with but an even more dangerous man to refuse.

The shah bade one of the Hollanders to take the ladle and fill our glasses. The ladle went around the table smartly considering the time of day. Servants entered, a cloth of gold was spread over the table and over that a leather cover. Over that, a long piece of bread no thicker than a piece of parchment was unrolled covering the entire table. This bread is never eaten. It is used to catch food dropped by the diners, after which it is rolled up and given to the poor. Placed before us were about twenty small dishes filled with broiled meat and smoked fish, sauces and other Persian delicacies. We commenced the feast, after which the dishes were removed and the bread rolled, and small bowls of water scented with rose petals were brought so that we might clean our hands.

The shah motioned me to come and sit by him on the dais. He wished, he said, to hear stories of my travels to the Indies. This was a ruse. What he had in mind was a test.

"Which of the great men of India have you met and done business with?"

Once I had listed them, he brought out a satchel and showed me a group of miniature paintings set in gold frames. "Which of these men do you recognize?"

I pointed out Shah Jahan, Aurangzeb and three of his sons, the king of Golconda, and two rajas.

His Majesty nodded and stroked his beard. He seemed little affected by the wine. Then I noticed that each time his cup was filled, he moistened his lips and passed it to a courtier standing just behind him who drained the cup.

He showed me miniatures of two Venetian women, one a widow and the other a virgin with a parrot sitting on her hand. "Which of these two women do you like the best?"

This seemed an odd question, but I answered truthfully that I liked the one with the parrot.

"Why do you choose her?"

"Because, Your Majesty, the other one looks as if she has renounced this world."

The shah found this very funny. He turned to Father Raphael: "Patri, Patri," he cried, handing him the tiny painting. "Is it possible that such a woman as this could have taken the veil?"

This led to a discussion of beauty in women. His Majesty demanded my opinion.

"Much depends on the custom of the country, Your Majesty. In the Japans they favor women with broad faces. In China they admire women with tiny feet. In the kingdom of Ava women with black teeth are greatly desired. On the island of Makassar they pull out the four front teeth of girls when they are very young and put gold teeth in their place. In Persia you admire women with their eyebrows grown together, but in France women pluck out these hairs by the roots."

"Very well said, my friend, but tell me, which do you prefer, the dark or the white?"

"Sir, were I to purchase women the way I purchase diamonds, pearls, and bread, I would demand only the whitest."

This answer set the shah to laughing. "For me, I like chicken breast meat for the most part, but I find the dark meat sweet and full of flavor." He slapped me on the back and ordered my cup filled to the brim. He then began to ask me questions about political conditions in Europe and of the king and nobles of France. By this time many hours had passed, and it had grown dark.

One of the Persian courtiers, a loud coarse looking fellow, had become quite befuddled and was loudly haranguing a holy man, trying to make him drink wine. The holy man had just returned from a pilgrimage to Mecca, what is called the hajj, and, by custom, was obliged to abstain from drink. The man did his best to ignore the bully who kept loudly plaguing him until he finally knocked off the holy man's turban.

The shah saw this. His dark eyes narrowed, and his lips formed a thin line. He motioned to the eunuch, who was chief of his guard. "This rascal has lost all self-respect. He thinks that he is no longer my slave. Drag him out by the feet, slit open his belly, and throw him to my dogs for their supper."

The eunuch made a small signal with his hand to two of the guards who stood on the dais. They ran over, grabbed the offending courtier by the feet, and started dragging him toward the door. The shah had ordered a particularly slow and cruel death. Once the belly is slit, a man's entrails spill from his body like a nest of snakes. The shah keeps a number of large, vicious hunting dogs. These animals are kept half starved to encourage their hunting instincts. I have seen them set upon and devour a man's entrails while the hapless victim writhes in agony. The drunken courtier, taken by surprise, at first did not understand what was happening, but he quickly sobered. He kicked his way free and threw himself at the foot of the dais.

"Your Majesty," he cried, "please, I beg you. I meant no harm. I meant only to play a joke. If I have offended you, please forgive me."

The shah was unmoved by this, sat stone-faced, and ignored the man. The guards came up from behind, grabbed the courtier's arms, and lifted him to his feet, but the courtier shook them off and again prostrated himself.

"Your Highness, please, I beg you, take pity in the name of Allah. I have a wife, a family." He began to blubber and cry.

The commotion caused the musicians to stop playing, and the dancers stood and stared. No one dared interfere.

The shah clapped his hands. "Bring on the dancers!" He cast a baleful eye at the musicians. "Have I given you permission to stop?" he demanded. "Play, play, and make it a lively air."

The musicians immediately resumed playing, and the dancers began to twirl and shake their tambourines. The chief eunuch motioned two more guards forward, and each took a secure hold of one of the man's limbs, and together they dragged him kicking, wailing, and fouling himself, across the chamber and through the door to his death.

As I said, no one interfered or even commented. In Europe if a king were to order such a thing, he would risk being thought a madman. The conceits and diversions of the French court would never be allowed in Persia. Can you imagine staging *Tartuffe* in Isfahan? Molière and the entire *Troupe de Monsieur* would become food for the dogs.

After a few minutes the shah asked, "Tell me, Monsieur Tavernier, do you enjoy our Persian music?"

"I do, Your Highness," I said, doing my best to act as if nothing unusual had happened.

"How does it differ from the music of the Ferenghi?"

I did not know how to answer, but there was a Monsieur Daulier present who fancied himself a musician. I think the scene he had witnessed had unmanned him. The man jumped to his feet and began to sing a court air, but he sang falsetto like a eunuch. The shah frowned. Persians prefer the bass. The man began to shake in fear. Though I am not a singer, I have a decent deep voice, and I was sufficiently in my cups that I rose and sang an old drinking ditty accompanying myself by dancing a little jig:

> *"Fill all the bowls, then fill 'em high*
> *Fill all the glasses there, for why*
> *Should every creature drink but I?"*

The site of a mature, overweight Ferenghi dancing about was too much for the shah. He laughed until the tears rolled down his cheeks. After this, His Majesty decided that the two of us were great friends, and I was frequently invited to the palace and always before the evening ended required to sing and dance. His Majesty found my songs amusing, and I constantly rooted among the Europeans, searching for new ditties to add to my repertoire. I did my best to play the role of the boon companion, but I felt much calmer in his presence after a few glasses of wine. Had I stayed much longer in Isfahan, I would no doubt have become a drunk. After several weeks of drunken evenings at court, I was able to make my excuses and arranged to take my leave.

Preparations began several hours before dawn. I had been in the Persian capital for better than two months. It was late February, it was at the edge of the monsoon. With some relief I packed up for Bander Abbās.

Torches lit up the dusty courtyard of the caravanserai like a scene out of bedlam. Shadows flitted between piles of goods and the night vibrated to the jingling of hundreds of camel bells. The proper packing of a camel is an art; if it is not done properly the beast will develop sores and even go lame. I had traveled the road from Isfahan to the gulf many times. Bullocks are better in India because of the heat, but in Persia, I prefer camels. They are nasty, smelly brutes, but they can carry three times the weight a horse can manage, and the road to the coast is quite dry during this season.

A great commotion erupted at the gate. There was still enough light from the waning moon that I could see a man gesturing and arguing with my guards, who were refusing to allow him entry. I knew that whining voice. I signaled to the guards to let him enter.

Danush ran up to me breathless, dragging the halter of a donkey which obviously had been packed in a great hurry. The beast was loaded to overflowing.

"Aga, aga!" His turban askew, he looked like someone who had dressed hurriedly and in the dark. "Your faithful servant is here," he announced. "Aga, I am coming with you to India."

I crossed my arms and addressed him sternly: "So you have changed your mind. What about your wife?"

Danush stopped and looked up at me, crestfallen. "Are you not pleased to see your loyal servant?" He cast a nervous glance back over his shoulder. "And please, aga, do not speak of that woman. She gives me no peace."

"I thought you had promised her that you would not come on this voyage."

He shrugged. "She made me promise, aga. I tried to reason with her. I told her; the aga needs his faithful servant. She would not listen. Women are impossible."

"What about your children?"

"They will be fine, aga. They give the woman something to worry about. I have left them with money enough. Besides, how can I support my family if I do not work? My travels with you, aga, have brought many blessings, praise God!"

I was pleased. Danush was a trustworthy and amusing companion. Nevertheless I could not resist having a bit of fun. "I am not sure that it is God who deserves the praise. Perhaps we can make room, but it is almost dawn and we must leave immediately."

Danush looked around nervously. "You should not speak that way, aga. Allah will be angry. Your servant is ready and has everything that is needed except a horse. Perhaps you could spare your loyal servant a horse."

"A horse, hmm. As it happens I do have a spare horse, and it is one I paid very dearly for, and I am very fond of. I suppose you may ride him until we can find you another, but. . ." I shook my finger at Danush "see that you do not abuse him. Do you have even a saddle? I have no extra saddle." I looked at the sky, it was beginning to lighten. "Quickly, go to the market and buy yourself one."

"No, no, aga," he said looking alarmed. "Your servant does not wish to hold you up for even a moment. You know that I am an excellent rider. I will ride bareback until we reach Shiraz."

By now Danush had caught his breath. He kept glancing fearfully towards the gate as if he was expecting his formidable wife to appear like an apparition out of the gloom.

"I won't have you riding bareback. I think we can delay long enough to secure a saddle."

"No, aga, please," he put his hands together and began to plead. "It will take too long. Please, let us go now while it is early and the air is still cool."

"What did you think, worthless fellow, that I rose in the middle of the night merely to amuse myself? We must put several leagues behind us if we are to reach our lodgings before the sun is high. We are packed and ready, but you are not. Repack that animal. As it is, we shall eat dust for several hours, and we will not make a league from the city before that pack will be dragging the ground and your goods will be scattered along the road from here to Shiraz."

Danush favored me with one of his big toothy smiles. "Yes, aga, right away. It will be good to be on the road again, aga, will it not?"

Chapter 44

The Great Mogul's Treasure

I am the only Frank who has been allowed to see the jewel collection of the Great Mogul. In September of 1665 after landing at Surat, I traveled directly to Jahanābād and was gratified to be able to sell several of my finest jewels directly to the Emperor Aurangzeb. I had requested the honor of viewing his treasury of gems. He kindly said that if I remained for the celebration of his birthday fête, he would be pleased to grant my wish.

Figure 18: The birthday ceremony of weighing the Great Mogul. Subjects were expected to give gifts of gold and gems equal to his weight. 17th Century engraving.

By tradition, the emperor is weighed each

year on his birthday, and his subjects are obliged to collect and offer him a tribute of his weight in gold. The celebration goes on for four or five days. First a great red velvet awning is erected to cover the great hall of the palace at Jahanābād. The awning, which is embroidered with gold, is so heavy that it requires thirty-eight poles, each the size and girth of a ship's mast, to support it. These poles are covered with plates of gold the thickness of a ducat.

The emperor has seven magnificent thrones; the chief throne that is placed in the great hall is the size of a camp bed, six feet long and four feet wide. The throne has four feet and between each of the feet are four bars which support its base. Attached to these are twelve columns supporting the canopy over the throne. Each of the bars is inlaid with gold and encrusted with diamonds, rubies, and emeralds. Each of the columns is surrounded with pearls which are between ten and twelve carats each. Above the dome-shaped canopy is a peacock with an elevated tail made of blue sapphires. This famous throne was commenced by Tamerlane and finished by Shah Jahan at a cost of 160,500,000 livres of French money.

The fête itself was magnificent. The emperor's guard alone was composed of six-thousand troops magnificently attired and arrayed in ranks. Each day the royal elephants pass in parade and one by one, each of the principal officials of the empire come forward, each with his own retinue amounting to 2,000 armed retainers. Each comes forward in turn and presents his gift to the emperor.

In the mogul empire, the crown owns every acre of land. The Emperor Aurangzeb surrounds himself with appointed officials, called omrahs, many of whom are Persians. These men hold no hereditary titles, but serve at the emperor's pleasure, and upon their deaths, all their wealth, excepting only their wives' jewels, reverts to the crown. In practice the father's office is often granted to his eldest son, but it is by no means assured. To curry favor, each courtier scours the kingdom for rare items in an effort to outdo his rivals in presenting the finest gift to His Majesty at his birthday fête.

Aurangzeb is a very crafty ruler. Several months before his birthday, he consigns jewels from his treasury to some of the most trusted merchants in the city. The courtiers then buy the jewels from the merchants and, thusly, the mogul is able to transform his jewels into gold and get the jewels back again.

One morning, just after the fête, six officers called at my lodgings with a summons from the emperor. At the palace, I was conducted to a small audience room where I found His Majesty seated on a throne. The mogul is tall for an oriental and very thin, almost wasted from his ascetic practices. He has a long straight nose, deep set dark eyes and eyebrows and a dark beard which he wears full. I made my salutation. With a gesture, the emperor bade me rise.

"We have heard that you wish to leave us." His Majesty raised an eyebrow.

"Regrettably, yes, Your Majesty. I have business in Agra."

"You enjoyed our birthday celebration?"

"Yes, Your Majesty. It was magnificent, and I thank you for inviting me to witness the fête."

The emperor nodded, "Excellent. You expressed a desire to see the royal jewels. Today it is our pleasure to grant your wish. We will be pleased to hear your opinion." The emperor clapped his hands twice and nodded to an attendant.

"I thank Your Majesty, and may I beg a further boon? May I be allowed to make drawings of some of Your Majesty's jewels so I may show my king the magnificence of Your Highness's collection?"

The emperor smiled and nodded.

Akil Khan, keeper of the royal jewels, came forward and prostrated himself before the throne. He was a short furtive little man, a Persian, with a richly appointed turban and just a scrap of beard clinging to his chin. Akil Khan means prince of wit, though prince of thieves would have been a more accurate title. I had had dealings with him in the past. He had attempted to extort money as a bribe, which I refused. We were not friends.

"Akil Khan, the Lord Tavernier has asked to see the royal jewels, and we are pleased to grant his request. See to it."

The khan knocked his head against the floor. "Your wish is my command, oh lion of the faith. Had I known that it was your wish, I would have made preparations immediately. The jewels have never before been shown to an infidel, but if it is Your Majesty's wish, I shall begin arrangements this very day."

"Begin arrangements?" the emperor glowered and his deep set eyes burrowed into the skull of Akil Khan. "Did you not hear me speak, dog? Would you embarrass us in front of this Frank? It is our desire that the Lord Tavernier will see our jewels now in our presence."

The keeper seemed about to offer an objection but thought better of it. "As you command, majesty, so shall it be done!" Akil Khan bowed and backed slowly from the emperor's presence, but when he walked by me his mouth was set in a grim line and his eyes were flinty with hate.

He summoned four burly eunuchs and commanded them to bring the jewels. Two other servants ran ahead and placed cushions in an alcove under a group of latticed windows at the end of the chamber within view of the throne.

The eunuchs, accompanied by three scribes, returned carrying two large gold leafed and lacquered trays with fitted covers of silk brocade. One was covered in green, the other in red. The trays were so heavy that two fat eunuchs were required to carry each of them. With his mouth set, Akil Khan made an elaborate bow, stepped aside, and motioned me to precede him.

The late morning sun cast charming patterns of light and shade on the white marbled walls. The scribes arranged themselves cross-legged on the floor. The trays were uncovered, the jewels counted three times, and a list prepared by the scribes. This procedure took quite some time. The Indians do everything methodically and with great ceremony, and it is necessary to be patient. I once saw a Dutch trader become angered by all of this ceremony. The Indians said nothing at all, just gazed and smiled at him as if he were a madman.

An embroidered cushion was placed before me. On it was a huge gem known as the Great Mogul's Diamond. I held it up in a beam of sunlight that filtered through the latticework. This diamond shone like the sparkling water of a pure mountain spring. A delicate blue-white glow hovered and clung to the surface of the gem and a rainbow flashed from within its depths, sending out shards of colored light that danced about the walls of the chamber. The stone is a round rose cut, and it weighs 279 and nine sixteenths French carats. The stone was mined at Kollür. When the Emir Jumla originally gave the rough stone to the Great Mogul's father, Shah Jahan, it was the size of a small hen's egg and weighed 787 ½ carats. The Mogul is the largest and most beautiful diamond anyone has ever seen. It is said to be worth all the gold in the world. I measured the stone, made a few notes, drew its outline and quickly sketched in its facets.

I gingerly replaced the Great Mogul onto the cushion and into the hands of Akil Khan. He nodded curtly and presented another gem. This was a pear shaped diamond of fine water which weighed over 60 carats. The third stone was a marvelous rose cut, about the size of half an English walnut. It was clean and crystalline and weighed in the neighborhood of 70 carats. I was awestruck. These were jewels

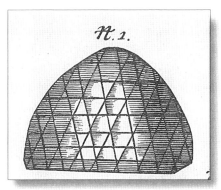

Figure 19: Tavernier's drawing of The Great Mogul's diamond.

such as I had seen in my dreams and though I had searched for more than thirty years, bought and sold many fine and beautiful gems, never had I seen the like. Would I ever possess such a gem?

One by one I examined each jewel and made sketches of the most important. The ability to make a quick drawing is a skill I learned from my father. Akil Khan dared not say anything, but he made his disapproval plain enough by snapping orders to his staff and moving about the room making inarticulate sounds.

After I had seen all the treasures, I walked back to the other end of the chamber. Aurangzeb still sat upon his throne surrounded by several omrahs, scribes, and other court functionaries. He looked up and motioned with his hand that I should come forward.

"Tell me, Senhor Tavernier, did my collection meet your expectations?"

"Your jewels are beyond anything that I have ever had the privilege of seeing, Your Highness."

"Even greater than those of the king of the Franks?"

"Far greater, Majesty." Truthfully, I had not at that time had the opportunity of viewing King Louis's cabinet, but I felt it would be impolitic to mention that fact.

He nodded, "Good, very good, you are known to be an honest and knowledgeable dealer, and we thank you for your opinion. May Allah bless you and may your trip be a safe one, and, senhor, it is our wish that when you are next in our realm we will be the first to see any of the curiosities you bring from your country."

I bowed deeply, "It shall be as you command, Highness."

I now burned with a desire to find and purchase a gem equal to those I saw in Aurangzeb's collection. Little did I realize just a year later I was to have my opportunity?

Chapter 45

Shah Jahan

I left the mogul's court and proceeded to Agra where I had some business to attend to.

Just after breakfast one morning I received a messenger with an invitation to visit the Great Mogul's father, Shah Jahan. The former emperor and builder of the Taj Mahal had been dethroned and imprisoned by his son after a bloody war during which Aurangzeb killed two of his three brothers and took the throne for himself.

I first met the ill fated shah during my second voyage to the Indies. He was a small but robust man with a barrel chest and a wiry build. He had the small dark almond shaped eyes of his Mongol ancestors; these were his most prominent feature and were as piercing as those of a hawk. When we first met he still held the throne, but now he was kept a prisoner in the Red Fort at Agra and closely guarded by troops loyal to his son.

The shah smiled and signaled with a hand gesture that I might approach him.

"Greetings, My Lord Tavernier. I heard that you were in the city and knowing your love of gems, I thought you might like to see a stone. It is a gift to my son from his uncle, Ja'far Khan."

"It has been many years, and it was kind of Your Majesty to remember his poor servant and condescend to instruct me."

I could see that my manner of speaking pleased him. He had lost none of the haughtiness of an emperor, but he looked tired and worn. He sat on a raised dais and was dressed in trousers and a simple, long Persian style white silken coat embroidered with gold and pearls. A magnificent double strand of large matched white pearls hung around his neck.

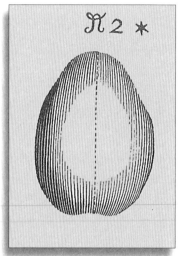

Figure 20: Tavernier's drawing of the Balas ruby shown to him by Shah Jahan.

"Nonsense, my friend, I have little to do these days, and this stone is a curious one. I know your love of the curious." With an imperious wave he dispatched one of his servants to fetch the stone.

The servant brought the gem in a small leather pouch set on a silk cushion. The Shah gestured and the servant presented it to me. I picked up the gem. It was exceptionally large for a ruby, perhaps half the length of my thumb and roughly pear shaped weighing twenty-five Indian rati, or about twenty of our French carats. It was of a pinkish-orangey red color of excellent water with no visible flaws. A flawless stone of such a large size was unusual in a ruby and I said as much to His Majesty.

"Just so, friend Tavernier. My son sent this one to me; he flatters me that I am the best judge of the quality of rubies, though not—unfortunately—of good enough judgment to rule my own empire. He wishes me to tell him if the stone is a true ruby or a Balas ruby." He gave me a sardonic smile. "The court jeweler and all the others my son has consulted, save one, say it is a ruby. What is your opinion?"

In Asia two types of ruby are known, the true ruby and the Balas or spinel ruby. Although it resembles the true ruby, the Balas ruby is considered much inferior and will fetch barely a tenth the price that will be paid for the true ruby.

The shah was a true connoisseur, and few men can resist the urge to teach others so I held my council to allow him the pleasure of instructing me. "Your Highness, this stone is a puzzle. I would value your wisdom."

"Harrumph," he said eyeing me with mock annoyance. "A puzzle you say? Doubtful my Frankish friend, but attend: what of its weight?"

I hefted the stone. "It seems a bit light."

"Just so and its polish?"

"I do not like its polish or its luster."

"Precisely, my friend, and that tells the tale. The gem you hold in your hand is a spinel ruby, and my son has been cheated. The spinel, you see, lacks the hardness of the true gem and takes a slightly inferior polish. The question now is," he said with a mischievous smile, "what should I tell my son."

It seemed best to remain silent.

"Hmm. Well I suppose I must tell him the truth. The jeweler charged Ja'far Khan ninety five thousand rupees, about one and one half million Frankish livres, and it is worth barely five hundred. I can see no reason to allow the jeweler to cheat him."

"Your Highness is famous for his wisdom."

"Wisdom, you say?" The aging prince smiled ruefully. "I might have chosen a wiser course with regard to my offspring. Do you know anything of the mogul tongue, My Lord Tavernier?"

"Very little, Your Highness."

"We have a saying about royal princes; we say *"taktya"* or *"takhta."* The two words rhyme, do you see? The first means *throne* and the second is our word for *tomb*. It is either one or the other. Well, no matter, what is written is written." He held the stone up to the light and rotated it in his fingers. "A beautiful spinel, though, and worth every bit of five hundred gold rupees! You have a good eye, my friend, for a Frank, though not so good as mine."

I learned a great deal during that short audience, and as the Bible says, "The price of wisdom is beyond rubies." Unfortunately this was to be the last time I saw this unfortunate prince. He died still a prisoner, barely a year later. His body was buried in the Taj Mahal next to the woman for whom it was built, his wife, Mumtaj Mahal.

Chapter 46

A Very Brief Affair

As I left this last audience with Shah Jahan and was making my way out of the fort, I spied a fully veiled woman walking along the corridor toward me. As soon as she saw me, she skittered though a side door like a rabbit bolting down its hole. Though she moved quickly, I recognized that proud carriage; it was Princess Jahanara, Shah Jahan's favorite daughter.

Before I leave the unfortunate Shah Jahan, let me tell you the story of my first meeting with this ill starred princess, in the year 1642.

While Shah Jahan's wife, Mumtaj Mahal, was alive, she was his closest advisor. The empress kept her own court and signed imperial decrees in her own name. When she died, the emperor turned to his eldest child, the Princess Jahanara. At this time, the princess was twenty-eight years old and, after the emperor, the most powerful noble in the empire.

One day I received a summons to the Agra Fort. I immediately presented myself at the gate, expecting to be brought before the emperor, but to my surprise was taken to a separate mansion within the fort's walls and ushered into the presence of Princess Jahanara. She sat in a gilded chair perched upon a raised dais. Her dark flowing hair shone blue in the light that filtered through the jalis screens. Female attendants stood on either side of the dais. The princess wore only a gossamer thin veil which barely hid her full red lips. She addressed me directly in beautifully accented Portuguese.

"Senhor Tavernier, I have summoned you because I am curious about one of the beautiful jewels you showed to my father, the emperor. Also, I am curious about some of the customs of your people."

"I am yours to command, Highness."

"This may seem an odd question, senhor, but please tell me, is it your custom to bathe regularly?"

I fear my face turned red. I was totally flabbergasted and began to stutter. The princess's obsidian eyes danced mischievously over the rim of her veil. Her ladies giggled and tittered like birds.

"Come, come, senhor, it is a simple enough question."

"Yes, that is, yes, I do bathe, er regularly, Your Highness."

"Truly? I have been told that it is the custom among certain of the Franks never to bathe."

"Well, Your Highness, it is true that some Europeans believe that bathing is not good for the health. They feel that it disobliges the humors and causes sickness."

"Who could believe such nonsense?" The ladies giggled. "Do you believe that, senhor?"

"No, Your Highness, I do not, but you must consider that the country where we are from is much colder than it is here in India."

"Yet you come from that same country and you bathe?"

"Yes, as I said, my lady, I find a hot bath very relaxing."

"I thought so. Many of the Franks who have come to the court stink, but you do not smell in the least gamey.

My face was now red as a winter beet. I stood speechless.

"Truly, Senhor Tavernier, I congratulate you for your civilized habits. Many of your countrymen stink so badly that it is difficult for a civilized person to converse with them, particularly in an enclosed space. The ambassador of the Hollanders is hairy and smells like a dead fish. The English are the worst of all. My father only gives audience to the English ambassador in the palace garden. Just to be sure, he orders several eunuchs to station themselves behind the throne with large fans to keep His Excellency downwind."

The princess beckoned me forward and abruptly changed the subject. "I am also curious about your coupling habits. Is it true that in your country a woman is supposed to go to her marriage bed a virgin?"

"Yes, Your Highness, but in that respect our customs are not so different, I believe, from your own." I felt like I was beginning to regain my footing, that is, until she asked the next question.

"Senhor, tell me how are your women instructed in the amorous arts?"

"Instructed, my lady?"

"Yes," she said a bit peevishly, "instructed. Are you having trouble understanding my manner of speaking, senhor? I dislike repeating myself. My teachers tell me I speak excellent Portuguese. Have I been misled?"

"No, Your Highness. I mean, yes, Your Highness, you speak beautifully."

"Then answer the question. Do you have books and such as we have to teach women the different positions and techniques and methods for prolonging the pleasure of the act of intercourse?"

"No, Your Highness. No gentleman would read such a book and if a book on this, er, subject existed, it would be considered a sin to read it, and it would be banned by the church."

"Then how are young women to learn? Surely they are not instructed by your filthy priests."

"No, Your Highness. Priests, that is, Roman Catholic priests are expected to remain celibate and would never discuss such things with a young woman. After a woman is wed, I suppose, she is taught by her husband."

"I see," she then spoke to her ladies in the mogul dialect. They listened intently, then all smiled and nodded gravely.

"Tell me then what positions do Frankish men prefer."

"Positions, Highness? I really don't know," I said, the sweat now rolling down my face. "I don't think they have names. Such things are never discussed—certainly not among gentlemen."

"Then how do the men learn enough to instruct their wives?"

"Well, a man is expected to have some experience, you know, before he is married."

"With prostitutes you mean! Tell me, Senhor Tavernier, are you familiar with a book called the *Kama Sutra*?"

"No, Highness, I have never heard of a book by that name. What is the subject?"

"The *Kama Sutra* is the Hindoo manual of love. A moment, senhor, if you please!"

Princess Jahanara motioned to one of her eunuchs, a hugely fat man who came forward. She spoke a few words of command, and he hurriedly waddled out of the chamber.

"As I was saying, the *Kama Sutra* is truly a manual of the amorous arts, and it is used to educate young women and prepare them for the marriage bed."

The eunuch returned with a thick book set on a velvet cushion. "Here you are, Senhor Tavernier, a copy of the *Kama Sutra*. Please accept it as a gift. It is a translation made by a Portuguese friar who has made a fortune selling copies to other Franks. I am surprised that you do not have one. The pictures, I believe, speak for themselves. I wish you to study it and return here just after the sun sets the day after tomorrow so that we may speak further."

I bowed and backed out of the chamber. I never felt so glad to get out of a place in my life, but my elation was short lived when I recalled that I was required to return in two days, prepared to discuss the intimate details of western love making with this beautiful, demanding young woman.

I had little choice, I did as I was bidden; I studied the manual and found it both intriguing and titillating. I had no idea that there were so many ways for men and women to perform the act—in truth, some seemed quite impossible—so many delightful ways for men and women to bring each other pleasure.

I returned to the palace, as I had been commanded, determined not to allow myself to be intimidated. Princess Jahanara was one of the most powerful nobles in the Mogul Empire, but she was still only a woman. If she wished to ask questions, I would answer them straightforwardly without blushing like a silly girl.

After spending some time cooling my heels in an anteroom, a eunuch came and to my surprise led me not to the audience room, but up a flight of stairs then down a series of corridors. He opened a door for me, stepped back, and bade me enter. I stepped through the entrance and before I could turn and ask my escort a question, the door closed behind me with an audible click. The room was quite large and richly appointed. Braziers, set around the room, burned scented wood, golden lamps glowed in niches in the walls, thick carpets covered the marble floors, and richly woven tapestries depicting scenes from the *Kama Sutra* covered the walls.

I had just a few minutes to take in my surroundings when Princess Jahanara swept into the room. She was dressed in a pair of pantaloons of the thinnest red silk, topped with a tight jacket which accentuated her slender waist and showed off her breasts to great advantage. She wore a thin veil that did nothing to hide those full red lips.

"Greetings, senhor, I see that you have returned. Have you studied the book as I asked?"

"I have, Your Highness."

"Excellent." The princess seated herself on one of a pair of velvet divans with a small table set in between. "Please sit down; will you join me in a glass of wine?"

"With pleasure, my lady. What a lovely chamber!"

Princess Jahanara smiled, lifted a beautifully worked crystal decanter, and poured wine into two golden goblets. "I am pleased that you like it. I had it specially built. It is very private. Even the servants do not enter unless they are summoned. The latticed screens let in the breeze off the river. I have a view of my mother's tomb, the Taj Mahal. I suppose you could call this my play room."

"I see."

"Do you?" She raised her glass and saluted me, and her eyes searched mine over its rim. "Bottoms up, senhor!" she smiled mischievously, tipped her cup, and drank off the wine. I followed suit. She refilled the goblets. Her hands were very beautiful; the backs and her long tapering fingers had been painted with henna in graceful Arabic design, and her fingernails were scarlet. She wore a single ring, set with a cushion shaped ruby the size of a quail's egg. She held it up to the light. The gem glowed like a hot cinder.

"A beautiful stone, is it not?

"Magnificent, Your Highness!"

She shrugged. "It was a gift from my father, the emperor. You have heard the stories I expect?"

"Your Highness?"

Her almond eyes turned hard. "Don't pretend, senhor, that you have not heard them." She tossed her head as if to rid herself of the thought. "Everyone has heard that I have taken my mother's place at my father's side and in his bed. It is a vicious lie!"

"No one believes such things, Your Highness."

"But, you have heard the rumors?'

I nodded.

Her eyes softened: "You would be surprised what people believe, senhor, but let us talk of other things. You realize why it is that I have asked you here?"

"Your Highness wishes me to inform her concerning the bedding habits of my people?"

The princess reached up with both hands, removed her veil, and smiled beguilingly. "Yes, senhor, in a manner of speaking, but what I had in mind is a demonstration."

I held her eyes. "Princess Jahanara, are you trying to seduce me?"

"Exactly, senhor. I have never bedded a Frank, and I find you most desirable. I confess that I spied on you during your audience with my father. I hope that does not upset you. I know that it is the custom in your country to approach such matters indirectly, but I prefer to be direct. I wish you to become my lover."

"I am honored, my lady."

"Then let us dispense with formalities. You must call me Jahanara, and I will call you Jean-Baptiste, if that is the name you prefer."

"Yes, that will do nicely. So long as we are being direct, may I ask a question?"

She tossed her head. "Yes, of course. What is it you wish to know?"

I smiled and looked into her eyes. "Is this to be just a short dalliance?"

"That, of course, depends, but you must understand, senhor, I am a princess of the blood. Anything longer would be difficult."

"Then you are just toying with me. I will not be required to enter your harem?"

The princess's eyes lit up, and she laughed merrily. "What an amusing fellow you are, senhor. Upon my word, but surely you know that a woman, unfortunately not even a princess, may keep a seraglio."

"Yes, but you are a most unusual woman."

"Yes," she said, "that is true."

She stood and raised her arms above her head, which lifted and accented the shape of her full pear-shaped breasts. A lump formed in my throat. She smiled and slowly turned in a circle. Her cinnamon skin shone in the lamp light.

"Come, senhor, do you not find me attractive?"

"I think so, but I cannot quite tell."

"Cannot tell?" she stamped her foot and glared at me, her arched brows poised like twin scimitars above her piercing black eyes. "Are you blind?"

"No, but I have very poor eyesight. I see well enough up close, but at a distance everything blurs. Perhaps if Your Highness came a little closer."

Princess Jahanara smiled, sat herself gently onto my lap, placed her arms around my neck, and looked into my eyes—her full crimson lips just inches from mine. I detected a scent of jasmine. "Tell me, Jean-Baptiste, can you see better now?"

"Yes, Jahanara, that's better!"

She looked into my eyes. Her lips trembled slightly, and our mouths came together as she pressed her breasts against my chest and slid her tongue into my mouth. We kissed for a long time.

She pulled back her head and looked into my eyes. "And now?"

"Much better!"

"You know, Jean-Baptiste, a woman, especially a woman like me, becomes very used to having men do her bidding. In matters of love, a woman likes to feel that a man wants her for herself, not because he is afraid to say no."

"Yes, Jahanara, and a man likes to feel that he has some choice in the matter."

"I do hope that I have not been too forward, Jean-Baptiste ," she said, her voice becoming soft and girlish. "A woman likes a man who is strong and masterful, she likes to serve a strong man, to do his bidding."

Jahanara stood, then knelt down in front of me, and looked up, her eyes were no longer hard but soft and adoring. "May I serve you now, Jean-Baptiste?"

By this time I was so erect that I had to stand to disengage myself from my small clothes. I let my cotton salvi drop to the floor."Here," I said sitting down. I leaned back against the cushions. "You may pleasure me now!"

"Oh yes," she sighed.

We remained in her chamber for the best part of a day. She had a sumptuously appointed bathing chamber with a deep tub. The bath was fed by golden pipes with hot and cold water that flowed on demand.

It was a short, delightful affair, and we parted friends. Two years later, I heard, there was an awful accident in the palace. The princess brushed against a lamp, and her gown burst into flames. In the privacy of the seraglio, the royal women wear thin, very finely woven muslin which is woven in one particular village and reserved for their use only. The cloth is anointed with fragrant oils and though four of her personal servants did their best to put out the flames, she was horribly burned on her chest, hands, and back. The princess almost died, and it is said that Shah Jahan himself attended and nursed her.

The last time I saw Princess Jahanara was shortly after the death of her father. I caught just a glimpse of the procession. She rode in a curtained palanquin on the road to Agra, to the court of her brother Aurangzeb. She presented her brother with her father's jewels and was restored to favor. The new emperor returned all her estates, sat her on a throne, and honored her with the title of Badshah Begam, a name that means princess queen. She died a year later, some say from poisoning. I will always remember Princess Jahanara with affection. She was a woman of notable quality and fully capable of governing the empire. True, she was arrogant and often headstrong, but she was a woman much like Madeleine, a proud, free spirit. It was sad to see how the awful trial she endured had broken that spirit.

Chapter 47

A Dream Fulfilled

One of the most remarkable things about the Great Blue diamond is the manner in which I acquired it. In March 1666 l arrived in Rammalakota. I first secured lodgings, as is my custom, and then called upon my friend and factor Hiresh Dhawan. With the exception of a bit of gray at his temples, he seemed hardly to have aged at all. I had sent word well ahead. I had a great deal of capital, and I was hoping that my factor had found something of interest.

Hiresh's wife bustled officiously about the outdoor kitchen. Unlike her husband who had remained rapier thin, she had put on a good deal of flesh. The gold bangles on her wrists and ankles tinkled like poorly tuned bells as she slapped and prodded the portly cook who moved too slowly to suit her. She personally served us tea, set on a low table under a huge spreading plain tree which shadowed the back of the house. Drinking boiling hot tea on a stiflingly hot afternoon might seem odd to those who have never visited the Indies, but it is very refreshing.

As always I carefully avoided actually entering my factor's home. We played a little game. He would insist that I enter and accept his hospitality, and I would pretend that I preferred the out of doors and insist on sitting beneath this tree. Although I was his friend and honored guest, as an orthodox Hindoo, he would be obliged to clean and purify the house each time it was soiled by an unbeliever.

Hiresh wrung his hands, smiled, and bowed. "I am sorry, my dear friend. Please forgive me. I have made constant inquiries, but the mines have yielded little of quality these past months, and I have nothing to show you, but I think, perhaps, that you have come at the perfect time. I have seen one marvelous stone, quite an oddity, a very large indigo diamond.

"A blue diamond, you say? I have never heard of such a thing."

He smiled and nodded serenely. "Just so, dear friend. I have seen it. The stone weighs 124 1/3 ratis—that is over 100 of your carats, isn't it?"

I did a quick calculation. "Yes, just under 113 carats." I felt my pulse quicken. That would make it larger than any diamond in Europe save one, the Tuscan Yellow. "That is indeed a large stone. Was it found at Kollür?"

"Yes. No. That is, I am sorry, my dear friend, I do not know… at least, not for certain. The gem seems to have come from nowhere. It is very curious. I have seen many small fancy colored diamonds from the mines at Kollür but rarely a blue of any size and nothing so large. The owner will say almost nothing about it. There seems to be some sort of mystery surrounding this diamond."

"Can you describe its shape?"

"The table is kite shaped, not flat." With his finger he sketched an outline in the air. "It is quite thick and has a great deal of bottom, do you see? The back side is shaped like a triangle. Its water is perfect."

I felt a tingle along my backbone. "I must see it. Can it be brought here to Rammalakota?"

"A thousand apologies, my dear friend. Please forgive me, but the owner will not let it out of his sight." He fluttered his hands. "The owner is being most difficult. I have done business with him for many years, and I have explained that you are an important Frankish lord and my very dear friend. Honestly, I do not understand it, but if you wish to see the diamond, my dear friend, I fear that we must travel to Kollür. I will send a runner to ask the owner to hold it. Not many have seen it. He seems very reluctant to show the stone."

"If he won't show it, how can he sell it?"

"Just so, my dear friend," he said, shaking his head solemnly. "It is very odd. He is a man of business, my dear friend. I have known him for thirty years. A man of business does not act in this way."

The trip to Kollür took seven days over dusty roads. The dry season was just ending. The road was hot. My nostrils filled up with sand, and my mouth turned gritty from chewing dust.

Kollür is located on the Kristna River, seven days journey from Golconda. These mines have been known to produce very large gems. The Great Mogul Diamond was found at Kollür. Unfortunately, many of the stones from these mines are of inferior water, either inclined toward the yellow or brown or green.

Between the river and a crescent shaped mountain lies a plain, and it is on this plain where the diamonds are found. The country is dry and decidedly unfriendly, with sparse vegetation made up mainly of thorn bushes, and there are many snakes.

When I last visited, there were sixty thousand people engaged in the mining, including men, women and children. The men do the digging; the women and children carry the earth. The miners at Kollür do not dig tunnels as at Rammalakota; they dig open pits. The miners select a likely spot where the soil is of the type where diamonds are normally found, the closer to the mountain the larger the stones. The miners then pace off a square section and dig down, usually no more than twelve to fourteen feet until they reach a layer of clayey dirt with large rounded pebbles in it. This is the layer that usually contains diamonds.

The gem-bearing dirt is hauled out in buckets and brought to a nearby space that has been smoothed and surrounded by low clay dikes. The thick red gravel is spread across the bottom of the tank, water is poured over it, and it is allowed to sit. After several days the water becomes muddy and is drawn off, leaving behind a thick layer of muddy gravel.

The gravel is allowed to dry, which does not take long in the fierce heat, and then it is winnowed like wheat in large, flat, loosely woven baskets which permit the soft gravel to sift through, leaving behind the pebbles and larger diamonds. The larger chunks of clay are spread across the pit. The men break up the clods using heavy wooden bats shaped like pestles. The dirt is then winnowed in baskets.

We arrived in the village and went straight to the dealer's home. He was an old, ascetic looking Banian, bare-chested and dressed in the usual baggy white dhoti which fell to his knees. The old gentleman resembled a chicken, a stringy, tough old chicken with tiny eyes set close together and a large beak-like nose between and skin wrinkled like old parchment. His dwelling was a poor one though it was plastered and the floor was covered with old but costly rugs. He smiled and invited us to refresh ourselves.

We squatted, as is the custom, facing each other in a rough circle. A servant brought tea and placed the tray on a low table set between us. An hour or two was consumed by the inevitable polite chit-chat. It was necessary that I act as if time meant nothing, but I will confess to you that although I have done business in the Indies for many years, I have never quite gotten used to the Oriental manner. I burned with impatience to see this gem. It is odd—I can picture the old man's face and thin brown frame, but I cannot remember his name. I have a very good memory for names. After the tea and talk had taken up most of the afternoon, the gem was brought forth wrapped in a scrap of dirty calico.

Diamonds come in many colors. White diamonds, that is, those that are colorless, are most desired and are by far the most abundant. Diamonds of the finest water are pure with a slight blue tint, what we call a blue-white.

Of the fancy color diamonds, yellow and brown are the most common. Blue, green, orange, and red are the truly rare colors. These gems are so rare that the Banian merchants are never sure what to charge for a colored diamond, though when he is unsure, a Banian will always ask an outrageous price.

Finally, when my patience was almost at an end, the dealer

unwrapped the stone and placed it in my hand. I hefted it; it was flat, quite thick, and shaped like a rough triangle. My heart began to pound in my chest. I had never seen such a stone. The diamond showed almost no brilliance, but when held to the light, it was a perfectly transparent, rich, lovely blue, like the afternoon sky, with just the slightest touch of gray.

Some compare the color to that of sapphire, but this is quite wide of the mark. The quality of the color depends on the light in which one chooses to view the stone. In Europe we believe that northern daylight at noon is truly neutral and is the best light in which to view a diamond. In India, the sun is much brighter, and the best light for viewing colorless diamonds is to be found in the shade of a tree. If the stone is a blue-white, the subtle blue tint is most easily seen in shaded sunlight.

The Banians, however, use an entirely different method to light and judge the color of a diamond.

The dealer lit a lamp that sat in a square niche in the wall in a dark corner of the room and placed the blue diamond next to the lamp. I have never understood this method. It hides the blue tint in a blue-white and brings out the yellow. The Great Blue looked distinctly inky under this light, and the gray was more prominent. I have asked several dealers why they insist

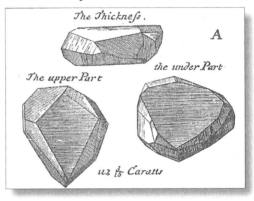

Figure 21: Tavernier's original drawing of the Tavernier Blue Diamond.

on this method. I was told that it was done this way because this is the way it had always been done. The Hindoos have a great reverence for tradition.

My heart continued to pound, and I was having difficulty swallowing. I have studied many of the great jewel collections of Europe, India, and Persia and I had never seen anything that compares with the Blue. It was the finest and rarest diamond I had ever seen, and I was with child to have it.

The dealer squatted and rocked back and forth on his haunches while I examined the stone. He batted at a fly that repeatedly landed on his nose.

Finally I asked: "My factor, Senhor Dhawan, has told me that you wish to sell this diamond."

The dealer nodded, looked up at me, and smiled sheepishly. "Forgive me, senhor, the stone is such a rarity that I do not know what to ask for it. Would you care to make an offer?"

I make it a strict rule; I never make the first offer. I can still recall Sheik Arash's words; 'An offer tells the seller many things without his revealing anything.'"

"Excuse me. You said you wish to sell?"

He nodded gravely. "That is true, senhor."

"Come, come, then, senhor, if you wish to sell, tell me your price?"

The old man wrinkled his brow, turned to my factor, and shrugged helplessly.

"Why do you look at me?" Hiresh responded angrily. "Are we not serious men, men of business my dear friend? Will you embarrass me in front of this great lord? Enough of this foolishness. State your price."

The dealer remained silent. We drank more tea. We were getting nowhere. An hour later, the day was almost gone, and the old dealer had yet to put a price on the blue diamond. I signaled to Hiresh and rose to leave. The Banian stood up. "Senhor," I said, "I thank you for your hospitality, but I have no more time to waste. Good day to you." Hiresh said nothing and followed me outside.

"I am sorry, my dear friend. You see, it is as I told you—the man is being very difficult. But please wait just a moment. Let me speak to him alone. Perhaps I can induce him to be more reasonable."

I shook my head. "I am tired, Hiresh. We have been here all afternoon. You have done your best, but this man has yet to name his price. I don't believe he ever will. It is hopeless!"

My factor looked up at me plaintively. "Please, aga, just give me a moment?"

I shrugged.

Hiresh walked back into the house. I heard angry voices. I could hear my factor loudly berating the other Hindoo. I had never heard him sound so angry. Finally he walked outside to the tree beneath which I was standing to ward off the sun. He was breathing heavily, and his eyes flashed with anger.

"Well, my dear friend, he has named a price. It is ridiculous, my dear friend, ridiculous! I am ashamed to even mention it. I have told this man that you are a very important merchant with many years experience and not someone to be trifled with. I also told him that he has made me look the fool and that if he does not choose to be reasonable, we will simply leave and have nothing further to do with him. He promised me that he will think about it over night. We will return at noon tomorrow, and he must name a reasonable price."

That night I tossed, I turned, but sleep would not come. I was obsessed by the blue diamond, and I feared I might lose it. But how do you value something so unique? What is such a gem truly worth? I have been asked this many times and that night I struggled with that question. A gem has no practical use. It is worth everything and nothing. Rare and beautiful, yes, but it will not feed you when you are hungry, nor clothe you, nor keep off the rain. Its value is totally dependent upon what someone will pay for it. It has been said that the Great Mogul's diamond is worth all the gold in the world. Yet a starving man would trade it for a crust of bread.

Thoughts of this kind occupied my restless mind, and I slept fitfully and awoke with the first cock's crow. In the late morning, we returned to the old dealer's home. The sun was high and hot. A mangy old dog, lying in the shade of a tree outside the dealer's door, raised his head as we approached, then recognizing us, yawned, closed his eyes, and lowered his chin to the ground.

The dealer greeted us politely, and again we squatted in the center of the room, and again he had a servant bring tea. He had set his price: 200,000 golden rupees or about 300,000 livres in our French money.

Hiresh gazed at me, shrugged, and spread his arms helplessly.

All I could do was smile.

"Enough of this nonsense. My offer is 35,000 rupees."

The old man's jaw dropped. He stared at me open-mouthed. I suppressed a smile—what actors these old Banian dealers are: "Thirty-five thousand rupees for a diamond so rare that no one has ever seen its like?"

With effort I kept my face passive and spoke softly: "I agree, senhor, that it is an unusual stone, a curiosity. Perhaps one of my clients will find it amusing. It turns almost black in lamplight. The color of the diamond makes it sudra, does it not—a gem of the lowest caste? Would you offer such a stone to another merchant of your own religion at such a price? You think that because I am a Frank I do not know that such stones of this color are of the lowest value? Thirty-five thousand is a fair price for such an oddity."

The old man slowly shook his head and blinked his watery eyes. "No, senhor, the sudra is a gray or black stone. So, senhor, perhaps you could make a better offer?"

I pinned the old Banian with a cold stare. "I must make a better offer? Did I not sit here half the day yesterday while you toyed with me? If it is, as you say, so rare, why have you not sold it. Where is the line of merchants outside your door clamoring to buy? Do you think I have nothing better to do than sit here while you amuse yourself? Today I come back ready to talk serious business, and you make sport of me."

The old man lowered his eyes doing his best to look contrite. "Truly, I am sorry, senhor. I did not mean to insult you. Perhaps you would care to make a better offer."

"Senhor, I leave that to you. You have stated your price, and I have made you an offer."

"Perhaps I could part with the stone for one hundred seventy five thousand rupees."

I smiled at the dealer. "Yes, I am sure that you would if I were foolish enough to pay such a sum." We went back and forth, and two hours later the price stood at one hundred fifty thousand rupees, with the Banian refusing to make any further concessions. There was no point in continuing. This was twice the price I was willing to pay. There remained only the buyer's final gambit. If it did not work the game was lost. I rose and bowed politely to the old dealer. "Senhor, I thank you for your hospitality, but I believe that we are too far apart in price to do business. Perhaps," I said with a shrug, "some other time. I regret that I have other business to attend to, and I must leave the day after tomorrow. Goodbye."

The old Banian rose, nodded, smiled his toothless smile but said nothing. My gambit had failed. Hiresh got up and without a word followed me out the door.

I returned to my lodgings. I have walked away from many negotiations. There is always another day and another opportunity. Yet this gem continued to haunt me. I was out of sorts. The servants noticed and kept out of my way. I took my dinner alone and spent the balance of the evening drinking wine and thinking about the blue diamond. I fear I drank too much because early the next morning, I awoke from a deep fog with my servant Danush shaking me by the shoulder.

"Aga, wake up, wake up. Someone is here to see you."

I emerged from the fog with a headache. My mouth tasted like dried parchment. "Danush, what? Stop that! What on earth is the matter?"

"You must wake up, aga. The old man, the diamond dealer, he is here. He says that it is urgent. He must speak with you immediately."

My heart leapt into my throat. "The old man here? Why, what does he want?" A cock crowed just outside the window. The sound pierced my temple like a sharp needle.

"I do not know, aga, but he seems quite uneasy. He is downstairs." Danush stood holding my clothes, gazing at me meaningfully. "I am sorry to wake you, but I think you should speak with him."

I stepped into my salvi, the light cotton drawers I habitually wore during the hot season, buttoned on a light singlet, and made my way downstairs. The bright sunlight streaming through the open doorway felt like someone had driven a spike through both my eyes. The old fellow was pacing back and forth.

"Good morning, senhor," he said, raising both hands in supplication, "please forgive me for calling at this early hour, but something has happened, and I must visit my uncle on important family business and so…"

"Senhor, it is no trouble at all, I do assure you. Please, sit down." I called for tea. "You will take some refreshment? I hope there is no trouble."

The tea came quickly. The servant poured two cups. The steaming liquid seemed to calm the man somewhat. He sat looking down at his cup, then lifted it and noisily slurped the steaming liquid. "Senhor," he said, barely pausing between sips, "do you still wish to purchase the blue diamond?"

"Yes," I said, "it is a curious novelty. I am interested, but it seems impossible for us to agree. We are so far apart in price."

He raised his head, met my eyes, and smiled. "I know I have been difficult, but, senhor, I think we both know that this diamond is far more than a curiosity. The truth is I can hardly bring myself to sell it, but I find that I now have an immediate need for capital. I came in hopes that we might reach an agreement?"

The dealer was being unusually candid. It put him at a great disadvantage. After a bit of bargaining we agreed to a price, much less than the 75,000 that I had been willing to pay. The old man kept glancing at the door as if he expected someone. I gave him all the golden rupees that I could spare. He was more than willing to accept a draft for the balance on my factor in Agra. He wrapped the money in an old rag, bowed and hurried off.

A few moments later, Hiresh stumbled into the room, rubbing the sleep from his dark lidded eyes. "Senhor, is it true what your servant told me? You have purchased the diamond?"

Triumphantly, I held out my hand, and the blue diamond glowed like the blue sky in the morning sun. "Yes, and at a very good price."

He raised his eyebrows questioningly.

I told him the price.

He stood for a moment stroking his chin and shaking his head. "This is strange, my dear friend, very strange. First the man will not even name a price, and then suddenly he drops it far below the gem's value. In the twenty years I have known him, he has never left this town, and now he suddenly speaks of an uncle in Goa, an uncle of whom I have never heard. I do not like this. No, no, I do not like this at all. There is something very, very wrong here! If you will take my advice, my dear friend, I believe we should leave this place, now, this morning."

My mood changed from elation to concern. Hiresh Dhawan was not an excitable sort of fellow. The old Banian's behavior had, indeed, been very odd. I decided to take my factor's advice. I ordered my servants to pack up my goods. Very little had been actually unpacked and our beasts had had three days of rest and good fodder. Dhawan became more and more excited as the morning wore on. He prodded and kicked the servants, shouting and flapping his arms about like an angry hen. Danush loaded and primed the muskets I customarily carry and handed them out to my most trusted servants. In just three hours we were packed and ready. Counting bearers, servants, and guards, our party numbered about fifty.

Chapter 48

The Goddess' Revenge

bout two hours out of Kollür we encountered what appeared to be a large body of men blocking the road. There were perhaps sixty, most on foot. We stopped about half a league from them, and I sent Danush to reconnoiter.

Danush reined in his mount. "Aga, these men have been waiting for us. They say you have stolen a treasure that belongs to their god, and they will not let us pass unless you give it to them. They are armed, aga. I think they want the diamond. They ask to parley with you."

Taking Danush and one of the servants who spoke the local language, I rode slowly toward the group. Three men broke away from the mob and walked toward us. We met about halfway between the two groups. One was a fakir, one of the so-called holy men who infest the roads of India. He was a skeletal-looking fellow with a pinched face, dressed only in a filthy loincloth. His fingernails had not been clipped, and they curled around his thin fingers. His hair

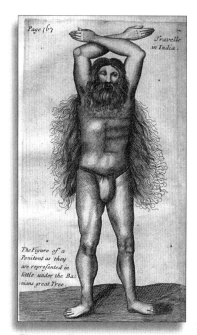

Figure 22: Tavernier's drawing of
a fakir from the 1st French
edition tion of his Six Voyages
published in Paris in 1677..

and beard were gray, ratty, and unkempt and reached past his waist. With him was a large burly man, an acolyte, younger and with a full dark beard. He looked like he had once been a soldier. He was barefoot and wore a soldier's breastplate, buckler, and sword. The old man carried only a walking stick. The third man carried a basket.

The fakir began to make a speech with words spewing from between his rotted teeth. The younger man translated. "His holiness says, the blue diamond that you have stolen has been promised to Rama-Sita, the wife of the god Rama. You must give the diamond to him, or the goddess requires that we kill you and take it."

"I must give you my diamond? Give you? Do you claim that it has been stolen from you?"

"It was stolen from the goddess. Many years ago the wife of Rama was carried off by a prince named Revan, who ravished her. In the struggle, her great blue diamond was lost. It is written that the diamond will be found buried in the earth. It is the eye of the god. It must be placed in the temple as an offering to the goddess."

Now my blood was up; I have always disliked being threatened, particularly with death. "Who has told you that I have such a stone?"

The soldier turned, issued an order, and the third man reached into the basket and held up an object for inspection. I felt my stomach lurch. It was the severed head of the old diamond dealer, dangling by his hair. The eyes were open, staring vacantly, the neck still dripping gore.

"So you are murderers as well as bandits. I purchased the gem from its legitimate owner, and you have murdered him."

"The diamond belongs to the goddess."

"Nonsense, it belongs to me. I have heard enough. I bear the passport of the emperor's uncle, the Nabob Shaista Khan. He shall hear of this outrage."

The mention of my protector seemed to have a momentary effect. The younger man looked alarmed. He translated my words, but his holiness was not impressed. The old man stank of curdled milk. He trained his wild eyes on me and responded with a stream of curses, and although his gibberish meant nothing to me, the import was clear: "We will have the diamond."

I looked the bearded soldier straight in the eye. "If you want my diamond, then come and take it. But be warned, you will not find the work as easy as killing a helpless old man." I turned my horse and with my two servants, galloped back to the rest of the party. I had instructed them to take up a defensive position behind a barren rocky outcrop just off the road. It was late afternoon.

I dismounted and arranged my men. A few of the local porters had run off so our party was reduced by ten or so, but our position could hardly have been better. The rocks were shoulder high and made excellent props for our muskets. Danush passed out spears to the men without firearms. The old sword in the worn leather scabbard which he habitually carried dangled from his belt, and a pair of silver inlaid pistols jutted from his waistband. I buckled on my own sword, checked the priming of my pistols, and took up a position just behind my musketeers, with Danush standing grimly at my side.

I could see the old fakir clearly. He was screaming and waving his arms, doing his best to whip his troop into a religious frenzy. It took a while. Finally he finished his harangue, and the mob began to advance. They moved forward slowly at first. It was a motley lot, most armed with homemade spears, though a few carried short stabbing swords. The bearded soldier took the lead. They were quite far off so we had plenty of time to prepare. I spoke calmly to my musketeers, urging them to pick their targets and hold their fire until I gave the signal.

My plan was simple enough: let them get well within range, then fire a volley into the front ranks, kill a few, and hope that the noise, smoke, and blood would panic the rest. I knew what a musket volley could do at close range, and I was fairly confident the plan would work. My men, however, were not soldiers. They were familiar with muskets but had never fired at a man charging at them with murderous intent, and I feared that they would panic. The wind began to rise out of the east; I wiped the sand out of my eyes and waited.

The plan worked, almost. My men nervously held their fire, but as the mob began to close, the old man started babbling, screaming, and hopping about like a rabid squirrel. The soldier raised his sword, and the mob charged, brandishing their spears and screaming like devils. This unnerved my people, and they began firing. It was a ragged volley, and it came too early. Still, with our attackers bunched close together they could hardly miss. Six of the devils fell, several howling in pain.

The soldier was not hit. He bellowed and waved his sword to rally the remaining rabble, then turned and charged forward like a maddened bull. I pulled my two pistols from my belt, waited until the soldier gained the rocks, and discharged my left pistol full in his face. The ball took him in the forehead, and its force blew out the back of his head. His eyes flew open, and he dropped like a stone. This turned the tide.

The old man stood his ground surrounded by the dead and the dying. The soldier lay dying, his body draped over the rocks, his brains leaking into the dirt. The others broke and ran, leaving the old fakir babbling alone with the wind-whipped dust swirling about him like a vision from the netherworld. Danush and the spearmen surrounded the old man. Danush raised his sword and looked at me for a sign. It was then that I made a serious mistake.

"No," I shouted and shook my head as I strode towards him, "let him be!"

Danush looked stunned. "Master please, let me kill him."

The fakir grabbed at something around his neck.

Danush darted forward and knocked him senseless with the flat of his sword.

"Danush, stop, do not kill him!" I grabbed my servant's sword arm. "Lord knows he deserves death for killing the old dealer, but I do not want his blood on my hands."

"But, aga, we will never be rid of him. He will follow us. Look!" He knelt down and lifted one end of a thin round circle of metal which the fakir wore as a necklace.

"What is it, a neck ring?"

"It is a chakar, and it is sharp like a razor's edge. It is thrown like a child would skip a flat stone, but this is no child's toy. I have seen one slice a man's head from his body. He meant to kill you with it, aga."

I looked at the pathetic figure lying crumpled in the dust. He seemed wholly defeated. "I thank you, old friend, but let him be." I put my arm around Danush's shoulders. "You know how superstitious the men are. Killing a holy man is bound to cause trouble. What more can he do?—even his own followers have deserted him. Tie him up. By the time he gets loose we shall be far away."

Danush shook his head sadly, but found a rope and did as I bid him. We left the old man, trussed up like a chicken, in the shade of the rocky outcrop and resumed our journey.

We reached Raolconda without incident though on two occasions my people thought they saw men following us. The first night after we set up camp, I sent out guards to scout our back trail, but they returned without seeing anyone. I spent several days in Raolconda. There was still no sign of the old fakir. I then took the road for Patna.

My plan was to be in Surat by early January, in time to catch the remains of the northeast monsoon, take ship and return by sea to Persia. The trip from Raolconda to Surat takes about thirty days, but I had business in Patna and in Agra, and little realizing the danger I was in, I continued along with my plans. The trip to Patna took seven days.

Patna is a one of the largest cities in India. It is situated on the western side of the river. The Hollanders maintain a large, well protected establishment in the city. I knew the Dutch president, a Herr Wachtendonck, and I hoped to take lodging at the Dutch fort.

Herr Wachtendonck expressed great joy at seeing me once

again and kindly insisted that I lodge with him. We were old friends. On my last trip to India, I had obtained two parcels of diamonds which he had sold in Amsterdam for a very good profit, and profit is a thing very dear to a Dutchman's heart.

The trouble began about a week later, early one morning just after sunrise. I had accompanied the Dutch president on an inspection of the saltpeter works in Chopra, and our party was returning to Patna. We had left Chopra in the early morning hours and traveled the forty leagues or so to Patna while it was still dark to avoid the heat of the day and the dust along the road. It was market day, and we had just passed through the main gate of the city. My palanquin was leading with two of my servants up ahead, clearing our way through the crowds along the narrow street.

I thought I heard a familiar voice shouting, opened the curtain, and leaned out of the side of the palanquin. That action saved my life. I caught a glint of something metallic. I flinched as a spinning iron disk passed through a narrow gap between my head and the window and buried itself in the wooden side of my palanquin. I sat for a moment stunned.

"Guards!"

My men along with several of the Dutch guards crowded around. I showed them where the chakar was imbedded. Everyone began talking at once.

Herr Wachtendonck's palanquin was half a cable length behind mine. He dismounted and rushed forward, pushing his way through the thickening crowd of curious gawkers. He arrived breathless.

"My dear fellow, what has happened?" The Hollander was a thin balding man with a bird-like beaked nose. He was well into his middle years and looked more like a minor clerk than the chief Dutch official of the whole of Bengal. His close spaced eyes grew almost owl-like when I showed him the wicked circle of metal embedded inside of my conveyance.

"As you can see, my friend, someone has attempted to filet me."

Danush ran up. "You, you and you," he said pointing at three of my servants who stood gaping. "Cannot you see that our master has almost been murdered? Close your stupid mouths, spread out, and find the man."

I grabbed Danush by the sleeve. "It was the old fakir, who else could it be? Fifty golden pagodas to the man who captures him," I shouted. The men scattered into the crowd, but, as I feared, it was too late. The old man and his accomplices had had plenty of time to melt into the market crowd.

Herr Wachtendonck put his hand on my arm. "Come, my friend, let us go to the factory. It is very near, and I for one will feel much safer once there are strong brick walls between us and these heathens."

Two of our bearers who had panicked and run off returned looking sheepish, picked up the palanquin, and we were once more on our way. Danush trooped grimly along at my side with his sword drawn.

"Did you see him, aga?"

"I caught just a glimpse. At first, I wasn't sure, but it could be no one else. He called out the name of his goddess."

Danush looked about nervously. Tears filled his eyes. "Oh, aga, I am sorry. Your stupid servant should have slit the throat of that filthy old devil when he had the chance."

"No, Danush, don't blame yourself. It was my decision. You were right. I should have let you kill him."

"Yes, aga, but now he has followed us here, and we will never be rid of him. I know these people. He means to murder you as a sacrifice to his filthy goddess. But do not worry, aga. He will not get another chance. Your faithful servant will guard you every minute. I shall not sleep, and the next time I see him," he raised his sword and shook it, "that stinking old devil will not escape. By the beard of the prophet, I swear it."

Seeing my stout balding old friend striding down the middle of the road with his paunch protruding, brandishing his sword, and swearing revenge was about the most hilarious thing I had ever seen. I am sure that it was just nerves, but after what I had just experienced it seemed hilarious. Danush would do his best—that I knew. What I didn't know, then, was the terrible price he would pay.

Several nights later I lay asleep behind the walls of the Dutch factory. An awful racket coming from the courtyard awakened me. Danush, who had insisted on sleeping in my chamber, jumped up and rushed from the room. He was back a moment later, out of breath.

"Aga, we are being attacked."

Just then I heard several muskets go off. The sound came from the direction of the courtyard.

I grabbed my drawers and looked about for my sword belt. "What, who is attacking us?"

"I do not know, aga. It is too dark to tell for sure."

"It must be the fakir and his followers." I buckled on my sword.

Just then we heard a noise in the corridor. A voice screamed "Rama-Sita," the door burst opened, and three bare-chested, fierce looking Banians rushed into the room with drawn swords.

These attackers were younger men, dark, wild-eyed, lean, and unshaven. Each carried an unsheathed khanjar. The long curved blades gleamed wickedly in the candlelight.

Then there was an explosion somewhere close by, and the sharp tang of gunpowder filled the air. One of the heathens grabbed his chest, screamed, and fell forward. Out of the corner of my eye, I could see Danush standing with a smoking pistol in his hand. I drew my sword. The two remaining zealots began to move in warily. Even in the dim light, I could see by their berserker eyes that they had been fed hashish.

One fellow, his hair falling around his head like a nest of greasy snakes, raised his knife, screamed the name of his goddess, charged forward, and practically impaled himself upon my lowered sword. The blade pierced his breast while I was still a foot beyond the range of his knife. His eyes widened and he fell backward. I jerked my blade from his chest. Pink blood bubbled between his lips. His eyes rolled up into his head as he fell.

The remaining attacker was not so foolish. Finding himself alone, he glared, and then glanced quickly around, obviously looking for reinforcements. From the racket coming from the courtyard, with muskets popping like champagne corks echoing down the corridor, it sounded as if the Dutch had gotten the upper hand. Danush moved in on the man, sword at the ready. The zealot was caught between us. His reddened eyes flicked back and forth trying to watch us both at once. I waited, hoping for an opening. Then he feinted toward me, stepped back and slashed right. The move caught Danush unaware; the zealot's sword severed his hand just above the wrist.

Danush's sword clattered to the stone floor. My servant's face went white. Blood gushed like a fountain from the stump of his severed arm. There was nothing I could do. I tore my eyes away and focused on my attacker. The man began moving in, a small smile played around the corners of his mouth. The sound of running feet echoed in the corridor, and men appeared at the doorway behind the zealot. The lips widened in a smile of triumph just before a Dutch musket ball tore off the back of his head. His eyes widened with surprise as he fell dead at my feet.

Danush stood stock-still staring vacantly at the blood pouring from his arm. He seemed not to know what was happening. I quickly tore a length of fabric from a shirt lying on my bed, wrapped it around his arm as I had seen the surgeons do and pulled it tight. The bleeding slowed. Danush's face was a ghostly mask. The floor was slick with blood.

His eyes met mine and he smiled. "Aga, you are all right. Allah be praised." he said and fainted.

I beckoned the soldiers and, with their help, raised his considerable bulk and laid him gently on my bed. I sent one of the men to fetch the doctor. A few minutes later, Herr Aerntssoen, the Dutch surgeon, came into the room.

The doctor bent down and examined Danush's arm. It was still dripping blood at an alarming rate. "Ja, I believe we can save him, but we must cauterize the wound before he bleeds to death."

"What is happening outside, doctor?"

The doctor was a short thin man with a pinched face and protruding eyes. He turned and his eyes met mine. "We have beaten them back, Mein Herr, at least for now. It was you they were after, you know?"

I nodded.

"They are very determined. Who would have believed that the bloody heathens would have the nerve to attack us here, inside the walls of our own fort? What have you done to provoke them?"

I shook my head.

He motioned four of the men forward. "Each of you take a corner of the blanket. Gently now. We must move this man to the courtyard." He turned toward me, "You did very well stopping the blood, Herr Tavernier, but we must act quickly now, or he will lose the arm."

The servants had already begun cleaning up. Several of the Dutch wounded sat or lay sprawled in the dirt. One of the guards had been stabbed in the stomach. He sat with his back against a tree moaning pitifully. My eyes queried the doctor. He glanced at the man and shook his head. The man took two days to die.

The bodies of a dozen or so of our attackers had been thrown like so much cord wood into a heap on one side of the courtyard. The men lay Danush gently on a bench near the blacksmith's forge.

"He is still unconscious. That is good. He will feel nothing until he awakens. Still we must hold him down," the doctor said. With three of us holding down his arms and legs, the blacksmith pressed the flat of a red-hot sword blade against the bleeding stump. The scorching smell of searing flesh made my stomach turn. Danush's eyes flew open, and he screamed and passed out.

"He was lucky, Herr Tavernier. It was a clean slice," the doctor said leaning over and examining the stump. "The bleeding has stopped. Now we must seal it off with tar. Then, with God's help, I believe it will heal."

The next morning Danush opened his eyes. I had sat by his bedside for most of the night dozing in a chair. "So my friend, you are awake."

He tried to speak, but all that came out was a croak. I lifted his head and fed him some water. He sputtered and coughed, then drank greedily.

"Oh, thank you, aga. Tell me, what has happened?"

"You don't remember?"

He shook his head. "I remember that we were attacked.

That is all."

"What happened is that you fought bravely, my friend, and we have beaten them, but you have been badly hurt. Here drink some more water."

"No, aga, thank you. Oh, now I remember—my hand. Oh aga, that filthy beggar cut off my hand!" Danush began to cry.

"Yes, but the doctor has cauterized it. It will heal, and soon you will be as good as new."

"I fought well?"

"Like a tiger."

He smiled weakly. "Good! Oh, aga. My arm, it hurts."

"The doctor said it would. Here," I said raising his head, "drink this. It will dull the pain."

"Oh, it tastes terrible. What is it?"

"Poppy juice."

Danush drank and lay back. Soon his eyes flickered, and he fell peacefully asleep.

I had a problem. Danush's prophetic words kept repeating themselves in my mind. I had underestimated the fakir's determination. He was a true zealot, and he would pursue us until he either recovered the Great Blue diamond or until one of us was dead. I had been lucky. I was usually lucky, but luck favors those who prepare.

A thought struck me. I was overdue in fulfilling my promise to visit Aurangzeb's uncle, the Nabob Shaista Khan. We had done a great deal of business in the past, and during my last voyage, he had made me promise to give him first pick of the rarities I brought from Europe. Due to the emperor's order, I was unable to fulfill that promise, but I still had several rare jewels and pearls to show him. Word was that the great man was in Dacca with an army. I traveled with the nabob's passport. I decided that as soon as Danush was fit to travel, I would go to Dacca and seek the nabob's protection. He was a devout Mussulman as well as a great prince. He would not be pleased to hear that an idolater had attacked a man who traveled under his protection.

We spent another two weeks in Patna waiting for Danush's wounds to heal. The Hollanders trebled the night guard and brought in a platoon of soldiers from Chopra. They could not have been more gracious. Still our presence put a great deal of strain on their resources, and I knew that Herr Wachtendonck would be more than pleased to see us on our way.

The fakir and his followers were watching. I did not know how many men he commanded. He had lost at least a dozen in the attack on the Dutch factory, but time, I knew, would only make him stronger. Some of my own men were unreliable, and I feared the consequences should he attack us on the open road. Many of the Banian porters would run away if they felt any real danger. It would be impossible for a large party to leave the Dutch fort without being seen and followed. Finally after much thought, I hit upon a plan that I thought might allow us to escape, but it would require the active support of the Dutch president. Despite our friendship the man had grown distinctly cool in the days following the attack on the fort. My first task was to warm him up.

That evening just after dinner, I found M. Wachtendonck working alone in his office. I entered and saluted him. He was sitting at his desk going through his paperwork. Before he could say anything beyond mumbling the usual pleasantries, I got right to the point.

"Herr Wachtendonck, I am much obliged to you for your kindness and protection, and I wish to express my appreciation. Please accept this small gift as a token of my thanks." I removed a leather bag from my girdle and placed it on the desk.

"Herr Tavernier, what's this?" He picked up the bag and poured its contents onto the desk in front of him: fifteen small uncut diamonds and one large stone weighing almost fifteen rati, all flawless and of fine pure water, approximately forty carats in all. The man's tiny eyes lit up with pleasure. "A magnificent gift, Herr Tavernier. How kind. I don't know what to say."

"Please, there is nothing to say, my dear fellow. You have lost men and money, and you have treated me with the utmost care and friendship, and I simply wish to say thank you."

"Well, you are certainly welcome," he said as he held the large stone up to the light. "If I may be of any further service…?"

"As a matter of fact, Herr Wachtendonck, there is one further service that you can do me. That is to say, I have a plan and if you will aid me in it, I believe I can solve both of our problems, and I can resume my journey without further delay."

"Really?" The Hollander looked worried, but as I laid out my plan, his pinched face began to light up. He even managed a smile.

Early the next morning, two palanquins, together with a large party of Dutch guards and native bearers carrying heavy loads, set out from the Dutch fort. The palanquins had closed curtains so that a watcher would not be able to tell that they were empty. The bails that the bearers carried were stuffed with bricks and old clothes. The party would march north to Chopra where it would overnight within the factory walls and make the return journey to Patna late the next day. While the fakir and his men pursued the caravan, we would slip out of the fort and take a boat down the Ganges to Dacca. By the time the idolaters realized their mistake, I hoped to have a two-day head start.

Soon after the Dutch party left, my servants, bearers, and guards began to filter out of the fort. I had instructed everyone to rendezvous by a dry streambed on the south road two leagues beyond the main gate. Toward midday, dressed in the clothes of a Mussulman servant, I departed with a small party of my servants leading a bullock ridden by Danush, who was dressed in woman's robes and veil.

It was the hottest part of the day, and the road was crowded with people going about their normal business. I kept my head down and looked quickly to my right and left. No one seemed to be paying us any attention. Then to my right I noticed a thin, young bare breasted Banian dressed in a dhoti, staring curiously at Danush and walking along directly paralleling us. He started gesturing and pointing and talking to another man who walked along beside him. The other fellow laughed. I do not speak the language. Was he making a joke of Danush, or was he one of the fakir's men? Had he pierced my servant's disguise? Danush certainly looked ridiculous in his feminine garb as he rode serenely along, veiled like an orthodox Muslim woman, his right arm held tight against the folds of his robe to hide his missing hand.

The man now walked toward us and, bent crab-like, began capering in front of us with one hand shading his eyes, peering up at Danush. He pointed and shouted something. His companion and several of the other people on the road laughed. Encouraged, he hunched down and began to waddle and cavort alongside Danush's mount laughing and making obscene gestures. Everyone along the road stopped and watched. I was at a loss as to how to react. In my role as a servant I dared not speak or otherwise call attention to myself.

While I pondered, Danush twisted around in the saddle and beckoned one of the guards. Danush leaned down and whispered a few words. The guard took hold of the bridle with one hand and extended the other. Danush took the hand and playing the feminine role, dismounted as delicately as his substantial bulk allowed. He then made a show of carefully picking his way, avoiding the offal and the puddles in the road, to where the Banian stood and with one hand holding his veil tightly to his face, confronted the fellow.

After a brief, angry exchange, Danush suddenly swung up his wounded arm like a club and struck the Banian clown full across the side of his head. The Banian fell, like a pole axed mule, face down in the muddy dirt road, and lay still. The crowd erupted in mirth while the man's friend ran over and attempted to minister to his fallen comrade. Ignoring this, Danush turned, drew himself up, and with his head held high, sauntered delicately back to the bullock, took the guard's hand, and remounted.

We managed the rest of the way without incident and rendezvoused with the rest of our party at the river bank. The Dutch president had arranged for a boat large enough to carry our party and all of our goods to be waiting by the riverside. The Ganges was in flood and the current is strong at that time of the year. We sailed all night and stopped at dawn in a town called Beconcour. It appeared that we had our head start, but as I now knew the old fakir was no fool, and a party the size of ours, particularly one led by a Ferenghi, would be remembered, but with luck we would reach Dacca before they could catch up.

We spent over a week making our way along the river, traveling by day and refreshing ourselves at riverside villages by night. With the monsoon waters at height, it would have been foolish to attempt to navigate that section of the Ganges after dark. In the afternoon of our eighth day, our party entered Dacca through the north gate, a high narrow vaulted affair made of beautifully decorated plastered brick.

The next morning I went to salute Shaista Khan. He had set up his headquarters at the governor's residence, a rather squalid affair enclosed by high walls. The Moguls were at war with the king of Arakan, and the emperor's uncle had a large army quartered in the city. I found the nabob reclined on a cushion in one of several large tents pitched in the middle of the courtyard.

"So, Senhor Tavernier," the nabob said with a frown. "I see that you have finally come to me. Where have you been? I expected to see you long before this."

"Your pardon, Excellency, but you are a difficult man to keep up with."

The nabob smiled. He was at this time sixty-three years of age with a full gray beard, a long face, and a long prominent nose. "Yes, I suppose that is true enough. Well, what have you brought me?"

"Several things, Your Highness, I have shown to no one else. But, first, may I be allowed to present you with a few gifts that I hope will not displease you." I motioned my servant forward with a mantle of gold brocade edged with point d'Espagne, a fine scarf, and a jewel set with a beautiful large emerald. I also brought along a watch with an enameled gold case, a pair of silver inlaid pistols, and a telescope that I presented to his ten-year-old son. Together, the gifts that I presented to the nabob and the young prince cost me more than five thousand livres.

The nabob was well pleased with his gifts. "Senhor Tavernier, tonight you shall dine with me, and I hope that you have brought with you some of that excellent Shiraz. It has been a very dry campaign."

I returned to the caravanserai. I had barely sat down when Danush rushed into my room.

"Aga, aga, I have bad news. The bashi says that there were two men here this afternoon asking questions about us."

"This afternoon? How and who can they be? No one knows we are here. Could it be that filthy fakir has found us so quickly?"

"The bashi did not know, aga, but who else could it be? Did not your loyal servant warn you? The bashi had never seen them before. He said that they were low caste Banians."

"It must be he. We shall see about this. I am growing weary of this madman. Danush fill a large borracho with our best Shiraz and put it down the well to cool it. I dine with the nabob tonight."

Dinner was served in the nabob's tent. The night was unusually hot for the season, and His Excellency ordered all the flaps to be lifted to take advantage of a light breeze off the river. There were only a few guests and several officers of his guard. We reclined on pillows in the Persian manner. Dozens of brass lamps hung like tiny moons from the tent's roof. The dinner was excellent. Shaista Khan is Persian and favors the delicately flavored dishes of his native land, which included an excellent pilaf, a dish to which I am particularly devoted. I made sure to keep his cup filled.

Shaista Khan lifted his cup and saluted me. His face was slightly flushed, and his gray eyes glittered in the lamplight. "Excellent wine, my friend. Now tell me how long can you stay, and what I may do to make you more comfortable?"

I raised my glass and met his eyes. "Since you have asked, my lord, I have a problem." I explained the circumstances to the nabob, reminding him that I traveled under his passport. "The man seems to believe that I have insulted his god."

Shaista Khan's face turned red with anger. "What," he said, turning to his officers. "Who is this filthy dog of an unbeliever who dares to attack a friend who travels under my protection?"

The officers eyed each other nervously.

"None of you have heard of this man? Very well, bring the chief of the Banian priests before me tomorrow morning!"

The next morning I waited upon the nabob. I was grateful that His Excellency had not pressed me further concerning the fakir. I did not wish him to know of the existence of the blue diamond. Shaista Khan was a proud man and a great lover of jewels. I feared if he knew of the gem that he would wish to buy it and I had my own plans for the great blue stone. Fortunately, the nabob cared little about the source of the dispute, only that an infidel had dared defy his will.

A platoon of guards marched toward the dais with a wrinkled, bare-chested old man with a bewildered look, walking between the ranks. The man was dressed in the long snow white diaper-like dhoti that wound around his waist and private parts and extended to his knees. He was the chief priest of the town.

The nabob sat just outside his tent on a raised dais covered with rare Persian carpets and sheltered by a broad awning of gold cloth which was supported at each corner by a narrow column of carved teakwood. Several dozen courtiers stood around the dais. A tall bare-chested Banian slave stood on either side of the dais and fanned His Excellency with a long handled fan of peacock feathers.

The old Hindoo was a thin, bird-like fellow with sunken eyes and chest and a white beard that touched the ground. He knocked his head against the dirt in the most abject fashion.

"Speak, dog. I wish to know of this fakir who dares to attack the Lord Tavernier, a man who travels under my protection!"

The old man shook his head. "Your Highness, I know nothing of this. Do you know the name of this holy man?"

"You do not know this man? Senhor Tavernier, please enlighten this priest."

I bowed and described the fakir.

"I do not know of him, Your Highness. If, as the lord says, this man has followed him from Patna and just arrived here in Dacca, I have not yet heard anything of him or of his followers. Which of the gods does he serve?"

"He claims to be a priest of one of your filthy goddesses, Rama-Sita," the nabob said.

The priest turned to me: "Lord, I know of them, of course, but there are no temples consecrated to the goddess here in Dacca."

Shaista Khan spoke: "Then you will find out where he is. You will locate this arrogant dog and bring him, his stinking followers, and your miserable self before me tomorrow, before the sun sets."

"But Highness!"

Shaista Khan's eyes bored into the man like cold steel. "Do not toy with me, priest! You have until tomorrow. Do not fail! Now go!"

The old man stood blinking stupidly in the bright morning sun, looking as if he was about to protest, then thought better of it. "Yes, Your Highness!" He prostrated himself again, rose, and backed slowly from the nabob's presence, stopping to bow every few feet.

The following afternoon I returned to the nabob's court. He was very busy. The nabob acknowledged me with a nod and returned to his work. Shaista Khan had an interesting method of organizing his paperwork. Messages arrived much faster than he could respond. Those he wished to keep handy, he tucked between his toes. Every once in a while he would pause and pluck a paper from where he had placed it.

Just before sunset one of the nabob's guards came forward. A large mob of Banians were at the gate. "Bring them to me now," the nabob commanded. The men reluctantly lined up before the dais. I immediately recognized the old fakir flanked by two guards. He had with him about a dozen of his ragged followers. The chief priest approached the dais, kneeled, and knocked his head on the ground.

"As you commanded, great prince, I have brought the fakir and his men. They arrived in the city only two days ago."

The nabob gestured impatiently. "Show him to me."

The two huge Banian acolytes came forward dragging the struggling fakir between them before the dais. They bowed and backed away leaving the man standing alone, dressed in his filthy loincloth, grinding his teeth and glaring at Shaista Khan.

The captain of the guard stepped forward. "Kneel before His Highness," he ordered.

The old fakir ignored the soldier and stood defiantly, staring and mumbling into his beard. With a single sweeping motion, the captain kicked out his legs, and the old priest collapsed onto the ground like a rag doll.

He struggled to his feet, covered with dust. The captain stepped forward again, but Shaista Khan raised his hand to restrain him.

"Speak, idolater. Tell me why you have attempted to kill this

Frankish lord who travels under my personal passport?"

Would this old man hold his tongue or reveal the existence of the great blue? I held my breath and waited.

The old man spat into the dust. "You command me to speak! Why should I speak? I do not serve you or any other man. I serve the great goddess Rama-Sita. This Ferenghi" he said pointing at me, "has offended the goddess and for that he shall die."

Shaista Khan's eyes narrowed. He regarded the old man silently for a few moments and then spoke. "Be warned, old fool. In Bengal it is I who decides who shall live and who shall die. You would do well to remember that, and I say now that if you and your men do not renounce your evil intentions, I will separate you from your head."

The old man drew himself up. "Who are you, unbeliever, to speak to me thus? Men have bowed down and raised temples to the goddess wife of Lord Rama long before your false prophet was breached." He spat in the dust. "I do not fear you. No blade can harm me. The will of the goddess protects me."

Shaista Khan's face turned so red I thought he would explode, but he paused for a moment, and then a wicked smile spread slowly across his face. "So your goddess protects you, does she?" The nabob clapped his hands. "Let us put your goddess to the test. Captain of the guard, your sword," the nabob ordered, holding out his hand. The captain drew his blade, kneeled, and presented it to the nabob. Shaista Khan tested the edge and smiled. "It seems sharp enough. Take this dog out and separate him from his head and bring it to me." The captain raised his hand; a guard appeared on each side of the fakir, each grabbed an arm and marched the fakir away, kicking and spitting curses like a feral cat.

The nabob's order caused a great stir among those assembled. Shaista Khan took no notice and calmly returned to his work. A short time later the captain returned, carrying a basket. He placed the basket at the foot of the dais and bowed, and at a nod from the nabob, reached in and raised the fakir's head, holding it aloft by its greasy tresses for all to see. A hush fell over the crowd. It was a ghoulish sight: blood dripped from the severed neck, the face was drained of color, the eyes stared vacantly, and the mouth drooled.

The fakir's followers stood mute, exchanging fearful glances.

"Tell me, captain," the khan asked in a strong voice, "was this dog's head difficult to remove?"

The captain grinned. "No, my lord, it required but a single cut."

"I see. So it seems," the nabob said smiling wolfishly, "that the power of this goddess is inferior to mogul steel." The courtiers and the soldiers laughed. The nabob then addressed the fakir's men. "How say the rest of you? Which of you will be next to test my steel? Come now, do not be shy, step forward." The fakir's followers threw themselves onto the dusty earth and began beating their fists on the ground and loudly begging for mercy.

The nabob observed all this for a moment and raised his hand for silence. The men fell mute. "Who speaks for the rest of you?"

One man, thin and unkempt like his dead leader, stood and bowed deeply. "Please, Your Highness, we are but poor men with wives and children. I beg you to spare us!"

The khan's cold gray eyes bored into the man. "You have seen, dog, what happens to those who defy me. Do you renounce your vengeance against this lord?"

The man lowered his eyes, and his voice shook. "We do, Your Highness. The old priest threatened to curse us if we did not do his bidding. We bear this lord no ill will."

"Good. Then kneel and beg his forgiveness."

The men threw themselves down and began yowling like a bag of cats, begging for mercy.

Shaista Khan looked at me. "You are satisfied, senhor?"

I nodded. "Yes, thank you, Your Excellency."

The nabob turned back to the fakir's man and raised his hand. "Enough! Get up. Claim your priest and drag his filthy carcass from my sight. My men will escort you to the city gate. I have already wasted too much time with you. Be sure that I do not have occasion to see any of you again or you will all share your leader's fate. Now, in the name of Allah the Merciful, be gone!

Chapter 49

Last Business

The danger was now passed, and I could get about my business. Shaista Khan and I had not yet settled on a price for my goods. The nabob was a canny trader, and he was not above playing tricks on an honest merchant. Several years prior he had expressed a desire to purchase a large West Indies pearl that I had brought with me from Europe. After many days of wrangling he agreed to my price, but desired me to accept payment in old pagodas. When I took these to the shroffs, as the Hindoo money changers are called, they discounted them 2% on account of the gold lost through wear. When I protested to the nabob, he became red in the face and threatened to have the shroffs beaten.

I remained the khan's guest for two weeks. I was invited to dine with him almost every night. I, of course, supplied the wine.

As I said, the nabob was a canny trader but he did not have a very good eye for gems. I had with me another very large, drop-shaped pearl weighing fifty-five carats. It too came from the West

Indian fisheries and though its water was quite dead, it was the largest pearl ever seen in India. Princes are impressed by size, so I decided to ask a very high price and, perhaps, recapture some of the profit the nabob had done me out of on our last transaction.

"This pearl is magnificent, Senhor Tavernier, but 60,000 pagodas! I am a poor man. How can I possibly pay such a price?"

"It is the largest pearl ever found, my lord, and note its perfect

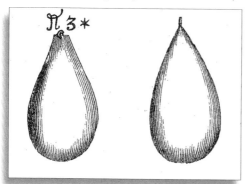

Figure 23: Tavernier's drawing of the 55 carat pearls he sold to Shaista Khan.

shape. No one has seen this pearl but Your Excellency. However, that is of no consequence," I said offhandedly. "If you do not wish to buy it, I will show it to the shah when I am next in Persia. He will, doubtless, wish to purchase it."

The nabob eyed me sourly. He disliked being bested. It seemed the perfect time to press my suit on behalf of the French company. I still had Colbert's gold, but as I had not expected the French fleet to arrive before the end of the year, I had held back. Mogul princes are famous for their short memories, and while I waited I was able to employ the capital to good advantage.

"Your Highness, I have spoken to my king, of your great wisdom and he has asked me to bring a petition before you. He has sent a gift in hopes that Your Highness will look with favor upon his request."

The nabob leaned back, looked at me warily, and cocked his eye. "A gift, you say? What sort of gift?"

I clapped my hands and four of my servants came into the tent weighed down with heavy leather bags.

I signaled Danush, who took out a knife and cut open one of the bags. A shower of gold spilt out upon the carpeted floor. "Three hundred thousand golden pagodas, my lord."

The nabob sat up and licked his lips. "Three hundred thousand, you say? Upon my head, senhor," he said beaming, "this is a princely gift." He leaned back against the cushions and began solemnly stroking his beard. "May I ask, senhor, what the Frankish king requires in return for such a gift?"

I spread my arms helplessly. "My Prince, His Majesty requires nothing; he seeks only your friendship. His Majesty wishes to establish trading relations with the empire and seeks only those privileges that the emperor has already bestowed upon the English and Dutch. He hopes Your Highness might support his petition with the emperor."

"Really," he looked at me askance but could hardly keep his eyes from straying to the money bags. "If I understand you, your king wishes trading rights and permission to build factories?"

"Just so, Your Highness."

"I see! That seems perfectly reasonable, senhor, but as you know the final decision is in the hands of my nephew, the Emperor Aurangzeb."

I bowed. "Yes, of course, Your Highness. I have already placed the petition in the hands of his vizier, together with a suitable gift."

The nabob smiled and nodded. "Wise, very wise. Tell me, senhor, are your king's ambassadors presently in residence at the emperor's court?"

"No, my lord, they have not yet arrived. I expect a fleet to arrive at Surat within months."

The mention of a fleet caused Shaista Khan to raise his eyebrows. "A fleet, you say. Hmm, I see. Well, I shall dictate a letter to your sovereign, and you may rest assured, Senhor Tavernier, that I shall write to my nephew, the emperor, at once. I believe that broader trade between the empire and the Franks is very much in the interest of our empire. I shall send him a portion of your gift," he smiled slyly, "perhaps a third. That should aid him in reaching a favorable decision."

I bowed. "Your Highness' name is a watchword of wisdom. And the pearl?"

The nabob regarded me for a moment. "Well, senhor, since you have now provided me with the means, I will buy it. Now," he said, arching one eyebrow, "let us discuss the manner of payment. I just happen to have exactly the right sum in old pagodas?"

Chapter 50

Final Homecoming

For most men it is enough to live on through their children. For my part, to pass along the shape of my nose or the cleft of my chin has always seemed, somehow, trivial. If a man is to achieve true immortality, he must do so through his own efforts. The blue diamond was the chance that my name, too, would echo down through the ages. Am I being foolish? Perhaps so, for what good is a man's name, after all, once he is dead.

Now that I had acquired the great blue diamond, to whom would I sell it? I had given the question much thought. There was but one choice. The finest gem in the world must ornament the crown of the greatest monarch in the world, Louis XIV of France. Colbert had commissioned me to find such a gem, and I had succeeded. His majesty would name the stone, but history will always footnote, at least, the man who sold it to him. How and at what price? It would be a long trip home; I would have plenty of time to think about that.

After making one last visit to Agra, I made my way to Surat. In one respect I was to be disappointed; when I arrived at the port, I found no sign and no word of the French fleet. There was very little to be done, the fleet might never arrive, and I could wait no longer. I had not had a letter from Madeleine in over a year. I left a long letter with my factor with instructions to deliver it to the French admiral, boarded an English barque on February 20th, 1667, and set sail for Bander Abbās.

At dawn on the morning of the 6th of December, 1668, my entourage passed through the gates of Paris. Guards with muskets mounted on their shoulders, a bevy of servants in bits and pieces of exotic garb with fifty fully loaded pack mules, must have made an exotic sight that morning on the Rue de Cardinal. I halted the procession at the front door of my chateau, dismounted and knocked. The door opened; it was Madeleine's servant Shadeh. Her eyes brightened with surprise at the sight of me. She looked older. I was surprised and somewhat shocked by the network of fine lines around the chin and mouth of the young girl who had played such a prominent part in a young man's fantasies. Well, I was now 63 years old and had been away from home for the better part of seven years. I smiled, placed a finger to my lips, and silently slipped by her.

Madeleine was standing on the lower rung of a ladder looking up at a plasterer who was perched above her putting the finishing touches on a decorative cornice. The floors and walls were draped with rough cotton drop cloths. She wore a simple dark blue frock with a stained workman's smock which fell almost to her knees.

"Shadeh," she called without turning, "what is all the commotion? If it is that bloody mason, tell him he must go around to the back entrance. I will not have him tracking plaster dust all over my new floors."

When Shadeh did not reply, she turned toward the door with a quizzical look. Her eyes fluttered wide in surprise. "Jean?" she cried," Jean is it truly you?" She hurriedly stepped off her perch, rushed to me, and threw herself into my arms.

"Jean, my darling, where have you been? I have been expecting you this age."

"When did you get my last letter?"

"It has been almost a year. I have been very worried."

My wife couldn't wait to show me what she had accomplished with the house in the time I had been away. Outside the façade looked pretty much as it had when I had left, but inside the house had been transformed. I gazed about me in awe.

She stood silently. Her eyes watched me as I surveyed the room.

"Madeleine, what you have done? What joy! Such elegance! I can hardly believe it!"

She laughed happily. "Do you really like it, Jean? Wait until I get these awful drop cloths down, but wait, you have only seen the foyer." She took me by the hand. "Come!"

The sitting room was a jewel. The floors had been refinished, and I recognized the largest of the four carpets, the lovely Kerman with its floral pattern in red and blue, that I had sent Madeleine from Aleppo.

"The carpets arrived the first year you were gone. So quickly, I couldn't believe it, and this one, where did you find it? So perfect, Jean. I composed the whole room around it."

"You will recall that you presented me with a list."

She laughed. "Yes, but you chose the carpets."

Madeleine had created a lovely blend of Persian and French style: the furniture—a sofa and several chairs—upholstered in a light blue watered silk embroidered with a floral pattern. The wood was elegantly carved but ungilded. The glow of dark wood blended perfectly with the rich fabrics and in each corner, Persian columns anchored a gracefully vaulted ceiling decorated with geometric designs. Along the floor the walls were edged with inlaid marquetry: small squares of turquoise, carnelian, and lapis lazuli arranged in a geometric design, putting me in mind of designs I had seen in the palaces of Persia.

"Come, Jean, there is one room I am particularly anxious for you to see," she said as she led me up two flights of stairs. The treads and risers had been redone in the Persian style.

"I do hope you like it. Now close your eyes." She led me by the hand. "Now stand here, keep your eyes closed, and give me a moment. Shadeh, help me light some candles!" I smiled, listening with pleasure to the swishing of her skirt as she bustled about the room.

"Now you may look."

I blinked in the dim light.

"I created this just for you, your own library."

One wall had built in shelves of dark cherry from floor to ceiling. My books and many of the odds and ends I had picked up on my voyages were neatly displayed. My eyes filled with tears. Gifts, Persian miniatures, shadow puppets from Pegù, the golden spurs that had been given me by the king of Ava, the souvenirs of a lifetime of travel, most of which has been packed away for so long I had forgotten about them, were all laid out.

I picked up a turquoise encrusted, silver drinking cup that had been a gift from the Shah Abbās. A large mogul tapestry with a hunting scene, a gift from the Emir Jumla, filled the opposite wall. Two small Kermans graced the floor, and there was a large plain walnut worktable in the center of the room. Light colored drapes framed the windows. Two comfortable looking chairs faced the hearth, and several maps of Persia and the East Indies, hand drawn by my father, had been framed and arranged above the mantle. I wiped at my tears.

Madeleine stood silently biting her lip while I walked about surveying her handiwork.

"I hope you don't mind, Jean, but when we made an attic apartment for Shadeh and Marcel, I was afraid to move the crates you left to the basement. It is so dank and dirty down there. Marcel brought them down here, and we unpacked them. So many treasures, what joy! I had no room for all the maps, but I found this old cabinet and it seemed just the thing, Marcel laid them out. Perhaps we should have something a bit grander made to store them."

"No, that was my father's map table." I pulled open a drawer. "The maps are just where they should be." I raised her hand to my lips and kissed it. "You have done a marvelous job, my love. I feel right at home here, and I don't mind at all that you unpacked those cases. The Lord knows when I would have found the time to do it. I love it all. Everything!"

"There are several crates left that we have not had time to unpack, and oh, Jean, I almost forgot the garden. There will not be much to see before spring. There is the fountain, and I can give you the general idea of the layout…"

"A moment, my love. I am sure it is beautiful, and there will be plenty of time to see the garden. I have brought something for you. I took her hand and slid the ring onto her finger. I drew back the curtains and light flooded the room.

"My God," she said, looking at me, her eyes glistening with tears. "How beautiful!" She held it out to arm's length and laughed, "I love it."

"It is your betrothal ring, a bit late, forgive me, but…"

She held the ring close to the windowpane and studied the gem. It was a long narrow cushion shape, set as a simple solitaire.

"Oh, Jean, there is nothing to forgive. Such a color, so delicate! I can't quite decide, Jean, is it pink or orange? I have never seen such a color or such a gem. Forgive my ignorance, my love, but what is it?"

Madeleine's pleasure was so obvious it made me smile. "It is a very rare sapphire. I had it set for you before I left India. The natives call it 'padparadscha.' The word means, color of the lotus flower. The people of the island of Serendib value it above all other gems. This one weighs a bit over ten carats and is of the first water. I have seen only three in all my years in Asia, and this is the finest. The moment I saw it I knew it must be yours."

She put her arms around me and kissed me. "Oh, Jean, you were so right. It is the most beautiful ring I have ever seen. A sapphire, and I thought that they were all supposed to be blue. Well, never mind, I love this color. I am sure that no one has one like it. I will wear it always."

Epilogue

(1668-1669)

Chapter 51

The Presentation

While he was alive, Cardinal Mazarin held the title of first minister and ruled France in all but name. Mazarin had now been dead for nine years, and Louis had grown into his kingship. His experience during the Fronde of the princes had made him distrustful and canny in the ways of power. He respected Colbert and trusted him, but never granted anyone the title of first minister. As finance minister, Colbert was the most powerful official in the kingdom.

My plan was to show the blue diamond to Colbert and through him seek an audience with His Majesty. I was promptly granted an appointment with Colbert. High office takes its toll; the black clad minister had aged in the nine years since our first meeting. He had taken to covering his graying hair with a periwig, but neither the deep pouches beneath his eyes nor the spidery lines could be hidden beneath his false tresses. Colbert exuded an aura of quiet gravity. His greeting, never warm, was friendly in a matter of fact sort of way.

Colbert informed me with some pride that the three ships flying under the flag of the French East India Company had arrived in Surat in January of 1668. He had received a report sent overland. I was surprised to hear that M. Caron, the former governor general of the Dutch company had been given command of the French expedition.

"Caron is most fulsome in his praise of your efforts, monsieur. He tells me that the arrangements you made smoothed our embassy's path to the emperor. Apparently you were able to win over the emperor's uncle, and he was most supportive. Caron was able to obtain a charter from the emperor and has already established a factory. It was money well spent. His Majesty is most pleased, as am I. Now may I ask if there is any way that I may be of service to you?"

I bowed. "Thank you, my lord. I did what I could, and I hope that your efforts may prosper. You will recall your request that I look for larger gems. I have brought something that I think will please you." I removed the pouch containing the blue diamond from my waistcoat pocket and let it slide out onto the desk in front of him.

He raised his eyes and looked at me quizzically. "Beautiful! What is it, a sapphire?"

"No, my lord, it is a diamond. You are looking at the rarest diamond on earth."

His eyes registered surprise. "A blue diamond? Good God, I have never heard of such a thing. How much does it weigh?"

"Exactly 112 7/8 French carats, my lord."

The minister clasped his hands in front of himself and studied the diamond intently for a minute, and then raised his eyes. "A blue diamond! May I touch it?"

"Oh course, my lord."

Colbert gingerly picked up the stone, turned it this way and that, then rose, and walked over to the window. Happily, it was a sunny day. He held it up and turned it in the light.

"Beautiful! Marvelous! The king must see it. I have seen the Tuscan diamond, you know, the Great Yellow," he said studying the stone intently. He turned and faced me. "His Majesty's appetite for diamonds has grown. As you know, Cardinal Mazarin left the king his entire collection. It is His Majesty's ambition to own the largest diamonds in Europe. I confess I have never heard of a large blue. Is it really so rare?"

"Without question, Your Excellency. In my thirty-five some years of travel to the Orient, I have seen many yellow gems, none as large or as beautiful as the Florentine, but I have never before seen a blue diamond as large as a single carat."

"Truly? The rarest in the world, you say? Perhaps His Majesty may wish to buy it. This would suit you well, I believe, and it will be my pleasure to tell him of it. If it is agreeable, monsieur, I will arrange an audience."

I rose and bowed. "I am at His Majesty's service, but may I beg, my lord, that the audience be private? You are the first to see the blue diamond, and I would not like it generally known that I have such a treasure in my possession."

The minister thought for a moment and nodded. "Yes, I quite take your point, monsieur. We would prefer to keep the matter confidential as well. It may take some time. His Majesty is very busy, but in view of your many services I am sure something can be arranged quite soon. In the meantime I will mention this to no one." He rose, walked around the desk and placed the diamond in my hand, and with a curt nod I was dismissed.

It was a particularly cold December. A harsh breeze off the Seine cut me to the bone as my carriage carried me along the quay toward Torreles. The people walking along the street were hooded and wrapped up like walking corpses in their shrouds. The years in the Indies had thinned my blood. I had on wool smallclothes, breeches, and doublet, two pairs of stockings, and one of the newly fashionable, fur lined *casaques*. I pulled my cloak up tighter.

Making a sale warms the blood considerably, and I had a great many gems to sell. The smaller parcels were the easiest. As always, Pierre had first pick. The years had been kind to my dear cousin. He was a little bent, but he retained a full head of hair, though by now it was completely white beneath his fashionable wig. He remained nonplussed, that is, until I brought out the Great Blue.

"Mon Dieu, is it real?"

"Real enough, cousin!"

"Mon Dieu, just when I thought that I had seen everything! Fabulous! Jean-Baptiste, fabulous!"

"I thought you would be impressed."

"Impressed? Tell me everything. Where in the world did you get it and how?"

After I told him the story, we repaired to his favorite tavern, a dark paneled pub just a few blocks from Torreles. It was between hours, just after the businessmen went home to their wives and before the serious evening drinkers became too boisterous. I filled him in on the details of my meeting with Colbert.

His pale blue eyes danced with amusement. They reminded me of my father's eyes. "You are a sly devil, Jean-Baptiste, a private audience with the king. Marvelous, marvelous, my boy! I am proud of you."

"Thank you, Pierre, but I think it would be best to save the congratulations until after the audience."

"Don't worry. The king will be astonished. The blue is marvelous. He will buy it, never fear. I wish that your father were still alive to see this. He was very proud of you, you know."

"You think the king will buy it?"

"He will buy it if only to make sure that no other monarch shall have the prestige of owning it. He is ambitious, our Louis, obsessed with his *gloria*. He truly believes all this nonsense about being the Sun King. He has made the French court the grandest in all the world, and whatever he desires, Colbert will see that he gets it— even if he has to beggar the whole kingdom in the process.

"Is it as bad as all that?"

Pierre glanced around the room. A few tables were filled but no one was paying us any attention. He leaned forward and spoke softly. "Worse, Jean-Baptiste, taxes have become horrendous, especially for the peasants. The tax collectors have always been a grasping lot, but, you know, a bribe here, a bribe there, and a man could purchase some relief. No more, your friend Colbert is relentless. He has sacked many of the officials with whom one could do business and made the system much more efficient, curse the man. Pierre leaned closer and grasped my shoulder. "But now with your new relationship with the minister, we will get some relief, hey?" He leaned back and grinned.

"Relief? I wouldn't depend upon it, cousin. Mazarin called me by my Christian name. He made you feel like he was a friend, but there is none of that with Colbert. It is always very proper and businesslike. I don't believe I have ever heard the man laugh."

"Nothing? No reaction? Even when you showed him the Blue?"

"Even then. He was curious, but he showed no real passion. Cardinal Mazarin was a true aficionado. If he were still alive, there would have been no talk of an audience with the king. He would have insisted on buying the stone himself. Louis would never even have gotten a smell of it. Colbert cares nothing for gems!"

"Did he ask the price?"

"Oh no, Colbert is far too subtle for that. He spoke of the Florentine. He wished me to know that he has seen it, of course, but the Florentine yellow diamond cannot be compared to the Blue."

"What is it really worth, Jean-Baptiste?" he asked lifting his glass.

"I calculate the yellow is worth over two and one half million livres, 2,608,335 to be precise. The Blue should be worth twice that."

Pierre's cup slammed onto the table, his eyes widened, his face turned red, and he began coughing. He looked as if he would choke on his wine. "Five millions?"

I pounded his back. "Are you all right?"

Yes, yes, I am sorry, Jean Baptist, but five millions?"

"I don't expect to get nearly that much."

Pierre shook his head slowly back and forth. "No one would ever call you shy, Jean-Baptiste, but if you succeed in getting even a quarter of that price, you will be the greatest gem merchant of this age."

"Pierre, I have been waiting for this gem my whole life, and I will not sell it cheap—that I promise you. Between us, cousin, I am finished with traveling. I do not plan to go back to India. I have seen all that I wished to see and have done all that I can do. Thirty-eight years is enough."

Pierre nodded. "Has it been as long as that? Well, yes, you said as much before you left on your last voyage? I agree, you have done your share, and your wife will be pleased. I too am thinking of retirement. Let the next generation handle it. How is young Pierre coming along, by the way? Surely he has learned Persian by now."

"He is still in Isfahan. You should hear him. He babbles away like a native. He has the gift, and Bharton is very pleased with him."

"Then you feel optimistic about our Persian venture?"

"Yes, so long as the shah continues to protect the Armenians. The Persians despise them as unbelievers but truly hate them for their control of the silk trade."

"Are we so tied to the Armenians then?"

"No, not absolutely, though our connection with Bharton's family is more than useful. Their contacts are very wide. I was personally in high favor with Shah Abbās, but now he has died, and with this new shah, who knows? Princes are fickle and Persian monarchs are notoriously short lived—so nothing is certain. "

"Madeleine will be very pleased. Have you told her?"

"It was the agreement between us. I promised her that this would be my last voyage. You have seen the town house? I feel like a great lord whenever I walk through the door. I shall retire and grow old and fat. You must come to dinner."

"I visited her and had dinner with her as often as I could. She is a charmer, your Madeleine, but she led a lonely life these past few years, Jean-Baptiste. Her maid, I can never quite pronounce her name, what a marvelous cook. Such flair! Madeleine has made you a most elegant home. As to your retirement; I shall believe it when I see it."

"You think she is happy?"

"Yes, of course she is—now that you are home. You were gone a long time, Jean-Baptiste."

"Well, that is over. I believe that she still pines a bit for her lost title. She denies it, but I know she did so enjoy being a marquise."

"Well, cousin, with the money you have made and what you will get for the Blue…. You already live like a royal duke. Buy yourself a title. Other successful men have done it."

"What? Spend half a million livres of my hard earned gold just so that some bumpkin will call me 'Your Lordship?' I have worked too hard for my money to spend it on such frippery."

Chapter 52

The Audience

 wo weeks after my interview with Colbert, I received an official summons with the date and time of the audience. I was pleased to see that it was scheduled for the afternoon.

The Louvre is laid out in a square surrounding a central square courtyard. The king's apartment is on the second floor. You enter through the east entrance off the Rue de Auriche, turn right, and ascend a wide staircase to the king's apartment. I presented myself to the lord chamberlain at precisely the time specified and was shown to a small private antechamber to await His Majesty's pleasure.

After about an hour the Chamberlain came to fetch me and ushered me in to the king's bed chamber. Several servants and court functionaries were present, including Lord Colbert. The King was at the far side of the room seated on his bed. I was somewhat shocked by this. I suppose I expected that he would be seated on a throne like the Great Mogul and indeed there was a bed on the east side of the room, gilded, canopied, and ignored.

I made my bow. Surprisingly, the king rose, came forward with a smile, and shook me by the hand. "Well, Monsieur Tavernier, we meet again. It has been a long time, has it not?"

"Your Majesty. Yes, it has been a very long time. May I compliment Your Majesty on a prodigious memory? I had no idea that you would recall a meeting that took place twenty years ago."

"But of course, monsieur, I remember it very well. You came and told me such wonderful tales of India. How good it is to see you again."

His Majesty was formally dressed, complete with a hat in the style of a musketeer, with a huge ostrich plume, a long doublet embroidered in gold, red silk Gally-Gascoignes, red hose, and a pair of high heeled, chamois boots.

"Come, monsieur," he said sitting down on his bed and motioning for me to sit beside him, "my lord," he said raising his voice to get Lord Colbert's attention. The minister was conversing with the chamberlain a few yards away. "If you please! My Lord Colbert tells me you have a diamond that will truly amaze me. That is all he will tell me. He refuses to give me any details. What do you think of that?" he said staring into my eyes with a bemused look on his face.

I could not help but laugh. The king had a charming way of putting a man at ease.

Colbert walked over to the bed and bowed solemnly.

"Your Majesty, I think it is best that I show you the diamond, and I believe you will say that My Lord Colbert has not deceived you." I drew the pouch containing the Great Blue from my doublet and placed it into the king's hands.

The light in the center of the chamber was murky despite dozens of candles blazing in golden chandeliers and in sconces along the walls. His Majesty squinted at the stone for a moment then, as I had hoped, led us to the west side of the chamber where the late September sun filtered through the high windows.

"Ah, that's better."

The king held up the blue diamond and rotated it in the

sunlight. The stone seemed to light up in his hand. Perhaps he truly is the Sun King. At any rate the stone came alive; deep blue flashes emanated from the diamond's heart.

"You were right, my lord," the king said glancing at Colbert with wide eyes. "A blue diamond. I have never seen or even heard of such a thing. It is truly magnificent. Would it be inopportune to ask, monsieur, how and where you obtained such a gem?"

I bowed. "Not at all, Your Majesty. It comes from northwestern India, in the kingdom of Golconda from a mine called Gani in the Persian tongue and Kollür by the Hindoos. As you can see, the diamond has pure crystalline water and is absolutely without flaw."

"You don't say. The kingdom of Golconda, how exotic! The words conjure up all sorts of pictures in one's mind. Yes, it must be newly found, for if it had been in Europe, I should have heard of it. How much does it weigh?"

"Just under one hundred thirteen carats."

"Ten carats less than the Tuscan Yellow?"

"Just so, Your Majesty, the second largest diamond in Europe, but the Blue is far rarer than any yellow diamond."

"Yes, I believe you, monsieur. I know of no other."

"There is one other, my liege." Colbert said.

The king caught my eye and raised his eyebrows. "You see, monsieur, be warned. Colbert never sleeps." The king laughed. "Tell us, my lord."

"After Monsieur Tavernier showed me his gem, I began making enquiries, Majesty. My sources report that a blue diamond just over thirty carats formed part of the gift that Philip IV of Spain gave his daughter the Infanta Margareta Teresa upon her betrothal to the Emperor Leopold in the year '64."

"Ah, yes, now the Holy Roman Empress. A great beauty, one hears. Pity, Emperor Leopold is old enough to be her grand sire. Very good, my lord! What do you say to that, monsieur?"

I was shocked; I knew nothing of this gem. "My Lord Colbert is very well informed. I too have heard a vague rumor of a gem fitting my lord's description, Your Majesty, but I have found that it is best not to put too much stock in rumors, and I have not heard the name of the owner, nor its exact weight." I said turning and bowing to the finance minister. "May I know what you have found out about the diamond's quality, its water and clarity, my lord?"

Colbert shrugged. "That is all the information I have been able to obtain."

"With the greatest respect, Your Majesty. If this gem exists, and I am sure Lord Colbert's sources are impeccable, thirty carats is quite a long way from one hundred twelve, and the Great Blue is flawless."

The king nodded and raised an eyebrow. "Is that what you call it? I would have thought the Tavernier Blue?"

I blushed. "Well, yes, Your Majesty, for the moment, but the honor of naming the diamond goes with its purchase."

"Quite. I suppose, were the crown to acquire it, it would be the French Blue or something similar. I am surprised that I have not heard of your diamond's existence from one of my jewelers."

"I have shown it to no one, Your Majesty. I could have easily sold it to one of the great princes of India, but I knew that a gem so rare must first be offered to Your Majesty. My Lord Colbert was the first man in Europe to see it."

The king studied me for a few moments and then smiled. "Truly, monsieur, I am flattered and grateful. It is my wish to build the greatest collection of gems in the world, to the glory of France."

I bowed deeply. "Your Majesty, it is only fitting that the rarest diamond in the world should adorn the reign of the most glorious monarch of our age."

The king raised his hand in dismissal, but I could see that my words pleased him. "Before I become too enthusiastic, may I ask the price?"

"Your Majesty, how does one set a price on a gem so beautiful and so rare? Were I to offer it to the emperor of India or the shah of Persia, my price would be four million livres or more. But this diamond is not for them. The price to you, Your Majesty, is 1,500,000 livres."

Colbert's jaw dropped. "A million and a half livres? Surely you jest, monsieur! My God, has anyone ever paid such a price for a diamond?"

"I believe the Tuscan stone has been appraised for over two million, and in my opinion the true value of the Blue is closer to five and one half million."

The king stroked his chin. "Monsieur Tavernier, I can think of no one among my subjects who can boast half your experience. What is your opinion? Is the Tuscan Yellow the largest diamond in the world?"

"No, Your Majesty, it is not. The Grand Duke's gem is the largest diamond in Europe, but to my certain knowledge there are several larger to be found in Asia. The largest and most beautiful of all lies in the treasury of the Great Mogul of India. It is a gem of the finest water, pure, like a clear mountain spring. It weighs 279 9/16 carats and there is nothing in Europe to touch it. The next largest is a flat table like stone. It weighs 242 7/16 carats, and its water is a beautifully limpid light pink."

The king's brow furrowed. His Majesty was a good listener. His dark eyes searched my face. I could see that he was carefully weighing my words.

"I have bought and sold at least fifty large white diamonds over the course of thirty years. I have travelled over 40,000 leagues in my search, and I have never seen another blue of any appreciable size. I believe when all factors are considered—size, color and clarity— excepting only the Great Mogul's gem, the diamond you hold in your hand is the rarest of them all."

The afternoon was advancing; the westering sun cast long narrow shadows across the polished marble floors and the richly patterned carpets.

"Hmm and I take it that the Great Mogul's gem is not for sale?"

"It is not, Your Majesty."

The king placed his hand in my shoulder and smiled graciously. "Upon my word, monsieur, I could listen to you discourse for hours, but then I would be in trouble with my esteemed minister who has many important items for me to consider." He smiled at Colbert. "Is that not so, my lord?" Colbert's face remained as placid as if carved from a block of wood. The king laughed. "You see, monsieur," the king said placing his finger beside his eye, "the man is a veritable sphinx. But, never fear, Monsieur Tavernier, I shall carefully consider all that you have said."

Chapter 53

The Negotiation

I returned the next afternoon and showed the king the balance of my goods. After His Majesty had looked them over, Lord Colbert motioned me aside.

"His Majesty is considering a number of your gems. He asks you to leave them with his chamberlain so that he may examine them at his leisure."

I bowed. "Of course, my lord, I am honored. May I know which of the stones His Majesty is considering?"

"All!" he said rather curtly.

I was not sure that I had heard him correctly. "Did you say 'all,' my lord?"

"I did, monsieur", he said with a sour look. "His Majesty is considering your entire stock. He wishes to have Monsieur Pitau evaluate the gems. You are acquainted with the king's diamond expert, I believe?"

"I have had that honor."

"Good, if you will submit a receipt to my secretary, I will sign it and let you know His Majesty's decision in due course. And now I must bid you good day."

"Excuse me, my lord, I am pleased to serve His Majesty and I do not wish to give offence, but this will tie up all my goods. May I ask how long His Majesty will require making his decision?"

"Monsieur, don't be impertinent. The king is the king. He has many important affairs of state that take precedence, as do I. Such things cannot be rushed. He will make his decision at his own leisure. He has honored you with his interest. That should be sufficient."

I bowed, "Yes, my lord."

Colbert turned to go, paused, turned back and said in a softer tone: "Monsieur Tavernier, I will do my best to expedite this matter, and now I must bid you good day."

I went to Torreles to see Pierre. I knew that he fairly ached to know how I had fared. It was near dusk. The streets were growing quiet. My carriage passed a lamplighter lighting the candles in the newly installed street lamps near the Place Royale. The bright flame made a charming counterpoint against the darkening winter sky. A gentleman scurried along in the opposite direction, head down, his hands thrust into a muff against the cold.

Pierre did not share my dark mood. He clapped me heartily on the back.

"Jean-Baptiste , you could not very well expect the king to make a decision on the spot. He is not a fish-wife, for all love. From what you said, I would be hopeful. You have had a private audience, two in fact. I think this bodes very well for future business. Pay no attention to Colbert. He is a notorious cheapskate, the creature. If it was up to him he would gather up all the gold in the kingdom and bury it in the ground beneath the palace. What I wouldn't give to have seen the look on his face when you named your price for the Blue."

"I asked too much!"

"Too much? Well, cousin, as I believe I have said, no one would ever call you shy when it comes to pricing your goods, but if Colbert thinks your price is too high, perhaps he can find another at a lower price."

"I was very nearly destroyed when Colbert described this other blue diamond. Pierre, I have never heard even a whisper of this gem. Lord above, the man must have eyes and ears everywhere."

Pierre waggled his finger at me. "Have a care, cousin. Colbert is a canny devil, but you covered yourself very well. Do not forget there are others—jewelers, men you know well—who will soon hear of this and, never fear, they will do their best to queer the deal."

"Perhaps, but you know, Pierre, I wonder if that was really the first the king had heard of that stone. He certainly seemed surprised."

"Not as surprised as you were when Colbert dropped his bomb, I'll wager, ha, ha! It is best not to underestimate our Louis, cousin. His Majesty is young, but he is no babe in the woods. They probably cooked up the whole thing between themselves just to see how you would react."

"Do you think so? I must be on my guard, but, in the end, Pierre, there is no other, nothing can match the Blue!"

"What will you do if Louis refuses to pay your price?"

"If the king does not want the gem, I suppose I would take it to Duke Ferdinand. I am on good terms with His Grace. He already owns the Yellow, and he is a great lover of beautiful stones. As I am sure you have guessed, I am asking more than I am prepared to accept."

"But, of course. You are far from being a fool, Jean-Baptiste. This is just the opening gambit. Colbert is a wily negotiator, and you have been down this road many times before."

"You are right, Pierre, but the truth is I am tired of the hauteur of kings and princes and endless negotiations."

"Sounds like you are in need of a rest, Jean-Baptiste. Why not take Madeleine and go out to the country or go to Vichy and take the waters."

In the end I did not have that long to wait. I was able to spend a restful two weeks at home puttering about, arranging my books and collections in my new library and getting reacquainted with my wife before I received a summons from Lord Colbert.

Winter had come early. Snow had fallen the previous night. The sky was lead gray, and there was a wicked north wind. A lackey announced me. I found Colbert stalking back and forth across his office like a black crow on his perch. The minister barely raised a hand, and then continued his pacing. Finally he stopped and faced me.

"Well, monsieur, His Majesty has commanded me to make you an offer."

"His Majesty has made his selection?"

"His Majesty wishes to purchase your entire stock."

"Everything?"

"Yes, monsieur, everything. His Majesty is quite pleased with the quality of your goods and wishes to buy the entire collection."

I had left His Majesty with a large number of gems, forty-six large and medium sized diamonds, one thousand one hundred and two smaller diamonds, and the Great Blue.

Colbert picked up a paper from his desk, glanced at it, and spoke matter of factly. "First, let us talk about the smaller gems, monsieur. His Majesty will pay 678,731 livres in gold—67,000 Louis d'or for the white stones."

Colbert and the king had clearly done their homework. Monsieur Pitau had advised them well. The offer was almost to the sou what a dealer would have offered for the lot. It was a fair offer. I nodded without saying anything and held my breath waiting for the offer on the Blue.

"For the large blue diamond, monsieur, His Majesty offers 220,000 livres in gold, making a total of 898,731 livres or 89,000 Louis d'or."

I was stunned. The offer was much less than I had expected, and a great deal less than I was prepared to accept. It never pays to respond hastily. I took several deep breaths to calm myself while I pretended to ponder His Excellency's offer. I began to feel calmer and raised my eyes to meet Colbert's.

"Your Excellency, I am prepared to accept His Majesty's offer for the smaller gems, but with regret, I cannot accept his offer for the Blue."

Colbert did not appear surprised. His tone remained even. "His Majesty has been advised that the Blue is worth less than the Sancy, for which Monsieur Le Cardinal paid 360,000 livres. The total offer is the equivalent of 598.6 kilograms of pure gold, monsieur, a princely sum by any standard."

I dislike justifying my prices. Silence is usually best, but I could not help but respond. "The Sancy, my lord, is the largest white diamond in Europe. It is an exceptional gem, flawless and of the first water, but it weighs only 53 3/4 carats. With respect, my lord, the comparison does not hold. By dint of its rarity, the Blue is worth much more than the Sancy."

The minister's dark eyes remained fixed on mine for several moments. I assumed that this was the end of the negotiation, but Colbert was a subtle one. I was soon to learn just how subtle.

"Monsieur Tavernier, do not make a decision you may later regret, I beg. Take your time; consider His Majesty's offer. Let us meet again in a week. I beg you also to consider that one does not haggle with His Majesty. The offer is for all or none."

We made an appointment to meet the following week.

Chapter 54

Parry and Thrust

A few days later while I was still seething over Colbert's offer, a gray liveried messenger knocked on our door with a sealed letter. I left the fellow in the hallway and sought out my wife. Madeleine put down her needlepoint and smiled as I came into her room.

"Madeleine, a lackey has just brought a mysterious invitation."

"Who is it from?"

"That's just it. I don't know. It is signed by a 'Lady A' who requests my presence, but the rude fellow refuses to name his mistress."

"What is the address?"

"The Rue de l'Échelle. It is close by the Tuileries. Do we know anyone in that neighborhood?"

Madeleine thought for a moment and then gasped. "Lady A! Jean, it can only be Athénaïs de Montespan, the king's new mistress."

"The king's mistress? What has become of Louise de la Vallière?"

Madeleine reached up and patted my cheek. "You mean the Duchesse de Vaujours, Jean?"

"La Vallière is a duchess?"

"Oh, yes, for over a year now. You are sadly out of date, my dear. Before Louis dismisses a mistress, he always grants her a title. He has legitimized her three bastards as well. Athénaïs de Montespan is His Majesty's current favorite. She is the daughter of the Duke de Mortmart and the wife of the Marquis de Montespan. The king is besotted with her."

"And how does Monsieur le Marquis feel about being cuckolded by His Majesty?"

"By all accounts he has taken it rather badly. I have heard that he has torn down the gates to his chateau. The fool is telling everyone that his horns are so high that he cannot get through the archway. Can you imagine? Well, he is a Gascon. You know how proud they can be."

"Yes, quite right, my love."

"Oh, and you haven't heard the best part. He threatens to visit the meanest brothels in Paris, catch a disease, and then force himself upon his wife so that she will infect His Majesty. "

"Extraordinary! Sounds like the fellow is playing a dangerous game. Would he not be better off to retire quietly to his estates and await his dukedom?"

"Exactly! Some men are such fools!"

"I suppose that I should answer the lady's summons."

"Why, of course, you *must* call on her, Jean. It would not do at all to insult her. You must go. I am dying to know what she is after. I have heard that she is a great lover of jewels."

It was a frosty winter afternoon and the horses' hooves made a brittle sound on the hardened earth. I alighted from my carriage in front of a small stone house with a garden enclosed by a high wall. I found out later that it had also housed Louise de la Vallière during her early days in the king's, ah, service. It was the royal hatchery, where the king's mistresses stayed while they awaited their chicks.

I presented my card to a servant dressed in the king's livery. Madame la Marquise received me *déshabillé*. La Montespan is said to have created the style. The term is one our betters use meaning that they wish to appear as if they are too lazy to dress themselves. Lord, what a woman—she received me in her bedroom—huge blue eyes, a naughty red mouth, a lusciously ripe figure, and dewy skin with the softness and color of a rose just coming into bloom.

Madame was half-reclined on a Greek chaise, her lustrous corn-silk hair flowing artlessly like a waterfall about her shoulders. The chaise was set by a bay window that looked onto the frosted winter garden. One of His Majesty's famous orange trees sat in a chased silver planter between the chaise and the window.

"Monsieur Tavernier." She extended her hand with a languid grace and fastened those azure eyes upon me. "How good of you to come."

I bowed. The lady wore a voluminous silk dressing gown that brought out the color of her eyes and did little to hide the fact that she was quite obviously with child.

"As you may know, monsieur," she began, "His Majesty and I are very good friends. I have seen your diamonds—so beautiful, monsieur—and one hears everywhere of the exploits of the famous Jean-Baptiste Tavernier. I must confess I was fascinated and wished to make your acquaintance myself."

"Madame is too kind." I bowed quickly. I caught her scent, and my breath felt constricted and my face turned the color of red cabbage.

"Monsieur, please do sit down." I glanced quickly around the room. The chaise was the only piece of furniture other than a large canopied bed set in the other corner.

Figure 24: Tavernier's drawing of one of a pair of diamond briolettes that he sold to Louis XIV in 1689.

"Please do not stand upon ceremony, I beg you," she smiled and patted the cushion next to her. "I do so adore hearing about exotic places. I wish to hear especially of the diamonds and the other jewels you have acquired."

I sat down gingerly on the edge of the chaise, still blushing like a schoolboy. My lady favored me with a beguiling smile.

"I have seen the blue diamond. It is magnificent, monsieur, but it is rather dark and flat, is it not?"

"Yes, Madame, it is, but once it is re-cut into the modern style, it will be stunning."

"But it will be so much smaller. I wished to ask you what you think of the two large diamonds that you have offered His Majesty. They are almost the same size. They look rather like a pair of turnips."

"They are called pendeloques or briolettes, my lady. They were cut in India, and they are of very fine water. Together, they weigh a trifle over thirty carats."

"Would they not make lovely earrings?"

I looked into her eyes. "Perfect, my lady. They require only a pair of equally lovely, ah, ears, my lady." I felt myself blush again and dropped my eyes.

The marquise laughed and clapped her hands with delight. Her voice was like the tinkling of silver bells. "Oh, là, upon my word, you are a naughty one, monsieur. I was not told that you were such a gallant." She leaned forward slightly and a shoulder strap slipped, exposing a charming décolleté. Her smile seemed faintly mocking.

"I only speak the truth, my lady. Perhaps you noticed that the gems do not quite match."

"Yes, but with a nose between, who will notice?" She giggled prettily. "They are stunning, upon my word, and it would be a sin to sacrifice even one lovely carat, would it not?"

I bowed. "My lady has the soul of an aficionado."

She smiled and lifted an eyebrow. "I had hoped for a pair of *girandoles*. Might you be able to find just four smaller ones of a similar quality?"

I bowed. "I shall closely examine my stock. I am sure something can be found, My lady. I will send several over for your inspection."

Madame de Montespan idly picked up a fan from a small table next to her chaise and with her eyes still fixed on mine, snapped it open, and raised it to her face so that only her eyes were visible. The eyes were thoughtful.

"Tell me, monsieur, I am curious about the blue diamond. One hears that you are asking a great price for it?"

"It is a magnificent diamond, my lady, a gem truly fit for a king."

Her eyes held mine for a moment and then looked away. "So you say, monsieur, but one hears that the king's experts are advising him that your price is far too high. I believe the king's jeweler, Montarsis—do you know him—actually laughed out loud when he was told of it. He has offered to obtain for His Majesty another diamond, a bit smaller, but at a much better price."

Beads of sweat broke beneath my wig. Who had put her up to it? Montarsis? I detected Colbert's deft hand. I knew M. Montarsis fairly well. We had done some business in the past. He was the king's jeweler at that time and something of a blowhard, and he did not love me. I had taken away too much business from him. I also knew that my answer would soon reach the ears of the king. I took a long, deep breath.

"Another blue, my lady? Blue diamonds, it seems, are popping up everywhere. I know of no other blue diamond of size for sale at any price."

The fan moved gently back and forth in front of her face. Her eyes took on a sly look. "Apparently Monsieur Montarsis does," she replied.

"Truly? As you know, my lady, I have made five voyages to India in the search for great treasures, and I have not heard of another large blue diamond, and, to my certain knowledge, Monsieur Montarsis has never been outside the environs of Paris. But one man cannot see and know of everything. Is it a beautiful stone?"

The fan froze in mid-stroke and Madame's eyes regarded me warily. "Why, I have not seen it, monsieur—that is, not yet?"

"I see, how odd? Given your standing with His Majesty and your excellent eye for gems, I would have thought Monsieur Montarsis would have shown the diamond to you straight away."

Madame's eyes narrowed. The fan twitched back and forth like the tail of an angry cat.

"Forgive me but in this business, my lady, one hears many rumors. If a gem exists such as Monsieur Montarsis says and is available, I would consider it an honor to be allowed to purchase it myself and present it to His Majesty as a gift."

Behind the fan, Madame's eyes widened. "Indeed, monsieur, that would be a princely gift."

I bowed. "It would be an excellent, ah, accompaniment to my blue, don't you think? I have shown the Great Blue only to His Majesty though I could have sold it easily to one of the nabobs of India, and, as you know, I have had the honor of being appointed court jeweler to His Imperial Majesty, the Shah of Persia, and he too is a great lover of fine gems."

"Then why, monsieur, did you not sell it?" The fan snapped closed. "Isn't that what merchants do?"

"My lady, I am a Frenchman. The Blue is one of the world's greatest jewels, and it is my belief that the finest jewels in the world should adorn the crown of the greatest monarch in the world, His Majesty, Louis XIV of France."

"Well spoken, monsieur. You can be *sure* that I shall convey your very generous offer to His Majesty." The fan once again passed languidly back and forth in front of her face.

"Thank you, my lady."

Madame lowered her fan. "Now tell me, monsieur, your lady wife, I trust she is well."

I could not help but smile. "Yes, madame, she is quite well. I shall tell her that you asked after her. You are acquainted?"

"I have not had the honor, monsieur." The fan opened and fluttered twice. "I was a mere child, still stuck in the provinces when the marquise was at court, but even after all these years, one still hears stories of the mysterious Persian beauty. There were rumors that she was the daughter of an emperor, and Paris was quite taken aback when you married," the lady smiled. "So romantic giving up her title to marry for love, but that was so many years ago, and one hears little of her these days."

"Yes, she gave up a great deal for me, and I am truly honored."

"One can see it in your face. You truly love her—how very quaint, monsieur."

After a few more pleasantries, she put down the fan and offered her hand. I was dismissed. Had the lady gotten what she was after? I guessed that I would soon know.

"Do you think I came at it a little high, Pierre?"

"Never in life, cousin! You handled the royal harlot perfectly, and did I not warn you? Montarsis is a snake."

"Yes, I believe you."

"He is jealous. Montarsis has never been further than the Quai des Orfèvres. He and the others—Le Tessier, Bosc and Pitau—have made a fortune turning out jewels for His Majesty's stable. They have their little club. La Vallière never much cared for jewels, but now they are in ecstasy. La Montespan would fill a tub and bathe in them if she could."

"Pierre, you are beginning to sound a little jealous."

"Jealous, me?" Pierre looked at me and laughed. "Well, perhaps a little. I will tell you what, Jean-Baptiste, I am tired of being on the outside looking in, and now, thanks to you, and your Great Blue, we will wipe their eyes for good and all."

"I don't believe I have ever heard you speak so." Pierre had always been the soul of rectitude.

Pierre's face had reddened with passion. "This has been coming on for a great while, Jean-Baptiste. Torreles has always been in the back tier. Oh, we have done well enough, but how many times have I been required to sell my best jewels to these bastards so they, in turn, could sell them to the palace and make the lion's share of the profit? They had the entrée to His Majesty, and, oh, they will indulge any fantasy, no matter how gauche. Such toadies! 'Oh yes, Your Majesty, such a magnificent concept.' And they run off and throw together some gaudy confection that makes a mockery of all standards of good taste."

"Pierre, are you saying that His Majesty has poor taste in jewels?"

Pierre looked around and leaned close. "Pedestrian, Jean-Baptiste, not to put too fine a point on it. His Majesty missed his calling. He should have been a baker. He wishes to slather frosting on every one of his tarts."

I threw my head back and laughed. "Lord, Pierre, I hope you have not said these things to anyone else."

Pierre sat back in his chair and glared at me. "No, I have not. In truth, I have hardly dared say them to myself." He took a deep breath. "Forgive me, cousin. I don't know what came over me."

"Cousin," I said wiping my eyes, "there is nothing to forgive."

"Montarsis put de Montespan up to it, of that you can be sure, but he has nothing to rival our Tavernier Blue, I will tell you that, nothing that comes even close."

"I am pleased to hear you say that as I am pledged to buy it if he does."

"Ha, ha, do not worry. He never will! You handled it brilliantly, Jean-Baptiste. Check and mate. Lord, how I would love to be a fly on the wall when His Majesty demands that Montarsis produce his diamond. And, when he cannot, that will be the end of him. The king dislikes being toyed with. You have destroyed him, believe me, Jean-Baptiste, I know. Montarsis will not be able to show his face at court."

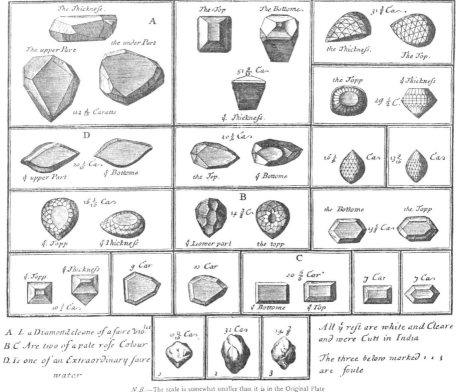

A Representation of 20 of the fairest Diamonds Chosen out among all those which Monsieur Tavernier sold to the King at his last return from the Indies, upon which Consideration, and for several services done the Kingdome His Majesty honored him with the Title of Noble.

N.B.—The scale is somewhat smaller than it is in the Original Plate

Figure 25: Copy of the original invoice of Louis XIV's purchase from Tavernier (with English translation added) as published in the 2nd English Edition of Tavernier's Six Voyages. Actual document is on file in the Louvre. The text reads: "A Representation of 20 of the fairest diamonds chosen from among those which Monsieur Tavernier sold to the King at his last return from the Indies upon which consideration and for several services done the kingdom, His Majesty honored him with the title of noble."

Chapter 55

Final Gambit

I called upon Lord Colbert a few days later. I found him seated behind his great desk. He motioned me to a chair set just in front of it.

"Well, monsieur, you have decided, I trust, to accept His Majesty's offer?"

I bowed. "I am sorry, my lord. It pains me to say it but I cannot."

The minister stared at me. "You will refuse the King?"

"My deepest apologies, my lord, but, as I said at our last meeting, the price is simply too low, and much as it pains me to disagree with His Majesty, I cannot sell at that price."

Colbert sat in his chair staring at me. That was it. The interview was over. My heart sank. I had rolled the dice and lost. There was no going back. I had lost my one chance to sell the Great Blue to His Majesty, and as Colbert said, His Majesty wished to buy all or none. Well, I had been at this point before. I stood and bowed, "Good day to you, my lord."

The minister raised his hand. "Just a moment, I am not quite finished, Monsieur Tavernier. It gives me great pleasure to tell you that His Majesty proposes to pay you the sum he has offered and, in addition, in recognition of your many years of service to France, wishes to honor you with a patent of nobility."

Colbert's words took me completely off guard. The minister knew, of course, my personal history and more importantly that of my wife's. He now dangled before me the one jewel he knew would please her more than any other.

The selling of offices and titles had proved an excellent way to raise funds and if it displeased the old nobility, so much the better. After the Fronde, the king never really trusted them.

The old aristocracy affects a public distain for the new men, but while they are rich in land, they are constantly strapped for cash. They are forbidden to engage in ordinary business and as time has gone on, basking in the reflected light of the Sun King has become very expensive. They marry off their sons and daughters to the offspring of these rich burghers in return for huge dowries.

The going price for a patent of nobility was 500,000 livres. What Colbert was now offering on the king's behalf, effectively trebled his offer for the Great Blue diamond. For a commoner it was the fulfillment of a dream, for who amongst us does not wish to raise himself to the nobility.

I felt my heart swell. What a wonderful surprise for my darling wife. She would be so happy to once again have a title—countess or baroness or the wife of a chevalier at the very least, depending upon the estate. With the money and a patent of nobility, I could purchase an estate and with it the title.

As if he had read my mind, Colbert spoke. "I know of a barony, Aubonne, a lovely estate, monsieur, in Savoie, in the hill country near Geneva. I believe it can be had for less than 100,000. Beautiful country, wonderful place to retire, and they make a very tolerable wine." Colbert kept his dark hawk's eyes fixed on me. A thin smile spread slowly across that usually stony visage. I knew the price of that smile, and he knew, at that moment, that he had me.

"I accept your offer, but would ask one favor, my lord, if I may?"

Colbert eyed me suspiciously. "Yes, monsieur?"

"You know I have long been associated with Torreles. If the firm could receive some recognition, perhaps a commission from His Majesty?"

The minister smiled "Yes, of course. I am sure something could be arranged. I cannot promise you understand, but I will speak to the king."

Chapter 56

To the Manor Raised

nnobled by His Majesty, I can hardly believe it. Oh Jean, how wonderful!" Madeleine's eyes flashed with excitement. "Lord knows, you deserve it. When? Will there be a formal ceremony?"

"I don't know. Colbert said nothing about a ceremony, only that we should be received by His Majesty."

"Received by the king! Well, of course, it comes to the same thing. An audience with the king, my God, and all that lovely money, too. Jean, you are a genius."

"I still can't believe it."

"Believe it? Why, what do you mean, my dear?"

"Colbert played me, played me like a violin. I must be getting old."

"Oh Jean, don't be ridiculous. To be raised to the nobility—it is a wonderful coup. You know what such things cost."

"It is Colbert who got the best of the bargain. The Blue is worth at least a half million more."

"I am sure you are right, but, as you said yourself, there was only one other possible buyer, and you were asking a great price. What would you do if the grand duke could not, or would not, buy it?"

I smiled at her. "Find a deserving woman and pin it to her bosom, I suppose."

My wife turned to me and placed her hands on my shoulders. Her dark eyes searched mine, and she slowly shook her head. "Jean-Baptiste Tavernier, you are a great tease. The blue diamond is magnificent, breathtaking! What woman would not wish to possess it? The world will never forget the man who found the stone, but I believe that for ordinary people, it would be a curse. I have a feeling, and I think it is best to be rid of it. Such things are the province of the great."

"A feeling…?"

"Yes, just that. Oh, I know it sounds silly, but yes I have a feeling that the Blue is an unlucky stone, unlucky, that is, for the likes of us."

"Well it certainly proved unlucky for its former owner."

"Yes, what an awful story, Jean. The poor man, to have died like that!"

"You may be right, my darling. I hope for the king's sake that you are wrong, but at any rate the deal is done, and as Pierre would say, there is nothing to be gained by dwelling on it. Now we must look for an estate. Colbert told me of one, a barony, Aubonne. It is in Savoie, in the wine country, and there is a lovely old chateau that I am sure is in need of work. The deceased baron was a famous physician by the name of Sir Theodore Turquet De Mayerne.

"I have not heard of him?"

"Nor should you have, my love, unless you suffer from the gout? He immigrated to England and wrote a very well regarded book on the subject of gout, do you see? He has been dead now for thirteen years, and the estate has languished since. His daughter Adrienne inherited it, and she married the Marquis de Montpouillan. From what I was told, they rarely visit the place and wish to sell."

"So many years? It might be falling down. We must see it."

"Yes, of course, but first we shall celebrate the New Year in Paris, go to Geneva, and then pop in to see the king."

"'Pop in', indeed. Where will the ceremony be held, the Louvre or Versailles?"

"I am sorry my dear, I do not know."

"Well you must find out. There is a great deal to be done. You have no idea! I need a new gown and shoes and—well, everything— and we must do something about a proper suit of clothes for you. You absolutely cannot appear before His Majesty dressed as you are. I shall be a laughing stock. We must find you a new coat and breeches, something more stylish.

I bowed deeply from the waist. "I shall leave everything to you, my dear baroness."

"Truly, Jean-Baptiste, you bow like a common oaf."

I wrote to the Marquis de Montpouillan concerning the barony at Aubonne and made arrangements for us to journey to Aubonne in early January.

We left for Versailles early that frosty morning, February the 28th, 1669. Madeleine hired a gilded coach with six matched blacks— magnificent

Figure 26: Early 18th Century antique engraving of Louis XIV's Palace at Versailles.

animals! I do love a fine horse! What a sight they were, with breath rising like steam in the early morning chill. They were curried and brushed until their backs gleamed like satin in the pale winter sun.

"Appearances!" Madeleine said. "It is not every day, Jean-

Baptiste, that a man is raised to the nobility." The horses tossed their heads. They were as nervous as we were and anxious to be off. Then we were on our way. The sharp staccato of the horses' hooves echoed off the stone walled buildings as we passed through the narrow streets and out the city gates.

Pierre accompanied us. The trip was not particularly pleasant. The road to Versailles is very well traveled. The autumn had been warm and wet and the first freeze had frozen the mud into deep ruts. We were tossed about like ninepins as the heavy carriage dipped and bounced along the road. I ordered the driver to pull up as we crested the hill overlooking Versailles.

The palace complex was only about half built at that time. It was laid out geometrically and from the overlook it reminded me of a children's toy, a village of spun sugar and marzipan. You could see the long rectangular buildings fade down the long valley towards a gap in the hills to the east. Versailles cannot compete with the elegance and perfect proportions of the Taj Mahal, but the Taj was built as a monument to a dead queen. Versailles has beggared a kingdom to pander to the vanity of a living man who has set himself up as second only to God.

The last mile of the road is flanked by an avenue of tall pines which leads into a large round parking area, cupped between two semi-circular walls that open on one end and lead to the main gate. It was almost noon. Carriages came and went, stopping only long enough to deposit their fashionable cargo at the gate. Empty carriages were scattered like dead leaves all about the waiting area. Liveried servants stood huddled in small groups, stamping their feet to keep warm while they waited, sometimes for many hours, for their masters' or mistresses' return.

We queued up, and when our turn came, we alighted, and I presented my summons to a chamberlain. We were led across a courtyard into the palace and down a long hall with marble floors lined with mirrors on one side and tall windows on the other, and through a vaulted chamber bounded on either side by tall marble columns, topped with ornately carved arches. The ceiling was frescoed with scenes by Le Brun, celebrating the king's reign. Ornate chandeliers hung from the high ceiling. We passed workmen painting and plastering, and groups of courtiers gathered in the sunny alcoves by the huge vaulted windows, smiling, nodding, sharing the latest gossip, and preening like exotic birds in their gaudy plumage.

Madeleine had never looked more beautiful, dressed in a gown of red watered silk with her hair cascading in ringlets, just touching her bare shoulders. Her hair was still a lustrous raven black, untouched by frost. She walked with her head held high, regally bestowing a nod here and a smile there as she recognized old acquaintances. That day she looked every inch a shah's daughter. Some courtiers stared, others smiled and nodded as we passed, others pretended to take no notice, but I could feel their eyes following our progress wondering, no doubt, who we were, and how we stood in the pecking order.

When we had been ensconced in one of the waiting rooms, Madeleine turned to me. "Jean, why so somber? You have hardly said a word since we left Paris. You seem pensive. Is something bothering you?"

"No, my love."

"On this of all days, Jean, you should be happy. We are about to be received by His Majesty. Please try and look, at least, as though you are pleased to be here."

"Don't worry, my love, I shall rally, never fear."

Madeleine stamped her foot. "Rally, rally! I swear, Jean-Baptiste, sometimes I despair, I truly do. Here you are about to receive a great honor and you seem not the least pleased with it."

"I was thinking about all this magnificence, the cost of it and all these useless aristocrats hanging about like ornaments on a Christmas tree. Do you see those orange trees? One hundred and ten livres, each!"

"Really!"

We had been deposited in a small parlor with four heavily gilded chairs set in a circle and a potted orange tree sitting in a silver pot by a floor-to-ceiling window that looked out on a formal garden.

"Yes, they remind me of a line from that writer of farces, you know the one who calls himself Molière: 'people of rank know everything without ever having learned anything.'"

"Ha, ha, exactly right, cousin," Pierre said.

"Shh!" Madeleine put her finger to her lips to quiet the both of them. Her eyes darted anxiously about the room.

"Please, Jean, not so loud. Someone might hear you, and, Pierre, please don't encourage him. Try to remember that you are about to become an aristocrat yourself, Jean-Baptiste. Will you then be a useless ornament? These men are your clients."

"Yes, some, but in India and Persia the omrahs must work for a living. Our nobles contribute nothing."

"It is the king's wish that they reside at court."

"Yes, I know, since the Fronde, he has built this…this magnificent gilded cage so he can keep them here—prisoners under his thumb."

"His Majesty is no fool," Pierre said.

Just at that moment one of the king's lackeys with four of the King's guards came to escort us. We were taken to Madame de Montespan's lavishly decorated apartments.

Figure 27: Louis XIV, the Sun King of France. From a 17th Century engraving.

The chamber was of modest size by the standards of Versailles, which means that it was quite large and sumptuously decorated with high gilded vaults and frescoed ceilings. The walls were papered and the doors carved and gilded. The floors were marble. Though it was mid-day, the room was lit by several large chandeliers, perhaps fifty candles, and it was filled with people.

There were at least sixty courtiers and half as many liveried servants, all circling the king and his mistress like planets revolving about the sun. The courtiers milled about greeting friends and talking amongst themselves while each kept an eye on the man upon whom all their fortunes turned.

"Ah Monsieur Tavernier," the king rose smiling from his chair and beckoned us forward, and the courtiers moved aside like the Biblical parting of the Red Sea. "So good to see you again, and I see you have brought a charming companion."

"Your Majesty." Following Madeleine's lead out of the corner of my eye, I made a leg, bowed deeply, keeping time with Madeleine's graceful curtsy.

The King doffed his hat with a flourish. It was another musketeer's hat with a wide brim and a long feather stuck into the crown. "What a pleasure to see you once again, my dear marquise."

Madeleine blushed deeply. King Louis was very polite. He acknowledged my wife even though she was no longer, strictly speaking, a marquise. It is said that he even tips his hat to his maids.

"Your Majesty, may I name my dear friend and cousin, Pierre of Torreles."

"Why of course you may, monsieur. A pleasure to meet you. The House of Torreles enjoys a high reputation at court."

"Your Majesty!" Pierre bowed deeply.

"Perhaps, Master Pierre, if you would not mind staying behind for a few minutes after the ceremony. There is a matter upon which we wish to seek your advice."

Pierre blushed, "Of course, Your Majesty, I am at your service." He caught my eye and bowed again.

The king was dressed in scarlet with an elaborate black periwig with tresses tumbling about his shoulders. He wore an embroidered silk doublet and a pair of the newly fashionable Rhinegrave pantaloons tucked into a pair of brown chamois high-heeled boots. His shirt was a brilliant white and beautifully ruffled at the wrists and throat.

"May I present the Marquise de Montespan? Madame, I believe you have met Monsieur Tavernier," he said arching one eyebrow, "but perhaps not his charming wife."

Madeleine and I turned slightly and bowed again, and if I do say so myself, in perfect unison.

"Come, come, Monsieur Tavernier. I have had this document prepared for you," the king said, indicating a rolled parchment held by one of the servants.

"Monsieur, a small token of our esteem in view of your most valuable services to the crown." The king smiled. "I trust you already know its contents." He raised his hand. The room went silent. "Gather around, everyone. You all know or have heard of the famous traveler, Monsieur Jean-Baptiste Tavernier. Herald, read the patent so that all may hear!"

The herald unrolled the parchment and read. The language was fairly standard though I was gratified by several obliging things His Majesty included about my service to the kingdom. I could not prevent tears from coming to my eyes as it was read and wished only that my mother and father had lived to see this day. His Majesty bade me kneel.

"By order of His Majesty, King Louis XIV of France," the herald intoned. "Jean-Baptiste Tavernier Is hereby raised to the rank of noble."

I looked over at Madeleine. Pierre stood beaming by her side. Tears were streaming down her face.

His Majesty reached down and took my hand: "You may rise, my lord."

The End

Afterword:

    Jean-Baptiste Tavernier was one of the most remarkable figures of the Seventeenth Century. Between the years 1630-1668, Tavernier made six voyages to Persia and India. Prior to this, by age twenty, he tells us, he had *"…seen the best parts of Europe, France England, Holland, Germany…and I spoke fairly the languages which are the most necessary…"* Though he is most remembered for the acquisition and selling of the great blue diamond to Louis XIV, that was just one event in a life crammed full of adventure.

    In telling Tavernier's story I have tried to keep as closely as possible to the real time line of his life (the historical timeline can be found on the book's website, www.thefrenchblue.com). Most of the events described in the book are the actual events Tavernier described. Tavernier was not a boastful man. He wrote three books, all 17th Century bestsellers, describing his travels but rarely dwelt upon himself. There are broad gaps during which we have no clear idea of his activities. It is within these gaps that I have felt free to speculate and invent.

    In all cases the fictional portions of the novel are meant to provide a plausible context for the true events of Tavernier's life. For example, of the five year span between his first and second voyages we know almost nothing. By the beginning of his second voyage, his first to India, we see him established as a jewel trader and well capitalized. How did the son of a mapmaker achieve entrée into the highest aristocratic circles of France? How and where did he learn the gem dealer's trade? The events described in Chapters 7-9, though wholly fictional, do provide a plausible explanation. The entire factual basis for Tavernier's apprenticeship under Torreles rests upon a single mention of the name by Tavernier's biographer, Charles Joret.

    During the early years of the 17th Century, most of Europe was caught up in the ravages of the Thirty Years War. Tavernier served in the Holy Roman Emperor's court, did know Père Joseph and did serve for a brief time under Colonel Walter Butler. He could have been of great use to Cardinal Richelieu and his participation in the plot to assassinate the Austrian Generalissimo, though completely fictional, is, at least, plausible.

The main characters are mostly real. Tavernier met and did business with many of the most important men of the age. Wherever possible, I used biographies and studied contemporary portraits to develop their personalities.

One central character, Madeleine de Goisse (Madame Twelve Tomans) is completely invented. Jean Chardin, another 17th Century French traveler writing at this time, mentions the famous courtesan Madame Twelve-Tomans, as maintaining a mansion in the Persian capital of *Isfahan*. I found this name sufficiently intriguing to create a history for her and fashion her fictional daughter into Tavernier's great love and eventual wife. We know that between his fourth and fifth voyages Tavernier met and married Madeleine Goisse, whom Joret describes as a jeweler's daughter, with some family connection. I added the *de* to provide her with a noble lineage.

Tavernier was a 17th Century man. No attempt was made to sanitize his opinions or make him politically acceptable to the 21st Century reader. His comment about "the whitest women" for example is taken word for word from *The Six Voyages*. He expressed personal opinions so seldom, that, whenever I discovered one, I felt honor bound to include it. The reader who is familiar with *The Six Voyages* may find a phrase or two taken directly from Tavernier's narrative. To flavor the language, I made it a point to sprinkle some of Tavernier's typical turns of phrase throughout the novel.

That Tavernier did acquire the 115.28 carat blue diamond is a fact beyond dispute. The gem was originally called *The Tavernier Blue*, then renamed by Colbert, *Le diamant bleu de la couronne de France*. (The Blue Diamond of the French Crown). Five years after acquiring the gem, Louis XIV had the gem recut by Pitau, his court jeweler, into a 68.97 carat heart shape. From that time until it was stolen from the Garde Meublé in 1792, the stone was known as *The French Blue*. Thirty years later the gem re-emerged as the 45.52

carat Hope. Additional information can be found on The French Blue website.

Tavernier is particularly closed mouthed about this gem. He only mentions it in passing and says nothing at all about how, when or where he acquired the stone (luckily we do have his drawing of the gem which is reproduced in the text). We do not even know for certain at which of the several active mining areas the stone was found.

Tavernier mentions the mines at Kollür, a defunct mining area located in the modern Indian province of *Andrea Pradesh* as a source of colored diamonds. This is the only clue. This is really not surprising. As a gem dealer I can well understand his reluctance. Even today, trade sources are closely guarded secrets.

At the time of the purchase, Louis XIV granted Tavernier a patent of nobility and though most writers simply accept the statement that Tavernier received this honor for services to the crown, that is what today has become known as the "spin"?

With the connivance of His Majesty, Finance Minister Jean-Baptiste Colbert ran a lively business selling offices to raise money to support the Sun King's lavish lifestyle. The highest and most expensive was an outright patent of nobility. An elevation to noble status sold for between 400-500,000 livres.

From reading Tavernier's Six Voyages, it is clear that the French gem merchant did not sell his wares cheaply and that Colbert was a notorious skinflint. It is more than probable, given the timing and the price paid for the blue diamond, that the patent of nobility was part of the deal. Farges states that the Tavernier Blue was worth twice what Louis XIV paid. If we take the stated price and add the going price of a patent of nobility we get 620-720,000 livres, a sum much closer to the blue's real value.

Some scholars believe that Tavernier acquired the blue during his 5th voyage. I see no real basis for this claim. Gem dealers are always in need of capital. It is doubtful that Tavernier would have tied up his money for so long.

Acknowledgements

In the interest of historical accuracy, I consulted a great many sources in the writing of *The French Blue*. Tavernier's own *The Six Voyages of Jean-Baptiste Tavernier*, itself a 17th Century best seller, was a basic template. The book was written at the behest of Louis XIV as a manual for his French East India Company. Thus many of the actual adventures and much of the political, cultural and geographic detail comes directly from my protagonist. I consulted both the 1679 1st English edition which included *Tavernier's Travels in Persia* and Valentine Ball's second translation (1889). Ball's copious footnotes, preface and time line were very useful. Charles Joret's biography, *Jean-Baptiste Tavernier* (1886), contained much good detail.

I consulted several contemporary travel accounts written by French travelers who visited Persia and India and wrote during these years. Sir John Chardin (1686), a Huguenot jeweler who fled Protestant persecution in France and settled in England, wrote a very thorough account of Persian life and mores *(Ferrier, A Journey To Persia, 1996)*. Abbé Carré (1674) and Abbé Françoise Bernier (1668) also wrote interesting accounts of travel in India. Chardin knew Tavernier and Bernier traveled with him for a time in 1652.

For a historically accurate picture of 17th Century Paris and its suburbs, as well as details concerning the purchase of offices and titles, Trout's *City On The Seine* was very useful. I consulted three biographies of Louis XIV: Mitford (1966), Louis (1997), and Dunlap (2000). Antonia Fraser's *Love and Louis XIV, the Women in the Life of the Sun King* (2007) was a great help in filling out the chapter on Louis' mistress Athénaïs de Montespan as was Barker, *Brother to the Sun King* (1989), for the chapter on Philippe, Duke of Orleans. The three volume Memoirs of the Duc de Saint-Simon and those of Liselotte, the second Duchess of Orleans, gave a good overall feel of life at the court of the Sun King. I consulted De-than, *The Young Mazarin* (1977), and Trout's *Jean-Baptiste Colbert* (1978) aided me in defining the personalities of these two important French ministers.

The Counter Reformation and The Thirty Years War defined and shaped the politics of Europe during this period. Although the chapters dealing with Tavernier's part in the assassination of Wallenstein are fictional, between his service under the Viceroy of Hungary and at the Imperial Court in Vienna and his acquaintance with Père Joseph, it is difficult to believe that he was not somehow involved. In his own book, Tavernier mentions Père Joseph (Richelieu's eminence grise) and he served under Walter Butler, one of the actual assassins. For an overview of the political situation, I consulted Parker's and Asch's similar titles: *The Thirty Years War* (1987) and (1997) and Schiller's trilogy, *Wallenstein* (1799).

For information on the Mogul Court of India, Bakshi & Sharma's *Aurangzeb* (2000) as well as *Cities of Mughal India*, Hambly & Swaan, (1968), was useful. I also consulted *The Worlds of the East India Company* (2002), Rawlinson, *British Beginnings in Southeast Asia* (1920), and Priolkar, *The Goa Inquisition* (1961).

For Chapter 36, "War At Sea", I found a contemporary account on-line which was written by a participant in the battle. *The Shah's Silk for Europe's Silver,* (McCabe 1999) was an excellent account of the history of the Armenian people in Persia in the 17th Century. I took details of the topography and climate of Golconda from Kurin's *Hope Diamond*. Will and Ariel Durant's *The Age of Louis XIV* (1963) contains a breadth of relevant cultural information. To Alan Villiers's *Son's of Sinbad* (1939) I am grateful for a wealth of detail about the day-to-day operations of the pearl trade in the Persian Gulf; to him as well I am grateful for some of the character development of Tavernier's mentor Sheik Arash.

For gem and jewelry information I consulted Tillander, *Diamond*

Cuts In Historic Jewellery1331-1910 (1995) for information and descriptions of diamond cutting, Huda's *Arab Roots of Gemology.* Themelis' *Valley of Rubies and Sapphires and Gems & Mines of Mogok* was also useful for the chapters on Burma. Morel's *The French Crown Jewels* was a treasure trove. The details of Richelieu's liturgical set come directly from Morel as well as some of the names of goldsmiths and gem cutters used in the narrative. I am indebted to Pogue's *Turquois* (1915) for information on the gem as well as details of the geography in and around the turquoise mines near Madan. Khalidi's *Romance of the Golconda Diamonds* (1997) provided much information on early diamond mining in India. Ronald's *The Sancy Blood Diamond* was important in gaining a real understanding of the role played by important gemstones in the history and politics of Europe.

Then there was the internet! *Google* was extremely useful both for references, out of print sources and contemporary images of many of the main characters in the novel. It is difficult to imagine a part time writer constructing a novel with the historical, geographic and political sweep of this one without the aid of the internet.

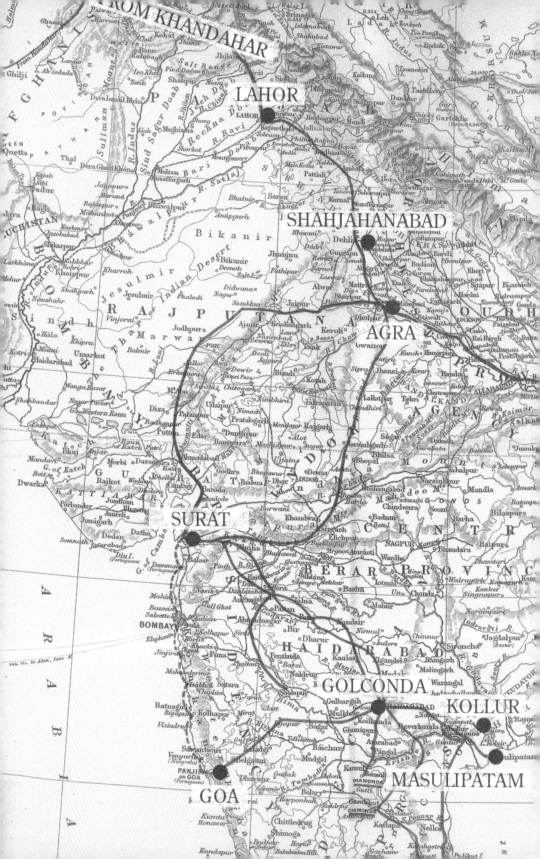